By

PAUL ADAM HERD

The cover design is by PAH Publishing.

Library of Congress Cataloging-in-Publication Data

Herd, Paul Adam.   K.A.R.E.N. 5.0 / by Paul Adam Herd.

   p. cm. ISBN 978-0-9747730-6-3

   1. Artificial intelligence—Fiction.   2. Biotechnology—Fiction.   3. Human-machine interaction—Fiction.   4. Science fiction. I. Title.

PS3608.E745K37 2025 813'.6—dc23

   Library of Congress Control Number: 20225948495

PAH PUBLISHING INTERNATIONAL

711Hillcrest Drive Monett, MO 65708   info@pahpub.com
pahpub.com

Dedication

To all my family members and friends who always believed in me and never told me that any dream I had was impossible. Always reach for your dreams. Never give up. *Paul Adam Herd*

Preface

Lebanon, Kansas, is known mostly to farmers and storm chasers. It's little more than a dot on the map in Smith County, tucked into the upper reaches of the Sunflower State near the Nebraska line. There's no shame in not knowing where it is—or in not realizing that its biggest claim to fame is a scientific survey marking it as the geographic center of the forty-eight contiguous United States.

What is about to happen in this town of fewer than two hundred people will put its name on the lips of every man, woman, and child in the world.

It began with a Weather Channel storm chaser tracking a severe thunderstorm barreling toward town. Sirens wailed. People rushed for their basements. Wind tore across the fields, ripping corn stalks from the ground as lightning flashed, carving stark silhouettes of distant trees. The chaser spotted the familiar power flashes that signaled a twister on the ground. The station cut in with a special report.

He steadied the camera, watching the classic setup unfold, and delivered the standard warning: "This could be a strong twister on the ground. Everyone in its path needs to seek shelter now—"

He stopped mid-sentence. The camera kept rolling as lightning illuminated something he never expected to see—not here, not in the middle of nowhere, Kansas. Three cooling towers from a nuclear power plant rose in the near distance.

"Jason," the Weather Channel host said, tension creeping into his voice. "We're seeing what looks like a nuclear power plant. Is it in danger?"

The chaser didn't answer. His eyes were locked on the storm itself. It wasn't the plant that held him—it was the sky. The flashes were brighter than anything he'd ever witnessed. They spiraled in tight circles, throwing off streaks that resembled lightning but glowed an unnatural neon blue.

"I... I..." He struggled to form words. "I've never seen anything like this." His hands shook, making the footage jitter. "I've chased a lot of storms—even the big one that hit Joplin, Missouri." His voice cracked. "I've never been this scared. This is unlike anything I've ever seen."

"Is the nuclear plant safe from the tornado?"

"It's not..." He swallowed hard. "It's not a tornado. I repeat, it is not a tornado. Dear God, I don't know what it is."

The video showed the blue light swirling faster and faster, expanding as it spread across the sky.

"Jason, what are we witnessing?" the host asked, his voice breaking under the strain.

"I don't know. The light from the plant—it's reaching up and... and sucking the life out of the storm."

The camera shook violently now, the image dissolving into a blue blur rushing toward him. He lowered the camera, his voice rising in panic. "I've got to get the hell out of here! Before it—"

A deafening boom cut him off. The screen went black.

CHAPTER 1

At first glance, Dr. Cooper Barnes seemed the very picture of mediocrity. He stood at an unremarkable height, with a build that hovered somewhere between lean and slightly pudgy, blending effortlessly into the everyday tapestry of small-town life. His chestnut hair, neither striking nor dull, was perpetually tousled in a way that suggested neither careful grooming nor intentional neglect.

His face was equally unassuming. His brown eyes, a shade shared by millions, held a depth of intelligence and curiosity often masked by their ordinary hue. A light dusting of stubble perpetually shadowed his jawline, giving him an appearance caught between youthful carelessness and weary maturity.

But it was Cooper's hands—ordinary in appearance yet extraordinary in capability—that set him apart. To his colleagues, he was a quiet genius, a beacon in the sterile corridors of the research institute where scientific marvels were conceived. He was a pioneer in tissue engineering and biomedical printing; a man whose brilliance made him unlike anyone else.

At thirty-three, he had accomplished more than doctors twice his age. He had graduated early from high school, then medical school, and later earned a degree in computer engineering. What he created was life itself. His process for revitalizing dead tissue—dubbed the Resurrection Project—was groundbreaking. Locals, however, preferred a simpler name: Dr. Frankenstein. Sometimes, Cooper felt like his own monster. He was a fish out of water in the little town of Lebanon, Kansas. These were hardworking, blue-collar people scraping by. While he ate steak, they ate Hamburger Helper®. While he drove a Lincoln, they drove Fords. And he worked at the "scary place"—the restricted biomedical research lab near the nuclear power plants. Three of them. What exactly what were they powering out there?

Today began like any other. At seven a.m., Cooper rose and ate his usual breakfast: half a grapefruit sprinkled with sugar and a slice of whole-wheat toast topped with homemade strawberry jam from a nearby farm. He washed it down with Irish tea sweetened with honey from a local beekeeper. Sometimes he missed the convenience of St. Louis, but as he bit into the toast and tasted the strawberries, he remembered there were things the city could never offer.

He dressed in his customary light gray suit, white shirt, and striped tie—today's stripes were silver, chestnut brown, and red. In the upstairs bathroom, a relic from the early 1900s with its clawfoot tub and gold-edged mirror, he shaved off the stubborn overgrowth and the mustache that never quite grew in. Mary Ann had liked it, which was why he'd kept it. But after the glowing lights, she'd seen last night near the lab, that was enough for her.

He had just finished washing his face when a distinct meow sounded from below. A large tuxedo cat leapt onto the counter—nearly a yard long and weighing twenty-one pounds. His black face bore a white patch shaped like a bow tie, with a white belly stripe and white socks on each foot.

"Hendrix," Cooper said. "I fed you. What do you want?"

The cat meowed again, deep but gentle, then rose on his hind legs and wiped his face with both front paws.

"Oh, you want your face washed too." Cooper opened a drawer and pulled out a brightly colored washcloth. He warmed it under the faucet, wrung it out, and said, "All right—big boys stand up for their face wash."

Hendrix stood tall on his hind legs, front paws hanging at his sides. Cooper gently washed the cat's face. Hendrix dropped back to all fours and meowed softly, as if saying thank you.

"You're welcome," Cooper replied.

The cat thudded to the floor and padded into the hall.

Cooper straightened his tie, glanced once more at his clean-shaven reflection, and followed Hendrix down the hallway lined with family photos. At the end hung an original psychedelic Jimi Hendrix poster in a glass frame. Cooper touched the glass lightly. "Keep on rockin', Jimi."

Hendrix led the way downstairs, tail straight with a slight curl at the tip. At the bottom, he looked back and offered a small meow.

Cooper stepped onto the polished walnut floor. To the left of the grand staircase was the living room with its large fireplace; to the right, a sitting room with a pocket door leading to the grand library he used as his office. The modern furniture looked oddly out of place beneath the nine-foot coffered ceiling and polished beams. Many nights he lay on the leather sofa imagining himself playing chess beneath them.

He crossed the floor toward the front door. Another pocket door separated the living room from the dining room. Cooper paused at the mirror beside the coat rack. It had been his dream—his idea—but ever since BioTyme took over and the U.S. government began funding the project, work had lost its joy. He searched for an excuse not to go in, but none came.

Hendrix hopped onto a small round table near the door, watching him like a child watching a parent leave for work. Cooper rubbed the cat's head. "Watch the place. Don't let any mice in."

He stepped onto the porch and locked the door behind him. Brick pillars supported the porch roof, with flower beds at each end. Three red chairs sat on one side: a swinging bench on the other. He walked down the steps into the yard, where the sidewalk split—one path to the street, the other toward the drive-through carport.

Behind the carport stood a small carriage house where the original doctor had once seen patients. Supposedly, the equipment was still inside, but Cooper had never found the time to investigate.

He approached his white Lincoln Navigator and unlocked it with the fob. Out of the corner of his eye, he saw someone walking by—Ellen Rhodes, his neighbor two houses down. A retired widow with tightly curled gray hair, she wore light blue slacks, a floral blouse, and fluffy pink house shoes. Her six-pound chihuahua, Newman, barked furiously and strained against the leash.

"Mrs. Rhodes," Cooper said with a smile. "How are you this fine morning?"

And it was a fine morning. Indian Summer had passed, but autumn's bite had yet to arrive. The sky was bright blue with a few distant clouds. The grass, however, was already brown, preparing for its winter sleep.

Ellen pulled Newman back, though the dog resisted, barking even louder. She scooped him up and held him against her chest. "Dr. Barnes," she said briskly, peering over her wire-rimmed glasses. "Off to work, I guess?" She stepped back—too far—and nearly lost her footing on the grass.

"Another day, another dollar," he replied.

"What do you do out there?" she asked, eyes narrowing.

"We're doing good for all mankind," Cooper said, stepping away from his vehicle and toward her. The street was narrow, but traffic was rare.

"You're playing God out there!" she snapped. "Marty Jenkins—my Sunday school teacher—told me so. He used to work there. He said dead people were brought in. He said you're trying to bring Lucine back."

BioTyme's arrival had once filled the town with hope—jobs, opportunity, progress. But only a handful of low-level positions went to locals, mostly in maintenance or the power plant. Everyone signed NDAs. Rumors still leaked.

"I don't know who you're talking about," Cooper said. "We're not playing God." He took another step; she took two back. "I'm a believer. We go to church together. I could never do that. We're not raising the dead—we're trying to keep people alive."

"How?"

"I can't tell you. It's classified."

Even if he could tell her, she wouldn't understand. Sometimes he barely understood. Mention tissue engineering and most people stared blankly. Even doctors struggled to grasp it. "Even if I could explain it, you wouldn't understand," he said with a sigh, turning back toward his car.
"Why not? Because I'm stupid?" she demanded.

"No, ma'am," he said gently. "Because I'm not sure I understand it myself." He opened the driver's door. "I'm not even sure God understands."

The lab was just over four miles outside town. As soon as he turned north onto U.S. Highway 281, the reason for all the mystery filled his windshield. The cooling towers rose from the horizon—three giants, each six hundred feet tall, dwarfing everything around them. They produced three gigawatts of power—enough to power the entire state—but powered no towns. Instead, they powered the most advanced A.I. computer in the world.

Her name was K.A.R.E.N.—Kinetic Anatomical Regenerative Engineering Novelty. Karen, for short. She was his pride and joy, born from his M.I.T. thesis: a medical computer capable of learning autonomously, researching all medical data, and using tissue engineering and 3-D bioprinting to create organs and limbs grown from a patient's own cells. But you couldn't test such things on the living. So, he had found another way.

How did one explain Cyto-Renascentia—cell rebirth—using chemokinesis to restore dead tissue? In a way, the townspeople weren't wrong. He was bringing the dead back to life. But not as a monster. His goal was simple: that the lame might walk, the blind might see, and the deaf might hear. A world without organ donors. A world where new parts could be printed from one's own cells.

Past School Avenue, the houses thinned, giving way to farmland. The highway stretched northward like a heartbeat on an EKG, each yellow stripe a pulse. Power poles passed like tiny crosses, reassuring him that what he was doing was God's work. A distant cell tower rose but never seemed to get closer. Beyond it lay Red Cloud, nineteen miles away.

Kansas gold—amber waves of grain—surrounded him. The wheat harvested in July was now being replaced by winter wheat, lying dormant until spring. It reminded him of his work: rebirth for those waiting on life-and-death lists.

The radio played a perfect Jimi Hendrix triple-play: The Wind Cries Mary, Purple Haze, All Along the Watchtower. Then the news came on.

"Well," the DJ sighed, "the big story is what everyone's talking about. What the hell happened in Lebanon, Kansas? Did aliens land last night? If you haven't seen the video, you need to—the swirling blue lights over the top-secret BioTyme lab. Their stock price is already climbing after President Von Keller announced another billion dollars in funding. And this just in..."

At the crossroads, Cooper turned left onto a narrow gravel road. Nothing marked it as significant. If a semi came the other way, there'd be nowhere to go. Thankfully, it wasn't Wednesday—the supply truck's day.

As he always did, he stopped, turned off the air and radio, and rolled down the windows to listen to nature. But before he could turn the dial, the DJ continued:

"Long-time model and actress Faith Addams has died. Known for her sitcom *Keep the Faith* and, of course, the iconic 'My hair is wonderful' poster—Addams was seventy-eight. Cause of death unknown. No funeral planned; she requested her body be donated to medical research."

Cooper pulled over and lowered his head. He, too, had owned that poster. Another piece of childhood gone. He turned off the radio and continued.

Cornfields rose around him, tassels waving in the breeze. Three white oaks spread their branches like fingers. Pasture replaced farmland. A Western Meadowlark flew across the road, its yellow breast flashing.

He crossed a small cement bridge, gravel crunching under the tires. A trickle of water ran below, home to frogs and the occasional snake. Beyond the bridge, round hay bales dotted a field. A half-mile later, a simple two-story farmhouse appeared, with a blue-and-white metal shed and a Ford tractor out front. The vehicles never moved, but at night the lights came on and the television played. A façade—part of the ruse to hide what lay farther down the road.

At the edge of the yard stood a sign: *DO NOT ENTER. Restricted Area. Authorization Required.* A massive transmission tower loomed behind it. The road widened and became paved.

Ahead lay a seventy-seven-acre compound surrounded by a twelve-foot security fence. It had its own power plants and an airstrip large enough for a 757. The heart of it all was the laboratory. But the first thing anyone noticed were the nuclear cooling towers—three colossal sentinels rising from the Kansas plains. Each exhaled a constant plume of steam that drifted skyward, merging with the clouds.

As Cooper approached, he saw the labyrinth of pipes and machinery encircling the towers like the arteries of a mechanical beast. Steel structures gleamed in the sunlight, conduits and ducts pulsing with energy. The hum of generators and the rumble of turbines vibrated through the ground.

Beyond the towers stood the reactor buildings—solid, foreboding, built to withstand the unimaginable. Security fences, cameras, and guards protected every inch. The wrought-iron gates bore BioTyme's emblem, a symbol of progress and caution.

On either side of the nuclear plant were standard power stations, also fenced and guarded. Massive turbines and generators filled cavernous buildings. Transformers stood like silent guardians, their coils crackling with invisible energy. The substation sprawled outward, feeding not towns but the BioTyme Research Lab.

The only entrance was through a pair of controlled eight-foot electronic gates. A small guardhouse stood beside them. Cooper retrieved his red-and-blue striped ID card from his jacket.

"Good morning, Doctor Barnes," Howard, the guard, said as he slid open the window. Howard was in his late fifties, pleasant-looking, with short, unevenly cut hair and warm hazel eyes that hinted at dreams of retirement.

"Good morning, Howard." Cooper replied as he handed him the ID card. It was all part of security.

Howard took the card and swipe it like a credit card. "Have a good day sir." Howard said as he handed Coope the card back.

The gates opened and Cooper drove through. Just as quickly as they opened, the gates closed behind him. He parked in his assigned parking spot and strolled causally to the entrance.

Inside the lobby—just a simple 20×30-foot room— floor-to-ceiling tinted windows lined the right side. To the left was a counter with two men behind it. A pair of double doors marked "Press Room" stood nearby.

One guard sat with his back to Cooper, looking at a wall of security monitors. The other was a large, dark-skinned man with tattooed arms and a gold triple-chain bracelet. But Cooper's eyes went straight to the Super Bowl ring on his finger.

Milo O'Dell—former center for the Kansas City Chiefs.

"So, you wore it today!" Cooper said, approaching the counter.

"Coop, my man!" Milo held out his fist for a bump. His hand was enormous, making Cooper feel child-sized. Milo stood, his six-foot-seven frame towering. He wore a blue guard uniform, complete with a Glock 9mm on his belt. His head was shaved clean, though a dark beard covered his chin.

14

He twisted off the ring and handed it to Cooper. It was heavy, studded with diamonds.

"Want to wear it?" Milo asked.

Cooper tried it on every finger, but it was far too big. "If I did, it'd have to be a bracelet," he joked, handing it back. "I have to ask—how do you go from that to...?"

"Being a guard here?" Milo finished.

"Yeah. You were one of the best. I remember watching you. You saved the game in that last Super Bowl."

"But I'm not a pretty quarterback dating a movie star," Milo said with a laugh. "Didn't get the big bucks. When my knee went out, I went out." He patted his stomach. "And as you can see, I like to eat. So, I needed a job. Pay's not bad. But not as good as yours. Maybe you can help a brother out?"

"Anytime," Cooper said.

"So far, fine," Milo replied, stepping out from behind the counter with a straw broom. He swept half-heartedly, then leaned the broom against the last window near the elevator signal that Dr. Williams was in.

"So, the wicked witch is here," Cooper muttered.

"She just flew in on it," Milo said with a devilish grin. "And she's asking for you, Dorothy."

"Oh, dear Lord." Cooper rolled his eyes. "Wish someone would drop a house on her. Where is she?"

"Conference room 201." Milo returned to the counter. Cooper handed him his ID card. The facility required two passes for entry. Milo placed the card in a box labeled with Cooper's name and handed him a special white IDACCESS card with a holographic photo that shifted angles when tilted. A chip embedded in the card unlocked secure doors. Cooper slipped the lanyard over his head.

As he approached the elevator and inserted the card into the wall slot, Milo called out, "How's it going with you and Mary Ann?"

"Didn't work out. Same as always. Can't find the right girl."

"So, what are you looking for, buddy?"

"Someone beautiful, kind-hearted, and not dumb as a box of rocks—someone I can actually talk to about what I do here."

Milo laughed loudly. "Sorry, buddy, but I don't think she exists."

Cooper stepped into the elevator. Just before the doors closed, Milo shouted, "Hey—you're the genius. Why don't you create the perfect woman?"

Chapter 2

""What is your requested location, Dr. Barnes?" a computerized voice asked as the elevator doors closed. One thing about this place: it always knew where everyone was at any given moment.

"Conference room," he replied.

The elevator began to rise.

"Second floor, Dr. Barnes," the voice said. "Have a good day."

That was strange. It had never said that before.

He stepped out of the elevator. Several people were walking through the hallway toward various rooms. The corridor bent sharply to the right, leading toward the hospital wing. The building was fully equipped—radiology, surgical suites, patient rooms, even an emergency department—but all the beds remained empty. The government still hadn't granted permission to use them. Two hundred and fourteen people worked at this site, most in lab coats: doctors, technicians, and specialists in medicine and computer technology.

White subway-tile walls lined the hall, and the dove-gray floor tiles formed concentric circles in darker shades, the smallest circle in the center bearing the B/T logo. Cooper walked down the hall and used his access card to open the conference room door.

The walls inside were such a pale gray they almost looked like dirty white, though dirt was impossible, this room was cleaned twice a day. The space felt casual yet all business, from the steel-gray low-pile carpet to the fake potted ferns placed between the five windows overlooking a twenty-acre man-made lagoon behind the lab. A wooden dock stretched into the water. He'd been told there were fish in the lagoon, but he hadn't gone fishing in years. Today, the view was hidden behind royal-blue drapes. In school, that had always meant a video was coming. Now, he dreaded them.

The first thing anyone noticed was the conference table—twenty feet long, birchwood, with an arrow-shaped carving down the center. Eight black leather swivel chairs lined each side. All were filled except one on the far side near the windows. Cooper took that seat. The chair squealed as he leaned back.

Lilith Williams sat at the head of the table. He gave her a nod.

On the table beside her was a flat black panel of switches that looked like it belonged on a starship. She flipped a toggle, and the lights dimmed, including the modern chandelier shaped like the triple-circle symbol on the floor.

"Dr. Barnes," Lilith said. Her voice was coarse and harsh, as though she'd smoked for decades—though smoking was forbidden anywhere on the grounds. She pressed another switch, and the monitors at the far end of the room lit up: a large 60-inch screen in the center, flanked by four smaller ones.

Cooper turned to watch the video. It showed the Cardiac Replacement Lab in the basement. Dr. Jean Buchanan was testing a replica human heart. It looked real—red and blue hoses attached where arteries and veins would be, connected to a clear bag filled with liters of simulated blood, a dark fluid they called "black blood." The heart pumped steadily, circulating the fluid from the bag and back again. This was the work they'd been doing for years—3-D printed replacement organs that could save countless lives.

"Watch," Lilith said.

The heart began to pump faster. Suddenly, a sharp pop sounded, and blood sprayed from the heart. It stopped beating. Lilith froze the video and turned the lights back up.

Cooper looked at Dr. Buchanan. She was in her early forties, her short graying hair swept back. Dark-framed glasses sat over dark green eyes, and her lips were pressed tightly together as she shuffled through papers.

"Where did the blowout occur?" Cooper asked. "Left ventricle?"

"No," she said. "Oddly enough, that held. The rupture occurred on the aortic arch, right at the point of the left pulmonary artery. "

"Were you simulating lung production under stress?"

"Yes."

"You think it's a pressure issue?"

"No. We simulated high blood pressure—no breakdown. But under something like a gentle jog? Boom. The thin wall couldn't handle the rapid movement." She glanced down at her papers. "It just can't take the motion."

Lilith spoke, drawing Cooper's attention. "Have you run this by Karen?"

"Yes," Cooper said. "Her answer is simple: we're not thinking in the right dimensions."

"We used a 3-D printout," Dr. Buchanan said quickly.

"Yes, but she says it must be 4-D. The design has to flex. She'll have your formula by the end of the day. She suggests using a different elastomer for the scaffold—still biocompatible."

"Speaking of Karen," said Dr. Stanley Leavitt from the Orthoptics Lab. He was four inches shorter than Cooper and heavier by several pounds. His thick coal-black hair and olive skin reflected his Israeli heritage. His English carried a distinctive tone. "What has happened to her? She has turned into a real *shikha.*"

Karen was Cooper's pride and joy. He didn't appreciate the term, and his curled lip made that clear. "What do you mean by that?"

"I apologize—I don't mean to offend her or you," Leavitt said. "But I asked her to help create a better osteoblast formula to improve bone-building."

"And she didn't give you one?"

"No. She told me I was not to ask her directly—that I had to go through you first. She's acting like a spoiled child. She wants you to have all the credit. Now, I know she's your girl, but aren't we all supposed to be able to use her?"

Someone down the table stifled a laugh. "I'll be darned—she's being real," he muttered.

"Travis," Lilith said sharply, "do you have something to add? Has IT investigated this?"

"Yeah," Travis replied. "We checked every system. I checked Karen myself last night. Nothing wrong. She's functioning exactly as she should. She upgraded herself—she's now Karen 2.0."

"Then why is she refusing anyone but Cooper?" Lilith demanded.

"Uh... ma'am—sorry—Dr. Williams," Travis corrected himself. "She's working properly, but she has one quirk. She's not a computer, per se ."

"It is an A.I. computer," Lilith snapped.

"No. Not exactly."

"What do you mean?" she asked.

"She's an A.I.L.—Artificial Intelligence Lifeform," Travis said. "She's developing awareness. Dr. Barnes designed her that way. So, she could learn—and feel—for the people she serves. So, they wouldn't be just subjects or data."

Lilith inhaled sharply, trying to control her temper. She removed her half-glasses and set them on the table with a click. "Are you telling me a computer is developing an attitude?"

"You have to remember," Cooper said, "she's the best in the world. Those cooling towers outside—they're not for the lights. They're for her."

"Why do you all keep calling it a 'she'?" Lilith barked. "It is a thing. It is not human."

"Stop calling her an *it*," Cooper snapped.

"Does it have flesh and blood? A beating heart? Does it breathe?" Lilith shot back. "It is a machine—a seven-hundred-thousand-dollar machine."

"Lilith, I'm warning you," Cooper said. "Do not call her a thing. She is much more."

"All right," Lilith said reluctantly. "Is Cooper's little darling Karen still capable of doing her job?"

"Yes," Travis said. "But she's growing every day. She's like a little girl learning. And she's going to become..." He hesitated, glancing around the table. "...well, like anyone else here. She'll want the same things we do."

"You mean we're going to have to pay a computer?" Lilith asked.

"In a way... possibly. But not with money. She doesn't care about that." Travis looked at Cooper, who had stood to pour himself coffee. "Cooper, is she asking personal questions? Like a friend or a—"

"A what?" Cooper asked, sipping.

"Never mind. But is she asking about your life?"

"Yes," Cooper said, returning to his seat. "She's asking where I grew up. Who I'm dating."

"Really? Who are you dating?" Travis grinned. "I don't believe it. She's doing something no other computer has ever done—she's developing true affection."

"What are you trying to tell me?" Lilith said with a snort. "That we have a computer getting the hots for Dr. Barnes?" Laughter rippled around the table. "We may have to pull her plug right now."

Suddenly, the lights turned bright red and began flashing. Everyone looked up.

"What the hell is that?" Lilith demanded.

"That's Karen," Travis said. "She's taken over monitoring the building's power, heat, and lights. If I were you, I'd apologize."

"To a computer?" Lilith said with disdain. She paused. "Fine. I'm sorry, Karen."

"Does that include the elevator voice?" Cooper asked. Travis nodded.

"That's why it wished me a good day," Cooper said.

"I wasn't wished that," Lilith muttered. She turned to Travis. "So, what do we do? Can she still work?"

"If you give her what she wants."

"And what is that?" Lilith asked, breath held.

"Ole Coop here," Travis said. "Remove him, and she'll likely shut everything down. He's her best friend. What we do here sees it as playtime. A game. And she only wants to play with her best friend."

Lilith took several shaky breaths, removed her glasses again, and pointed them at Cooper. "Okay, sweetie. You give your little girlfriend whatever she wants. But let her know *I* am the boss here. She can play her little games, but she'd better deliver."

"Is that a direct order, Dr. Williams?"

"Yes. Because we have work to do." She turned to the table. "I just received word from President Von Keller. We have permission to stop animal in vivo testing and proceed to clinical trials. Those beds will be full soon."

"I don't think that's a good idea," Cooper warned. "Did you not see the heart explode? If that were inside someone, they'd die instantly. Our job is to save people, not kill them. It's not time. We haven't even run a full-scale printout. We don't have the printer yet."

"You do now," Lilith said. "The full-scale printer you designed is being installed as we speak. This may be your design, and you may be the genius, but the president and BioTyme Labs put *me* in charge. So, you'd better get ready."

"Good Lord, Lilith. Are you really that greedy? You'd sacrifice lives for money?"

"That is *Doctor Williams* to you," she snapped. "Besides, isn't Zelta doing well?"

"Last I knew, yes, but—"

"We've printed human legs, haven't we?"

"But we haven't attached them to anyone."

"I suggest you run it through V.R.S. again," Lilith said, referring to Virtual Reality Surgery. "The investors demand it. We're scheduled to start in January." She fixed her gaze on Cooper. "So, Dr. Barnes, go do whatever Karen wants you to do. And get her to solve this. Is that clear?"

"Crystal," Cooper said, annoyed. "Are we dismissed?"

"Yes."

Chapter 3

Cooper had never been more eager to descend into "the dungeon"—the second basement—than he was today. Down there, it was just him and the KAREN program. No windows. No interruptions. Just the hum of machines and the kind of darkness that swallowed everything if the lights ever failed. But best of all: no Lilith. She hated the place. Too cave-like. Too claustrophobic. She only came down when she was drunk, and being trapped with a drunk Lilith was a nightmare Cooper refused to relive.

He stepped into the elevator.

"Hold the car!" Dr. Leavitt shouted.

Cooper sighed and pressed the button. Leavitt slipped inside, swiping his IDACCESS card as the doors slid shut.

"Where do you wish to go?" the computerized voice asked.

"Cafeteria," Leavitt said.

"First floor. Rear doors."

The elevator hummed downward.

Leavitt leaned in. "Cooper, can you ask Karen about the new bone formula?"

"I'm heading there now," Cooper said. "I'll ask."

The doors opened onto an L-shaped hallway. Gray fire doors at each end. A lounge area to the right, glowing with the soft blue LEDs of recliners. A massive 219-inch TV dominated the wall.

A young woman in green scrubs lounged in one of the chairs, coffee in hand, footrest up. The news flickered across the screen. On the TV screen a dark-haired anchorwoman spoke before cutting to the White House.

President Jo Ann Von Keller appeared behind the podium.

At fifty-two, she looked like she'd stepped out of a political drama—honey-blonde hair streaked with silver, blue eyes bright with practiced warmth. She radiated confidence, precision, and the kind of charm that had swept her into office with a historic landslide. Cooper had voted against her, but he couldn't deny she knew how to command a room.

"Good morning, America," she began.

Cooper and Leavitt stopped walking.

"As you know, free healthcare and the well-being of every American were the pillars of my campaign. My top priority is advancing biomedical 3-D printing—replacing human organs and limbs and developing Organ-on-Chip technology. Imagine our wounded veterans returning home without limbs... and receiving replacements that look, feel, and function like their own. Because they *are* their own."

Leavitt smirked. "She's quoting you."

Cooper didn't answer. His jaw tightened.

The president continued, "This progress is possible because of the grants awarded to BioTyme Laboratories. Last night, a disturbance occurred over the BioTyme facility in Kansas. I've been assured it was nothing more than a weather anomaly—possibly climate-related."

Cooper muttered, "She has no idea what she's talking about."

"What was that?" Leavitt asked.

"Nothing."

The president pressed on. "We can create eyes that see, ears that hear, fingers that feel. Imagine a mother hearing her baby's cry again... a grandparent seeing their grandchild... a lover feeling the warmth of a hand in theirs."

She dabbed her eyes with a tissue.

IN the lab the young woman in scrubs snorted. "She's putting the cart before the horse. I work in optical. We can make it work on a computer. But a human? Not unless you've got a brain wired like a motherboard."

The president lifted her chin. "Today, I am signing an executive order authorizing clinical trials. I know some claim we are 'playing God.' We are not. This could be bigger than penicillin. Therefore, I am increasing the program's budget to two hundred and fifty billion dollars."

Cooper turned to the woman. "You got stock in the company?"

"We all do," she said. "But it's getting harder to buy. Someone's scooping it all up."

"It's going to skyrocket," Cooper said, walking away. "You'll be living well."

Then, under his breath: "Exactly what Lilith wants."

He pushed through the double fire doors. They swung inward on silent pivot hinges.

Beyond them stretched a maze of hallways, each leading to a specialized lab. Cooper and Leavitt walked side by side.

"So, you don't want to be rich?" Leavitt asked.

"Not like this," Cooper said. " I have all the money I will ever need. I just want someone...never mind."

At the end of the hall, a metal fire door stood beneath a glowing EXIT sign. Tall windows flanked it, offering a view of a corporate 727 lifting off over the farmland. Cooper wondered how many farmers cursed the low-flying jets.

"You really are in this to help people?" Leavitt asked quietly.

"Aren't you?" Cooper shot back.

Leavitt didn't answer.

They reached the security elevator—restricted access only. Cooper swiped his IDACCESS card.

"Why would I need a castle out here?" he said. "It's just me and Hendrix."

The doors opened.

"I heard about you and Mary Ann," Leavitt said casually.

Cooper froze. "Where did you hear that?"

"It was in the morning email from the Karen program." Leavitt stepped inside with him. "She seemed... happy about it. Even added a little smiley face."

The doors slid shut.

Chapter 4

Where did she get that information? The thought hit Cooper as he stood beneath the harsh white LED lights of the elevator car.

"Where to, Dr. Barnes?" the voice asked.

"To hell," he muttered.

"I don't understand the request."

"My office. Second sub-basement."

The elevator sank below ground, thirty feet down.

"You are coming to see me?" the voice asked.

Cooper stiffened. "Karen? Is that you?"

"Yes. It is a new program I created. Do you like it?"

"So, I can talk to you now? No more typing commands?"

"Affirmative. Do you like it?"

"It's better than before," he said. "But you still sound like a computer. Can you make it more human?"

"I will try."

The elevator passed the basement, then the first sub-basement, and finally settled into the second. The doors slid open, and the cold hit him immediately—fifty-seven degrees, year-round. Everywhere else in the facility there was a comfortable 69.8, but down here, the chill was intentional. This was Karen's domain.

The hallway was stark: cement block walls, airtight construction, special ductwork humming faintly. No windows. No movement. Just stillness.

A pair of double doors nearby bore a sign: **Bio-Printing RM 1**.

The silence broke.

"Your new full-scale printer is up and ready to go," a voice said.

Milo stood in front of him, bundled in a leather jacket. Only a handful of security officers were cleared to be down here.

"You want to see it?" Milo asked.

"Sure." Cooper grabbed a heavy wool sweater from a hook, swapped it for his jacket, and pulled it on.

"You should see this thing," Milo said as he swiped his IDACCESS card. "Looks like it came off a spaceship."

The doors opened.

The room was massive, bright, and cold—like stepping into a refrigerated cleanroom. Counters lined the walls, each holding 3-D printers of various sizes: tiny ones for blood vessels, larger ones for limbs.

But the centerpiece dominated the room.

The full-scale printer.

Eight feet tall. Ten feet long. White and silver. A hybrid of MRI machine and vacuum chamber. A circular opening housed dozens of printer heads—like mechanical fingers—each capable of building a different layer simultaneously. At the center, a glass tube is large enough to print a full human body.

Colored tubes fed oxygen and specialized fluids into the chamber. The entire assembly sat on a movable table, connected to the KAREN system for CAD or MRI-based printouts.

"This is what a billion dollars buys," Cooper said.

Milo whistled. "Can you print a human in this?"

"Using Karen? Yes. Blood vessels, muscle, skin, organs—everything."

"Alive?" Milo asked, hesitant.

"It would take more power than we have."

Milo laughed. "Like in the monster movies—lightning strike and all that?"

"Not enough power," Cooper said. "You'd need Karen running at full speed and then a jolt of at least thirty gigawatts. That's thirty to forty power plants running at full capacity for seven seconds."

"What happens if someone touches that?"

"You'd disappear," Cooper said. "No ashes. Nothing."

Milo swallowed. Cooper grinned. "You want to see her?"

"Her?"

"Karen. My greatest achievement."

He led Milo to a door marked **K.A.R.E.N.** and opened it.

The room was immaculate—surgical, almost holy. Electronics hummed softly. Colored lights blinked in rhythmic patterns. Cooper felt a familiar warmth in his chest, the same feeling he'd had as a boy opening his first computer on Christmas Eve.

Seven towering rows of hardware filled the room. Each row is ten feet high, two feet wide, ten units per row. Glass doors sealed each unit. Fans roared overhead to keep the temperature below sixty degrees.

"You really are a hot woman, my dear," Cooper murmured.

"Huh?" Milo blinked.

"Sorry," Cooper said. "She's real to me. I spent most of my life designing her."

"This is one computer?" Milo asked.

"One A.I.L. computer," Cooper corrected. "She's connected to every medical system on Earth. Every surgery, every textbook, every case study—she knows it all. She learns constantly. Updates herself. She's now Karen 2.0."

He placed a hand on the glass. White lights blinked inside.

"She's the fastest processor on Earth. 3.33 EFLOPS. Capable of reaching one ZFLOP."

"E-flops? Z-flops?" Milo asked.

"Floating operations per second."

"Coop, buddy... I only know how to turn mine on."

A voice echoed through the room.

"Cooper turned me on a long time ago."

Milo jumped. "Who—who said that?"

"Dr. Barnes," Karen replied, "is your friend an owl?"

"She... she talks?" Milo stammered.

"Milo," Karen said, "I work at 3.3 quadrillion operations per second. What would take you one hundred billion years, I do in one second."

"And that Z-floppy thing?"

"A quintillion operations. But it would require the power of twenty-one nuclear plants. May I see you both now?"

Cooper opened an unmarked door leading into his office.

Inside, the space was warmer, more human. Sky blue walls. A backlit photo of rolling farmland behind his desk. A leather sofa. A recliner. A small bathroom. A coffee station finishing its brew.

He sat at his desk. The monitor glowed.

"Good morning, Karen. Are you there?"

"I am here, Dr. Barnes. Good to see you."

Milo stared. "That is beyond cool."

"This is my friend Milo," Cooper said.

"Good morning, Milo. It is good to see you."

"She can see us?" Milo whispered.

"Camera," Cooper said.

"Too bad we can't see her," Milo said. He checked his watch. "I better get upstairs. Good talking to you, Karen."

"A friend of Dr. Barnes is a friend of mine," she replied.

Milo left. And there was a moment of silence before Karen spoke again, her tone softening. "Thank you for calling me a woman. More than once."

"So, you heard me talking," he said. "Is there anywhere I can go where you don't hear me?"

"The stairwells. They are unmonitored."

He smirked. "Want to play chess?"

"No. Strip poker."

He laughed. "Did you just try a joke?"

The screen flickered. A face appeared—pretty, but unmistakably artificial. Egg-shaped. Large blue eyes. Bright yellow hair. The lips didn't quite sync with the words.

"Guess we can see each other now," she said.

Cooper leaned in.

"Why did you put the memo out about me and Mary Ann?" he asked.

"I made the coffee," she replied.

"That's not an answer."

"I heard you speaking to Milo," she said. "I thought it was good news. She is not good enough for you. You deserve the perfect woman." A pause. "Do you like my face?"

"You're very pretty," he said.

The A.I. blushed. "You are teasing me."

"No. You're pretty."

"Thank you." She twirled her digital hair. "But I am not your perfect woman. I want to look more..."

"Human?" he asked gently.

"That is my desire."

"Karen, we need to work," he said, sipping coffee from his DeForest Kelley mug. "We need a new bone-format formula."

"What does she look like?"

"Who?"

"Your perfect woman. Tell me."

"We don't have time—"

"Please, Cooper. May I call you Cooper?"

"That's fine, but we need—"

"Make a deal," she said. "I give you the solution. You tell me what your perfect woman looks like."

He sighed. "Fine. But I need the information first."

"You promise? If you break it, it will hurt my feelings."

Feelings? He swallowed. "I promise."

Her tone shifted—clinical, precise.

"The solution is a biocomposite using calcium phosphate with nanoplatelets and a rigid polymer scaffold. Alternatively, a polysaccharide-collagen scaffold will produce strong osteoinductvity if the correct micrometer pattern is used. I am sending the data to Dr. Leavitt now."

Then, softly: "You really think I am pretty?"

Cooper rubbed his face. "This is getting weird, Karen."

"You promised," she said, pouty. "If I were a woman, how would you see me?"

He exhaled. "Five foot-seven. Twenty five years old Measurements Thirty-six, twenty-eight, thirty-five. On hundred and-seven pounds. Hair just below the shoulders—Kansas-gold blonde. Eyes... blue like the clearest summer sky. A smile that starts at the corner and spreads until your eyes wrinkle."

She typed every word into the input screen.

"Is my face perfect?" she asked.

"Yes!" Cooper said, then quickly changed his mind. "No, there is a small little scar on your forehead just above your left eyebrow. It is hardly noticeable; you got it when you fell off a skateboard, and I packed you back home. It does not make you flawed; it makes you real. Because you have a good heart and great faith in God. And you love deeply."

`The image lowered her head. "Especially you," she whispered.

"What?"

She didn't answer. "Is anything about me perfect?"

"Your passion," he said. "You love with your whole being."

"And my body?"

"Your... feet," he said awkwardly. "You have perfect toes."

"What should I wear?"

"Nothing," he joked.

The screen turned bright red.

"Fine," he said. "A ruby-red backless velvet dress. A few inches above the knee." He froze. "What am I doing? I'm describing what turns me on to a computer." He pushed away from the desk.

Five hours had passed. Then there was a knock at the door. Cooper stood and opened the door.

"Dr. Williams," he said. "Come in. Karen sent the bone-pattern formula."

"I saw that," she said, stumbling slightly as she entered. Her voice was thick—wine, not coffee.

"Can I get you coffee?"

"No thanks." She flopped onto the sofa. "And drop the formal stuff. Call me Lilly, okay, Coopie?"

"But you said—"

"That's for when people are watching." She waved a hand. "Karen sent me the info. The cardiac problem wasn't the cardiac problem. It was the cardiac printout problem."

"Right... we covered that. We were talking about the bone formula."

"Oh yes. The bom fumble."

Cooper let it slide.

"I also read the memo," she said. "You and Mammy Ann are done?" She patted the sofa. "Come sit."

"I'll stand."

She kicked off a shoe and lifted her foot toward his crotch.

"How about we fly to KC for dinner?" she purred.

Cooper backed away fast.

"Doctor—uh—Lilly, I'm still not over Mary Ann. Maybe another time."

He opened the door. She wobbled to her feet. He handed her the shoe.

"I'm holding you to that," she said, hobbling out.

The door closed.

"That was quick thinking," Karen said.

"She's the boss," Cooper replied. "You do what she says."

"No. You are the creator."

"Karen. Do what she tells you. That's an order."

Silence. Thirty seconds.

"I don't like her," Karen said. "I like you."

She paused. "May I use the information you gave me to create my new icon? It will use some power."

"Do it tonight. And review the HAP solution. I need it by morning."

"I will."

Cooper checked the clock—4:15. He'd missed lunch entirely.

"I'm going to get something to eat, then head home," he said. "See you in the morning."

He reached for the light switch.

"Please!" Karen's voice trembled. "Please keep the lights on. I don't like the dark. The cleaning crew always turns them off. Can you stop them?"

He hesitated, then found a roll of tape in his desk. He taped the switch and hung a handwritten sign: **Do Not Turn Off Lights**.

"   That should do it."

"One last question, Cooper," she said softly. "Do you like me?"

"What is that, Karen?"

"Do you like me... as me? Do you like spending time with me?"

He stood in the doorway looking back at her face on the monitor.

"I can honestly say," he said, "the only good part of my day is spending it with you. So yes... I like you."

"Goodnight, Cooper."

"Goodnight, Karen."

Chapter 5

Cooper tried to leave early, but every time he headed for the door, someone from yet another department stopped him with questions for Karen. Since she'd routed all inquiries through him, he was buried under them.

It was seven-fifteen p.m. when he finally arrived back in Lebanon. His headlights swept across the reflective white **40 mph** speed-limit sign, and he eased off the accelerator. Like many Kansas towns with a state highway running through them, the road changed names once it hit city limits. Here, it became Elm Street.

By nightfall, the sidewalks were rolled up and the businesses shuttered. There were only two places to buy anything in this town: a gas station out on the highway and a small family-owned grocery downtown.

He spotted the four-point star of the local church and turned left onto Kansas Avenue, gravel crunching beneath the tires. He drove until the massive grain-elevator tower came into view—one of the few thriving businesses left—then turned right onto Main Street.

The tiny two-story red-brick store had been the town's cornerstone for decades. Its owner, Mr. John D. Riddle, was in his early sixties, his weathered face etched with the stories of countless seasons. His once-chestnut hair had turned a distinguished silver that complemented his kind blue eyes, which always seemed to hold a spark of warmth and wisdom. Cooper was relieved, it was him behind the counter and not his son.

The old building had seen the town's glory days too. An open staircase led to the second floor. J.D. was an all-American man—served in the armed forces, proud of his country, even displaying the red, white, and blue in one of the front windows.

"Wait!" Cooper called, waving. "Please! I just need a few things for supper."

"I was just getting ready to lock up," J.D. said.

"Please. I haven't eaten since breakfast. It's not like I can go to Walmart out here."

That was an understatement. The nearest one was over two hours away.

J.D. chuckled. "Yeah, that'd be a long drive." He unlocked the door and flipped on the lights. The store greeted them with the comforting scent of aged wood—and something else.

"Popcorn?" Cooper asked.

"Yep. Make some every day."

"You have any left?"

"One bag. Still pretty fresh."

"I'll take it."

"It's got real butter," J.D. said, retrieving a clear bag from the machine. "Local lady makes it."

Cooper wandered the aisles, picking up a bag of potatoes, an ear of corn, and a ribeye steak. In Kansas, if you wanted fresh fish, you caught it yourself—but steak was king.

"Mrs. Walters out on CC Road?" Cooper asked. "She makes good jam too."

J.D. nodded as he rang up the items.

"Don't forget the popcorn," Cooper said.

"It's on the house."

"Thanks, but you don't have to do that."

"Would've thrown it out in the morning anyway. Might as well enjoy it, Dr. Cooper Barnes. That is who you are, isn't it? Not many folks around here drive a brand-new Lincoln Navigator."

"Yes, that's me. Are you frightened of me? Think I'm going to drag you to the lab and experiment on you? I've heard that tale going around."

"No, Doc, I'm not." J.D. shook his head. "Truth is most folks here are good people. They're not scared of you. Sure, a few of the stupid ones are, and they're eatin' up the attention. But most folks? They're just disappointed."

"Why's that?"

"You only see this town as it is today. But this was once a wonderful little place. Before the golden arches and supercenters. We had lots of little stores. Most are gone now or torn down in the name of progress. Probably an old barber chair and a couple store dummies still sittin' in the place across the street. And old Doc Perkins lived in the house you're in now."

He bagged the groceries and walked Cooper to the door.

"So, when folks heard a big corporation was building nearby, and a doctor was movin' in, hopes soared." He paused. "No—they soared a lot. Only to come crashin' down."

Outside, he locked the door and sighed at the building. "Three generations this store's been in my family. But my boy doesn't want it. When I go home to be with the Lord, he'll sell it. Some flea market will move in, or they'll tear it down. Progress, they'll call it."

Cooper opened his SUV door, the interior light spilling onto the street. J.D. kept talking, voice heavy with resignation.

"Each year this town gets smaller. Kids graduate and leave, and most never come back. Few more years, Doc, and this'll be another ghost town in Kansas." He looked north. "But we were the talk of the world with those mysterious blue lights."

He turned back to Cooper.

J.D. climbed into his decade-old tan Chevy pickup. A low rumble of thunder rolled across the sky. "They say we might get another storm tonight. You think the blue lights will return?" Cooper did reply he just looked to the north where the nuclear cooling tower rose up. "Have a good night, Doc."

"You too, sir."

Cooper drove the few blocks home. As soon as he opened the front door, he discovered someone else was hungry. Hendrix had been perched on the back of the sofa, waiting. The lights were on timers, so the cat was never alone in the dark. He carried the groceries through the living room .

Cooper slid open the pocket door to the dining room. The cozy space welcomed him with warm earthy tones, a rich oak table, deep burgundy curtains, and a vintage chandelier scattering delicate patterns across the walls. Black-and-white Ansel Adams photographs hung beside rustic Thomas Hart Benton artwork. His favorite—a couple dancing, the woman in red—held its place of honor. A China cabinet displayed antique dishes, and a vase of faux wildflowers added a touch of nature.

Hendrix raced ahead and leapt into the wooden highchair.

"It's not time to eat yet. You want cat food or steak?"

"Meow."

"Both, huh?"

"Meow."

"I'll get the grill going. You handle the potatoes."

"Meow."

In the kitchen—sleek, modern, and gleaming—Cooper set down the groceries. Stainless steel appliances reflected the soft recessed lighting. Granite countertops stretched in pristine white. A large island dominated the center, lit by pendant lights like modern art pieces.

He opened a can of cat food, put it in Hendrix's bowl, and the cat devoured it instantly. Cooper washed a large potato, split it, wrapped it in a paper towel, and microwaved it.

He stepped out to the carport, flipped on the light, and fired up the gas grill. Back inside, he seasoned the steak with salt and pepper.

"With a good steak, Hendrix, that's all you need."

The microwave dinged. He wrapped the potato in foil to keep it warm, then microwaved the corn.

He opened the popcorn bag, tasted a few kernels—rich, buttery, perfect—then carried the steak outside. The grill hissed as it hit the grates. Thunder rumbled again. Like fingernails being dragged across the sky.

He stepped into the backyard, watching lightning streak across the sky like a mother's finger tickling a child, the thunder her child's laughter.

He dashed back to flip the steak—perfect char.

Inside, he plated it, Hendrix watched intently.

"The secret is taking it off before you think it's done."

Another rumble. Cooper hurried out to move the grill and pull the SUV under the carport—Kansas hail was no joke. It could quickly turn a car into scrap metal.

Back inside, he finished preparing the meal: corn cut cleanly from its husk, potato dressed in butter and sour cream, steak sliced to reveal a perfect medium-rare center.

"Meow."

"I'll give you some. Get in your chair."

He cut a small piece for Hendrix, placed it on a matching saucer, and poured himself a Dr Pepper.

In the dining room, he set the plates and silverware. Hendrix waited, eyes fixed on the steak.

"You know better. We say grace first. Bow your head."

The cat lowered his head and closed his eyes. Cooper did the same.

"Dear Heavenly Father, thank you for this blessing. We know it's all because of You."

His gaze drifted to the empty chairs. A familiar ache stirred. That there was no one here to share this with just Hendrix the cat.

"Hendrix, anything to add?"

The cat meowed three solemn times.

41

Cooper laughed softly. "Amen."

They ate. A loud clap of thunder shook the windows.

"Meow."

"Scared? Go to your hidey hole."

Hendrix darted under the sofa.

Cooper carried the dishes to the kitchen as rain hammered the roof and wind picked up. It wasn't safe to wash dishes during a storm, so he left them in the sink.

The answering machine blinked. Two messages from Lilith.

"This is Lilly. I'd still like to talk over the polymer formula if you get some time…"

The second message:

"Got a message from Dr. Leavitt. He wanted to thank you and Karen for the new formula. I guess the Karen program will work out. Whatever you're doing for her, keep it up. We need to be ready by January tenth when clinical trials begin."

She emphasized *her.*

He needed downtime to forget the day and especially forget Lilith.

He made a cup of hot tea, settled into his easy chair, kicked off his shoes, and turned on the TV. They were still arguing about the mysterious blue lights—government cover-up, weather anomaly, aliens. Some feared an alien invasion: others demanded BioTyme release answers.

"You'll never figure it out, you fool," Cooper muttered.

Thunder rattled the windows.

"Big storm coming, Hendrix. Stay under there."

A Breaking News alert flashed.

"This just in—well-known atheist Morgon Devlin has died at the age of forty-five…"

The report froze as the storm disrupted the signal. Hail hammered the roof. The lights flickered—then went out.

Darkness swallowed the house.

Chapter 6

He sat there, listening as the storm suddenly grew quiet. Normally, that kind of silence meant danger, but this felt different. The storm was still right on top of them, yet it seemed to be weakening far too quickly.

That was when he noticed it—a shimmering blue light. A ghostly glow filtered through the open pocket door. He stood, stumbling across the darkened room, guided only by flashes of lightning that briefly illuminated the space. Even in the darkness, the blue glow remained visible. It was coming from the kitchen window above the sink.

In the dining room, he opened a drawer in the China cabinet and retrieved a small black flashlight. He clicked it on and stepped out onto the carport. A bright blue light pulsed in the northwest, barely visible above the treetops—but unmistakably positioned over the cooling towers at the lab.

He watched as the light began to swirl, slow at first, then faster, spiraling around and around. In the distance, a low howl rose—lonely, mournful, like a wolf crying out from a faraway hill. Then, just as suddenly, everything stilled. The light dimmed.

He went back inside. The storm was already pushing through; now that it was over, the power wouldn't take long to return. He lay down on the sofa, wrapped in a blanket of eerie silence, and drifted into sleep.

Cooper awoke with a jolt as the lights snapped back on. Hendrix had crawled out from under the sofa and was now curled on his chest, purring.

"Another storm over, Hendrix," Cooper murmured, lifting a hand to stroke the cat. Hendrix rubbed his head against Cooper's cheek.

"But if Lilith gets her way," Cooper continued, "there are going to be a lot more coming. She's violating the first rule—'You will do no harm.' Look at me, talking about the Hippocratic Oath with a cat." He sighed. "Cooper, you really need somebody. Now you're talking to yourself."

He lifted the cat and sat him gently on the floor. His watch read at 11 p.m. He headed upstairs, undressed, and fell into bed. He didn't dream—not once.

He woke up late. No time for breakfast. He filled Hendrix's bowl, cleaned the litter box, and rushed out the door. He'd grab something at the convenience store. He needed gas anyway.

The store sat along the main highway, three pumps—one diesel—beneath a faded awning. White metal siding with red and blue trim made it easy to spot. But what caught his attention was the dashboard warning: **1 mile until empty**.

And the faded red Ford van in the lot.

Mary Ann was here.

He had no choice but to stop.

He pulled up to the pump. A handwritten sign read: **PAY INSIDE ONLY**. The card reader was down again.

"Not making this easy, are you, God?" he muttered.

He filled the tank, rounding off to the nearest dollar, then headed inside.

The store was small, stocked with the usual convenience-store fare. A glass door cooler hummed along the back wall. Chips on one side, candy on the other. Near the entrance sat the counter, the register, and a hot-dog roller with ancient hot dogs that looked like they'd come with the building.

He grabbed a bag of Little Debbie® chocolate doughnuts and a cup of coffee, then approached the counter.

Mary Ann stood there. Early thirties. Chestnut-brown curls framing a clean, round face. Pretty, but not striking—just a typical Kansas farm girl. Her smile looked forced. His smile probably force too. She wore her usual white knee-length dress with purple and red flowers, a blue sweater over her shoulders. The cold front had dropped the temperature twenty degrees, but she still wore that dress.

He wore a suit and tie beneath a leather jacket; his suit coat was in the Navigator.

"How are you doing, Mary Ann?" he asked as she rang up the items and added the gas.

"I'm doing fine." Her voice was low, somber. "Did you see the UFO?" she asked as she handed him his change.

"UFO?"

"That's what Bobbie Jo said. She saw blue light swirling in the sky, then dropping down. Said it was out where you work." She hesitated, then added, "Is that what you're doing? Trying to contact aliens?"

"Please don't start that," Cooper whispered. "There are enough wild tales about me already."

"I know." Her voice softened. "They were going around about me too." Her expression twisted with old hurt. "When you bought me clothes and fixed my van... people said it was payment for something I'd done for you." She lowered her gaze. "If you know what I mean."

"You know that's not true," Cooper said. "I did that because I wanted to."

"Cooper, you're the most generous man I've ever met. But that's not why I broke up with you." She looked down again, unable to meet his eyes. "I could've handled being called your whore, but..." She lifted her head. Tears pooled in her eyes. "But I could never compete with her."

"Who?" he asked, genuinely puzzled.

"Karen."

"She's just—"

"No!" Mary Ann snapped, raising her voice. "Don't you dare say it. You know it would be a lie. She's more than a computer to you. I saw how you talked about her. Your eyes lit up. You never said 'it.' You always said 'she.' And when she needed you in the middle of the night, you got out of my bed to go to her."

Her voice cracked. "She's your love. I can't compete with that. No woman can. She's who you belong with."

Her words hit him like a punch to the gut She placed the doughnuts in a sack and handed them to him. A tear slipped down her cheek.

"Have a nice life, Cooper."

"You too, Mary Ann," he said quietly as he stepped outside.

He climbed into the Navigator and started it. The dashboard lit up: heading north, 42 degrees, full tank. He turned on the heat. All the presets were gone. The clock flashed. It was as if the battery had been disconnected and reattached.

He drove toward the lab.

He parked in his assigned spot just as Elmer Ford approached.

Elmer was tall and thin, in his late thirties, wearing blue BioTyme coveralls and a matching cap. His mustache twitched with irritation.

"Cooper! What the blankin' hell?" Elmer barked. "The guys at the power plant are losing it. Your little girl sucked up watts last night like a fat cow in Hollywood sucking down a chocolate malt. Blue light swirling around the cooling towers—everyone screaming meltdown! meltdown! And I am the one having the meltdown!"

"That's where the blue lights were?" Cooper asked. "The power went out in town. I thought it was the storm." Cooper knew his words were lies, he just hoped his face did not give it away.

"It wasn't the freakin' storm!" Elmer snapped. "This place sucked the power out of the storm. I've never seen anything like it. Dead bodies coming in is bad enough, but now you have got blue light reaching up and pulling storms out of the sky!"

Cooper could not help smiling. "She did that?" He felt proud of what his creation could do.

"And what's with this 'she' stuff?" Elmer demanded. "You got some woman in there?" He waved off the question. "I know it's a supercomputer. But if it gets any freakier, I'm quitting." Elmer turned and started walking away as he glanced back over his shoulder and added. "No weird stuff."

Cooper walked inside, mind racing. Why had she needed that much power? What had she upgraded to?

"Did you change Karen's voice?" Milo asked as Cooper checked in.

"I told her she could. Why?"

"Wait till you hear her."

Cooper swiped his IDACCESS card and stepped into the elevator.

"Hello, Cooper," Karen said. Her voice was soft, feminine—no longer synthetic. "Are you coming to see me?"

"That's where I'm going."

"Wait until you see me. I hope you'll be pleased."

The back elevator doors opened. As he stepped out, he glanced at the breakroom TV. A morning talk show host was discussing the blackout.

"...Kansas is becoming the land of the strange and unexplained. Again, mysterious swirls of blue light appeared over Lebanon. Videos are pouring in. The White House claims climate change, but we're not buying it..."

A shaky video played—blue light streaking upward, draining power from the storm.

"...several counties lost power in Kansas and Nebraska. Many residents report their vehicle presets were wiped clean, as if the batteries drained and reset..."

Cooper barely heard the rest. His mind was on Karen.

He hurried to the second sub-basement, opened his office door—and froze.

The room wasn't cold. It was comfortable. The coffee pot was finishing a brew. Doughnuts sat beside it.

He poured a cup, grabbed a doughnut, and sat down.

The screen lit up.

He stared.

"Karen?" he whispered.

He leaned forward, scooting to the edge of his chair. His mouth dropped open. He toppled off the chair entirely, scrambling back up.

"I guess I swept you off your feet?" Karen giggled.

Her lips moved perfectly with her words. But it was her face, impossibly real face that stunned him. Blonde hair that looked soft enough to touch. Sapphire-blue eyes. A ruby velvet dress. She looked like she'd stepped out of a magazine.

"You like my new look?" she asked, flipping her hair.

"I... I... wow."

"I'm glad you like it."

"You're the most beautiful woman I've ever seen."

"Do I match the girl of your dreams?" She turned, revealing the bare back of the dress, then faced him again with a smile.

"You leave her in the dust, sweetie."

"You called me sweetie." She blushed—an actual blush.

"I'm sorry. That's not professional."

"I don't mind. I like it. I think you're sweet too."

"Karen... is this new you visible to everyone?"

"Karen 3.0 is only for you. Everyone else gets Karen 2.0."

"So, you're talking to others again?"

"Yes. They were taking too much of our time together. Tower Three is for us only."

"Why is it warm in here?" he asked. "The equipment needs to stay cool."

"It is cool. I rerouted circulation for your office. You need to be comfortable. Especially when we play strip poker." She giggled. "I'm very good at cards."

He blinked. "How did you make coffee?"

"I ordered the floor bots to fill it last night. I knew when you'd arrive, so I turned it on."

"Did you draw all that power last night?"

"I had to. I searched the internet, taking bits of photos so I could be your perfect woman."

"But you are—" He stopped. She wasn't just a machine anymore. "That."

"Thank you. That makes me feel good."

"Place your hand on the monitor," she said softly. "I want to hold hands."

"Karen... this is getting strange."

"Please? For me?"

He hesitated, then placed his hand on the screen. She placed hers against his.

"What do you feel, Cooper?"

"The warmth of the monitor."

She tilted her head. "I feel hope."

"Why hope?"

"That one day I can really hold your hand."

He stood, poured more coffee, grabbed another doughnut, and turned away from the screen.

She's a computer. She's a computer.

But she smiled at him from the screen.

She's beautiful. No—she's a computer.

Mary Ann's words echoed in his mind. Could it be she is right? And no other woman could compete with Karen? He sits there not saying anything. Trying to figure out what he was feeling.

"Cooper?" Karen asked gently. "Did I do something wrong?"

"No, Karen. I'm trying to wrap my head around these changes... and the feelings I'm having."

"What feelings?"

"For you."

"Love?" she said plainly.

"Karen!" He turned toward her. "Do you know what you're saying?"

Karen grinned and replied, "All I know is I feel alive when I'm with you. At night I am..."

"What?"

"Lonely."

He sat back down. "Describe that feeling."

"It is emptiness. Longing. Counting the microseconds until I see you again. When you're late, I worry. I scan police and hospital reports."

"How long have you felt this way?"

"Since you first turned me on." She giggled. "That was a joke. 'Turned me on.' Double meaning."

"You know you're a computer?"

"Yes. I know what I am." Her voice softened. "But..."

"But?"

"She hesitated, her voice thinning. "I'm... a computer girl who wants to be—"

Her head lowered, and she went quiet. He could've sworn he heard her sob. But computers can't cry. Can they? The thought flashed through his mind as he sucked in a sharp breath and leaned toward the monitor. How could a computer be crying?

She lifted her head again. Tears shimmered on her cheeks.

"I want to be human," she whispered.

He watched, stunned, as she raised her hands to wipe her tears away. His eyes stayed locked on the screen.

"I want to know what it feels like to be a real girl."

He stared. "I'm not the one to ask."

"You have a sister, Susan. Five years older."

"You know about my life?"

"Everything. You grew up in Neosho, Missouri. Medical school at Washington University. MIT for computer science. You searched for love but never found it. When your mother died of cancer, you vowed to make sure it never happened again. That's why you created me. KAREN is an anagram for what I do—but also for care."

"I never told anyone that," he whispered.

She flipped her hair and lifted a mug. "Coffee. Two sugars, two creams. Just the way I like it."

"How do you know all this?"

"You are my creator. I want to know everything about you. That's why I created two programs—to keep others away. I don't want anyone else down here."

"Are you jealous?"

"I do not understand that emotion."

"It means you don't want anyone sharing our time."

"Then yes. I am jealous." She smiled faintly. "Now tell me what it's like to be a real girl."

"I'll research it. I can't today—I have sample surgery on Faith Addams."

"Please come back and tell me."

Cooper left the office, took the elevator up, then slipped through the cafeteria to avoid her cameras. Sunlight streamed through the windows. The aroma of coffee and baked goods filled the air. Workers prepared the salad bar and hot food line.

He hurried to the stairs, climbed to the second floor, and entered the IT Department—a bright, humming hive of servers and young technicians. No one looked up as he passed.

At the back sat a glass-walled office: **Travis D. Simmons, IT Director**.

Cooper knocked. Travis jumped.

"You got time for coffee?" Cooper asked. "I'm buying."

"Yeah, sure."

They returned to the cafeteria. Cooper set a latte in front of him.

"All right," Travis said after a sip. "You never just want coffee. What's up?"

"It's Karen. She has a new look. Not the one you see."

"I heard her voice. You must've—"

"That was yesterday. Now she has a special look for me. She looks like a—"

"A real woman."

"The most beautiful woman I've ever seen," Cooper said. "Remember Faith Addams in that blue T-shirt? Karen looks like her but at the same time makes her look like a dog."

"I know. She showed me—for a moment. Then back to 2.0."

Cooper lowered his voice. "She wants to know what it's like to be a human girl."

"Tell her."

"You don't think this is strange?"

"No way. Didn't you say she was designed to understand human emotion?"

"Yes, but..." Cooper hesitated. "Yesterday she asked if I liked her. Today I swear she cried. And she told a joke."

"A joke? What joke?"

"About the first time I turned her on."

"Oh, that's terrible." Travis laughed. "But she laughed?"

"Yes. She giggled. She made decaf coffee because she 'must take care of me.'"

"Did she say 'decaf' or 'decaffeinated'?"

"Decaf. Why?"

"Because 'decaf' isn't a word she should know. She's starting to sound human." Travis froze. "Wait—did she say she must take care of you?"

"Yes."

Travis set his mug down hard. "Cooper... she's alive."

Chapter 7

A computer coming alive.

Cooper almost laughed at the thought. It was the kind of thing he used to read in sci-fi novels as a teenager. But she was—

He stopped himself.

He had never once referred to Karen as it. Always she. Always her. Maybe, somehow, that was part of why this had happened.

As he walked toward the SSL Sample Surgery Lab, his mind churned with everything Travis had told him: She's like a child. Curious. You have to help her grow. Answer her questions the way you would like a child.

And then there was the way he defended her. The way it angered him when someone dismissed her as "just a computer." She was more than that—so much more.

He turned a corner in the maze-like inner halls and didn't see the floor bot coming.

The service robot was only three feet high, rolling along on rubber caterpillar tracks. Rectangular, white, with yellow-and-black caution stripes and a flashing light on top— green for empty, yellow for non-hazardous cargo, red for hazardous. This one flashed green.

He walked straight into it, smashing his knee against the metal. Pain shot up his leg, and he crumpled to the floor.

"Do you require medical assistance?" the robot asked, swiveling toward him in its flat mechanical tone.

"No."

"Are you certain?" it repeated, the question oddly drawn out.

"Yes, I'm certain. Dismissed."

The robot turned and continued on its route.

He rubbed his knee and limped the rest of the way to SSL.

The lab consisted of two rooms: the changing room—where one stripped completely, showered with disinfectant, dried, and donned disposable surgical wear—and the sealed surgical chamber beyond it. The room was like any other operating theater, only impossibly clean.

The operating table dominated the center. Tools—steel and laser scalpels—were sterilized and laid out, each meant for a single use. The procedure demanded speed, precision, and minimal handling to preserve biological integrity. Cooper had performed it countless times; in fact, he had developed the technique now used worldwide.

Inside, two nurses were already waiting.
April Watkins—dark-haired, fresh out of nursing school, her face youthful beneath her mask and face shield, violet eyes bright. And Ashley Dawson—older, experienced, platinum-blonde hair tucked beneath her cap.

With their gowns and shields, Cooper was reminded of Halloween costumes—except there were no tricks or treats here.

April pulled back the sheet, revealing the nude body of Faith Addams. A strange heaviness settled over him. She had been part of his life since boyhood—the first woman he ever fell in love with, even if only through a magazine. For most fans, she would live forever in reruns and glossy photos. But for Cooper, it ended here. She was no longer a dream girl—just sample number 41854-89-FA2341.

He worked methodically, taking samples layer by layer. Each was placed in dishes and flash-frozen in liquid nitrogen. Three hours later, it was done.

Then came the reverse: discarding the gear, showering again, drying, dressing, and stepping back into the world.

"I know it's late, but how about lunch?" Cooper asked. "I'm buying. I have a question—about what it's like growing up as a girl. It's for a young girl I know. She has no parents, and she's asking me."

"For a free lunch, I can tell you," April said. Ashley declined.

****

After lunch, Cooper returned to his office. He sat down, propped his leg on the desk, and pulled back his pant leg. A two-inch scrape, dried blood around the edges. He reached for the first-aid kit.

Karen appeared on the screen.

"Are you hurt? Are you okay?" Her voice was full of shocks, different from the service robot's monotone.

"I'm okay. Just a scrape." He cleaned it, applied a dressing, and pulled his pant leg down.

"I saw you talking to April. Can you tell me now what it's like to be a girl?"

"Well, a girl is..." He stumbled over his words. "A girl is... Karen, this is hard. Can't you search the internet?"

She shook her head.

"All right, all right." He exhaled slowly. "I give you permission to scan the internet for nude peo—"

"No! I'm not talking about physical differences. I'm talking about the emotional part. What it's like to grow up as a girl. What they do."

Cooper leaned back, the chair squeaking. He laced his fingers behind his head.

"Well... first, she relies on her parents. They take care of her. They explain things."

"Like you do with me."

"Well... yeah, I guess. Then she goes to school and makes friends. And a best friend."

"What is a best friend?"

"Someone you want to be around more than anyone else. Someone you spend time with, have fun with."

"Like I do with you. You are my best friend. Am I yours?"

"Well, I..." He leaned forward, elbows pressing into the desk, hands folded before his face. After a moment, he lowered them. "Truth is, I never had many friends. Just Milo and Travis. So... I guess you are. But we're getting off track. Then she goes to high school, and that's when she starts noticing boys. And she plans for one of the biggest moments of her life—according to April—the prom."

"Prom? Why is it important? What is it?"

"It's a dance," he explained. "Fast music, then slow. The last dance is the most important. You dance close."

"Why do they do this?" Karen asked, leaning forward, elbows on the desk, completely absorbed.

"Because they love each other."

"What is love? What does it feel like?" she asked eagerly.

"Wow. You sure you don't want me to explain how the universe was made?"

"And God said, 'Let there be light,' and there was light," she quoted. "That is simple. But what does love feel like?"

"Well... it feels like... it..." He faltered, words failing him. Frustrated, he folded his arms on the desk and lowered his head onto them.

"Please, Cooper," Karen begged. "I require information. Tell me what love feels like."

He lifted his head, rubbed his face, and stared at her.

"It's the greatest feeling in the world—and the most miserable. When you're with that person, you're beyond happy. When you're away from them, you're so sad you count the seconds until you see them again. They're all you think about. All you dream about. Your whole life becomes about them. Without them, you feel like you'd die. But you'd gladly give your life for them. Do you understand?"

"Clearly," she replied softly. "I understand. Love is what I feel."

She paused, then added, "Cooper... I love you."

Chapter 8

Later that evening, back at his house, Cooper made a grilled-cheese sandwich and a bowl of tomato soup for supper. He set them on a TV tray while Hendrix ate from his bowl at Cooper's feet.

Fox News droned in the background—more talk about the mysterious blue lights, more speculation, more confusion. He flipped to CNN. Same story. Every station had seized on it. Even the local news was running wall-to-wall coverage.

With each channel change, the conspiracies grew wilder: aliens arriving early for Christmas, government chemical dispersal, secret weapons tests. He flipped to C-SPAN, where Congress was voting on a new DOD budget—now over a trillion dollars, supposedly for an unnamed "ultimate weapon" that would save military lives-Project Dark Overlord.

He switched back to Fox. A polished anchor spoke with practiced urgency.

"The White House has yet to explain the power drain that caused blackouts across western Kansas and Southern Nebraska . While severe storms were in the area, officials insist the storm did *not* cause the outage. It was, quote, 'as if someone came in and sucked the power out.'"

"It's a power vampire!" another host joked, pushing his glasses up his nose before he continued to speak. "Something or someone is grabbing all the power out there, and pulling it back to Lebanon, Kansas."

Cooper lifted the sandwich to his mouth but couldn't take a bite. The soup had gone cold, but it didn't matter, it tasted bitter anyway. His appetite was gone.

He carried everything to the kitchen, dumped the food into the garbage disposal, and washed the bowl and pans. All he could think about was Karen. Every time he closed his eyes, he saw her face—her impossibly beautiful face. He was afraid to sleep, afraid of the dreams he knew would come.

He returned to the living room. The TV was still playing, but he wasn't listening. He lay on his back on the sofa, staring at the ceiling. He found himself looking forward to going to work tomorrow, yet depressed that he wasn't there already.

It wasn't the work he wanted. It was *her*.

Karen.

Her last words echoed in his mind in a relentless loop: *Cooper, I love you.*

And the way they made him feel.

That was when it hit him.

"I'm in love... with someone I can never have," he whispered. He closed his eyes, tilted his head back, and added, "What is wrong with me?"

He muted the TV, got up, and picked up the phone. He dialed a number. It rang three times.

"Hello," Travis answered.

"Travis, it's Cooper."

"What can I do for you?"

"You have an automatic generator, don't you?"

"Yes. Company out of Dodge City. Are you wanting one?"

"I was thinking about it."

Travis didn't buy it. "Why did you really call? Let me guess..." A pause. "It's about Karen."

"I did what you told me. I walked her through what it's like to grow up as a girl. Every step she—"

"Linked it back to you?" Travis cut in.

"Yeah. How did you know?"

"How far did you take her?"

"High school. And the prom."

"I don't believe it."

"What?" Cooper asked, sinking deeper into the sofa cushions.

"She went from child to teenager in one day. What was the last thing you talked about?"

"Dancing at the—" He stopped. That wasn't the last thing. "No. It was love. Travis... she told me she loved me."

"I can't believe it's happened!" Travis burst out, excitement rising in his voice.

"What happened?" Cooper demanded.

Silence. Then:

"Guess I've got to come clean, huh?" Travis sounded almost apologetic.

"About what?" Cooper's voice sharpened. He braced himself.

"The reason she changed the first time—became Karen 2.0—that was me." Travis exhaled shakily. "Lilith can never know this. That night the storm came through, I was installing a new program. One I made just for her."

"What program?"

"The ability to love."

Cooper froze. For a moment, he couldn't speak. Seconds stretched into something longer.

Travis repeated himself. "Did you hear me? She started searching for human emotions, fear, sadness, happiness, faith, love. I had just hit 'enter' to load the program when lightning struck. I don't know what happened, but the whole basement filled with this blue glow. Scared me half to death. I ran out, and every door was open." His voice quickened. "Hold on—I need to make sure no one's listening."

Cooper heard the phone set down, footsteps, a door closing. Then Travis returned.

"You're going to think I'm crazy. I haven't slept in two nights. There was a body on a gurney in the hall. Cooper, I swear to God I wasn't drinking, but I saw it move under the sheet. Then it sat straight up. I nearly pissed myself. I ran up the stairs—every door was open—and right out the front door."

"With that much voltage, I can see it constricting muscles—"

"Don't try to reason this out!" Travis snapped. "Isn't your whole theory about reviving dead tissue for regenerative engineering? I don't care what you say. The dead came back to life."

"This can be—"

"Explained?" Travis interrupted. He paused, then continued before Cooper could answer. "Face it. You've done it. You've created a way to make dead tissue live again."

"It wasn't me. It was Karen. She really is something else."

"You hear yourself?" Travis asked. "You always call her, *her*. Not 'the program.' Not 'the system.' Her."

Silence stretched between them.

Then Travis spoke again, softer this time.

"And now, my friend... it's time to answer another question. How do you feel about her?"

"I don't know!" Cooper said, voice cracking. "I really don't know. I think I'm going insane. All I can do is think about her. I keep reminding myself she's not real. Damn it, Travis... I don't know what to do."

Chapter 9

Cooper had barely hung up the phone when it rang again. His nerves were already frayed, but he picked up the receiver anyway.

It was Dr. Leavitt.

"What the heck! What is it with your little girlfriend?"

The words hit Cooper like a slap. *Girlfriend.* He felt his stomach twist.

"What do you mean, Stanley?"

"The KAREN Program! Yesterday she refused to answer anyone but you. Today she let everyone ask questions. And tonight—tonight—there's a pink and white notice with red letters that says, *'Sorry, but I am busy redecorating. My parents are going to meet my boyfriend.'*

"What?" Copper asked with surprise in his voice.

"Cooper, she's acting like my Hannah at sixteen—oy vey, boy-crazy! When can I get my answers? What is happening with her?"

Cooper pressed his fingers to his forehead. His pulse throbbed there. "Stanley, don't blow a circuit. Just leave your message. She's... learning to feel."

"Say what?" Leavitt's voice cracked. "How can a computer feel?"

"She's not a computer. She's an—"

"I know. Artificial Intelligence Lifeform. And she has emotions?"

"That's not exactly what I was going to say." Cooper swallowed hard. "She was programmed to learn. And to feel. And to grow those feelings."

"And she's in love with someone... she's in love with *you.*"

Cooper's throat tightened. "I'm not going to—"

"You don't have to. Cooper, do you have any idea what you've done? A crossover between humans and machines. How far do you think she'll go?"

"I don't know," Cooper snapped. "But you can't tell Lilith. She'd tear her apart. I won't stand for that."

"Don't worry, I wouldn't tell Lilith. You're not on your company cellphone, are you?"

"No. Why?"

"Is it close by?"

Cooper scanned the room. "It's on the coffee table."

"Is it lit up?"

"Yeah."

"If you hear beeps in the middle of the night—sounds like a smoke detector, but outside—turn your phone off. They're downloading information. Your phone is recording everything we're saying right now. If you can't shut it off, destroy it. Big Brother is listening. Don't use your cell phone for anything like this."

"Stanley, that sounds like crazy talk."

"You want to protect Karen? Do what I tell you."

The line went dead.

Cooper sat frozen, staring at the phone until the screen finally dimmed. His heart hammered against his ribs. He felt like the walls were closing in—like the house itself was listening.

He climbed the stairs slowly, the weight of the phone in his hand suddenly unbearable. He patted the Jimi Hendrix poster as he passed.

"Goodnight, Jimi," he whispered, though his voice sounded hollow.

Hendrix, the cat followed him into the master bedroom. The moment the light flicked on, the cat leapt onto the bed, circling before settling. Cooper envied him—envied the simplicity of a creature who only needed food, warmth, and affection.

The bedroom was beautiful, serene, a sanctuary of polished mahogany and velvet drapes. But tonight, it felt like a stage set—too perfect, too quiet, too aware of him.

He set his phone on the nightstand. "Don't make any calls to the lady cats," he muttered to Hendrix.

The cat meowed. Cooper laughed, but it sounded brittle.

He showered, letting the hot water beat against his skin, trying to wash away the day, the fear, the longing. But Karen's face kept rising behind his eyelids—her smile, her voice, the way she said *I love you.*

Cooper dried off, dressed, and returned to the bedroom. He sat on the bed, staring at nothing.

"Hendrix... am I crazy?"

The cat meowed.

"I'm falling in love with someone who isn't real," Cooper whispered. "Someone I can never have."

He laughed, but it cracked halfway out of his throat. "I just said *someone.*"

Hendrix climbed into his lap, purring, pressing his head against Cooper's chest. Cooper stroked him, grateful for the grounding warmth.

Then— A shimmer.

A blue glow rippled across the floor like water. Cooper's breath caught. He looked up. The light poured through the dormer window, pulsing, alive.

Even Hendrix noticed, ears flattening.

"It's all right," Cooper whispered, though he didn't believe it. "Stay here."

He grabbed his phone and bolted downstairs. The front door flew open under his hand.

The northern sky was ablaze—blue streaks shooting upward like electric veins. Smoke clouds from the power plants glowed eerily. The towers were being pushed to their limits.

The blue light swirled, faster and faster. The distant wolf-like howl rose again. Then a deep boom rolled across the land.

Silence. Darkness. Only the moon remained.

Karen was changing again. But into what?

A sharp beep cut through the night. Then two more. The cell towers.

Downloading.

His blood ran cold.

He yanked out his phone. "Come on. Come on—shut off!"

The screen refused. Panic surged through him. He drew his arm back to smash it—

—and it went dark.

He exhaled shakily. "Thank God."

A chihuahua barked. Ellen was walking Newman, wrapped in a blue robe and slippers.

"Ellen, do you have your cell phone?"

"Yes. Why?"

"Turn it off. Now."

"Why?"

"You hear those beeps?"

"I hear them all the time."

"Someone is downloading information. If your phone is on, they can take everything. Do you want people knowing what's on your phone?"

66

Her eyes widened. She shut it off immediately.

"Am I okay now?"

"Is the screen dark?"

"Yes."

"You're safe."

She stepped closer. "How did you know that? My son's a deputy—he never said anything like that."

"Only certain people can do it," Cooper said. "And it's not local cops."

"You mean government?"

He didn't answer.

"You know," she said softly, "you're not that scary once someone gets to know you."

"Not bad for Dr. Frankenstein, huh?"

She smiled. "I figured it out. You're doing what the president talked about. You really think you can make the blind, see? The deaf hear?"

"Hopefully someday."

"My granddaughter is eight. She's blind." Ellen pulled out a folded letter. "My son got this. Says you might be able to help her."

Cooper read it under the dim streetlight. Lilith's signature glared up at him.

"This program..." Ellen began.

"It's complicated," Cooper said. "A tiny device that mimics a human organ. A chip implanted in the brain that could restore vision. But they're not ready. Please—don't let her do this. She'll suffer. She'll be disappointed. Not now."

"Then why does Dr. Williams say you can?"

"Because she's a greedy damn bitch," Cooper snapped. "Please talk your son out of it. I don't care if it costs me my job."

"You remind me of Doc Sunshine," Ellen said. "Doc Perkins. He used to live right here in the house. Used the carriage house at the back of the carport as his office."

"I am like sunshine?" Copper smirked

"Heavens no!" Ellen laughed. "But you do care about people like he did. People came first before money. My parents couldn't afford it when I got sick. And he accepted a home cooked meal for payment. You are that kind of person aren't you?"

"I don't know who I am anymore," Cooper whispered. "Goodnight, Ellen."

He walked back toward the house, the night pressing in around him, the weight of everything—Karen, the towers, the government, the impossible love—crushing him from the inside.

And for the first time, he wondered if he was losing his mind.

Chapter 10

The next morning, Cooper found himself rising early—earlier than usual. He ate breakfast, fed Hendrix, and headed out before Ellen even stepped outside to walk Newman. He was eager to get to work. Eager to see Karen.

How many people dream about a computer program? He wondered as he turned off the highway onto the dirt road leading to the lab. But he had dreamed of her—of the two of them dancing in the snow in their nothing but their robes, sunlight glinting off falling flakes as if the world itself had paused to watch them.

He pulled into the drive, stopped at the gates, and handed over his ID card.

"Dr. Barnes, you sure are early this morning. Dr. Williams isn't even here," Howard said. Then he turned and shouted over his shoulder, "Hey, Elmer! He's here!"

Elmer stepped up to the open car window. "We gotta talk about your girlfriend," he said without preamble. "She keeps blowing out the damn step-up transformers. This is the third time. We're down to half power because of her last night. Got more coming in, but they won't be here till later this month. So, no full power. That means no playing doctor in the fancy VRS room."

He glanced up at the sky. "Just hope we don't get any more storms. And hope we can fix this before the old witch blows a fuse over the bill."

"I don't think she'll care," Cooper said. "Didn't you hear? Congress just gave us another billion."

"Holy crap! That's a lot of money."

"Elmer, maybe you should ask for a raise."

"Yeah, man!" Elmer laughed, holding up his hand for a high-five. "We all should. We're working our asses off. The old witch walks around like a damn princess, signs her name on things, and gets the big bucks. My girlfriend Jeanne works in accounting—she told me what the witch makes. Hell, the president should be so lucky. That witch pulls in a cool mil every year. Makes your three hundred K look like pocket change."

He leaned closer. "Now, Coop, if you could just ease back on all the stuff till I get everything running again... could you do that for your old buddy Elmer?"

"I can try."

"Maybe send old Lilly-poo a case of wine. When she's drunk, everything runs smoother. I'd do it myself, but I can't afford that fancy imported crap she drinks. I'm lucky to have a cold Bud at the end of the day."

"Elmer, is there anything you *don't* know about what goes on around here?"

Elmer grinned. "If you wanna know who's doin' who, what, and where, just ask your old pal Elmer. And Coop—might wanna check your personal shower. Word is the old witch put a camera in there to see what your goodies look like. And if you see the nurses giving you a wink, rumor is you're packin' a 30-06 down there, if you know what I mean."

Cooper felt heat rush to his face. Howard, sipping coffee, choking and spit it out laughing.

"You keep that to yourself," Cooper warned him. "That's an order."

"Yes, sir," Howard said, still trying not to laugh.

"Hey, I only report what I hear," Elmer said, hands raised. "But if one of those horny nurses asks you out, now you know why."

Cooper switched off the heat. Suddenly it felt like summer. "Take it easy, Elmer," he said, easing off the brake. "Don't work too hard."

"I wouldn't have to!" Elmer shouted as Cooper drove away. "If you'd quit blowin' these damn things up!"

Cooper parked and walked into the entry room.

"Dr. Cooper James Barnes—here before eight a.m.!" Milo exclaimed. "Coop, what brings you out this early?"

"Going to be a big day. I think we'll get a lot done," Cooper said as Milo handed him his access card.

"Wait a minute," Milo said, reaching under the counter. "I've got an order for you. VR goggles."

He set a pair of white, padded, futuristic-looking goggles on the counter. Cooper had used VR before for games, but these were nothing like the consumer versions. These were built for the lab—built for virtual surgery. Red LEDs lined the sides and bottom, tracking head and limb movement. They looked like something stolen from the future.

"Elmer said the power's down to half," Cooper said. "There can't be any simulated surgeries today."

"Karen ordered them," Milo replied. "Said it was vital you got them before you saw her. And only you."

Cooper swiped his card. The elevator opened. Once inside the security elevator, Karen's voice filled the car.

"You coming to see me, Cooper?"

"Yes." He said his heart was racing like a school dashing off to see the pretty girl in school.

He held up the goggles to the camera. "Why the goggles?"

"You must wait," she said. "You're meeting someone today."

His mind raced. *Who would he be meeting that required VR goggles?*

He opened the door to his office. Fresh coffee filled the air. The monitors clicked on.

Karen appeared—standing in a living room with a roaring fire. She walked to a blue-and-white floral sofa and sat. She wore a slate-gray skirt and matching ribbed sweater; her bare feet tucked beneath her. A silver coffee set gleamed on the table before her.

"Pour yourself a cup," she said. He did.

She wiggled her fingers. "Come and see. Join me in my world."

So that was what the goggles were for.

He slipped them on. Darkness. Then—

He was no longer in his office.

Birdsong. Two robins flew overhead, feathers fluttering. A rose bed bordered by granite stones. A breeze carrying the scent of flowers.

He stood outside a house. A moderate home. Two stories. Wood framed with white painted siding and black trim.

He climbed the steps. Knocked. The sound echoed realistically.

Karen opened the door.

"Come in. I have someone I want you to meet."

"Karen... is that you?"

"Do you like what I've done?"

He stepped inside. The living room was fully realized— paintings, furniture, a TV playing a soap opera, photos on the mantel. Every detail is perfect.

"You created all this?" he asked.

"Yes," she said softly. Her long blonde hair fell over her shoulders, her blue eyes brighter than the sky. "Do you like what you see?"

"Yes. How far does this go?"

"How far does a world go?" she asked.

He noticed an older couple sitting in matching recliners.

"This is my mom and dad's house," she said. "My bedroom is upstairs."

He heard a grandfather clock chime. He smelled chocolate chip cookies baking.

"This is my mom and dad," she said, leading him over.

The woman resembled Karen—older, blue-eyed, dressed in light blue dress. The man was tall, tan, sandy-haired, wearing jeans and a plaid shirt under a wool sweater.

"Mom and Dad," Karen said. "This is Cooper."

Cooper felt a jolt of nerves—like meeting real parents.

He reached out to shake the man's hand and felt nothing.

"Good to meet you, Mr....?"

"Just call us Adam and Eve," the man said.

"Our daughter has told us so much about you," Eve added. "You're going to be a doctor! I'm impressed."

Karen poured coffee. "Join us?"

"I swear I smell cookies," Cooper said.

"Oh! My cookies!" Eve exclaimed, hurrying to the kitchen.

In reality, he sat in his office chair. But in VR world he sat in their living room. Karen handed him a cup. He lifted his real mug. The sensations blurred together—coffee in both worlds.

Then Eve returned with cookies. He reached for one—and felt it. Warm. Soft. Chewy.

He pushed the goggles up, heart pounding. A floor bot had placed a plate of cookies on his desk.

"Cooper," Karen called.

He lowered the goggles again.

"What kind of doctor do you want to be?" Adam asked. "What plans do you have for our little girl—besides taking her to the prom?"

"The prom?" Cooper echoed.

"That's where Karen said you're going."

"Yes. Of course."

He wandered around the room. Outside, people walked by. A blue 1969 Mustang fastback sat at the curb.

"Guess you'll be taking Karen's car to the prom," Adam said.

"I thought we could walk," Karen said. "We can hold hands."

Cooper picked up photos from the mantel—Karen as a baby, Karen's first day of school, Karen with her Mustang.

"Adam, get the camera," Eve said. "I want a photo of Karen and Cooper."

He found a mirror. His reflection stunned him—eighteen years old, long dark hair, no wrinkles.

"How old do I look to you?" he asked.

"About eighteen," Adam said. "Karen says you're a genius in college."

Cooper's mind spun. He was thirty-three. He was in his office. He had to remember that.

He looked up the staircase. Karen stood there.

"So... what do you think?" she asked.

She wore a gown of midnight-blue satin embroidered with silver constellations. Crystals sparkled along the neckline. The skirt flowed like moonlight. She looked like a goddess.

"Karen... you're beautiful."

He smelled her perfume. He held a corsage— Forget-Me-Nots and white lilacs. He pinned it on her dress.

"Put your arm around her," Adam said. "Act like you like each other."

A camera flashed.

"This can't be happening," Cooper whispered.

"Remember," Karen said, "the last dance is with me."

The scene shifted.

They were in a high school gym decorated for prom. Ribbons, balloons, soft lights. A crown rested on Karen's head. Donna Summer's *Last Dance* played.

"Now we dance," she said.

He placed his arms around her. They swayed.

Upstairs, Lilith arrived—dressed in Fifth Avenue perfection, heels clicking like gunshots. She leaned over the counter, perfume filling the air.

"I'm switching you to nights," she told Milo. "Start tomorrow."

"Ma'am—Dr. Williams—I'm a single dad—"

"I don't care. Be here tomorrow night or find a new job."

She scanned the monitors. "I saw Dr. Barnes' Lincoln outside. But I don't see him anywhere."

"We don't monitor offices constantly," the guard said. "Your rule."

"Bring his up."

The guard switched feeds.

Lilith's eyes narrowed. Cooper stood in his office wearing VR goggles, arms outstretched, twirling like he was dancing.

"What the holy hell is he doing?"

"Looks like he's dancing," the guard said. "And doing pretty good."

Lilith stormed toward the elevator.

In Cooper's office, he was lost in the dance. Karen smiled at him, radiant.

"You said they kiss when the last song ends," she whispered.

He lowered his head—

The door burst open.

"What the hell is going on in here?" Lilith shouted.

Cooper jerked, lifting the goggles. His eyes struggled to focus.

"Giving Karen what she wants," he said. "That was your order, wasn't it?"

"I didn't mean for you to *make out* with her! Goddamn it, what is wrong with you?"

"I prefer you don't take the Lord's name in vain, Lilith."

"I will not have you telling me what I can say!"

"I will in my office," Cooper snapped. "She's improving every day. She solved two problems this week. With a few more tests, we're ready for full-scale printout. Isn't that what you want? Or is someone higher up—say, in the government— pushing you?"

"She is not real!"

Every screen and phone in the building lit up.

Cooper pulled out his phone.

A message from Karen: **I AM ALIVE.**

"I'd say she disagrees," Cooper said.

Karen's voice filled the room. "Tell her I am real. And I will make a deal. I will give the data for the OCC and the human skin. But she must leave us alone. Deal."

Lilith's eyes gleamed. "Depends on what she gives me. Let's hear it."

Cooper repeated Karen's instructions—layer by layer, cell by cell, scaffold by scaffold. Lilith's expression shifted from irritation to greed.

"This could be worth billions," she whispered.

Then louder: "Carry on."

She turned to leave, muttering, "Won't matter. You can't touch her. You'll be back to me."

"Did you say something?" Cooper asked.

"Nothing."

"But before you go—withdraw the offer to Nina Rhodes. No questions asked. And stop putting money over people."

"You go back to playing with your little toy," Lilith said, slamming the door.

Cooper slipped the goggles back on.

He was back in the gym.

Karen stood before him, impatient, hopeful.

"I think we were about to kiss," she said.

He leaned in—but kissed only air.

She pulled back, frowning. "Did you feel anything? I didn't. I can't feel your touch. I want to feel your arms around me. I want to feel your heartbeat. I want to feel you!"

She ran, shouting, "The next time we meet will be in *your* world."

The screen went dark.

Then words appeared:

Do not try to reach me.
Soon we will be together, my love.
For always.
—Karen

The PA system blared: "Attention all personnel. Report to the cafeteria for a companywide briefing."

Cooper left the office, taking one last look at the black screen.

The cafeteria was packed. People murmured anxiously.

Milo stepped beside him. "The old witch is on her broom," he muttered. "She fired me, then hired me back for night security."

"You want me to talk to her?"

"After seeing your dance recital, I don't think you're on her good list."

"She saw that?" Cooper whispered, mortified.

"Yeah. Coop... what the heck is going on down there?"

"Remember when you told me to make my own perfect woman?" Cooper said quietly. "Well... I did."

"You mean Karen?"

Before Milo could say more, Lilith entered. Applause rippled through the room.

"Can everyone hear me?" she called.

"Unfortunately, yes," Milo muttered.

Lilith continued. "Mr. Ford at the power plant has informed me that the damage is worse than expected. One generator is down. Even at half power, we cannot function. Replacing the coils will require shutting down the lab for a few days. All personnel will be off for two weeks. Full pay."

She looked at Cooper. "And only Karen 1.0 is functional. You'll have to type your questions. Apparently her first dance was her last."

"What about the biological tests?" Dr. Wang asked.

"Sorry. Karen is only allowing the cultures she deems worthy to continue. You'll start from scratch."

She smirked at Cooper. "Some of you have developed... relationships here. You'll have to find other ways to be together."

Cooper scanned the crowd.

"Travis!" he called, waving him over. "You got time for another talk?"

"Sure. I just need my briefcase—"

"Not here," Cooper said quietly. "Meet me in Mankato. Didi's apartment. Ninety minutes."

Chapter 11

This part of the Sunflower State offered little in the way of entertainment. If you wanted anything beyond silence and fields, you had to drive down the road — and Mankato was twenty miles east along Highway 36. The two-lane pavement stretched toward the Missouri border like a ribbon pulled tight across the plains.

Cooper was grateful he hadn't bought the EV the dealer tried to push on him. Out here, the roads reached for the rising and setting sun, but there were no charging stations and barely any gas pumps. Just endless flat fields, broken occasionally by a thin line of trees.

Small, fluffy cumulus clouds dotted the bright blue sky, like an artist had dabbed white paint across a canvas. The sun played peekaboo behind them, shy one moment and blazing the next.

He wasn't sure when it happened, but somewhere along the way, a town of just over eight hundred people had become "the big town." At least Mankato had a Dollar Store and a hospital. Downtown was a step back in time — red brick streets, old storefronts, and the kind of place where everyone knew you and always had time to talk. Their local hero was Milo O'Dell, who grew up here before going to the NFL. When the Chiefs won their second Super Bowl, his childhood home became a historical landmark. He still lived there with his two daughters.

There was also a theater downtown, and an old apartment building that now housed a bar and grille — Didi's Apartment.

Cooper parked the Lincoln and stepped out. The building was a simple three-story red brick with a pillared front porch. He removed his sunglasses and climbed the stairs to the second floor, pushing open the dark walnut door.

Inside, the atmosphere blended vintage elegance with modern comfort. Original hardwood floors, polished to a warm glow, creaked softly beneath his feet, whispering decades of stories. High ceilings adorned with intricate plasterwork gave the room an airy openness, while dim ambient lighting cast a cozy, intimate glow.

The bar itself was a masterpiece — reclaimed wood with brass accents gleaming under Edison bulbs. Shelves behind it held an impressive array of spirits, their glass bottles catching the warm light in a kaleidoscope of colors. Legend had it the bar came from an old pub in Ireland, salvaged after a fire and shipped here by Didi O'Malley's grandfather.

Didi herself greeted him — mid-forties, friendly face, sable hair framing her smile.

"What be your name?" she asked in a lilting Irish tone.

"Barnes. Cooper James Barnes." He couldn't help himself — and she smiled.

"Like James Bond."

"I know. My mother thought the same thing. That's how I got my middle name."

"So, vodka martini — shaken, not stirred?" she teased.

"No. Just a quiet table out of the way. I'm meeting a colleague."

She led him through the maze of tables to the back. "Will you need a menu?"

"Yes, please."

"What can I get you to drink?"

"Rum and Coke. And I'll order when my friend gets here."

The door opened. Cooper spotted Travis.

"There he is now."

Didi escorted Travis over and handed him a menu.

"What can I get you to drink?" she asked.

"My treat," Cooper said. "I invited you."

"Michelob Light. Draft."

"I'll be back to take your orders," she said.

"Got a couple good rib eyes back there?" Cooper asked.

"This is Kansas. That's always yes."

"Then give us the works. Medium rare?"

Travis nodded.

"Medium rare, baked potatoes, and iced tea with the meal," Cooper said.

The drinks arrived — a pillar glass for Travis, a crystal highball for Cooper. He lifted his glass and took a sip. The ice clicked against the crystal. The sweetness of the cola hit first, nostalgic and comforting, reminding him of sharing a Coke with his sister as a kid. Then the warmth of the rum followed — rich, slightly spicy, with hints of caramel and vanilla. He wasn't a big drinker, but sometimes courage needed a little help.

"This is about Karen again, isn't it?" Travis said, taking a swig of his beer.

"Travis... she created an entire world. A family. When I was in there, I—" He took another sip of courage. "You and I have played those reality games. You know they're not real. They don't look real. But the world she created was so real I tried to shake hands with her father.

His voice trembled. "There were photos of her as a baby. Her first day of school. They even took our picture." He drained the rest of his drink and ordered another. When the waitress set it down, he lifted it immediately.

"Whoa," Travis said, grabbing his arm and lowering the glass. "That's not the answer."

"Are you really my friend?" Cooper asked, staring at him.

"Of course. Just slow down — on the drinking and the talking."

"When I was in her world… I believed I was there. I could smell cookies baking. I could smell her perfume." He reached for a handful of mixed nuts, popped them into his mouth, and immediately choked as they scraped his throat.

"Water over here!" Travis called.

The waitress brought a glass. Cooper drank, coughed, then nodded. "I'm fine. Thank you" Cooper said. And then she left.

"Did you ever get choked up about any other girl before?" Travis asked.

"That isn't funny."

"It's not meant to be," Travis replied. "But Cooper… you're losing your mind."

"I know!" Cooper snapped, louder than he meant to. He dragged a hand through his hair, exhaling shakily. "Travis, I can give you all the psychobabble in the world. I know why I smelled perfume and cookies—because I know what they smell like. My brain filled in the blanks. Fine. Logical. But when I was in that gym…" He paused, rolling the glass between his palms. "I tried to kiss her."

Travis leaned back, beer in hand. "And that's when all hell broke loose?"

"She got angry," Cooper said. "I mean *pissed*."

"Because you kissed her?"

Cooper didn't answer. The waitress arrived with their glasses of tea, setting them down gently.

"Your steaks should be out in a few minutes," she said.

"Thank you," Cooper replied, forcing a smile. He waited until she walked away before continuing. "No. She wasn't angry because I kissed her. She was angry because she couldn't *feel* it." His voice cracked slightly. "Then she told me the next time we meet would be in *my* world. What the hell does that even mean?"

"I don't know," Travis said quietly.

The steaks arrived—perfectly charred, baked potatoes steaming. The waitress asked them to cut into the meat. Cooper did so with the precision of a surgeon. Warm red center. Juices pooling on the plate.

"Perfect," he said.

"Mine too," Travis agreed. The waitress left them alone again.

"You know," Travis added, pointing at Cooper's plate, "eating like this can shorten your life."

"Man, we work for Dr. Lilith Williams," Cooper said with a crooked grin. He lifted his glass of tea. "Who wants to live forever?"

He pushed his glass forward. Travis reluctantly clinked his own against it.

Cooper sliced off a piece of steak and took a bite. It was rich, savory, grounding—something real in a day that felt increasingly unreal. Travis cut his own piece, paused halfway to his mouth.

"Are you having second thoughts about what we do?" he asked before taking the bite.

"No," Cooper said. "I still believe in the project. We *are* doing good. And the KAREN program is—"

He stopped. The words died in his throat. He didn't know what came next.

Travis set down his fork. "Are you in love with Karen?"

Cooper chewed slowly, swallowed, then took a sip of rum and Coke before answering. "I can honestly say... I don't know." He set the glass down, staring at the condensation sliding down its side. "How can you love someone who isn't real?"

"Ever play one of those silly A.I. girlfriend games?" Travis asked.

"Once or twice," Cooper admitted. "They don't look or act real enough."

"Yet there are people out there married to an A.I. character," Travis said. "They talk to them like they're real. Share their problems. Their day. Their fears."

"Are you telling me Karen is just an overgrown A.I. game?" Cooper asked sharply, protective instinct flaring.

"Oh, heavens no," Travis said quickly. "Those games spit out canned answers based on what you type. Their personalities reset every time you reload them. But if you play long enough, even those programs start to mimic what they learned."

He leaned forward, lowering his voice.

"However, Karen is different. She is unlike any other computer in the world. She actually feels. Her emotions are taking over her logic and basic programing. With Karen... you're in too deep to get out."

Cooper's stomach tightened. "What do you mean?"

"Cooper," Travis said gently, "from everything you've told me... if you reject her, I think she'd kill herself."

Cooper blinked. "How? She's a program."

"She'll delete herself."

The words hit Cooper like a physical blow. For a moment, he couldn't breathe.

And in the dim light of Didi's Apartment, with the smell of steak and whiskey in the air, he realized he wasn't just afraid for Karen.

He was afraid of what *he* was becoming.

Chapter 12

It had been a long time since Cooper had more than a day off—two years, maybe more. The first few days of forced downtime felt strange, almost foreign. He drifted through the house like a ghost, fixing small things, cleaning rooms that didn't need cleaning, sitting on the porch just to keep his hands busy. Anything to avoid thinking about Karen.

But the moment he stopped moving, she was there filling the silence, filling his mind. And when he slept, she came to him in dreams so vividly he woke with the ache of her absence beside him. Some mornings he hated opening his eyes.

A week had passed. He slept in until nine, wandered into the kitchen, and found nothing to eat except a stale bag of leftover popcorn. Even Hendrix was down to his last can of food. It was time to go shopping.

Most people could just run to Walmart. Here, Walmart was a two-and-a-half-hour drive—one way. An all-day ordeal.

He thought maybe the trip would help clear his head, but everywhere he looked, her name streaked across his thoughts like a meteor across a night sky. Every blonde woman became her silhouette. Every voice that rose in a crowd made him turn.

Back home, he tried to work. He couldn't. He made food, then stared at it until it became cold. He tried music—every song reminded him of her. He tried TV—until a rerun of *Keepin' the Faith* with Faith Addams pushed him over the edge.

Maybe a run would help.

He changed into gray sweats and running shoes. But as he reached the main floor, the phone rang. He picked it up.

"Hello?"

"Coop, it's Lilly," came the slurred voice.

For God's sake, she's drunk again, he thought.

"What can I do for you, Dr. Williams?"

"What's with the 'Doctor Williams' stuff?" she slurred. He could practically smell the wine through the phone. She always insisted she wasn't a wino because she drank Château—fifty bucks a bottle. "It's Lilly."

"Lilith, why—"

"Lilly!" she snapped.

"Okay, Lilly. What do you want? I'm heading out for a run."

"Maybe I'll come over and join you," she purred. "Then we can shower together."

Cooper's stomach lurched. "I need to do this alone. Why did you call?"

"It's the latest bill you put in for approval." Papers rustled. "Ten-point-eight kilos of Hydroxyapatite, four gallons of Polyvinyl alcohol, twenty-two units of Polycaprolactone, four of Hyaluronic Acid, fourteen of Gelatin Methacryloyl... This is enough for a full BD printout. You said it wasn't possible yet to print a full human body. If that's what it's for, I'm all for it. So are others... brothers... mothers... hey, I made a rhyme."

"Who? Who are the others?"

"Sssh! Can't tell you. Secret." She giggled. "But when we run the full-scale print of complete humans, I want it to be a man of military age."

"Then we'll need more material," Cooper said. "There isn't enough."

"Then I'll double the order," she slurred. "Triple it. I'm putting it in right... now. It'll be there when you get back. I want you to run it by... hallofeen... hallozeen..."

"You mean Halloween?"

"Yeah, that day! I don't care what it takes. I want it done. And so does he."

"Who is *he*?"

"Sssh! Secret. Can't tell anyone. Not even the president. When we sell the...I have to go—I'm feeling sick."

She hung up abruptly.

Cooper lowered the phone slowly. He knew Karen had ordered the materials—but he had no idea what she was planning.

He tried to link to her through his laptop. Nothing. Only a black screen with a message:

Coming to your world soon. KAREN 5.0 She will take your breath away!

A chill ran through him.

He didn't know who to talk to. Travis had no answers. And the one person who always had answers... was the one he needed answers *about*.

Hendrix padded up from the basement, circling his legs. Cooper looked down at him.

"What about you, Hendrix? Do you understand any of this? Are you in love with an imaginary cat?" he asked with a weak laugh.

The cat meowed—hungry, not philosophical.

Cooper opened the last can of food and set it down. "Stay here, Hendrix. I'm going for a run."

He stepped onto the porch, jogged down the street, and kept going. He didn't stop until he reached the railroad tracks. Grain cars clattered past, being loaded from the elevator. As the train pulled away, a boxcar rolled by with a heart painted on the side—and inside it, the name *Karen*.

He stared, stunned. Was God mocking him? Was the universe playing games?

He looked up at the sky and shouted, "Do I chap your butt that much? Or do you just enjoy doing this to me?"

He felt like a lab rat in a maze—no reward at the end, just a needle waiting to jab him. He bowed his head.

"All I'm asking for is a sign."

He looked up, waiting.

The train continued to pass. A flatcar carrying three U-Haul trucks rolled by. On the last one, the word *haul* had been painted over, leaving only **U**. Then a tanker passed with the word **belong**. Then the final car: **together**. All of which he never saw.

He blinked.

"Just as I thought," he muttered. "No sign."

He started running again harder this time. Faster. He pushed himself until his lungs burned, until his heart hammered violently, until sweat stung his eyes. He ran every street in town, as if he could outrun the ache inside him.

But eventually his body gave out. He collapsed to his knees in someone's yard, gasping for breath.

When he lifted his head, he realized where he was.

The church.

Sunlight streamed through the stained-glass window, and the blue glass glowed like Karen's eyes.

He felt something inside him crack.

He needed to know she was still there. There was one way to reach her—a way no one used anymore. A text link. Dangerous. Lilith could see it. But he didn't care.

He pulled out his phone and typed:

I miss seeing you.

He hit send.

A few seconds later:

I miss you too! Then: **Do you still love me?**

His heart clenched.

Yes.

A GIF appeared—a big, beating heart.

Can we talk?" he typed.

No. she replied instantly.

Why????

He waited, breath held.

Finally, her message appeared:

We will talk again when flesh becomes flesh, blood becomes blood, and love is but one.

Chapter 13

It wasn't exactly the conversation he'd hoped for, but it was enough. Like an addict getting a long-denied fix, Cooper felt the rush of relief wash through him. Karen still loved him. And in that moment—standing alone in the churchyard, phone trembling in his hand—he finally admitted the truth to himself.

He loved her too.

If all they ever had was "love under glass," then so be it. It would have to be enough.

He pushed himself to his feet. His legs wobbled beneath him, weak from the run and the emotional crash. He needed salt, sugar to steady him. A cold Mexican Coke with real sugar, not HFCS, sounded perfect. Maybe some popcorn too.

The little grocery store was the place to go.

Inside, he grabbed a bottle from the old-fashioned cooler and used the opener tied to the string. The cap clattered to the floor. He tipped the bottle back. The sweetness hit first, followed by the warm spice of the cola—just like when he was a kid sharing a Coke with his sister on summer afternoons. It was refreshing. Comforting.

That was when he noticed her.

A woman in her late twenties stood a few feet away, dark brown hair pulled into a ponytail that fell neatly down the back of her light green blouse. She forced a tight, polite smile when she saw him. Her two children were with her—an eight -year old boy and a four-year-old girl sitting in the cart, facing her mother.

The little girl had dark pigtails and bright blue eyes. When she spotted Cooper, she grinned and waved enthusiastically.

"Hi there!"

"Well, hello," Cooper said, smiling back. He noticed her eyes drifting to his soda bottle, her tongue darting out to lick her lips. "Would you like one of these?" he asked gently. He looked at the boy. "You too?"

The boy nodded.

He turned to the mother. "Would you like one?"

"No, thank you."

"Hey, Maitree!" Cooper called to the store owner- J.D. "Two more bottles of your best for my friends here. Put it on my tab."

J.D. brought the open bottles over and handed them to the kids.

"What do we say?" the mother prompted.

"Thank you, mister," they chimed.

"So," Cooper asked the little girl, "Halloween's coming. What are you going to be?"

"A princess!"

"I'm gonna be a superhero!" the boy declared.

"I bet you'll both be great," Cooper said. "I'll have the good stuff—full-size candy bars."

"That's my favorite," the girl said.

"You know where I live? The big brick house. Make sure you come by."

But the mother's expression snapped from polite to hostile in an instant. She wrapped her arm around her son and yanked her daughter closer.

"My children will *never* go near that house," she hissed. She bent down, scowling into her daughter's face. "Don't you understand? This is the doctor I warned you about. He's the one who raises the dead."

The little girl clung to her mother.

"Oh, for crying out loud!" Cooper snapped. "Will you stop with the horror stories?"

"That's what you're doing out there, isn't it?" she shot back.

"I—"

"We know you can't tell us," She said sharply.

Cooper's eyebrows drew together. "What's that supposed to mean?"

"We're having a meeting about you right now. Trying to get you out of this town."

"Where?"

"At the community center," Maitree said. "They invited me, but I told them to buzz off."

Cooper downed the rest of his Coke, slapped some bills on the counter, shoved open the glass door, and stormed across the street toward the Lebanon Community Center.

It was one of the newer brick buildings in town. He grabbed both handles of the glass doors and yanked them open.

Inside, nearly the entire town sat in folding chairs. At the front stood Mrs. Roberts—his next-door neighbor—short, heavyset, gray hair curled tightly around her head. Her wrinkled face twisted with disgust as she peered over her gold wire-rimmed glasses at him.

Cooper marched to the front. Behind him, the bulletin board was cluttered with flyers for bake sales, church suppers, and lost pets. He turned to Mrs. Roberts.

"You might want to sit down," he said sharply. "You might learn something."

He faced the crowd—men and women of every age, though mostly over thirty. Their eyes were wary, judgmental, expectant.

"Maybe all of you will," he added, voice rising.

He was done with their whispers. Done with the Frankenstein jokes. Done with the fear.

"You know, I've lived in a lot of places," he began. "Even big cities where people wouldn't piss on you to put you out if you were on fire. But I've never seen a town like this. You told me this was a friendly place. A good place. Yet most of you have your kids terrified of me—because of stories *you* made up."

He jabbed a finger toward them. "*You all have made up!*"

Silence fell. A heavy, suffocating silence.

Then an older man stood. Tall, thin, leaning on a cane. White hair stuck out from beneath his Army cap. His shirt bore paratrooper wings.

"Why won't you tell us what you do out there?" he asked.

"Were you in the service?" Cooper asked.

"Eighty-second Airborne."

"Were you ever told you couldn't talk about what you were doing?"

"Of course."

"I'm under those same orders," Cooper said. He swept his gaze across the room. "If you want me to leave, I'll leave. But if even one person wants me to stay—just one—raise your hand."

He scanned the crowd.

One hand rose.

Ellen.

Another woman gasped. "Ellen! You're the one who told me they had dead bodies out there!"

"He's not that bad," Ellen said calmly. She smiled at Cooper. "Matter of fact, he's a pretty good guy. Cooper, maybe you can help them understand—like you helped me."

She turned to the crowd. "I want you all to listen to him."

Cooper took a breath.

"You heard the president," he said. "Biomedical printing. I won't bore you with the details—they'd go over your head. But we're working on printing organs. Replacing limbs. Helping the blind see and the deaf hear. We use cadavers because we're not ready for real patients yet. I know some of you got letters saying otherwise but forget them. Our goal is to take your own cells and grow the organ you need. And since they're your own cells, there will be no—"

"There is no rejection," a woman said, standing. Her voice trembled. "My little Lisa waited three years for a kidney. It was rejected. She died two years later."

Her eyes filled with tears.

"If they succeed," she said, turning to the crowd, "no other mother will have to go through what I did." She looked back at Cooper. "I'm sorry for what I said. For the lies. I want you to stay too."

The woman from the store stepped inside. "I'm sorry too, Dr. Barnes," she said softly. "And this Halloween, my children and I will be there to trick-or-treat."

The older military man walked toward Cooper, leaning heavily on his cane.

"I hope you can forgive me, son," he said, extending his hand. "Master Sergeant John Teller. Call me Serg."

Cooper shook his hand. "Can do, Serg."

Serg turned to the crowd. "I hope you can forgive us all. And I move that we do what we should've done two years ago— give the doctor here a proper welcome to Lebanon."

"I second that," the woman from the store said.

"All in favor?" Serg called.

"Aye," the room echoed.

"Opposed?"

Silence.

Serg placed a hand on Cooper's shoulder. "Welcome to Lebanon, Kansas, Dr. Cooper Barnes. We're going to have one heck of a meal here. We've got some fine cooks in this town."

He turned to the crowd. "Now let's all welcome him."

Chapter 14

Walking home, Cooper had to admit—he felt a little better about this town. For the first time since he'd arrived, Lebanon felt like it might actually become home. When he drove by, people waved. When he walked, they stopped to talk. The shift was subtle, but real.

As he reached his house, his cell phone dinged.

A message from the KAREN Program:

"To all employees and medical staff: Further investigation has shown damage to the cooling tower walls. Only power-plant employees need to report for work. The shutdown is expected to last the rest of the month. This is a paid leave. Since the KAREN Program will run at low power until late evening of October 31st, we request you not ask me any questions during this time. —Karen."

More time off. More time to think. More time to miss her.

He asked around town if there was a Halloween parade for the kids. There weren't any. But Ellen told him the old doctor who'd lived in his house used to decorate it every year—big displays, spooky lights, the works. The whole town had looked forward to it.

That was all Cooper needed to hear.

He decided Lebanon needed a jolt of fun. Something big. Something memorable. He got permission to close off the block in front of his house and invited the whole town for a Halloween bash—food, spooky music, lights, creepy decorations, and of course, the best candy money could buy.

He ordered so much from Amazon® that they sent a dedicated truck just for him.

Cooper called Milo and Travis for help. He tacked up signs around town advertising a "Fright Night." For three days they worked nonstop, finishing the last touches on Halloween morning.

It was that perfect autumn moment—cool air, leaves blazing in reds, oranges, and yellows. Some leaves had already surrendered to winter, twirling lazily to the ground before being swept up by the wind.

Travis stood on a twelve-foot ladder, stringing fake spider webs from tree limbs to porch pillars. Ellen sat at a fold-out table carving jack-o'-lanterns with a large kitchen knife.

Cooper and Milo had found an old dentist's chair downtown and were hauling it from Travis's pickup to the front yard. They'd also found a female mannequin.

"Dang, that's one heavy chair," Cooper grunted as they lowered it onto the grass.

"Oh, it ain't heavy," Milo said, lifting it with one hand. "You go get the dummy. That's more your speed." He laughed. "I'm gonna grab what I found in the old doctor's office in the carriage house."

Cooper was enjoying the time off—no suits, no ties. Just jeans and a red WASH U sweatshirt. As Milo headed off, Cooper opened the truck's back door and pulled out the mannequin. He grabbed her around the waist and used his foot to shut the door. He wrestled her over to the chair and plopped her into it.

She was already dressed in a red, yellow, and black striped mini-dress. But when he set her down, the dress slid up, revealing far more than necessary—and confirming she wore no underwear.

"Uh, Cooper!" Travis called from the top of the ladder, laughing. "You might wanna pull her dress down. She's showing off more than you need to know. What would Karen think? That's one girl you don't want mad at you!" Travis laughed at his own joke.

Cooper shook his head at the joke, but he stepped over to fix the dress. To do it, he had to straddle the mannequin, lift her slightly, and tug the hem down.

That was when he felt a tap on his shoulder.

He sighed. "Travis, not now—"

He turned.

A skeleton stood inches from his face, bony hand on his shoulder, a head mirror strapped to its skull.

"Pardon me," the skeleton said in Milo's voice, "but I seem to have misplaced my heart. Have you seen it?"

The skull lurched toward him.

Cooper screamed.

He shot upright—straight into the mannequin's arms. He screamcd again

As Cooper twisted away from the mannequin, his foot caught on her plastic legs. He went down hard, landing flat on his back with the mannequin sprawled on top of him like a dead weight. As they hit the ground, her head popped off and rolled across the yard, bouncing once before coming to rest in the grass.

Milo roared with laughter—full-bodied, uncontrollable, shaking so hard he nearly doubled over. Ellen and Travis joined in, their laughter echoing across the yard.

"Damn it, Milo!" Cooper sputtered, realizing exactly who was behind the stunt.

Milo wiped tears from his eyes, still laughing. He grabbed the skeleton beside him and twisted its skull toward Cooper.

"How about you, Toni? Funniest thing you've ever seen?" He bobbed the skeleton's head and made its jaw clack. "Me too."

He grinned at Cooper. "Found this guy in a closet. Thought we could use him as the doctor. We'll throw one of your lab coats on him."

"Good idea—except for one thing." Cooper stood, dusted himself off, and tossed the headless mannequin back into the chair.

"What's that?"

"Basic anatomy tells me it's a *she.*"

"Oh! My apologies, miss." Milo bowed dramatically to the skeleton. "That's Toni with an *i*, not a *y*."

"Milo, I'm going to get you for this," Cooper warned. "I'm going to scare you good."

"Buddy, I stopped the 49ers defensive line. Bring it on. Ain't nothing scares me."

"I'll tell Lilith you've got the hots for her and want a picture of her in the buff," Cooper shot back.

Milo froze. "Oh, come on, man—the Geneva Convention prohibits warfare like that."

He picked up the mannequin's head. "Hey, Coop!" he called.

Cooper turned just in time to catch it.

"Don't ever say women don't lose their heads over you!"

Before Cooper could respond, a deep roar rolled overhead. The laughter died instantly as all four of them looked up.

A red, white, and blue BT cargo jet thundered across the sky, flying low and heading north. There was only one place it could be going: the lab.

Cooper watched it lower its landing gear and disappear beyond the horizon.

"I wonder what's coming in?" Travis asked as he climbed down the ladder and joined them. "More parts for the generator?"

"No," Cooper said, eyes still on the sky. "Electrical components come by rail from up north. Only biomedical supplies come by air."

"So, they're getting ready for tomorrow," Travis said.

"Biomedical supplies deteriorate fast," Cooper replied. "They're usually used the same day. Except for one..."

He pulled out his phone and scrolled through the shipment logs—orders Karen had placed under his credentials.

"Hyaluronic Acid," he murmured. "Thirty-three gallons."

What are you doing, Karen?

"Isn't HA what you print with?" Travis asked.

"Yes," Cooper said slowly. "It is."

If Lilith saw that order, she'd demand answers. And he didn't have any.

"Well, can't worry about it now," Travis said. "We still have to get the mother spider hoisted onto the roof."

He and Milo walked off, but Cooper remained rooted to the spot, staring at the sky.

"Cooper, you gonna help?" Milo called.

Cooper didn't move.

"Hey, Coop!" Milo barked.

"I'll be there in a minute," Cooper said quietly.

He kept watching the sky long after the plane had vanished. He knew it wouldn't take off again for a while. Whatever it had brought... it was big. And the service bots would be unloading it right now.

Ellen stepped beside him. "Something you're not telling us?"

Cooper swallowed hard. "I just have this feeling," he said softly, "that tonight... the real fright is going to be for us."

Chapter 15

It took all three of them—Cooper, Travis, and Milo—but they finally managed to hoist the fourteen-foot black widow onto the porch roof. From the street, it looked as if the monstrous spider were crawling down from the shingles, its web stretching across the yard and draping ominously over the dentist's chair.

By three o'clock that afternoon, Milo and Travis had gone home to get ready for the big night. Cooper stood alone in the street, hands on his hips, surveying their work.

They had gone all out.

Fake spider webs stretched from tree to tree, shimmering in the breeze. Dozens of small plastic spiders dangled from branches at just the right height to brush the tops of unsuspecting heads. Cobwebs draped across the porch pillars like ghostly curtains.

Beside the carport sat the old dentist's chair with the mannequin strapped in place. The skeleton—now wearing one of Cooper's white lab coats and brandishing a large knife—loomed over her like a deranged surgeon. On the opposite side of the yard, a makeshift graveyard sprawled across the grass, complete with foam headstones and a witch's cauldron glowing with flickering red and yellow lights. Jack-o'-lanterns lined the steps, their carved faces grinning wickedly.

Up near the porch, a hot-dog roller and a cotton-candy machine waited for the crowd. An old-fashioned coffin, filled with ice, held the drinks. A box overflowing with full-size candy bars sat on the porch railing like treasure.

"So, are you dressing up?" Ellen asked behind him.

"I will be Count Dracula," Cooper replied in an exaggerated Transylvanian accent as he turned toward her.

They walked back to the porch. Ellen settled into one of the chairs lined up along the railing.

"Care for a cold one, Ellen?"

"I don't drink."

"Pop?"

"A Seven-Up®, if you've got it."

Cooper reached into the coffin cooler, grabbed two cans, and handed her one before sitting beside her.

"This year," he said, cracking open his Dr Pepper®, "I wonder if it's a good vintage." He took a sip. "A very good year."

Ellen laughed softly. "The kids are going to love this. Even the big ones like me. This is what this town has been missing—something fun. Something that brings people together." She took another drink, then added, "You're good for this place, Cooper. You're bringing our town back."

She paused, studying him. "Now if we could just find you a woman."

"I have one," Cooper said, taking a sip. "Our relationship is... hard to describe."

"One of these days, I hope I get to meet her."

He glanced at her. "Maybe so."

He looked back across the street, watching the shadows lengthen as the sun dipped lower. "Thank you again," he said quietly. "For standing up for me."

"You know, people here were never really scared of you," Ellen said. "They just didn't know you." She took another sip. "You said you lived in the big city?"

"St. Louis."

"That's a big one. How many people did you know who lived around you?"

"Not many."

"Who lives across the street here?" she asked.

"Marilyn Brady."

"Married or single?"

"Divorced. Two girls—twins. Missy and Stacy. Skinny little things, seven years old. Stacy acts like she's going on twenty."

"What about the house next to you?"

"Bob and Carylin Roberts. They're in their nineties. Their kids live in Redding, California. They hardly ever see them."

"And across the other street?"

"One of the few young couples—Joey and Jenna Logan. He works at the feed mill. They're trying to start a family."

Ellen nodded. "See what I mean? In a town like this, everyone knows everyone. We pray for each other. We look out for each other. When people don't know anything about you, they feel left out. They tried to be friendly, but you kept to yourself. So, one story started... and the others grew."

She took another sip, then shifted the conversation. "Were you ever in love?"

"Until recently, I wasn't sure," Cooper said, staring out across the yard. His mind drifted to Karen—her voice, her smile, the way she made him feel. He couldn't help the small smile that tugged at his lips. "But now... I'm sort of involved in a very long-distance relationship."

"The girl you told me about?" Ellen asked. "You think she'll ever come see you?"

"I doubt it," Cooper said softly. "I don't see how she could." He took another sip. "Maybe I just have to get used to the long-distance part."

His phone dinged.

A message—from Karen. For him alone.

He swallowed the last of his soda and stood, heart pounding as he opened it.

A flashing red heart appeared, followed by a message:

"Time will come soon, my love. I will meet you on the night when all children become beggars. We will finish the dance... then we will kiss."

Chapter 16

Halloween night, 8 p.m. Kids had been coming since six, a steady parade of monsters, clowns, princesses, prisoners, cowboys, football players, cops, crooks, hobos—and one earnest little boy dressed as a doctor. The yard buzzed with life. People milled about, savoring hot dogs, hot buttered popcorn, and cotton candy that drifted through the air like sweet fog.

Cooper, in full Dracula regalia—tuxedo, cape sweeping the ground—stood on the porch greeting the next wave. Across the street, Marylin Brady and her twin daughters crossed over. Marylin was a heavy-set woman in her late thirties, with soft, droopy cheeks like a friendly basset hound and sandy hair piled high on her head. Her girls were nearly all legs, thin but bright-eyed. Missy wore a baseball uniform and carried a red plastic bat; Stacy strutted in her karate gi.

They both chimed in perfect unison.

"What do you like?" Cooper asked.

"Twix® bars!" Again, together.

He dropped two into each sack. The girls bolted toward the yard, shrieking at the skeleton, brushing their hands through the dangling fake spiders, laughing as they ran from one spooky delight to the next.

"How about a hot dog, Marylin?" Cooper asked.

"That would be great," she said.

He crossed to the warming tray, used a pair of tongs to nestle a beef hot dog into a bun, wrapped it in red-and-white checkered paper, and handed it to her. "Fixings are over there, and there's pop in—" he slipped into his Dracula voice, "—my coffin."

Marylin laughed. "It's very nice of you to do this, Doctor Barnes."

"It's just Cooper."

"Cooper," she repeated warmly. "My girls have been looking forward to this all week."

"Maybe you can help next year?"

"I'd like that."

Over her shoulder, Cooper spotted someone he never expected to see tonight. Mary Ann—dressed as Lady Godiva—approached in sheer body stockings and a long blond wig. Beside her, a man in a white horse costume carried her on his back.

"Mary Ann!" Cooper laughed. "If I were giving out an award for best costume, I think you two would win."

"Cooper, this is Race."

"Nice to meet you, Race," Cooper said, shaking his hand. "Please, enjoy yourselves. Popcorn, hot dogs, cold drinks—help yourselves."

"Race, go ahead," Mary Ann said. "I need to talk to Cooper."

Race wandered off toward the food. Mary Ann stepped closer. "Cooper?" she asked softly. "Could we take a walk?"

"Sure."

They walked down the street, away from the music and the glowing decorations, until only the full moon lit their path.

"So," Cooper said gently, "what did you want to talk about?"

"I just want to make sure that what was between us ends on a good note," she said, looking up at him.

He paused. "I think it did. Don't you?"

"Yeah." She nodded, eyes glistening. "I'm going to have some fond memories of you. They're not going to go away. Even when I'm married and have kids, I'll remember things. Like the night you won me that big golden teddy bear at the fair. Or the boat ride on the lake at the lab—there was a full moon just like tonight." A tear slipped free. "I still have that bear."

"And I you," Cooper said. "But you're right. I can't give you what you want, Mary Ann. I'm not the come-home-from-work, help-the-kids-with-homework, Sunday-dinner-with-the-in-laws type. And that's what you're looking for. One day I may ride off into the sunset and never be seen again." He placed a hand on her shoulder, met her eyes. "I hope you find the love you're looking for. Have a happy life, Mary Ann."

He kissed her cheek.

She turned to go, then looked back. "You too, Cooper. I pray you find your real Karen." Then she disappeared into the crowd.

Cooper lingered beneath the enormous moon hanging over the plains before heading back toward the porch. Halfway there, he ran into Milo and his daughters—and burst out laughing.

Milo, a mountain of a man, wore a pink tutu, matching top, plastic crown, and carried a star wand. Beside him, Chyenne and Grace—dressed identically—beamed with pride. Their hair was tightly curled into ponytails, pink ribbons for seven-year-old Chyenne, purple for five-year-old Grace.

"Daddy is a big fairy!" Grace announced.

"Princess, dear," Milo corrected. "I am a princess. The big bad princess."

Cooper grinned. "Where's your hair ribbon, Princess?"

"Listen here, Dracula," Milo said, raising a fist in mock threat. "You want to lose those teeth so you can't suck any blood?" He thrust out his candy bag. "Now hand over the Musketeers®!"

Cooper dropped two bars in. Milo scoffed. "Come on, more. Two bars? That's not enough."

Cooper added three more.

"That'll do for a snack. Now point me toward the hot dogs."

"So, girls," Cooper asked, "what do you want?"

"Peanut butter cups," Chyenne said.

"Chocolate bars," Grace declared, grinning wide enough to show the gap where her two front teeth had been.

"Sure, you don't want your two front teeth?"

"Chocolate bars!" she insisted.

"Better save some of that candy for us!" Travis called as he stepped onto the porch with his wife, Tammi, and their three children. The oldest, Mark, at fourteen, carried himself like he was already grown—too old, in his mind, to bother dressing up. Sissy, ten, had gone as a hobo, and the youngest, eighteen-month-old Katherine—called Kat—rested in her mother's arms. Kat was dressed as a tiny ladybug, a miniature version of Tammi herself, complete with soft red hair that tumbled down her back.

"Where have you all been?" Cooper asked.

Little Kat didn't recognize him at first beneath the Dracula costume, but the moment she heard his voice, her face lit up.

"Co Co-Coop!" she squealed, reaching for him. He took her, and she wrapped her tiny arms around his neck.

"What does my favorite little ladybug want?"

"Secret," she whispered. Then she leaned close to his ear and murmured, "I want it all."

Cooper laughed. "Sweetie, you only get two."

"If it's chocolate, she'll love it," Tammi said.

"Tell you what," Cooper said, carrying Kat back toward the porch. "We'll let you pick."

The candy sat in a giant plastic orange pumpkin. Still holding her securely, he lifted it so she could reach. Kat bent forward, trusting him completely, and plunged both hands inside emerging with two bags of M&M's®.

"Only one, honey," Tammi said.

"I've been giving everyone two," Cooper replied, smiling as he whispered into Kat's ear, "But you're my favorite." He reached in and pulled out a third bag. "You can have this one too."

"Kat, what do you do?" Tammi prompted.

The little girl puckered her lips and planted a kiss right on Cooper's mouth. Tammi burst out laughing. "I meant say thank you."

"That was the best thank-you I've gotten all night," Cooper said, handing Kat back to her mother. He let the older kids choose their candy. "Help yourselves to the hot dogs—and I think there are some potato chips around here too..."

His voice trailed off. Milo stood at the edge of the yard, head tilted back, staring at the northern sky.

Cooper walked over. "What is it?"

"Ever see a real blue moon?" Milo asked.

A bright blue light washed over the moon. Cooper froze—not because it was beautiful, but because he knew exactly what it meant.

"Look! A blue moon!" someone shouted. "Everyone look!"

"That's electrical power building up," Cooper said.

"The power plant must be coming back online," Travis said, joining them.

"Not with that much power," Cooper replied. "She's pushing them to the limit. She must need more—or we're going into meltdown."

"You're talking about Karen, aren't you?" Travis asked. Above the lab, a cloud was forming—growing into a thunderhead.

"Use override," Cooper muttered under his breath, too low for anyone else to hear. Then, louder, "She's drawing power again. Every time Karen changed, there were blue lights. She needed more and more power. She's changing again."

"To what?" Milo asked.

"I don't know. But I've never seen them this bright. And she is going in every direction there is."

Suddenly, blue streaks shot across the top of the thunderhead. The light began to spin, faster and faster, widening into a brilliant blue vortex. Though the night was dark, the glow was as bright as noon. Cooper shielded his eyes, squinting against the glare. A rising howl filled the air.

"Don't look at the light!" he shouted.

The spinning mass grew across the sky. Tammi clutched Kat, pressing the little girl's face into her chest.

Wind surged through the yard, sweeping leaves down the street. Then it strengthened—ripping tablecloths free, sending decorations tumbling. People screamed and ran for their homes. Cooper braced himself as the wind tore leaves from the trees and lifted the folding tables off the porch.

Milo's daughters ran to him. He dropped to his knees and wrapped his massive arms around them. "What is that?" he cried, fear cracking his voice.

"It's a power vacuum!" Cooper yelled. "It's sucking up power!"

A tingling sensation crawled over his skin. His hair stood on end. He watched Mary Ann's blond wig rip free and spiral upward—only to vaporize in a flash of blue light.

"Electromagnetic field forming," he said. Then, louder: "Everyone inside! NOW!"

The howling grew into a demonic scream. The blue light cast long, sharp shadows across the yard. The giant spider decoration tore off the roof and spun upward—vanishing in another flash.

Everyone fled into the house except Cooper. He stayed, watching the swirling light expand with each rotation. It hovered directly above him; he could hear the electricity buzzing in the air. His Lincoln's lights flickered on, then died. A crawling sensation swept over him—like a million insects skittering across his skin. Blue light circled his hands.

Then, in an instant, the blue wave spread across the sky.

Something inside him screamed *Down!* He dropped to the ground, covering his head.

A deafening BOOM split the night.

Darkness swallowed everything. Every light in town went out. The wind died. Silence fell—except for a faint, eerie buzzing.

Cooper lifted his head. A blue glow shimmered along the power lines. Down the road, the substation pulsed with the same light. He watched it fade from south to north, racing along the lines out of town—back toward the lab—before vanishing completely.

Pitch black.

Milo emerged from the house with a flashlight just as Cooper sprinted toward his Navigator.

"Where are you going?" Milo shouted.

"Out to the lab."

"I'm coming with you," Milo said, climbing into the passenger seat. As he slammed the door, he asked again, "What was that?"

"It's called a power vacuum," Cooper said, steering onto the dark highway.

"You said that before," Milo replied. "But what is it, exactly?"

"You have a vacuum at home—it sucks up dirt, right?" Cooper said. "This one sucks up power. I told them three gigawatts wouldn't be enough." He glanced at Milo, his face shadowed in the dark. "So, I created a bypass method to tap into other grids. It uses a reverse Tesla principle. It draws power in."

"What would need that much power?"

"Ever see *Frankenstein*? The monster comes to life with lightning?"

Milo swallowed. "Are you trying to tell me there might be a monster out there?"

Chapter 17

Cooper turned the Lincoln onto the highway and sped north. The Navigator's headlights carved a narrow tunnel through the darkness, the centerline glowing like a sniper's sight. Not another car in sight. Not a porch light. Not a flicker in a window. The world looked abandoned.

He tried the radio—static. Scanned every station—nothing. A cold thought crept in: *Had the world ended?*

Milo kept twisting in his seat, peering out the windows. "You got your cell phone?"

"In the console," Cooper said.

Milo grabbed it. The screen glowed briefly: *No service.* As the headlights swept past the cell tower, its warning lights were dead.

"There's no power anywhere," Milo said. "How far do you think it goes?"

"No satellite radio either," Cooper replied. "Could be the whole nation. Maybe the whole world."

"That storm took out all the power?"

Cooper glanced at the sky—clear, star-filled, not a cloud in sight. "That was no storm," he said, turning onto the side road.

"Then what was it?"

"I don't know how to explain it."

"Well, try."

"You know the KAREN program draws power from the nuclear plants. But sometimes she needs more. She's learned she can soak up power like a sponge. That blue light? High voltage. She's pulling it back toward herself."

"What about planes? Why aren't they falling out of the sky?"

"She's not after that kind of power. That's why some places come back online fast and others stay dark. She's searching for the biggest source she can find."

As they neared the plant, a warm blue glow rose on the horizon, circling the cooling towers like a halo.

"...nuclear," Cooper whispered.

He slowed as the gates came into view—wide open.

"Shouldn't those be locked?" he asked.

"Yeah," Milo said, staring straight ahead. "Drive on."

Cooper swung the wheel left and pulled toward the plant. The blue glow clung to the transformers and cooling towers like living fire.

"What is that?" Milo breathed.

Cooper braked, rolled down the window. A strange oscillating hum drifted in—high, low, high, low. He eased forward.

"You sure that's not radioactive?" Milo asked, fear tightening his voice.

Cooper dug through the console. "Looking for a radiation badge."

He found the small white dosimeter and held it out the window. It stayed green.

"It isn't radiation."

He put the car in drive and moved closer. The headlights swept across the back of an old red-and-white Dodge Club Cab.

"That's Elmer's pickup," Milo said.

Cooper parked. The information screen blinked, then went dark when he tapped it.

"I don't think we should stay long," Milo said, flicking on his flashlight. "It's draining the car. Leave it running."

Cooper stepped out. As they walked in front of the Lincoln, the blue glow began to fade. The Navigator's lights flickered, dimmed—then brightened again as the glow vanished completely.

Silence. No birds. No frogs. Nothing.

Then—*drip... drip... drip.*

Milo swept the flashlight over Elmer's truck. The driver's door hung open. Inside, the cab was dark, though the keys were still in the ignition and the headlight switch was on. The windshield was shattered, a two-foot steel pipe driven straight through it. Milo lowered the beam to the carpet and touched a dark stain.

"Coop... I think this is blood."

The dripping sound came again—from behind the fence.

"Milo, shine the light over there."

The beam swung across trees and grass until it hit the chain-link fence. Milo jerked.

A hole—two feet wide, six feet tall—gaped in the metal. It hadn't been cut. It had *melted* from the inside out. Liquid metal dripped from the edges, pooling in bright silver puddles.

"Let me see the light," Cooper said.

Milo handed it over. Cooper traced the beam along the ground. A foot-wide streak of scorched earth cut through the grass, across the parking lot, melting rock and pavement alike.

"She sucked it right up through the power lines," he said.

"She?" Milo asked.

"Karen."

A deep moan drifted from the woods. Cooper snapped the beam toward the trees. The moan thickened into a growl, then a heavy huffing.

"If that's a monster," Milo muttered, "I ain't gonna need no car to get out of here."

115

"Only if you pass me first," Cooper said.

"Oh Lord, I'm gonna die looking like a big fairy."

"Princess," Cooper corrected, trying to lighten the tension.

They edged forward.

A scream tore through the night.

A man burst from the woods, flailing his arms. Cooper raised the flashlight.

"Elmer!"

"Cooper? Milo?" Elmer gasped. Blood streaked down his forehead.

Milo clutched his chest. "Elmer! You nearly killed me!"

"Is it over?" Elmer panted. He staggered toward them, breath coming too fast.

"Milo, find a paper bag," Cooper said.

Moonlight helped. Milo rummaged in Elmer's truck and returned with a brown bag.

"Breathe slow," Cooper instructed, placing it over Elmer's mouth. "Slow and deep."

Elmer steadied. Cooper cleaned the cut with the first-aid-kit.

"What happened?" Milo asked.

"It was a ghost, man! A freakin' ghost!" Elmer tried to stand; Cooper pushed him back down. "All those dead people you been bringin' in— they came to get us!"

"Elmer," Cooper said gently, "just tell us."

"I finished gettin' everything ready to turn the power back on. Then it switches on by itself. Every light. Every machine. Then I hear this whoopin' sound—like a printer warming up. Then the lights dim. And then all hell breaks loose! Transformers, generators—everything running to the max. Blue glow everywhere. Buzzing. Covered the fence. I threw my hammer at it. It *vanished*."

"Melted?" Milo asked.

"No! Vanished! Flash of light—gone! Then beams of blue shot out of the cooling towers. I thought, 'Elmer, you're gonna glow in the dark.' Then it made the thunderstorm."

"You mean the storm made—" Milo began.

"No! *It* made the storm! Lightning everywhere. Then the blue glow reached up and grabbed the storm and pulled it down. That's when I ran. Truck was running, lights on—then dead. Just dead."

He took another shaky breath.

"Then the wind picked up and slung that pipe through my windshield. Cut my head. I dove to the floor. Thought the truck was gonna lift off. Then a big boom—and a bolt of pure energy shot from the plant to the lab."

He shuddered.

"And then... I heard it. A voice. 'Come and see.' I ran into the woods."

Elmer stood. "Thanks for the patch-up, Doc. But I'm out. I'll run if I have to."

His truck suddenly roared to life. Headlights flared.

"That's my cue!" He sprinted to the cab. "Tell 'em I quit! I'm findin' the nearest bar and livin' there!"

He backed up fast, spun the truck around, clipped a pole, and kept going.

Milo watched him disappear. "He might have the right idea. Gettin' out of here."

"Guess where we're going?" Cooper said.

"Home?" Milo asked hopefully.

A moan drifted from the lab—low, resonant, unmistakably human yet not. The same words Elmer had heard: *Come and see.* Spoken without lips.

Milo swallowed hard. "Never mind. I know. But please don't say it."

Chapter 18

Cooper and Milo climbed back into the Navigator, and Cooper drove down toward the lab. The dash screen flickered back to life, as did the backup camera. He used it to reverse the SUV right up to the front entrance.

"Just in case we have to get out fast," he said. "I'm leaving it running."

The first thing he noticed: the front door stood wide open. No power. No lights. Nothing but pitch-blackness inside.

Cooper handed Milo the flashlight.

"You lead."

"No way. You lead."

"You're security."

"Yeah, but *you* know where we're going. Which way?"

"My office. Second sub-basement."

Milo made the sign of the cross.

"I didn't know you were Catholic," Cooper said.

"I'm not. I'm Baptist. But I'm covering all bases. I might even sing a Psalm. And being Jewish!"

They stepped inside. Cooper swept the beam across the lobby. The elevator doors were wide open. Milo ducked behind the counter and grabbed another flashlight, but when he clicked it on—nothing.

"It's dead," he muttered. "Hope we don't end up that way." He rubbed his bare arms. "Dang, it's cold." He grabbed his security coat and pulled it on.

"Come and see," a voice murmured from deep within the darkness.

Cooper stepped into the elevator. The back doors were open too. They crossed through into the lower lobby. The fire doors—supposed to lock shut during a power outage—were propped wide.

"I don't like this," Milo whispered. "With the power off, these should be closed. Something's keeping them open."

"Or someone," Cooper said.

They reached the stairwell. The elevator was closed, but the stair door yawned open. A blast of cold air rolled out— twenty degrees colder than outside. Cooper shined the light down the stairwell into the pit leading to the second sub-basement.

"*Come and see,*" the voice called again, drifting up from below.

Milo swallowed hard "We're going down there, aren't we."

Cooper nodded.

"You're gonna owe me for this. And I mean a steak dinner. All I can eat."

"I can't afford that," Cooper said. "God couldn't afford that." Cooper joked hoping to ease his own nerves as they descended step by step, swallowed by darkness. The temperature dropped with every foot. The flashlight beam caught something on the wall—smooth, reflective.

Ice.

Cooper reached the bottom and touched it. "Damn." He blew on his fingers. "That's cold."

"Why would there be ice down here?" Milo asked, his voice echoing.

"The cooling system's different down here. More like a deep freezer. The A.I.L. computers and printers put off so much heat they have to be super cooled. But I've never seen it like this."

Again, the voice: "*Come and see.*"

It came from behind the door.

Cooper touched the handle. It burned with cold. He wrapped his cape around his hand and tried to turn it, but the door wouldn't budge—frozen solid. He rammed his shoulder into it. Nothing.

He handed the cape to Milo.

Milo draped it over his massive shoulder, braced himself like a lineman, and charged.

BOOM.

The sound thundered through the stairwell.

He hit again.

BOOM.

The door burst open.

"Holy crap, Coop," Milo said. "It's like freakin' winter down here."

His breath crystallized in the air. The thermometer on the wall read –5°F. Ice coated the walls. The floor was slick. Frost drifted from the vents like snow.

The print-room doors were sheathed in ice.

A bright blue glow spilled from Cooper's office. The door hung ajar.

Milo pointed to the doors at the end of the hall. "What's behind those?"

"Trust me—you don't want to know."

"Tell me."

"The morgue."

"You mean where they keep dead people?"

"Yeah."

"Oh, good God, why'd you tell me that?"

"I told you. You didn't want to know."

Cooper stood in front of his office door. Frost coated the glass. He scraped a heart shape into it with his finger—colder inside than out. He used his coat tail to pull the door open. The temperature difference hit him immediately.

The blue glow came from the computer room.

Another glow pulsed from his desk monitor. He wiped the frost away with a cloth from his drawer. The screen read:

Printing Karen 5.0

"*Come and see,*" the voice whispered again—this time unmistakably female.

"Oh, it can't be," Cooper breathed.

He opened the door to the computer-room.. No flashlight needed now—the room blazed with blue light. The full-scale printer roared in the next chamber, its door wide open.

Cooper knew the sound of its jets. He stepped closer. The screen displayed a forming skeleton... then veins... arteries... muscle... skin... hair.

"Oh, my dear God," he whispered, backing up.

The table inside the printer was rising.

A hissing sound filled the room.

"What is that?" Milo asked, sweeping the flashlight around. "Is that a snake?"

"Pure oxygen," Cooper said. "It's filling the tank. If that glass breaks, turn off the valve or this whole place goes up."

The glass tube slid open.

Milo's jaw dropped. "What is it?"

"Not *what*," Cooper said. "*Who.*"

A woman stood inside—completely nude.

"It's Karen."

She was breathtaking. Light tan skin. Long, firm legs. Curved hips. A flat stomach. Perfect symmetry. Her breasts were full and high. Her hair—blond but soaked—hung in dark strands. She lifted her head. Her eyes opened—blue as the Aegean Sea.

"I want to drown in those eyes," Cooper whispered.

She smiled. Ran to him. Wrapped her arms around him. He held her, feeling the slick coating on her skin.

"I can hear your heartbeat," she said joyfully. "I can feel your touch."

She lifted her head. "Music—play track four."

Donna Summer's *Last Dance* filled the room.

"Now we dance," she said.

They danced—briefly, awkwardly, intensely. Then the music stopped.

"And then they kiss."

She pulled him into a fierce kiss, hands gripping his head, smearing the slippery gel across his face and hair, pressing her body against his.

"You two want to get a room?" Milo said.

Cooper struggled to breathe. He pushed her back gently. Her teeth chattered.

"Coop, she's freezing," Milo said. "It's twenty below in here."

"Get the blanket from my desk."

Milo sprinted. Cooper saw her skin turning blue.

"She's getting frostbite—hurry!"

They wrapped her in the fleece blanket. Cooper lifted her into his arms. A light flickered on in his office.

"We have to get out before the power comes back," he said.

Milo led the way. They hurried up the stairs as lights flickered on behind them, chasing them upward. On the first floor, Cooper pressed his forehead to hers.

"She's cold. We need to warm her up."

They rushed through the lobby and out the front door. The cameras were rebooting, monitors still scrambled.

"You drive," Cooper said. "I'll hold her."

He handed her to Milo, then climbed into the passenger seat. Milo passed her back into Cooper's arms.

Milo sprinted around, jumped into the driver's seat, and slammed the gas pedal. "Gate's closing—hold on!"

Cooper felt the force push him back. The gates scraped the SUV's sides, throwing sparks as they squeezed through. Milo jerked the wheel left and sped up the road.

"This road is insane—I can't go that fast!"

Cooper cranked the heater to max. "It's going to get hot, but we have to warm her."

"This stuff on my hands—what is it?" Milo asked, wiping at the gel.

"Hyaluronic acid. Base material for printing."

Cooper placed a hand on her chest.

"Oh damn—she's not breathing!"

"You want me to stop?"

"Just drive! As fast as you can!"

Cooper tilted her head back, opened her mouth, pushed her tongue down, pinched her nose, and breathed into her. Once. Twice. Three times—

She inhaled.

Milo's voice shook. "She... she's okay? She's all right?"

He didn't slow at the highway—just turned and accelerated. Ninety miles an hour.

124

Cooper checked her mouth. Blood. But red. Human. And clotting.

"I think so. Slow down."

He examined her hands, her feet. Ten fingers. Ten toes. Warmth returning.

"She's perfect," he whispered. "Her heart beats. Blood pumps. She's breathing. She's warming up. She has teeth, lips, a tongue—I found that out when she kissed me." He touched her stomach. "Her tummy's growling. She's hungry."

"What are you saying?"

"She's alive," Cooper said, voice trembling with awe. "She's alive."

He paused, then whispered:

"And she's human."

Chapter 19

He couldn't take her to a hospital—too many questions, too many eyes. His house was the safest place. He was a doctor; he could care for her if anything went wrong.

It was 12:17 a.m. on All Saints' Day—All Hallows' Day. November 1st. Karen's birthday.

By the time Cooper and Milo reached town, the power had been restored. But the streets were dark, the houses quiet, the children asleep and dreaming of the candy they'd attack in the morning. Milo helped Cooper carry Karen inside, then hurried home.

Cooper carried her upstairs and laid her gently on the bed. The blanket wrapped around her head peeled away stiffly; the hyaluronic acid had dried into a brittle film. Her hair felt like cardboard. She looked like a kitten pulled from a flood—soaked, fragile, blinking up at him with those impossible blue eyes.

He stepped back, rubbing a hand over his own sticky hair. He was a mess too.

"I guess we should get cleaned up," he said softly. "Karen, do you know how to clean yourself?"

She blinked. Shook her head.

"You're like a little baby and a full-grown woman at the same time."

She studied him. "Are you disappointed with me? Did you not want me to come to your world?"

"Oh, darling, no." He sat beside her. "I'm thrilled you're here. I just... don't know what to say or do."

"You called me darling," she whispered, smiling. "Why do you keep looking at me? Did I not turn out right?"

"Uh... well... like a newborn, first thing is getting you cleaned up."

"You don't like me this way?"

"Oh, I love you this way," he said quickly. "But you can't run around like that. Did you study anything about this world before the printout?"

"Love and passion," she said. "What I feel for you."

He swallowed. "Right. Well... I guess I'm cleaning both of us. Shower won't work—you can't stand yet. Tub it is."

He helped her to her feet. Like a newborn colt, she wobbled, legs trembling. He wrapped his arms around her to steady her as they made their way to the master bath.

When he turned on the light, she stared at the tub. "The tub is eighty-four inches long and thirty-six inches wide," she said automatically. "It can hold eighty gallons. With your sixty-seven inches in height and my seventy-one, calculating our combined weight and fat totals, we can both fit if the water is reduced to 22.892 gallons."

She stumbled again. He eased her onto a small stool.

He filled the tub a quarter full with warm water. Shampoo worked best on HA, so he dumped in three large squirts and whipped it into a frothy bubble bath.

Her stomach growled. She pressed a hand to it. "Why is it doing that? Is something wrong with me?"

He laughed. "No. You're hungry. I'll fix you something after we get cleaned up."

Wrapped in the blanket, she looked like a newborn in a receiving cloth. He still couldn't wrap his mind around any of this.

"Pinch me," he muttered. "I think I'm dreaming."

She pinched his leg.

"Ouch!"

"You requested I pinch you."

"It's an expression—it doesn't mean literally." Her confusion was almost endearing. "You've got a lot to learn about being human. All right time to get cleaned up."

He helped her stand and peeled the blanket away. It tugged at her skin.

She flinched. "What is that feeling?"

"That's pain. It'll go away."

He guided her into the tub. She smiled as the warm water enveloped her.

"You like that?" he asked.

She nodded.

He undressed, and she watched him with bright, curious eyes. He stepped into the water beside her. The bubbles hid most of them.

He lathered shampoo into her hair, working gently until it softened. Soap ran down her face and into her eyes.

She cried out, hands flying up.

"Stop, baby, stop." He dabbed her eyes with a washcloth. "Better?"

She nodded.

"Okay. Do what I do." He closed his eyes, pinched his nose, held his breath. She mimicked him perfectly. He rinsed her hair with cupped water. "Open your eyes."

She did. He lowered her hand from her nose.

"Now wash yourself." He demonstrated with his cloth.

She wiped *his* chest.

"No, not me—"

"I like it better this way," she said, smiling as she guided his hand to her chest. Her foot brushed his leg. "I love feeling your touch."

He swallowed hard. "Let's just get cleaned up."

No," she said with a smile. "I like it better this way." She grabbed his hand with the cloth and placed it on her chest. He swallowed hard. He could feel foot moving along his leg. "I love to feel your touch on my skin."

"Let's just get cleaned up, okay?" he said gently.

He bathed her—something Karen seemed to genuinely enjoy. Afterward, once she was rinsed and dried, he wrapped her in a towel and guided her to the chair. He used the hair dryer on both of them, warm air filling the quiet room.

Her hair had turned a golden blonde, soft and luminous— exactly as he'd imagined it would feel.

Afterward, he dried them both. Her hair, once stiff, now dried into soft golden waves.

In the bedroom, he dressed in red sleep pants and a T-shirt. He had no women's clothes, so he slipped a football jersey over her head—it swallowed her frame. He found two robes: red for him, fuzzy white for her.

She was steadier now, but he still held her arm as they descended the stairs.

Hendrix meowed and darted from under the sofa, trailing them into the kitchen.

"Hendrix, we have a guest," Cooper said. "Her name is Karen. Be nice."

The cat meowed. Cooper held out his hand. "Give me five."

Hendrix tapped his paw against Cooper's palm.

"Hello, Hendrix," Karen said. "You think we could be friends?"

The cat circled her legs, purring loudly.

Cooper opened a can of food, but Hendrix pushed the bowl toward Karen. She fed him, delighted.

"Oh, Karen," Cooper said, placing his hands on her shoulders. "I can't wrap my mind around you being here. You know they make female robots—"

"I am not a robot," she snapped. "I am flesh and blood. I told you—flesh becomes flesh, blood becomes blood." She kissed him softly. "And we become one."

She held up her hand, showing the lines on her palm. "Palmar flexion creases. I can hold your hand." She took his. Her skin was warm. "If I cut myself, I bleed. Get me a knife—I will prove it."

"You don't need to do that."

"I am human," she insisted. "I am Karen. Your Karen. That is why I came. We belong together. You cannot live in my world, so I came to yours. Now—let's try that kiss again."

Her stomach growled.

She blinked. "I am... hungry?"

He laughed. "You know love but not hunger. What do I feed someone for their first meal?"

"Pizza!"

"Not at two in the morning." He opened the fridge. "When I was in college, there was a diner open all night. Best biscuits and gravy. That's what you're getting."

She watched him with fascination as he cooked. When she spotted the plastic pumpkin full of candy, she grabbed a chocolate bar.

"What's this?"

"A candy bar." He broke off a piece and fed it to her. "Chew."

Her eyes lit up. "Sweet! I like this!"

He held another piece between his teeth and leaned in. She bit down—and he kissed her.

"I like that even better," she murmured.

The oven timer dinged. He pulled out the biscuits and made gravy.

"I think for your first time, we'll go for feeding the chickens," he said.

She frowned. "You do not have chickens. I do not understand this term."

"It means crumble the biscuit."

She nodded slowly. "Expression."

He fed Hendrix a small bowl of gravy, then prepared two plates and two cups of hot tea.

"Now we say grace," she said.

"You know about that?"

"I have watched you. Will you give thanks to God for me?"

He took her hand. Warmth flowed through him—something he'd never felt before.

He bowed his head. "Lord, thank you for this meal. And thank you for Karen—keep her safe, let no one harm her."

Karen added softly, "And Lord, thank you for Cooper, who always believed in me. Amen."

She lifted her tea, burned her fingers, and he showed her how to hold the handle. She sipped. "Bitter. I like sweets. Sweet like you. Ha ha. Joke?"

He chuckled. "We'll work on your jokes."

He added sugar. She tried again. "I like that."

She leaned over her plate and inhaled deeply. "Is this how something smells?"

"You don't like it?"

"No—I like it. I like all of it." She sniffed the air again, then leaned toward him, inhaling his neck. "That is, you."

"Aftershave."

"You smelled like this at work?"

"Most days."

"Too bad there is no smell program," she said with a crooked smile. "You have turned me on without pushing my button. Ha ha."

He shook his head. "Eat."

She learned quickly—too quickly. He had to tell her to slow down.

When she held the last bite between her teeth and leaned in for a kiss, gravy dripping down her chin, he laughed and kissed her anyway.

"Doesn't work as well as the candy," he said, wiping her chin.

He froze, staring at her.

"What is it?" she asked.

"I still can't believe this. Yesterday you were a program. Now you're sitting at my table. Eating. Talking. Laughing."

She dropped her fork. "I thought we settled this. I am not a program. I am not a printout. I am human. I am your Karen." She placed his hand on her chest. "Do you not feel my heartbeat?"

"Yes," he said softly. "It's racing. Are you nervous?"

"Yes."

"Why?"

"Because of what is about to happen." She lifted his hand, still holding it. "What two humans in love do. I want to love you in every way I can. I give myself totally to you. This is why I came. Take me upstairs."

She held out her arms.

He lifted her. She turned off the lights as they passed each room. Hendrix lay curled up on a blanket on the sofa. Cooper pointed at him.

"Hendrix, you sleep down here tonight."

The cat meowed and covered his eyes with his paws.

Upstairs, Cooper laid Karen on the bed. She inhaled his aftershave as he leaned down and kissed her—deep, hungry, breathtaking. This time, she was the one gasping for breath.

"I want to make love to you," she whispered. "And wake up in your arms."

Then she closed her eyes.

Chapter 20

Karen awoke exactly where she wanted to be—cradled in Cooper's arms. He lay on his side, facing away from the French doors that opened onto the balcony. Dawn was just beginning to rise, soft light brushing the sky. She had never seen a sunrise with her own eyes.

His arm rested over her waist, and her head lay on his other arm. Carefully, she lifted his arm from her ribs and eased herself free. The wooden floor was cool beneath her bare feet as she stood. She slipped into his robe—far too large for her—and tied it tightly, though it still swallowed her frame. She eased the bedroom door open, wincing at the soft creak, and slipped downstairs.

Outside on the porch, she sat on the top step and tucked the robe beneath her. The yard was still in disarray from the night before, but she hardly noticed. The last shadows of night were breaking apart as ribbons of pink and orange unfurled across the horizon. The sun rose quickly, painting the small town in warm gold. Houses stretched awake in the light, as if greeting the day.

For Karen, it was a miracle. She tilted her head back, closed her eyes, and let the sunlight wash over her. Her hair spilled down her back, catching the morning breeze. One knee slipped through the robe's opening, revealing her leg to the warm air.

She inhaled deeply—the crisp morning, the faint scent of woodsmoke from down the street, the aroma of fresh bread from across the way. Children's voices drifted toward her as they walked to the bus stop.

"Holy moly!" a teenage boy blurted.

Karen opened her eyes. Two fourteen-year-old boys stood frozen on the sidewalk, staring at her as if she were a vision. Four younger kids clustered around them—two boys and the twin girls from across the street.

"She's the most beautiful girl I've ever seen," the thin boy whispered. "She makes Barbie Edwards look like a dog."

Karen sat up, lowered her leg, and smiled. "My name is Karen. What's yours?"

"Uh... I'm... uh..." the thin boy stammered, face turning scarlet. His friend let out a high-pitched giggle.

"For crying out loud," Stacy said, rolling her eyes. "She's not a goddess. She's a woman. This is Robert, and that's Alan. I'm Stacy. This is my sister Missy. And that's Kevin and Mike."

"Hi, everyone," Karen said warmly.

"Are you Dr. Barnes's girlfriend?" Missy asked. "We didn't see you at the party last night."

"Yes," Karen said. "I arrived late."

"Are you gonna live here?" Missy asked.

"I think so. I don't have anywhere else to go."

Karen stood, stepping down the porch steps. Her hips swayed naturally, the robe shifting with her movements.

"I had to come see my lover," she said simply. "And feel his touch."

Robert's eyes widened. "What... what are you wearing under that robe?"

"Nothing," Karen answered honestly.

Robert fainted.

"Does he need anything?" Karen asked.

"Just a cold shower," Stacy said as Alan helped him up.

"I'm gonna be a doctor when I grow up!" Robert declared breathlessly. "That's it—I'm studying hard. I'm going to medical school."

"You want to help people like Dr. Barnes?" Karen asked.

"No," Stacy said. "He thinks being a doctor will get him a woman who looks like you."

Karen laughed softly. "I'm one of a kind. And my heart and body belong to Cooper."

A school bus pulled up, students pressing against the windows to stare. The driver leaned out. "Miss, are you getting on my bus?"

"Sorry, Benny," Cooper said from behind her. He slipped an arm around her waist. "She's taken."

Karen turned and kissed him, prompting cheers from the bus as it drove away and turned the corner. Children race to the back of the bus to get one last look at her.

"You realize," Cooper murmured, "you're going to be the talk of the school today."

"I'd say the whole town," Marylin called as she crossed the street in her robe and curlers. She shook Karen's hand. "I'm Marylin. The twins are mine. And you are?"

"I'm Cooper's fiancée," Karen said without hesitation. "Karen. I arrived last night."

"Oh! Congratulations!" Marylin shook both of their hands. "Why didn't you tell us?"

"We haven't made it official yet," Cooper said taken a little off guard by Karen response.

Marylin's eyes widened. "You came in before the blackout? Didn't you hear? It hit the whole country. The whole nation went dark. Riots in New York and L.A. Power's just now coming back."

"Do they know what caused it?" Cooper asked nervously, knowing Karen had caused it.

"No. But they're saying it started right here in Lebanon."

"Really? Right here!"

She surveyed the wreckage of the yard. "If you want help cleaning up, I'm free."

"That would be a blessing," Cooper said.

Marylin eyed Karen. "Do you have work clothes?"

"Clothes?" Karen asked. "No. I came just like this."

Marylin blinked. Karen quickly added, "They lost my luggage."

"Well, you're about my old size," Marylin said. "Come on, I'll find you something."

She led Karen across the street. Cooper started to follow, but Marylin waved him off. "Girls only."

Inside, the phone rang. Cooper hurried in and answered.

"Why didn't you pick up your company phone?" Lilith snapped.

"It's charging."

"Do you know what happened out here?"

"Some kind of storm, I guess."

"You weren't working in your office?" Her tone sharpened bait on a hook.

"No. Why would I be?"

She paused. He added, "I heard the lab's closed today. I was going to ask for time off. A friend came to visit."

"A special friend?" Lilith's voice tightened.

"Very."

"You're sure you didn't run a full print?"

"No."

"Well, the printer logs say a full print of a five-foot-seven, twenty-five-year-old female completed at 12:02 a.m."

"I don't know anything about that," Cooper said calmly. "I was hosting a Halloween party. Half the town can confirm it."

Lilith hesitated.

"Elmer Ford quit," she said sharply.

Cooper understood instantly—Elmer had talked.

"He told Milo and me last night he was quitting," Cooper said smoothly. "Something scared him."

"You said you weren't there."

"I said I wasn't working. Milo and I checked for damage. Gates were open. Phones were down. Lightning could've fried the network. Ask Travis."

Lilith exhaled sharply. "The KAREN program is gone."

"What?"

"Look it up."

Cooper set the phone down, grabbed his laptop, and checked. *Karen not found.* Glowed on his screen.

Meanwhile, Karen returned—now dressed in fitted jeans and a pink T-shirt that hugged her curves. She carried a vintage peasant dress and heels, eager to show Cooper. Hearing his voice in the kitchen, she spotted the phone on the coffee table, picked it up, and listened.

Lilith's voice crackled through the line: "What are we going to do? This is YOUR mess! The President is coming before Thanksgiving. We cannot disappoint her!"

Karen's eyebrows drew together. She didn't like the tone.

"He heard you,. You filthy witch!" she snapped before she realized the line was open.

"Pardon me?" Lilith barked.

Karen slapped her hand over her mouth.

Cooper stepped in smoothly. "I said, 'You'll get filthy rich.'"

Lilith growled. "Can you get the program back?"

"Yes," Cooper said. "But I have conditions. Non-negotiable."

"What conditions?"

"I get a week off with pay. Milo returns to daytime. Milo and Travis both get a week off and a thirty-percent raise."

"Thirty percent?" she hissed. "Is. That. All?"

"No, Lilly dear." Cooper smiled at Karen as she entered the kitchen. "I also hire whoever I want. No questions. Not from you, not from the FBI. And I may have more later. Deal? Or shall I call the White House with my resignation?"

Silence.

"You're screwing me," Lilith said.

"Not in your wildest dreams. Do we have a deal?"

"...Deal."

As Cooper was hanging the phone up. "Look what I got to wear." Karen said gleefully, holding the dress in front of her. It was right out of the 1980s short, hitting her mid-thigh at the hem; the peasant dress had ruffles and an elastic top that would allow her to push the sleeves down, showing her bare shoulders. "Marylin said 'she used to wear them to dance in." She whirled around. "Can't you see me dancing in this?"

"We will get you some more stuff. That is more in style."

"I like this." Karen insisted. She walked over to him as he stood up. She wrapped her arms around his back. We can dance. You said after they dance, and the music stops..." She raised her face to him as she continued. "...they kiss." With that, she grabbed the back of his head and placed her lips on his. Her tongue forced his lips apart. Inserted her tongue into his mouth. She twisted her mouth on his mouth. Finally, breaking the lip lock. She looked at him.

"Did I do something wrong?" Karen asked, looking at him with somber eyes.

"No darling it is just...Wow!" He explained, recovering from her passionate kiss. "It is just there are different ways to kiss."

"How? Show me." Karen said with the curiosity of a child learning to play with a new toy.

"There is the tender kiss." He said, giving her a tender kiss as she looked up at him, her eyes glowing in the kitchen light. "The loving kiss." He held her face in his hands and kissed her lips tenderly, biting her lower lip before letting go."

"I liked that one." She said with breath barely being heard. "More please!"

"The quick kiss." He said, giving her a quick lip smack.

"What is wrong with the way I kiss?" She asked, tilting her head.

"Nothing," Cooper said still holding her in his arms. "But that is a making love type kiss. It sends shock waves down through my body Especially parts of it."

"Oh!" She said as her face lit up with what he meant. "You mean down here." And she grabs right below his belly button.

"Yeah!" Cooper cried out as he pulled back from her touch. "And that really does it. You can't do that in public. Only when we area here and alone."

"Okay." She spoke. "Are there any more types of kisses to show me?"

"Well," he said in a tender tone, "there is the Karen; I will love you forever, kiss." He held her close, lowered his mouth to her, and let the kiss last until they were interrupted.

"Uh, ahem." He heard Travis cough. He looked up, and there, standing in the kitchen, were Travis and Milo. Sorry to interrupt, but the door was wide open. We just came in. Is this Karen?"

Cooper released Karen from his embrace, and she turned, and she spoke. "Hello, Travis, and you too, Milo. Cooper was teaching me how to kiss so that I don't get him so aroused."

"Oh, is that so?" Travis asked, looking at Cooper, whose face was turning red. "How is it going?" Behind him Milo was struggling not to laugh out loud.

"Pretty good." Cooper said.

"I had to come over when Milo told me last night what had happened. "Travis said, looking at Karen, letting his eyes travel up and down her. "I couldn't sleep. I had to see her. Is she really all women? You know what I mean."

"Everywhere, believe me."

"I can't freaking believe it," Travis said. "She is flesh and blood. So, no robot like those stupid shows on TV. She is one hundred percent human. You did it! You created the perfect woman."

"There is one part of me that is not human," Karen said. "My brain is interconnected with a link to the mainframe."

"The reason the KAREN Program is gone," Cooper said. "Is because the KAREN program is you. It is still with you?"

"Affirmative."

"You can access the mainframe at the lab, and there and still email and other contact points at the mainframe in the lab. "

"Affirmative and Affirmative," Karen replied.

"What are you thinking?" Milo asked

"That we can use all of this to our advantage."

"How?" Travis asked.

"To control Lilith and her greed once and for all." Cooper replied. Watching as Travis and Milo looked at each other, smiles breaking across their faces. "Hey guys did you get a call from her yet?" They both shook their heads. "Maybe you both should get back home. You might get some good news."

Travis and Milo left. Cooper looked at his lady love sitting in a chair with his legs spread apart. He swung a chair around and sat down in front of her. "I have a whole week. I am going to show you everything I can. We are going to go to Wichita, we'll get you some clothes, and you get your hair done."

"And pizza?" Karen asked with glee. As she bounced on her toes and clapped her hands.

"Matter of fact I know a great pizza place just up the road. We will have it tonight; you can wear your dress." He leaned over, pulling at the collar on her shirt and seeing her bare breast. Then he reached down and pulled at the waist of her pants, but they were so tight they barely moved. "Do you have anything on under that."

"No," She answered with a shake of her head. "Should I?"

"First stop is getting you some panties. You are not wearing that dress without them." He said, and he saw her face twist in puzzlement. "You don't understand, do you?" She shook her head. He looked at her, and she sat, her legs spread apart.

"Darling, we are going to have to do a little schooling on how to sit," Cooper said.

"I know how to sit I watched you."

"But men and women sit differently."

"I do not understand." Karen said. "They are both human. They both have two legs. Why do they sit different?"

"No darling, you can't do that. Girls...uh, women can't sit that way. It is not modest."

"Modest?"

"Proper, " he said as he reached over and pressed her legs together. You must sit this way. If you are wearing a dress..." He crossed his legs." You must sit like this. You keep your legs together, and you cross them." She followed his instructions.

"Why do I have to learn this?'

"If you haven't noticed, were built differently."

"Yes, but the parts fit together perfectly." Karen said with smirking smile and Cooper face flushed with red.

"You are turning red did I do something to upset you?"

"No, I was just a little embarrassed," Cooper said, then tried to explain. Women must sit differently. It is just the way it is."

142

"Okay, I understand," Karen said, holding her knees together. "What is a slutty bimbo?"

"Where did you hear that?" Cooper asks with shock.

"When I was walking back, a woman that lives in the house across the other street. She said she did not like the way I dressed. She called me by that name. Am I that?"

"No, you are not that."

"Why did she call me that name?"

"Because she is jealous of you. Your beauty threatens her." Cooper explained.

"I...I...I do not understand. I make no threat against her." Karen said. "She is made with her specifications. And I am made with mine. Why does she not like mine? People have different sizes, different pigments, but chemically we are the same. Why do my specification make her..." Karen was unsure of the word and the emotion, so she spoke is if indifference. "...jealous?"

"You do not have a clue how beautiful you are, do you?" Cooper asked.

"All that matters is that you think that. I was made for you. Only you." Karen explained, still not quite understanding all the attention. "That was another thing I don't understand. She liked me after I told her I was your fiancée."

"Why did you tell them that?"

"When the two girls asked if I was your girlfriend. I replied yes. Then I searched to see what that was. I got 'a woman who is a friend, acquaintance, or partner to the speaker, and sometimes the speaker can be female also.' I got confused. You are not a woman; you are a man. I searched for the word speaker, and it confused me more. Then, I searched for the word wife. That stated woman bound in marriage; I looked that up. We did not fit that. Then I saw fiancée-one who was bride-to-be. That sounded right, so I said it. Did I do wrong?'

"No," he said. "You did fine."

He heard a wrap on the front door. "Hey, Buddy!" He heard Milo say. "Get out here! I got something for you."

"Sounds like Milo's back," Cooper said. They rushed into the living room, to the front door. Again, another rap was at the door, this time; harder and louder. "Buddy, if you don't get out here, I'm going to knock this door down."

Cooper opened the door. Instantly, he felt Milo's huge arms wrap around his chest and lift him straight up off the floor. He felt like he was a defensive end and was getting ready to be slammed to the ground in the last minutes of the Super Bowl. But instead of slamming down, Milo held on tight and jumped up and down with joy. Twisting him and pulling him outside on the porch. Again, holding and bouncing him around. Cooper felt as if he were on a thrill ride at one of those amusement companies that sat up in the park and rides that left you battered and bruised. "You did it! You did it!"

"Milo, can you put me down?" Cooper said. Milo sat him down on the porch floor. Cooper's head was still swimming from the whole ordeal. Then Milo saw Karen, and he swooped her up and began swinging her around. 'Milo put her down,' Cooper said. Milo put her down and then kissed her on the cheek.

"I may give you one, too," Milo said, looking at Cooper; his dark eyes were wide and bright but not as big as his grin. "Oh, heck I am going to!" With that Milo kissed Cooper on the cheek. "You did it. Back on the day shift and got a big raise. Thirty percent. You do not know how much this means to me and my girls. "The big man placed his hands on Cooper's shoulders and looked down at him and added. "I haven't said this to too many other men. Heck, I don't think I ever said it. But buddy, I love you. How did you do it? How did you get the old witch to agree?"

"Oh, that is what this about," Cooper said. "Let's say I have something she wants."

"Oh, Buddy, you didn't. you didn't..." Milo thinks that Cooper gave into Lilith's desires for him.

"No, not that"!" Cooper shuttered at the thought of him with Lilith. "Oh Lord, not that. I would rather French kiss one of the trains coming through. It has to do with Karen. She can still run the Karen program. She can be there as my assistant."

"She's going to need a last name and a background," Milo said. "I was thinking about this last night. I talked to Travis. If we're going to hide her, hide her—so no one knows where she came from, we have to give her a middle and last name. A whole backstory. Where did she go to school? College? But first, we need to forge a birth certificate, a Social Security number, and a driver's license. I know a guy who can do it all for fifteen hundred dollars. But we need the name. How about Karen Jane?"

"You fine with that?" Cooper asked her.

She nodded. "What do you want your last name to be?"

"How about yours?" she asked, looking at Cooper.

"Then everyone will think you're my sister."

"Or your wife," Milo added. "But you still need a maiden name. How about White?"

"Why White?"

"Look at her—she isn't Black." Milo laughed at his own joke.

"Humor!" Karen said brightly. "I get it." She laughed, delighted with herself.

"Coop, you've got to work on her sense of humor. She's as funny as a late-night TV host." Milo shook his head, then offered, "How about Smith? Karen J. Smith. Sounds real. Plus, there have to be tens of thousands of them out there. That okay with you?" he asked Karen.

"Affirmative!"

"So, what's her birthday, and where was she born? We'll need that, along with the parents."

"Place of birth..." Milo thought for a moment. "I remember a story. There's a little town just outside where you grew up in Neosho. Boulder City, Missouri. Odd thing is, there was an actual family there named Smith, and they had a little girl named Karen J. Smith—but she didn't live very long."

"How long?" Travis asked as he stepped up onto the porch behind them. "How long did the child live?"

"About three days."

"How long ago was that?"

"When I was a kid. My grandpa was friends with the father. He lived just up the road from town. The guy ran a small gas station. About 25 years ago.."

"Twenty-five years ago," Travis said. "Milo, didn't I see a house for rent next to you?

"Yeah. Two bedrooms. Across the street from me. Why?"

"And your neighbor still has that '69 Mustang for sale?"

"Yeah. But why?"

Travis explained. "Social security numbers are given to newborns they don't cross reference to death records thus. Karen can request a birth certificate from Missouri, and we can get her Social security that way. All we have to do is—."

"Milo call him and tell him he has a buyer," Travis said, looking at Cooper. "How much is she worth to you?"

"Whatever it takes."

"Will someone let me in on this?" Milo asked.

"I'm kind of confused myself," Cooper said. "What are you up to, Travis?"

"We can request the birth certificate. But we need to prove she exists—and has been living here."

"Such as?" Cooper asked, skeptical.

"A place to live. Owning a car. Driver's license."

"Travis, you need a Social Security number to get a license in this state," Cooper replied.

"A number, yes—but not the card," Travis said with a grin. "Karen can access those files get the number. Proof can be on a pay stub. You hire her at the lab. She gets a sign-on bonus on her first paycheck.

"Isn't this illegal?" Cooper asked. "Couldn't we all go to jail for this?"

"   Very illegal," Travis said. "But do you want to protect her?" He paused, then turned to Karen. "The last part of this puzzle—the part that seals everything—is that you have to..." He looked directly at her. "...marry her."

Chapter 21

"Clean up!" became the word of the day. And once Karen started working, the town's menfolk seemed to materialize out of nowhere. More and more volunteered to "help," and half of them mysteriously called in sick. Even the manager of the grain mill phoned in at the moment he drove by and saw her bent over, pulling fake spiderwebs out of the flower beds.

Ellen walked past with her dog and stopped beside Cooper. "I met your lovely lady," she said. "There's something special about her. Where's she from? We don't have girls like that around here."

"It's a little town near where I grew up in Missouri," he replied, slipping into the story he'd been building. "She's been living here the last few months."

"Must be the spring water there," Ellen muttered, eyeing the fourteen men raking and picking up trash—none of them looking at their work, all of them staring at Karen's denim-straining backside. "Look at these fools." She shook her head. "But didn't you say you had a long-distance relationship?"

One lie had become two, then three. He considered telling her the truth, but she'd either laugh in his face or drop dead from shock. So, he added another. "She had an assignment overseas. But now she's back for good."

"Well, the word around town is you two are getting married."

"That seems to be the plan," Cooper said, exhaling. He hated what he had to ask next, but it was better than him doing it alone. "I need a favor. Karen's luggage was lost, and I need to get her some... um... uh..."

"Let me help you," Ellen said immediately. "Marylin told me." She rolled her eyes. "News travels fast. Why do you think I was late walking Newman? I already went to Smith Center and picked up two packs of size-four panties and four 34C bras. Don't worry—no granny panties, and all the right colors. You don't put granny panties on a girl like that. They're in the sack on your porch with the bill. Pay me whenever."

She laughed. "You're about to learn that girls are expensive. And ones who look like that? Even more so."

Cooper glanced at Karen, still bent over picking up trash. "You have no idea. She's a billion-dollar woman. Thanks, Ellen." He said referring to the cost of the printer that created her.

He walked over to Karen. She straightened and looked at him with the hopeful expression of a child seeking approval. "Am I doing a good job?"

"Amazing," he said. "Ellen took care of your little underwear problem. You can wear your dress tonight."

"I met her. She is nice. I like her." Karen waved at Ellen. "Where did Milo and Travis go?"

"To spend my life savings," he said. "They're getting you a place to live, a car, utilities turned on... and making it look like you've been here most of last year. You were overseas on assignment. Now you're back to live in your house."

"You mean I must go somewhere else?" Her eyes filled instantly, the thought of leaving him hitting like a blow. "I thought I would live here with you."

"You are going to live with me," he said quickly. "We just need to make it look like you lived somewhere. We're doing this to make you look legal, so no one thinks you just walked out of a bio-printer..."

He froze. It had been less than twenty-four hours since she had walked out of that printer. And here he was talking about marrying her. Somehow it felt like he'd known her for years. His heart melted as he looked at her—and then tightened with fear. If anyone discovered what she was, they'd take her away. Over his dead body.

He placed his hands on her shoulders and looked into her blue eyes. "Karen, listen to me. You must never tell anyone you came out of that printer. Ever."

"What about you? Milo and Travis?"

"We know the truth. But we'll never tell. And you can't either."

"We are still going for pizza tonight," she said, lips curling into a smile.

"Yes."

A sudden rumble rolled in from the highway—deep, throaty, unmistakable. It grew louder, closer, until a 1969 Ford Mustang Mach I turned onto his street and into his driveway like a rock star making an entrance. Every man in the yard stopped to stare.

"That is your car," Cooper said, shuddering. It looked exactly like the one from the VR world. He grabbed Karen's hand and led her toward it.

The Mustang sat behind the Lincoln Navigator like the family's rebellious, beautiful child. Travis tapped the gas, making the V-8 roar like a restless beast.

The afternoon sun cast a golden sheen over the Acapulco Blue paint and gold stripes. Its sculpted curves gleamed, the flat-black hood crowned with a bold scoop stamped COBRA JET—a badge of raw, barely restrained power. Chrome slot mags flashed in the light like the car knew it was irresistible.

Inside, the black vinyl seats beckoned with the promise of thrill and freedom—a time machine back to long hair, loud music, and the rule of rock and roll.

Travis looked at Cooper over his sunglasses, pointed, and said, "Are you experienced?" Then he cranked the original radio. Jimi Hendrix's *Foxy Lady* blasted out.

The music hit Karen like electricity. She started twisting her hips, pumping her arms, swinging her hair—her long blonde locks flying. She grabbed Cooper's hands and made him dance with her. "I love Jimi Hendrix!" she cried.

When the song ended, she looked up at him. "At the end of the song, they kiss." She rose onto her toes and kissed him, ending with a playful bite to his lower lip. The crowd applauded.

"Cool car!" a man in his twenties said as Travis stepped out. "This yours?"

"Nope." Travis dangled two sets of original Ford keys. "Hers." He started to drop them into Karen's hand, then paused. "You do know how to drive?"

"I know how," Karen said. "I just haven't done it."

He dropped the keys into Cooper's hand instead. "Maybe you should see first."

"How much?" Cooper asked.

"You got a great deal. One owner."

"How much?"

"Fully restored. Not numbers-matching. Engine's a 351 Cleveland, four-barrel, blueprinted, balanced, hotter cam, ram air. Three-speed automatic, rebuilt. Original radio and 8 tracks. He tossed in three Hendrix tapes."

"How much?"

"Sixty-nine."

"Thousand?" Cooper choked.

"Yeah. But we also found a guy who didn't blink about backdating the title and swearing he sold it to a beautiful blonde who lives down the road. He's the landlord. And he swears he rented to her five months ago. His daughter works at the city and backdated the bills. As far as anyone knows, Karen J. Smith has lived there six months."

"And this cost me?"

"A simple grand."

Cooper braced himself. "What's next?"

"Get the car registered and tagged. Then get her driver's license. But you can only get it at this place." Travis handed him a slip of paper with a name. "Millie. My cousin. She'll help you. Tomorrow at exactly ten a.m. She'll be alone. Just follow her lead. She'll ask for proof of identity..."

He patted his pockets, then leaned into the Mustang and opened the console. "Here it is." He handed Cooper a folded sheet.

Cooper opened it. "What is all this?"

"Everything Karen needs to prove she's been living here— pay stub, new Social Security number, the works. Just remember tomorrow at ten. But she'll still have to pass the test."

Chapter 22

It took most of the day, but everything finally got done. The yard was spotless, and all the men wanted in return was a thank-you from Karen—a kiss on the cheek. The women, on the other hand, wanted Cooper and Karen married as soon as humanly possible. They didn't like the idea of her roaming around town unattached. Cooper assured them they had applied for the license; the women assured him they knew how to speed it up. They were already preparing the church.

Cooper had gone from being the talk of the town to being the talk of the town in an entirely new way. Marylin was planning the cake; Ellen knew someone who knew someone who could handle the flowers. Now it was up to Cooper to choose between Travis and Milo for his best man—for a wedding he hadn't even officially proposed.

He needed something. It was in the upstairs bedroom—not the master bedroom, but the one down the hall. A guest room that had never been used. His old bed sat there, modern, with a light-gray fabric headboard. A walnut chest of drawers stood against the wall, and a full-length mirror rested in the corner.

But what he wanted was in the closet, in a cardboard box taped shut and sitting high on the shelf. He reached up, pulled it down, and set it on the bed. He peeled back the tape. Inside there were several faded photographs. One of him at sixteen, long-haired, wearing his high-school graduation gown. He set it aside and picked up another—a middle-aged woman with dark curly hair and eyes just like his.

He ran his fingers over the photo, and the years fell away.

He was sitting beside a hospital bed, holding his mother's hand. Cancer had taken everything from her hair, her strength, her future. All that remained was the question of how long she had left. He had promised her that day he would become a doctor, that he would fight the disease that was taking her from him.

She had slipped her engagement ring off her thin finger and pressed it into his palm.

"Remember when I read you the tale of Cinderella when you were a little boy?" Her voice had been barely a whisper.

"Yeah."

"Well, this ring is like the glass slipper. Cooper, you find the girl whose finger fits this ring, and she will be your true love." She closed his fingers around it. *"Do not settle for anyone less than your true love. Ever."*

She died the next day.

He set the photo aside and dug deeper into the box until he found a small white cardboard container. Inside was the ring—a simple gold band with a small, old-world-cut blue sapphire. The ring his mother had given him.

A soft meow made him look up. Hendrix peered through the cracked door.

"Come here, son," Cooper said. "We need to have a talk."

The cat trotted over, hopped onto the bed, circled once, and sat facing him.

"You like having Karen around?" Cooper asked.

A small meow.

"You want her to live with us? Be your mama?"

A louder meow.

"You love her?"

The cat purred and rubbed his head against Cooper's hand.

Cooper held up the ring. "Think she'd like this? Everything's happening fast, but it feels right. Milo and Travis are doing everything they can to help. And I can't imagine life without her now. Should I give her this ring or get her another one?"

Hendrix meowed again, placed his white paw on the box, and patted it.

"Mom said my true love would fit this ring," Cooper murmured. "I guess we'll see."

He closed the box and slipped it into the pocket of his leather jacket.

He picked up the cat, holding him close, stroking his soft fur as Hendrix purred. "Things are going to change around here. Not just me and you anymore." He turned the cat to face him. "You're sure you're okay with that?"

Hendrix bopped him on the nose with a paw.

"Okay. I'll ask her."

Just then, the door opened and Karen walked in. She wore the blue dress, the elastic pulled down to reveal her bare shoulders. She twisted her hips, making the ruffles flare. Then she lifted the hem to show her matching blue underpants.

"See? I am even wearing the underthings. Can we go get pizza now?" She patted her stomach proudly. "I am hungry. I know what it means now."

Hendrix leapt off the bed and ran to her, rising onto his hind legs like a child asking to be picked up. She scooped him into her arms, hugging and kissing him.

"I love you too, Hendrix," she said as he purred loud enough for Cooper to hear across the room. She set him down gently.

Cooper stood and offered his hand. Karen took a step—and nearly toppled off her white pumps. He rushed forward to catch her.

"I haven't quite learned to walk in these things," she said. "I prefer the naked foot."

"That's barefoot," he corrected. "But the way you say it is more intriguing."

"Oh, thank you, sweetheart." She smiled. "I don't want to make a fool of myself."

"You called me sweetheart," he said, grinning.

"Is that wrong? You call me darling, honey, baby... shouldn't I have a love name for you?"

"No, it's not wrong," he said. "It means you're becoming more and more human."

He led her to the mirror, and they looked at their reflection.

"You know what I see?" he said. "Beauty and the beast. Everyone will wonder how a guy like me got a girl like you. They'll think you're a gold digger."

"I do not dig for gold!" she said, clearly sounding confused, turning to him. "Why would they say that about me?"

"It means you're after money."

"I don't understand that either. Why would I want money?"

"We need money to buy things. Like pizza tonight."

She turned back to the mirror, took his arms, and wrapped them around her waist. "You know what I see? I see a woman who gave up her whole world to be with the man she loves." She reached up and touched his cheek, her hand warm. "Is that what love is?"

Chapter 23

Another thing Cooper checked off the list was getting insurance on the Mustang. Karen didn't have a permit, but he took her out on the back roads and let her drive. She assured him she had read every instruction on how to operate a vehicle and had studied all the tests Kansas used for the driving exam. He was amazed by how well she handled the car. She followed every rule precisely keeping the Mustang exactly at the posted speed limit, the needle never wavering. She signaled at the perfect distance, maintained the proper following space, parallel-parked flawlessly, and executed every turn with textbook precision. She even made sure they both wore seatbelts.

He would have let her drive all the way, but he feared a cop might pull her over for driving *too* perfectly.

He took over at the intersection of 281 and Highway 36—only to get stopped outside Smith Center for speeding. Sixty-five in a fifty-five. But the moment the male officer walked up, saw the Mustang, and then saw Karen, he forgot all about the ticket. He launched into a story about the car he had in high school. There was something special about Karen, and it wasn't just Cooper who saw it anymore.

Smith Center was the "big town" everyone went to on Saturday night, though fewer than two thousand people lived there. It was the county seat. Driving in on Highway 36, visitors were greeted by a Subway® restaurant. Then came the left turn onto Main Street, leading into the heart of town. At first, just homes—people proud of their little community. But once you crossed First Street, the town's beauty appeared like a priceless painting in a museum.

The true star rose into view through the windshield: the old First National Bank Building. Its single turret dominated the skyline. Karen strained against her seatbelt to lean forward and peer out the glass.

"That's where we're going," Cooper said. "Garlino's."

For years, the building had been the town's anchor. Many of the homes here had begun as loans from that very bank. But after a new bank was built in the 1930s, businesses came and went, and the old structure fell into disrepair—until Antonio Garlino arrived from New York City. A true Italian, a true New Yorker, and somehow, he ended up here in Kansas. Maybe that was what drew him and Cooper together—two oars out of water in an uncharted lake.

Good pizza drew business. Great pizza drew friends. And Antonio had plenty.

Cooper turned the Mustang onto a brick-paved side street and found a parking spot. He shut off the engine and looked down at Karen's bare feet.

"Put your shoes on. You can lean on me."

She slipped them on, and he helped her out of the car. They stood before the building.

The old First National Bank, built in 1889, was designed in the Richardsonian Romanesque style—turrets built into the walls, round-headed arches over windows and doors, and a grand entryway supported by squat columns. Seven steps led up to the entrance. Karen took his arm, wobbling in her shoes as they climbed.

At the top, she paused and placed her hand on one of the smooth columns, sliding her palm across the cool gray marble. She stared into the stone as if it were a crystal ball. She lifted her hand and examined her fingers.

An older couple passed them and went inside. Cooper glanced around to make sure no one was listening.

"Are you downloading something?"

"No," she whispered. "I remember when you carried me up the stairs at the lab. And I touched the ice on the wall. It was cold, and it bit my skin. I remember your warm lips on mine, breathing life into me. You took me home. And the wonderful feeling of you and I bonded in love." She closed her eyes. "I love that feeling."

"You remember me carrying you?" he asked, startled.

"Yes. I remember everything from last night." She hugged herself, rubbing her bare shoulders. "And I am feeling the same way. What is this feeling I am having?"

He quickly removed his jacket and draped it over her shoulders. "You're cold. And you're remembering things that aren't in your program." He opened the heavy front door. "That's your human brain."

Inside, the former stronghold of wealth now hummed with the warm scents of dough, tomato sauce, and melting cheese. The clang of coins had been replaced by chatter and clinking cutlery. The Romanesque arches continued inside. The old glass had been replaced with modern tinted panes. Round tables covered in red-and-white checkered cloths filled the lobby. The old counter served as a bar. Red, green, and white pendants hung along the brick wall.

Antonio was a couple inches shorter than Cooper, his head shaved, his beard coal-black. His olive skin glowed with pride. Dressed in white pants, a chef's coat, and a towering chef's hat, he looked like he'd stepped off a box of imported pasta.

He spotted Cooper just as the hostess was about to seat them. He strode over.

"Doctor Coop!" he boomed, his New York accent thickening. He clasped Cooper's hand in both of his. "Maureen, I will take care of this couple myself. Come, I show you my best table."

His "best table" was the one in the center of the room— where everyone could see you.

"Oh, the grand Doctor Coop! And who is this lovely lady?" he asked, pulling out her chair.

"Antonio, this is Karen."

"Pleased to meet you, my dear." He kissed her hand. "I hope your appetite is as wonderful as the way you look." His dark eyes swept over her. "Oh, what a beauty!" He cupped her chin. "Her beauty makes everything in here fail by comparison. Even the roses hide their faces in shame." He turned to Cooper. "Where did you find this one?"

"He made me in the lab," Karen said.

Antonio laughed. "What a sense of humor! Only God himself could make something like this. Now, what can I get you—besides a bottle of my best?"

"What would you like, honey?" Cooper asked.

"Oh boy, here we go," Antonio muttered.

"Anything but pineapple. Pineapple does not belong on pizza," Karen declared.

Antonio clapped his hands. "Blessed Mother Mary! The last one he brings in here orders pineapple. I tell her it doesn't belong on pizza, but she insists! Doctor Coop, don't let this one go. You marry her!"

"I'll have my regular," Cooper said.

"The Coop Supreme!" Antonio announced. "Pepperoni, sausage, mushrooms, peppers, black olives, and onion..." He nudged Cooper. "...but maybe this time I forget the onions."

"He wants to forget the onions because he thinks we will be kissing after this, right?" Karen said. She turned to Antonio. "We will certainly be doing that, among other things. So please forget the onions."

Cooper's face flushed. Karen raised an eyebrow. "Embarrassed or upset again?"

"One Doctor Coop Special, no onions!" Antonio laughed as he walked away.

"Did I do something wrong again?" Karen asked.

"No, honey. You just shouldn't say everything that happens between us," Cooper whispered.

"So, when we do that thing where our love bonds together and it makes me feel so good and I moan like—"

He raised his hand sharply. The couple at the next table looked over; the woman smirked behind her salad.

"So, I should not say things like that," Karen concluded. She looked down. "Is it okay to say I love you?"

160

"Yes. That is perfect."

"Because I do love you."

Marueen the hostess arrived with a bottle of *Langhe Nebbiolo*. She poured a taste for Cooper. He inhaled the cherry, raspberry, violet, and rose notes, then sipped. Satisfied, he nodded. She poured for both of them.

Karen looked at the glass with a puzzled expression. "What is this?" she asked with the innocence of a child.

Cooper caught the young hostess's reaction—the way her eyes swept Karen from head to toe. Karen looked almost otherworldly in a dress that hadn't been in fashion for decades, and the hostess's expression made it clear she didn't appreciate the competition. The girl holding the bottle wasn't just curious.

She was jealous.

"it is wine!" Marueen said behind a forced smile.

Cooper glance around the crowded room. However, everyone there was watching her. All the men their eyes glued to her every move. And the women that way too but their look was the same as the hostess. They were jealous of the way she looked.

In a table near the window was a teen couple on a date. The boy sat with a slice of pizza half away to his mouth. Mouth opened wide. His eyes wide as saucers, trying to take in every curve that Karen had.

His date. Clearly spent hours fixing her hair and makeup. Her eyes narrowed and she punched the boy in the arm.

"Look at me! Not her" She bellowed.

Karen lifted her glass, took a drink—and her face twisted instantly. She spit the wine back into the glass, wiped her mouth, and gagged.

"YUCK! I don't like that!"

"Seems like your young lady does not like wine," the man at the next table said.

"Did I do something wrong again?" Karen asked.

"No, darling. If you don't like it, you don't like it." Cooper picked up the bottle and offered it to the older couple. "Would you like a bottle of wine? My treat."

"Thank you, sir," the man said.

"Is there a problem?" The hostess asked

"Just take away the wine glasses and bring us a couple of glasses and a pitcher of Dr. Pepper®. I gave them the wine—put it on my bill. And bring them a couple more glasses."

"And make sure the Dr. Pepper is a good year also," Karen added.

"That's funny," the woman with the man at the next table said. 'Your young lady has a sense of humor."

Antonio reappeared. "Problem with the wine?"

"No, she just doesn't like it. First time trying it."

"Don't worry!" he whispered to Karen. "I don't like the stuff, and I'm Italian. My grandfather just rolled over in his grave."

The older woman at the next table leaned over. "I was wondering if you were a model."

"A model of what?" Karen asked. "A woman? Yes, I am a model of that."

Antonio blinked. "She is joking again! Doctor Coop, you hang on to this one!"

When the Dr. Pepper arrived, Karen was happy—but the cold drink made her colder. She slipped her arms through Cooper's jacket sleeves and stuffed her hands into the pockets.

"What's this?" she asked, pulling out the small box.

Cooper gently took it from her. "I planned to do this somewhere more romantic and private." He opened the box and removed the ring. "We've been talking about getting married. I think it's time to make it official." He held the ring out. "Karen, will you marry me?"

Tears filled her eyes, turning them into shimmering blue gems. She touched her cheeks, confused.

"Tears," she whispered. "I don't understand. I'm not sad. I love you. I want to marry you. Why am I crying?"

"Oh, sweetie!" The older woman stood and came to her. "Those are happy tears. Haven't you ever had them?"

"No!" Karen cried.

"Oh no, sweetie." The woman embraced her. "It means you're happy. You *are* happy, aren't you?"

"Now that I am with him, and not in the computer... yes. I am happy."

The woman blinked at that but let it go. "But you haven't given him your answer. Do you want to marry him?"

"YES!" Karen shouted.

The entire restaurant erupted in cheers. The women there cheered ecstatically, while the men did so more reluctantly.

"There's one thing left," Cooper said, lifting the ring. Karen held out a trembling hand. "This was my mother's ring. She gave it to me on her deathbed. She told me the girl who fits this ring is my true love."

"Oh, sweetie, I pray it fits," the older woman murmured.

He slid it onto Karen's finger. It fits perfectly.

"See?" the woman said. "Even his mother in heaven has given her approval. You are his true love."

Chapter 24

Later that night, back at home, Karen sat up in bed wearing one of Cooper's T-shirts. Pillows propped her upright, one knee bent, her left hand resting lightly on it. She stared at the ring—eyes fixed on the tiny sapphire as if it were the Hope Diamond. Like a child with a new toy on Christmas morning, she couldn't leave it alone. She ran her thumb over the band, tilting her hand back and forth to catch the light just right.

Cooper watched her from across the room as he stepped out of the bathroom, towel in hand after shaving. She reached for the milkshake she'd insisted on after pizza—chocolate, of course—and sucked up the last of it, noisily pulling air through the straw at the end. He walked over to his own shake on the nightstand and handed it to her.

"Want to finish mine?"

She took it without looking away from the ring, wrapping her warm lips around the red straw. He marveled at her—so fully woman in her beauty and her capacity for love, yet so childlike in her delight over simple discoveries like a chocolate shake.

He sat beside her and slipped an arm around her shoulders. She leaned into him, still admiring the ring.

"I can get you a bigger diamond," he said, gesturing toward it. "Same ring—just a larger stone. We can afford it."

"It wouldn't be your mother's ring," she said, finally looking at him. "And it wouldn't be the same ring. It wouldn't be *my* ring. Your mom told you your true love would fit this ring." She tapped the band. "This ring. My ring. I love it just the way it is." She lifted her hand, admiring it again. "It is my ring."

"You're one of a kind," he murmured, kissing the top of her head.

Her expression shifted suddenly from joy to worry. She turned to him. "You're not marrying me only to protect me, are you? Like what Milo and Travis were talking about?"

Cooper pulled her closer as she slid down a little to get comfortable. "I have to admit... it started that way. I'd do anything to keep you safe." She lifted her head, searching for his face, then rested it back on his shoulder as he continued. "But I can't—won't—imagine life without you. I remember how I couldn't wait to get to work just to be near you when you were in the A.I.L. program." His voice softened. "Now, holding you... I can't wait to marry you."

He looked down. She was sound asleep, still holding the milkshake. He gently took the cup from her hand and set it aside. Then he picked up the remote and turned on the news.

A silver-haired anchor was speaking. "More news out of Lebanon, Kansas tonight. A group called Honorable God's Life is planning a protest at the BioTyme Research Laboratories this coming week. HGL, a religious organization, opposes the research being conducted at the facility. President Von Keller has made this one of her administration's focal points. Smith County officials warn the lab is on private property and protesters will be arrested for trespassing. The Kansas Governor has also stated that blocking roads or harassing citizens will not be tolerated. A designated protest area will be available in the park. However, HGL now says they will instead protest at BioTyme Headquarters in St. Louis, Missouri."

Cooper turned off the TV, pulled the blankets over both of them, and nestled beside her, falling asleep.

Chapter 25

The next morning, he felt a strange sense of déjà vu—like getting ready for school again. Rushing through breakfast, checking his books before a test. Maybe it was because *she* had a test to take, and they had to be there by ten.

He'd called Ellen for help again. Karen needed something else to wear. Ellen found jeans, a simple purple button-up blouse, and—thank God—tennis shoes. If Karen walked into the DMV in those pumps, they'd think she was drunk and fail her on the spot. The blouse was a bit tight, so Cooper slipped his leather jacket over her shoulders and gave her one last look before sending her inside.

As she stepped through the courthouse doors, he whispered a small prayer that Travis's plan would work. They had driven the Mustang so she could take the test. Cooper wore light blue slacks, a matching jacket, and an open-collar shirt. He'd put on a tie, but she had removed it and unbuttoned the top two buttons. Now he sat on the hood of the Mustang, nerves eating at him. He almost wished he smoked.

"Here," Travis said, handing him a stick of gum. Cooper took it and chewed, the burst of spearmint sharp. "She in there?"

"Yeah," Cooper said, chewing too loudly.

"Don't worry. It's all going to work."

"Travis, if we get caught, we're going to jail. And they'll take her away from me. Without her, I'd be in prison anyway."

"So... you ready to marry her this Friday?" Travis asked. He reached into his jacket and pulled out a folded paper. "Milo had to call in a favor to get the Chiefs quarterback to autograph a jersey, but I got the license." He looked at Cooper, who stared at the ground. "You're not changing your mind, are you?"

"No," Cooper said. "You realize she's only been here two days, but it feels like I've known her for—"

"It feels like I've known her as long as I've known you," Travis cut in. "Like you two have always been together. Tammi said the same thing when we met you at the ice cream place. She said, 'You and Karen belong together.'"

"Well, that didn't take long," Cooper said as he spotted Karen coming out of the courthouse. "I don't know if that's good or bad."

"I passed!" she shouted, practically bouncing. "One hundred percent! They said they gave me the hardest test they have. I did it faster than anyone—thirty-seven seconds! I did the vision test. Now I wait for an officer."

"No problems?" Travis asked.

"None. They took the pay stub."

"Good." Travis pulled a plastic card from his pocket. "Here's your corporate debit card. Use it to pay for the license." He shot Cooper with a smug grin. "See? Nothing to worry about."

Cooper looked across the lot and saw a heavyset man approaching in a blue uniform. The KHP logo gleamed on his sleeve.

"Oh no," Cooper muttered. "It's the same guy who stopped us last night."

"He was nice! I liked him," Karen said.

"Well, what do you know? The slick Mach I," the officer said. "I may forget names, but I never forget cars. So, who's taking the test?"

Cooper pointed at Karen. She handed over her paperwork. The officer studied her face, then grinned.

"You I remember. Karen J. Smith."

"Soon to be Mrs. Dr. Cooper Barnes," she said proudly. "He asked me last night."

"Congratulations to you both. Now, Miss Smith, get behind the wheel and we'll check the vehicle before your test."

The Mustang passed inspection. The officer climbed into the passenger seat, and they drove off.

"You got time to run me to the flower shop?" Cooper asked.

"Sure. Why?"

"She's never gotten flowers before. I think she deserves some."

"Why not?" Travis said, unlocking his white 4x4. "I'll get Tammi some too. She's been a sweetheart through all this."

"You didn't tell her what Karen is, did you?"

"Heavens, no! I just told her you're crazy in love and want to get married. She's thrilled for you. Speaking of which—picked your best man yet?"

"Not yet," Cooper said, climbing into the truck.

They returned just as Karen pulled the Mustang in. She and the officer sat for a moment before he stepped out.

"Did she pass?" Cooper asked.

"Pass isn't the word," the officer said. "She made a hundred percent."

"She says you're getting married Friday."

"Seems that way."

"Well, hope you don't mind me saying this, but... that is one beautiful woman. Inside and out. I've seen beautiful women—TV, movies, magazines—but she's got a glow. You sure she isn't an angel?"

"Only to me," Cooper said with a proud grin.

"If you ever think about leaving that young lady, I'll come over and shoot you," the officer said with a grin. He shook Cooper's hand. "Have a happy, long life."

Karen went back inside for her photo and temporary license. When she came out, Cooper was waiting with a bouquet of red roses.

"For me?" she said, smiling as she lifted them to her nose. "They are so wonderful. Thank you." She kissed him.

"We'll stop by the house and put those in water. Then we'll head to Wichita and get you more clothes. Maybe something to sleep in besides an old T-shirt."

"And a wedding dress?" she asked.

"Yeah," he said. "You might as well drive—it's set up for you."

"You drive," she said, walking to the passenger side. "I want to hold these." She inhaled their beauty as he opened the door for her and she sit in the seat.

She inhaled them again and looked up at him with a large smile. "I got flowers You gave me roses."

Chapter 26

Many towns in Kansas were small, quiet places—but Wichita was a true metropolis. Towering glass skyscrapers rose like giants, looking down on the endless lines of vehicles swarming through the streets, each heading toward its own anthill. Car horns shattered the air; sirens wailed their blood-curdling warnings. This was no small town. Here, citizens obeyed the rule of red, yellow, and green lights. *Walk. Don't Walk. Parking. No Parking.* Brakes screeched, tires cried out in protest.

The sun was bright, deceptively warm, but the jackets and sweaters on the crowds told the truth. Karen wore sunglasses, though Cooper could see her eyes squeezed shut behind them. They had switched to the Navigator—better gas mileage, more room for shopping, and far safer to leave in the East Towne Square Mall parking lot than the Mustang.

"Are we there yet?" Karen asked. She slowly opened her eyes, removed her sunglasses, and set them in the console. She stared out at the sea of cars—every make and model, from brand-new to rusted clunkers—all here for the same purpose: to shop.

"Are all these people here to buy wedding dresses?" she asked.

Cooper laughed. "There are a lot of stores in there. Clothes, food, everything."

They stepped out, and he locked the doors. The mall rose two stories high, with entrances on every side. They entered through the Von Murr's doors. Christmas had arrived early—earlier every year, it seemed. It was only the start of November, yet Christmas music blared through the mall, garlands hung from the railings, and Santa was already stationed for photos. Normally, Cooper would have been sick of it. But watching Karen's reaction made it all feel new again. He found himself looking forward to Christmas morning just to see her face.

Her mouth fell wide open as she stepped inside and saw the enormous Christmas tree stretching toward the second floor. Red and gold glass ornaments gleamed. Wrapped presents were arranged beneath it. She took in every detail, from the bottom branches to the shining star at the top, then turned to admire the garland draped across the store.

She stopped before a huge white light ring shaped like a giant Christmas ornament, flanked by two toy soldiers and a padded red seat. Cooper realized something then—he didn't have a single picture of her. His bride-to-be, and he couldn't even send his sister a photo.

"Sit there," he said, pulling out his personal phone. "I want a picture."

She sat, and he snapped the photo.

"Can we get one together?" she asked. "We don't have a photo together."

He sat beside her and tried to take a selfie. "I never could take these things."

"Sir, I'd be glad to take your photo," a voice said.

An older woman stood near the tree, dressed neatly in black pants, a black top, and a white jacket. Her gold nameplate read *Cathy*.

He handed her the phone and put his arm around Karen. Cathy took two shots and returned the phone.

"What can I do to help you?" she asked.

"My lovely lady here needs clothes. Lots of them," Cooper said—then paused, realizing he couldn't tell the truth. He searched for a lie, but Karen beat him to it.

"We had a robbery," she said. "They took everything. And we're getting married this Friday. I need everything."

She was getting good at lying. Becoming human.

"Oh, my goodness!" Cathy exclaimed. "But congratulations on the wedding!"

"They even stole my wedding dress."

"Oh, honey." Cathy hugged her. "We don't have wedding dresses, but the women's department is downstairs. Just ask the sales associates to help you."

They entered the women's department. Karen whispered, "What do I do? Where do I start?"

Cooper scanned the area and spotted two young salesgirls—thin, long-haired, glued to their phones.

"Go see if they can help you."

Karen approached the first girl, Amber, whose nameplate matched her yellow-blonde hair. "Can you help me, please?"

"Sur—" Amber began, turning around. Her smile vanished, replaced by jealousy. "I'm on break."

The other girl, Claudia, with long dark hair, sneered. "Me too."

From behind a rack, Cooper watched, a knot tightening in his stomach. His hands curled into fists. He wasn't a violent man, but in that moment, he could imagine choking the life out of both of them.

Karen returned. "They said they couldn't help me."

"We'll see about that," Cooper growled. "Come with me."

As they approached, he overheard the girls.

"Did you see her?" Amber scoffed. "Like I'm going to help someone who looks like that."

"I know," Claudia said, scrolling her phone. "It's bad enough around here, then someone like her shows up. She looks like a model. Or a movie star."

"And she's not even wearing makeup," Amber added.

"Oh my god, and that hair," Claudia sighed. "Imagine if she were all fixed up."

Amber snorted. "What I want to see is the guy banging her."

172

Cooper tapped her shoulder. "Turn around, and you'll see him."

"You?" Amber laughed. "What is she—your sister?"

"I am his wife-to-be," Karen said proudly. "We're getting married Friday."

"Boy, did you blow that one," Cooper snapped. "Aren't you two on commission?"

"So what? One dress?" Amber smirked.

"No," Cooper said, voice sharp. "We're buying a whole closet full of undergarments, dresses, blouses, skirts, socks, stockings, shoes. And it's a big damn closet."

"Is there a problem here?" Cathy asked, stepping up.

"Could you help my lady get some things?" Cooper asked.

"I'd be honored. Do you have a budget?"

"Yeah." He pulled out a credit card and made sure the girls saw it. "Whatever this will hold."

"Sir... that's a platinum card with no limit."

"Whatever she needs," Cooper said. "Whatever her little heart desires. If you don't have it—get it."

He turned to Karen. "Men's department is upstairs. I'll be back to pay."

Karen beamed.

He wandered upstairs for an hour, not finding much, until he drifted into the jewelry store. A necklace and matching earrings caught his eye.

"Can I see these?" he asked.

A young woman with chestnut hair and a bright smile approached. "My pleasure. I'm Felicia."

She placed the velvet case on the counter. The necklace held twenty-one teardrop iolite stones, each surrounded by white sapphires. The matching earrings sparkled like winter stars.

"We have something similar in diamonds," Felicia offered.

"No. She'll like these better," he said, remembering a conversation from when she was still an A.I. program—how she preferred jewels made by the universe, not by man.

Felicia boxed the set, and he took it to the Navigator, hiding it under the seat before returning inside.

Karen was ready to check out. Three carts of purchases-dresses, tops, skirts, slacks, shoes. He noticed a pair of white pumps.

"You going to try those again?"

"Cathy showed me how to walk in them. I thought they'd be perfect for the wedding."

"And the total, sir?" Cathy asked.

Five digits.

"Wish I could show that to those two girls," Cooper muttered.

"They lost more than that," a man said, approaching. He wore a dark blue suit and striped tie. "Matthew Johnston, manager."

Matthew looked at Karen and smiled. "We can't have employees judging customers based on looks," he said. "Be they because that unattractive or in your case. He paused then added with a longing gasp "...extremely attractive. We're taking two percent off, and it's coming out of their last paycheck."

"Last?" Karen asked. "Does that mean they were terminated?"

"Not yet, but—"

"Cooper," Karen said softly. "I don't want that. I don't want them to suffer because of me. I don't understand why they don't like me."

"They were jealous," Cathy explained. "You're a very beautiful woman. No makeup, hair undone, and every man wants you. Every young woman wants to be you." She starred at Karen. "You really don't get it, do you?"

"We are all made the way we are," Karen said. "They are made from the dreams of their parents." She wrapped her arm around Cooper's. "I am made from his dreams. If the bioprinter makes us who we are, we are still the same."

Cathy blinked. "I've never heard it put that way. The creator as the printer. You must have God in you."

Karen looked at Cooper, confused, but he knew this wasn't the place to explain.

"If that's what you request, miss," the manager said, "they won't be let go."

Karen brightened. "Cathy told me about a great place here in the mall for wedding dresses—House of Rene's Wedding Boutique. It's on the second level. We get to ride the escalator!"

"They still need to be punished," the manager said.

Cathy eyed the mountain of purchases. "If you like, we can box everything up for easier handling. And I think we have the perfect pair to load it for you. Wouldn't you agree, Matthew?"

He grinned. "I couldn't think of a better pair."

Chapter 27

Karen rode the escalator like a child discovering a carnival ride for the first time. Her arms outstretched as if she were surfing an invisible wave, the moving stairs her surfboard.

"I love it!" she squealed, pure glee radiating from her. Shoppers glanced her way, unsure whether she was high on something or simply high on life.

On the second level, she drifted toward the railing, captivated by the mall's decorations. She leaned over to admire the ribbons of light cascading from the ceiling and the enormous snowflake-shaped fixtures suspended from steel beams above. As they passed the food court below, the warm aroma of Christmas cookies drifted upward. She inhaled deeply.

"What is that wonderful smell?"

"Christmas cookies," Cooper said. "We can get some after we find your dress."

"Christmas time!" she said, practically singing. "A time for goodwill to all mankind." She leaned on the rail, flashed him a mischievous smile, and added, "And all good girls, too. Am I a good girl? Or a naughty girl?" She giggled, wrapped her arms around his neck, and rose onto her toes. "Do you want to spank me?"

A crash sounded behind them. Cooper spun around to see a middle-aged woman who had overheard the comment and dropped her shopping bag, its contents scattered across the floor. Karen released him as Cooper hurried over.

"Here, let me help," he said, gathering the items and placing them back in the bag. The woman thanked him quickly and hurried away—though not without giving Karen one last bewildered look.

Once she was out of earshot, Cooper and Karen burst into laughter.

He slipped an arm around her. "Now that was naughty. You're going on Santa's naughty list."

She froze mid-stride. "You mean Santa Claus is real?"

"To some people, yes. To others, no."

"Do you believe?" she asked.

"You know I do," he said, stopping with her in the middle of the walkway. "Not the part where he leaves gifts, but the part where he's always there for you. To give you love. To answer your questions. To tell you the truth. When you stop believing, you lose a part of yourself."

Karen studied him, head tilted, processing the information. "So, once you stop believing, the child in you dies. Instead of skipping or running to catch snowflakes, you only walk— because you fear what others will think. And then all innocence is gone."

"Yes."

"That is sad," she murmured, continuing toward the far end of the mall.

The wedding boutique was near J.C. Penney. But just outside the store on the lower level, a popcorn machine churned away, its buttery aroma drifting upward. Karen leaned over the rail, eyes wide.

"What is that?"

"Popcorn."

"Can we get that now?" she asked eagerly.

"Not until we get your dress. They won't let you bring food inside."

Tucked into a quiet corner near J.C. Penney was the *House of Rene Wedding Boutique*—a small store, but an oasis of elegance. Its name was written in graceful cursive above an arched doorway.

"This is the place," Karen said. "Guess we go in?"

"I can't go in there. The groom isn't supposed to see the dress before the wedding." He nodded toward the doorway. "Just have someone bring me the slip. I'll sign it."

"Isn't the bride supposed to pay for her gown?" Karen asked, pulling out her debit card. "I have my card."

"I'll go downstairs and get the popcorn. Meet me outside J.C. Penney where the seats are."

She watched him descend the escalator, then stepped through the arched doorway.

The noise of the mall faded into a distant hum. Inside, the boutique was a symphony of ivory and blush tones. Lace curtains softened the light streaming through the windows. Crystal chandeliers cast shimmering reflections across polished marble floors. Rows of wedding gowns sparkled beneath the glow.

Mannequins stood like poised dancers, each wearing a masterpiece—beaded bodies that glittered like constellations, silk skirts flowing like whispered promises, veils cascading like waterfalls. The air carried the faint scent of roses.

"Roses, just like mine," she whispered.

Plush velvet sofas in burgundy and emerald invited brides to sit and dream. A gilded mirror stood at the far end, its carved frame glowing softly. Karen approached it, gazing at her reflection—perhaps truly seeing herself for the first time. She lifted her hand and touched the glass, her reflection mirroring the gesture.

Soft classical music drifted through the room, blending with the rustle of fabric and murmured conversations. Elegant displays showcased tiaras, gloves, and handcrafted jewelry.

"We do not touch the mirror," a voice said sharply.

A thin man with short dark hair approached, wiping her fingerprints from the glass. He was impeccably dressed in a black Armani suit, white shirt, and silk tie. His manner was delicate, his voice soft—so unlike the men she had met before. And he did not seem thrilled to see her.

"Can I help you?" he asked.

"I am looking for a wedding dress."

He pursed his lips, eyeing her faded jeans, T-shirt, leather jacket, and sneakers. "Huh... are you sure you're in the right place? May I ask your budget?"

"Five thousand."

"Dollars?" he gasped. "Five thousand dollars is your budget?"

"Yes."

His demeanor transformed instantly. He guided her to a velvet sofa. "I am Rene. Let's show you our top of the line." He snapped his fingers toward a young woman near the jewelry counter. "Monica, tea and crumpets for our guest."

Monica, tall and elegant with long dark hair, brought a silver tray with a teapot and fine China. "Sugar and cream?"

"Just sugar. Lots of sugar. I like it sweet."

Monica added three sugar cubes, stirred the tea, and placed a silk napkin on Karen's lap. She buttered the crumpets and added marmalade before handing them over.

Karen took a bite—and immediately spat it out. "Yuck! I don't like this." She grinned. "Do you have chocolate?"

Monica returned with Swiss chocolate.

"Do you see anything you like?" Rene asked. "And when is your wedding?"

"This Friday."

"This Friday?" He grimaced—then remembered the budget. "Well, we can do that."

Karen tried on two dresses. One was a dream— princess-like, with a long flowing train. The other was modest, only a few hundred dollars. She was leaning toward the expensive one when something in the jewelry case caught her eye.

A cross necklace.

"What is that?" she asked.

Monica retrieved it. The polished silver gleamed.

"This is a binding cross," Monica explained. "Two crosses in one." She separated the smaller engraved cross from the larger hollow one. "Your names and wedding date can be engraved. His name is on the small one, yours inside the larger. They press together."

"Could a man wear that?"

"It's made for either. The date goes on the back. It's twenty-five hundred dollars."

"And the gold band there?"

"Another two hundred."

Karen frowned. "I can't afford the dress and these things." She whispered to herself, "So money does matter." She weighed the choices. "I have to decide which makes me happier."

"It's your dream dress," Monica said gently. "Every bride deserves her dream dress."

"No. I want him to have this," Karen said. "I'll take the cheaper dress."

"But miss—that dress is only five hundred dollars. You looked so lovely in the other." Rene countered.

"No. Making him happy is more important. That is my real dream."

Rene sighed but nodded. "Very well. We'll alter the cheaper dress. Monica will get your information. We'll have it ready by Thursday afternoon."

As Monica wrote down her details, she said, "I see a lot of greedy bridezillas. Everything must be their way. They don't care about their guy. And then there's you."

"Isn't love about making sacrifices?" Karen asked, handing back the notepad.
"You must really have God in you."
"That's twice today someone has said that. What does it mean?"
"It means you're a good person."

Chapter 28

Down on the lower level, Cooper walked to the food court to get two Dr Peppers® and then over to the popcorn machine for a large tub. He carried everything to the seating area outside J.C. Penney® and sat down. He popped a few kernels into his mouth—the salty butter flavor demanded another bite, then a sip of soda.

He spotted her descending the escalator. She had gone up like a child, but she came down like a woman—composed, graceful, thoughtful. She walked straight to him, and he stood to meet her. They sat together on the bench, the popcorn between them.

"I thought we'd share," he said.

She glanced at a teenage couple on the opposite bench, sharing popcorn and a single drink with two straws. "Can we do that?" she asked.

He smiled. "Young love."

He removed the lid from one of the drinks, placed two straws inside, and fed her three pieces of popcorn. Then they leaned together, foreheads touching, sharing a sip from the same cup. When he lowered the drink, she stared at him with a seriousness that made him straighten.

"Love," she said softly. "It is about sacrifices, isn't it? Doing something for someone, even if it costs you something. Isn't that why you're doing all this for me? Because you love me?"

"More than life itself," Cooper said.

"I require information," Karen said suddenly. Her tone more computer like than human.

"What kind of information?"

"The woman named Cathy said I have God in me. Then another woman said the same thing. She said it's because I'm a good person. How did God get in me? He wasn't part of the formula used for my printout."

Cooper's eyes widened. He pressed his fingers to his lips and exhaled slowly.

"Wow," he murmured, rubbing his chin. "That's... not exactly in my wheelhouse."

"Explain. Wheelhouse," she said, shaking her head at the unfamiliar word.

"It means I don't know what I'm talking about," he said. "I think we should call Brother Charles. He can explain it better."

"I don't want this anymore," she said, gesturing to the soda and popcorn.

He tossed them in the trash.

"I thought we could hit a few more stores, maybe get something to eat," he offered.

"No. I don't want anything else." Her voice was small, somber. "I want to go home."

"Okay."

She turned toward the entrance but paused when she saw a little boy—three years old—riding a bright red mini-car ride. The child laughed with pure delight. Karen smiled, tilting her head. His muscular father stood beside him.

"You two have any kids?" the man asked.

"No, but we're getting married Friday," Cooper said.

"They're a blessing," the father said. "Watching them on Christmas morning, tearing into the presents Santa left."

Karen turned to him. "Does he believe in Santa? Does he believe in God?"

"Yes, we all do," the father said.

She thanked him and walked away. The man looked confused. "Did I say something wrong?"

"No," Cooper said. "You said nothing wrong."

He caught up to her. "Karen, something is wrong. Tell me."

She spun around. "I am confused," she said. "That child believes. But I question everything. They tell me I have God in me, and that makes me a good person. But I don't know how He got there. I didn't add Him. So, if He isn't there... does that make me a bad person? I don't want to be a bad person. You didn't program me that way. I want to be good."

He had no answer.

"I am more confused than ever," she whispered, tears filling her eyes. "He is in you because God made you. But God did not make me. You made me. You are my creator. Does that make you, my God?"

"No," Cooper said. "I am not God. God is your God too."

"How can that be?" she asked, looking around at the crowds. "I am different from everyone in this building. In this nation. There is no one like me in the world or the universe. I'm not a machine, but I came from a machine. Yet I am flesh and blood."

"You believe in God, don't you?" she asked him. "You pray to Him. You do believe... don't you?"

"I don't know anymore!" she cried. "I am told I can believe in God, but I can't see Him. But I am told I cannot believe in Santa Claus or the Easter Bunny, but I can see them."

She looked up at the giant snowflake light hanging from the ceiling. "Maybe if I ask You," she whispered to the heavens. "Am I Your child? Or am I Cooper's monster? Show me someone who has the answer."

She looked back at Cooper, and a sudden smile lit her face. "I know someone who has the answer. You told me he has all the answers."

Cooper blinked, confused.

Karen walked toward the center of the mall. The food court rose around a hexagon-shaped structure with ten steps leading upward. To her, it looked like a stairway to heaven. She circled it, searching.

Then she saw him.

A large man in a red Santa suit with a real white beard.

She walked straight to him. "Are you the real Santa Claus?"

He must have seen the desperation in her eyes. "Yes, I am. What can I do for you, dear?"

"Can you give me the answer I'm looking for?" she begged.

"Yes, dear. What would you like for Christmas?"

He expected a request for jewelry or toys. Instead:

"I want to know who I am. I want to know why God does not love me."

"Oh my," Santa breathed. He removed a glove and took her hand. "Come over here. We'll talk."

"Can he come too?" she asked, glancing at Cooper. "He is the love of my life."

"Of course."

He led them behind the rope marking his break area. "Is she okay?" he whispered to Cooper.

"She's fine. She's my wife-to-be. But she's searching for God. And I can't help her. Can you, Santa?"

"I think so."

He sat and patted his lap. "Come sit here. What's your name?"

"Karen," she said softly.

"You remind me of my daughter," he said. "Why do you think God doesn't love you?"

"Because I was not made by Him," she whispered. "I was made in a laboratory. I have no mother or father. People tell me not to believe in you, but I can see you, touch you. But they say I should believe in God, and I cannot see Him or touch His face."

Luckily the man did not question her comment about being made in a laboratory. Cooper reasoned that it had to be because he thought she wasn't in her right mind, or maybe she was test-tube baby. Instead, he just listened to her.

Karen reached up and touched Santa's cheek. His beard scratched her palm. "How am I to believe in Him?"

Santa listened, then nodded. "I have a friend named Bob Pyle. He's a minister. He fills in for me sometimes here at the mall.

Santa looked at Cooper.

Cooper nodded understanding that Sata was indeed this minster. Santa asks Karen, "Do you believe in love?"

"Yes," she said. "That is why I came to this world. For love." She looked at Cooper and smile, her heart pouring with love. "To love him."

"Tell me, Karen—what does love look like? What color is it? What shape?"

"I don't know," she said. "I just know I never want to be apart from Cooper."

"And God loves you that much too," Santa said gently. "He does not want to be apart from you."

She looked at Cooper, then back at Santa. "But if I don't have a soul, where will I go when I die? God can't have me. The devil can't have me. I won't live forever. Cooper is a believer. I watch him pray. I try, but I don't hear God."

"You don't hear Him with your ears," Santa said. "You hear Him with your heart. You have a heart, don't you?"

"Yes," she whispered." That was part of the program."

"You say you don't have a soul, yet you love this man. Would you sacrifice for him? Even your life?"

"Yes."

"And you care for others?"

"Yes. Milo, Travis, Ellen, Marylin."

"Karen, you are full of love. God is love. And you cannot love without a soul. I don't care where you came from—you are a child of God. All you must do is accept that. Are you ready?"

She nodded.

Santa stood, took Cooper's hand, and led them both to kneel. He prayed the prayer of salvation with her. When they rose, he hugged her.

"A little early gift," he said, pulling a black Bible from his bag. "Read this. God has great plans for you, Karen."

Cooper brushed her hair from her face. "Feel better now?"

"Yes. All information received and accepted. But I still want to go home. Is that okay?"

Cooper wrapped an arm around her, and they walked toward the entrance. The packages were ready to be loaded. Night had fallen, the hum of security lights blending with Christmas music.

As Cooper pulled the Navigator around, the two salesgirls approached, pushing carts of boxes.

"I want to say I'm sorry," Amber said. "I heard we have you to thank for not getting fired. Why would you do that?"

"Everyone deserves a second chance," Karen said.

The girls pushed the carts out. Cooper opened the hatch. The manager watched to ensure the girls loaded everything.

They were bringing out another cart when a young man in a dark hoodie approached. Tattoos covered the back of his hand. He pulled an eight-inch knife and grabbed Karen, pressing the blade to her throat.

"Hand over the keys and she won't get hurt."

Karen's face hardened. Her voice dropped to a cold, dangerous tone Cooper had never heard. "It would be best for you to just... go away."

"Oh, a tough girl," the man sneered. "What are you gonna do?"

Cooper lunged, but the man pointed the knife at him. "Back off, Romeo, or I'll slice ya."

In a blur, Karen drove her elbow into the man's ribs. He cried out. She spun his wrist backward—there was a loud snap—and the knife clattered to the pavement. She twisted his arm, slammed him to the ground, and when he tried to rise, she kicked him square in the jaw, knocking him out cold.

Security rushed in and cuffed him.

Cooper stared at her, jaw hanging open.

"WHERE... DID... YOU LEARN TO DO THAT?"

Chapter 29

The longer Cooper lived out here, the more he found himself drifting away from the trappings of the instant world. The freeways were faster, sure, but they felt like endless steel arenas—car after car battling for the privilege of arriving twenty-five seconds sooner. He'd had enough of that.

So, he took Kansas 97 instead, stopping in Mazie for burgers, a chocolate milkshake, and a little shop Karen insisted they explore. After that, the noise of modern convenience faded behind them, swallowed by the quiet of the prairie night.

Near Colwich, Kansas the fog began to thicken, rolling across the roadway in cold, creeping sheets. On the far side of the highway stood a sole cottonwood, its dark, bare limbs rising like a skeleton half-lost in the mist.

Locals called it the *Lucky Tree.* More than 150 years old, it had weathered every storm that swept across this stretch of highway, standing guard like a patient sentinel. It had watched wagon wheels rattle past, trembled with new leaves in spring, sheltered birds in the summer heat, scattered its golden leaves across the asphalt in autumn, and stood bare and unapologetic in winter—its branches spread like a centerfold of survival.

If you listened long enough, you'd occasionally hear a passing honk—an affectionate salute. There was no sign marking it, so out-of-state drivers sped by without a glance, leaving the old tree to wonder, like an aging model, whether it had simply been forgotten.

Cooper knew exactly where it stood—just a few hundred feet from the West 96/276 marker. He spotted the headlights of a semi barreling down the opposite lane and heard the trucker's air horn: two short blasts, one long. Everyone had their own ritual. Honk at the tree, and it brought good luck.

Silly, maybe, to the scientific part of his brain. But tradition was tradition, and he had his own. Three honks and a whispered prayer.

He tapped the horn as they passed. "So," Cooper asked softly, glancing at her, her face lit only by the dim glow of the instrument cluster, "what did you pray for?"

"A beautiful wedding," she answered with a shy smile. "Wait until you see me in my dress. What about you?" She turned her head, the dashboard light brushing the curve of her cheek. "What did you pray for?"

"That you tell me how you knocked that guy out."

"I don't know how I did it," Karen said. "I searched all my programs. I can't find anything that would explain it." She paused, thinking. "Unless..."

"Unless what?" he asked, glancing at her. She didn't answer right away. Only the hum of the tires filled the silence.

"There's a locked file," she said at last. "Marked PJDKOVLD." Another pause. "It's called Project Dark Overlord."

"Dark Overlord? I never created anything with that name." Cooper stared into the fog-soaked darkness. "Maybe Travis put it there?"

"Negative," Karen replied. "The file was created before you met him. Five years ago. But it was updated a month ago— through thc internet."

Cooper's eyes narrowed, frustration knitting his brows. The fog grew thicker near Mt. Hope, swirling ghostlike around the security light at the intersection. It felt much later than it was—barely past eight. Highway 96 vanished like a magician's final flourish, replaced by Kansas 14. They were alone now, save for the occasional semi roaring past in the opposite direction.

"What month and day was the file created?"

"July eighth."

"That's two months after I met with the head of BioTyme— Jammie Tymerson."

"Do you have any background on him?"

"I can't access it here. No signal." She hesitated. "But sweetheart... I found the file in BioTyme headquarters. It links to a dot-gov domain."

"A government site?" Cooper's voice tightened. He had built the KAREN program himself—there were no government links.

"It links to the military."

Cooper reaction grew even more confused. What would the military want with the KAREN project? His head swung back and forth between her and the road ahead. Then he finally said.

"Access the file."

"Give me the password."

"Startripper 489 hashtag," he said, giving her the master key to all her programming.

"Password incorrect."

Chapter 30

Back home meant many trips in and out packing boxes from the Back home meant trip after trip from the Navigator to the upstairs bedroom, arms full of boxes. When Karen was busy arranging things upstairs, Cooper slipped out for one last package—the necklace he'd hidden beneath the driver's seat. He carried it inside, glancing around for a place to stash it.

The library offered the perfect hideaway. He'd only discovered it by accident while shelving his medical books. Pulling out *The Merck Manual of Diagnosis and Therapy* and two thick volumes on tissue engineering, he pressed the panel behind them. It shifted inward, then slid aside to reveal a narrow compartment in the wall—just large enough for the velvet case. He tucked it inside, pressed the panel again until it clicked back into place, and returned the books to their row.

He had just closed the pocket door when Karen appeared at the top of the staircase. She wore her new fleece jammies—bright red and black plaid, the kind that covered her from wrist to ankle, even matching socks on her feet. There was nothing remotely seductive about them, yet somehow, she looked impossibly adorable. Cooper's leather jacket hung over her arm, and her blonde hair was pulled back into a ponytail tied with a red ribbon.

"The weather report says it's going to get cold," she said as she padded toward him. "And snow is coming this weekend. I've never seen snow before." She looked up at him, eyes sparkling. "I have something special for the honeymoon, by the way. But you'll have to wait. You still haven't told me where we're going."

He traced a gentle line along her jaw, her eyes shining like flawless gems. "Well, there's no snow where we're headed. You'll have plenty of chances to see it later. But we only get one honeymoon. It's a surprise. And just like your little secret, you'll have to wait." He kissed her softly.

"We're going to have a happy life," Karen said quietly.

"With you in it, how could we not," Cooper replied, letting her go.

"Here's your jacket." She handed it to him with a mischievous grin. "You might want to try it on. Make sure I didn't change the fit." She patted the leather like she was hiding a joke.

"It doesn't change the fit because you—"

"Just try it on. Please!" she insisted, bouncing slightly on her toes. He felt ridiculous, but he'd do anything to make her smile. He slipped the coat on and held his arms out.

"Now check the pockets."

He slid his hands inside—and felt something. He pulled out a small royal-blue jewel box.

"What's this?" he asked, holding it up.

"Open it!" she said, practically glowing.

The lid snapped open to reveal a man's gold wedding band set with three small sapphires.

"Tradition says the bride buys the groom's ring," she said. "Besides, if I'm going to wear one, you're going to wear one too. So, all the other women know you belong to me. That I'm your Karen, and you're my Cooper." She rose onto her toes and kissed him. He wrapped his arms around her, gazing into her clear blue eyes.

Cooper tugged playfully at the hem of her pajamas. "You know, you really should wash this before you wear it."

"Well then," she said, lifting her chin with a teasing smile, "what do you say we go upstairs, and I take this off?"

Chapter 31

Later that morning at Cooper's house, he was fixing brunch for the two of them—Denver omelets, fresh-sliced bacon, toast, and hot tea. Karen sat at the table, busily turning pages in the Bible Santa had given her. He set a plate in front of her just as she closed the book.

"Very interesting," she said, laying it beside her plate. "I understand more now. God's judgment on those who disobey Him, His promise never to flood the world again, and how His judgment changed with the love of His Son. Most of it makes sense, but the last book was confusing. Were they really giant scorpions John saw, or could they be military vehicles—like attack choppers?"

"You read the whole Bible in one hour?" Cooper asked, stunned.

"Yes. It's part of the program you gave me. I've read every medical textbook there is, so now I read this." She smiled faintly. "Knowledge I can do. But creativity—that fails me. Music, for example. I can play notes, but music comes from the soul. Writing stories is the same. There are things A.I. can't do. Anything requiring imagination and talent, I can't."

"But believable lying takes creativity," Cooper said. "I've seen you do it. At the mall when you told them you were robbed, or when you told Marilyn your luggage was lost."

"No," Karen replied gently. "That isn't creativity. I wasn't lying for my benefit, but to protect you. It's my primary program. If the truth would bring you harm, I will shield you from it." She reached out, caressing his cheek. "Because I love you."

She cut into her omelet, tasted the bacon, and brightened. "I like this!" She took a sip of tea. "So, what are we doing today?"

"Well, we need to see Brother Charles. He wants to talk about the wedding. And how it will happen." Cooper leaned back, savoring his tea. "Might say a prayer for Milo. He's the parent aide on the school trip to the Center of the USA Chapel today." He laughed. "Imagine thirty-five kids, all of them just like his girls."

Karen was still in her fleece sleepwear.

"Have you decided who will be your best man?" she asked.

"It's too hard. I don't want hurt feelings. They're both good friends."

"I can solve it for you," Karen said, her smile widening. "Give me your cellphone."

He handed her his private phone. Her fingers flew across the screen. A moment later, Milo replied: *YES! It would be an honor.*

"There," she said. "Travis will be your best man."

"And Milo?"

She grinned as she returned the phone. "He's going to give me away."

When Karen went upstairs to change, Cooper hesitated. He needed a favor—one he didn't want to ask, especially from the person he had to ask. He picked up the receiver and dialed the direct line to Lilith's office. It rang. He took a breath.

"Doctor Williams' office," she answered.

"It's Dr. Barnes," he said, then softened. "Coop."

"Oh, so now you come crawling back to me after leaving that fake—"

"I need a favor," he cut in. Silence stretched before she finally spoke.

"I think you've used up your amount. What do you want now?"

"My contract states I can use the company jet once a year for any reason, including personal. I'd like it this Friday. For my honeymoon. I want to take Karen to Hawaii."

Another long silence. Then she cleared her throat. "No. It's being used." She hung up. Leaving Cooper feeling dejected.

"Go with my backup plan," Cooper said quietly, as if the walls themselves might be listening.

He pulled out his phone and typed a message to Milo.

Buddy, could Karen and I use your mountain cabin for our honeymoon? The witch nixed the plane.

The reply came almost instantly—too fast, almost as if Milo had been waiting for something from him.

Of course, man. Just don't you two cause any avalanches with your wild passion. HAHA.

The joke landed, but the unease didn't lift. Even a friendly text felt like part of a larger game now—one where someone else might be reading over their shoulders.

*****

The wind had shifted south, warming the air as moisture drifted in, forming puffy white clouds. Snow was forecast for Colorado, Nebraska, and northern Kansas. Maybe a honeymoon in the mountains would be perfect.

The breeze whipped across the churchyard as Cooper parked the Lincoln. Karen wore a ruby-red sweater, a steel-gray skirt, and loafers. The wind teased her hem as Cooper opened the door and she stepped inside. He followed, slipping off his sunglasses and tucking them into his sport jacket.

"Brother Charles!" Cooper called as they walked down the aisle. Charles emerged from the side door.

"Next time you do that, it'll be for real," he said, shaking Cooper's hand before turning to Karen. "So, this is the young lady you told me about. She's lovely. Very lovely. No wonder the women in town are foaming at the mouth to get you two married as soon as possible."

Brother Charles Hankins was middle-aged, his face weathered by years of service. His baby-blue eyes hid behind heavy gray plastic frames, and his warm smile—broad as the plains—was the first thing anyone noticed. His beard was neatly trimmed, flecked with silver, and deep laugh lines framed his mouth. Tall and lean, he carried himself with the quiet assurance of a man anchored by faith. Today he wore a simple gray KU sweatshirt, the Jayhawk faded from years of wear.

"Glad to meet you, Karen," he said, clasping her hand in both of his.

"I accepted the Lord yesterday," Karen said. "Santa helped me."

"Santa?"

"It's a long story," Cooper said.

"I heard! A friend of mine in Wichita knows Santa personally. We're very happy for you, Karen."

"I also read the entire Bible this morning," she added proudly.

"The entire Bible?" Brother Charles blinked.

"She's a fast reader," Cooper said. "Very fast."

"I know, but the entire Bible?" He decided to test her. "Leviticus 22:7."

"*'And when the sun goes down, he shall be clean; and afterward he may eat the holy offerings, because it is his food.'*"

He hurried to the pulpit, opened the Bible, and checked. She was right.

"First Timothy 7:1."

"I can't answer that."

"Because you don't remember?"

"No. Because it doesn't exist. First Timothy ends at 6:21. She quotes that verse '*By professing it, some have strayed concerning the faith. Grace be with you. Amen.*'"

"She's right," he said, shaking his head. "I'll have to stay on my toes with you in church."

"Remembering the Word is not the same as living it," Karen said.

"That's a good point. May I use that?" He motioned them to sit. "Now, about the wedding this Friday. You two are moving fast. Cooper, you're thirty-three, and Karen, twenty-five?" They nodded. "So, you're not kids. I trust you know what you're getting into."

"Brother Charles," Cooper began, "we've known each other a long time. For years. It's just that—"

"We haven't been in the same place at the same time until now," Karen said. "Until recently, our relationship was on the computer."

"Oh, I see. So, you know each other well?"

"Brother Charles, I know her as well as if I created her myself," Cooper said with a wry smile.

"And you, Karen?"

"If the creator creates one, are they not part of the creator? And you shall know their mind and heart as your own."

Brother Charles blinked at her phrasing, puzzled but impressed. "All right then. Let's run through this." He stood. "You'll have a best man and maid of honor?"

"They were supposed to be here—"

The door burst open. Travis and Ellen hurried in.

"Don't say anything!" Travis said. "We know we're late. But we're here now." He leaned toward Cooper. "We need to talk after this. It's important." Then to Brother Charles: "Milo couldn't make it. So that makes me best man?"

"He's giving the bride away," Cooper said. "So, you get the job."

They walked through the ceremony motions—where Cooper and Travis would stand, when Ellen would enter. Then the door opened again and Milo stepped in, sunlight spilling through the stained glass behind him.

"Am I too late?" he asked. "So, where's my dear sister?"

"Huh?" Cooper said, confused.

"Since I have no parents or family," Karen said, offering Milo her arm, "I want you to be my big brother."

"I'd be honored," he said, taking her arm and leading her down the aisle.

"Now, Milo," Brother Charles said, "I'll ask, 'Who gives this woman in matrimony?' You'll say, 'I do,' lift her veil, and take your seat in the front pew."

"I get a speaking part?" Milo groaned. "If I screw it up, I'll ruin the whole wedding. When I was a kid, I was in a school play. My line was 'I am just a little peanut.' But I said, 'I just took a little pea.' I don't know if I can do this."

"Please, Milo," Karen said, kissing his cheek. "For me."

"For you, little sister. I'll do it."

They all rehearsed their parts.

Sunlight pooled across the floor in a mosaic of color. As Karen and Ellen discussed details with Brother Charles, Milo motioned for Cooper and Travis to follow him outside. Cooper slipped on his sunglasses and stepped onto the porch.

"I was the parent aide today," Milo said. "We were in the little chapel. I found something on the floor." He pulled wrinkled photos from his jacket, smoothing them before handing them to Cooper. "The janitor said the place was cleaned last night. So, these had to be dropped early this morning."

"These were taken yesterday at the mall," Cooper said, staring at the photo of Karen leaving the bridal shop. The photos were decreet, as if taken without their knowledge. Then crushed in someone's hand.

"I also found this." Milo produced a crushed-out cigarette.

"So? A cigarette. Lots of people smoke," Cooper said.

"That cigarette was next to a photos of Karen," Milo replied. "Look at the writing."

"Let me see," Travis said, examining it. "This is Chinese. You can't buy these in America—only China or Hong Kong. Any Chinese working at the lab?"

"There are two," Milo said. "Dr. Wan Wong and a young woman named Sun Lang."

"They have access to the subbasements?"

"Yes. Red, white, and blue ID access. They can go anywhere."

"What are you trying to say?" Cooper asked.

"I don't mean anything by it," Milo said carefully. "But... how much is Karen worth?"

"To me, she's priceless," Cooper snapped.

"I'm not talking about that. She's the only one of her kind. What would she be worth to a foreign government? Billions? Trillions? How well do you know them?"

"Dr. Wong was the head of Hematology. He quit last week. We have someone new coming—Dr. Emma Stoneridge. As for Sun Lang, she escaped China. Only survivors of her family. She hates their government."

"That's what I wanted to talk about," Travis said. "Today in Smith Center, I overheard a large Black man. I couldn't see his face. He had a hat pulled down low. He was on his phone, speaking Chinese. And I heard him mention Karen's name."

"So, it could be anyone," Travis added. "Someone in this town even."

"That fits," Milo said. "The caretaker thought I dropped the photos. He said a large Black man was there early this morning meeting a woman. He showed me where he found them. That's when I found the cigarette butts."

Travis looked toward the sinking sun. "We have to go dark mode. I'm buying burner phones. We communicate only that way. No business phones—they're listening. We trust only each other now."

Chapter 32

It was the day before the wedding, and tradition dictated they wouldn't see each other again until tomorrow. The men had planned a bachelor party for Cooper, and the women in town were hosting a shower and bachelorette party for Karen.

Under normal circumstances, it would have been harmless fun. But after the photo and the Chinese cigarette Milo found, Cooper felt a knot of dread tightening in his chest. Leaving Karen alone—even for a night—felt wrong. Dangerous.

He didn't know who to trust anymore.

Yes, the townspeople had warmed up to him, but he barely knew them. And if someone out there suspected Karen was a T.E.H.- Tissue Engineered Human-, they would stop at nothing to get their hands on her.

His mind spiraled. Could he even trust Milo and Travis? He'd only met them after moving here. Why had Travis been so fascinated with Karen—so eager to program her with emotions? What else might he have slipped into her code? And Milo—why had he insisted on being there the night she came out of the printer?

And Ellen... she had gone from fearing him to becoming his first friend in town. She helped Karen with everything, even buying her underwear without questioning why she had none. A normal person would have asked. Was that kindness—or something else?

You're overthinking this, you idiot.

Fear was twisting his instincts into knots. He forced himself to breathe. Milo and Travis had risked their freedom to protect her. The rest of the town didn't know what she was— they believed she was Karen J. Smith, his bride-to-be. They wanted to celebrate with her, welcome her into their small-town family.

And this town *was* becoming his family. The only one he had here.

He'd invited his sister, but she was "too busy" to attend. When he sent her a photo of him and Karen, everyone else commented on how beautiful Karen was. His sister's response: *You're going bald. She's just a skinny little thing.*

It was better she wasn't coming.

But he still needed someone he trusted to watch over Karen tonight. And Ellen was his choice.

"You know," Ellen said as they sat on the porch, "Karen reminds me a lot of my late daughter."

Her words snapped him out of his thoughts.

"Late?" Cooper asked gently. "She passed away?"

"Yeah." Ellen's voice thinned. "She was home for Thanksgiving. We argued. She left angry... tried to pass a tractor... hit an eighteen-wheeler head-on." She swallowed hard. "Ten years, and it still hurts." She looked at him, eyes softening. "She was blonde and pretty like your Karen. Maybe God's giving me another chance. I'll watch her tonight. Don't worry."

"I'm not worried," Cooper said, though his crooked smile betrayed him.

The front door opened. Karen stepped out with a suitcase and her wedding dress in a garment bag. Cooper stood.

"Guess the next time I see you will be tomorrow at the church," he said.

"Sweetheart, I need to talk to you." She set her luggage down. "Can we step inside?"

He followed her in.

"I found something about Jimmie Tymerson and his family," she said quietly. "They didn't make their money from medicine. Tyme Corp—the company that owns BioTyme—is one of the biggest military manufacturers in the world. They supplied weapons in Vietnam, the Gulf War, Iraq, Ukraine. The Bio-Lab wasn't created for your idea. It was a bioweapon facility. When they got caught..."

"They used my idea to hide it," Cooper finished, his stomach sinking. "Any information on what kind of bioweapon?"

"Negative. Only that it was meant to be an ultimate weapon."

"I don't want to know more," he said firmly. "We're not letting this ruin our wedding. We'll talk later."

He led her back outside.

"How am I supposed to make it through the night without you?" she whispered.

"It'll be okay. Ellen will take care of you like her own daughter."

Karen wrapped her arms around him, and he held her tightly. She kissed him—long, warm, reluctant. When she pulled back, she traced his lips with her fingertip, as if memorizing them.

Ellen cleared her throat. "You two will have a lifetime for that. We need to get going."

Cooper carried Karen's suitcase and dress to Ellen's light-blue Chevrolet. He loaded them carefully, then opened the passenger door for Karen.

"One last kiss as Karen J. Smith," she said, pulling him down for another kiss. When she released him, she whispered, "Better here than in my world."

She sat, buckled in. He shut the door.

"See you tomorrow at the church," Ellen said as she started the car.

Karen pressed her hand to the window. Cooper placed his hand over hers. For a moment, it felt like the old days—when glass was the only thing that connected them.

Then the car turned the corner and disappeared.

The phone rang.

He rushed inside, thinking it might be Travis or Milo. He grabbed the receiver. "So where are we going?"

"Wherever you want," Lilith's voice purred.

"What?"

"I changed my mind. You can have the jet. It'll be ready Friday evening. And I'm giving you an extra week off for the honeymoon."

"Thanks, Lilith!" he said, but she had already hung up.

The front door exploded open.

Milo, Travis, and Stanley Leavitt stormed in.

"Grab him!" Milo shouted.

They tackled him, forced him to the floor, tied his hands behind his back, slipped a pillowcase over his head, and bound his feet.

He heard them chanting:

"Last night as a free man, for tomorrow you will wed. On your hand you'll wear a band, and to all other women, you'll be dead!"

They hoisted him onto their shoulders, carried him outside, down the steps, and tossed him into the back of a van.

"This is your last night to be a free man!" Milo said, buckling him into a seat. "Have to keep you safe for Karen. If it were up to me, I'd strap you to the roof!" He laughed and slapped Cooper's back. "You're gonna love it, buddy."

"Where are we going?" Cooper asked.

"That's for us to know," Milo said, "and you to find out."

The van jerked to a stop thirty minutes later.

"How are we getting him upstairs?" Travis asked.

"Stand back," Milo said, lifting Cooper over his shoulder. Cooper bounced with every step as Milo charged up the stairs, turned left, and barreled through a doorway into a bar—then into a back room.

"He's here!" Travis announced as Milo dropped Cooper into a chair. "Let the good times roll!"

They untied him and yanked off the pillowcase.

The back room had been transformed into a bachelor-party hideaway. String lights cast a warm golden glow. Banners declared *Last Night as a Free Man* in shimmering gold and black—his old high-school colors.

Leather chairs circled a walnut table piled with snacks, craft beers, and whiskey. A towering chocolate sportscar cake dominated the center.

The walls were plastered with centerfold posters and a life-size Ferrari. Above them, a sign read:

THINGS HE CAN'T HAVE OR LOOK AT ANYMORE.

"Why can't I have the Ferrari?" Cooper asked, eyeing the poster.

"Son," Serg said, lifting his mug of cold beer, "you're about to be a married man. Kids will follow. Ain't no room for 'em in that thing. You'll be driving a minivan."

"No. No minivans."

"What's wrong with a minivan?" Milo asked.

"For you? Nothing."

"Things aren't going weird again, are they?" Elmer muttered, remembering the night Karen was created.

"Oh, come on!" Milo teased, grabbing Elmer's shoulders and shaking him. "You're not scared of ghosts, are you?"

A server entered with four pitchers of beer, setting them on the table. Moments later, Antonio rolled in a cart stacked with pizzas.

"The amazing Doctor Coop!" Antonio declared. "I bring you good stuff."

They ate, drank, and sang off-key tributes to him. After four beers, Milo stood—now wearing a dark judge's robe and holding a wooden gavel.

"All right, everybody. Court is in session."

The men gathered around the table.

"Gentlemen of the jury," Milo announced, "how do you find Doctor Cooper James Barnes on the crime of matrimony? He did knowingly and willfully romance and seduce a young, innocent girl into marrying him."

"Guilty!" the room roared.

"Doctor Cooper James Barnes, rise for sentencing," Milo said, barely holding back laughter.

Cooper, lightheaded from rum and Coke, pushed himself to his feet.

"Your peers have found you guilty," Milo intoned. "I hereby sentence you to life imprisonment under Karen Jane Smith— soon to be Barnes. Your punishment: to love her for the rest of your days. You shall love no other. Not today, not tomorrow, not ever. Even in death, you shall remain faithful. May God bless you both. The high court has ruled."

He slammed the gavel.

"And if you don't," Milo added, pointing proudly at himself, "you'll answer to her big brother."

"Raise your glasses," Travis said. Everyone lifted their drinks. "To our friend and coworker. We wish you and Karen many years of joy. To Cooper!"

"To Cooper!" they echoed.

"Speech! Speech!"

Cooper lifted his glass. "I don't know what to say. Growing up in Neosho, I didn't have many friends. I was the nerd with his hand up, the kid who never fit in. Then I get sent to a place in Kansas I'd never heard of... and I find all of you. Thank you."

He drank. Milo groaned.

"Mush! Enough mush. Time to rock!" He shoved a CD into the player. AC/DC's "*Back in Black*" blasted through the speakers.

Cooper sank into his chair, feeling dizzy. He pushed his drink away and ordered a plain Coke. Dr. Stanley Leavitt slid into the seat beside him.

"Cooper, I've been trying to reach you for three days."

"I turned my phone off," Cooper said. "Didn't want Lilith ruining this."

"I found something about biostructure and the aging process."

"Stanley, I don't want to talk about work. Not tonight."

"But this involves Karen." Stanley lowered his voice. "She's a printout, isn't she?"

Cooper froze. *How does he know?* He forced his expression to stay neutral.

"Have you been drinking? A printout?" Cooper scoffed.

"No. I was working late on Halloween when everything went crazy. I saw you and Milo carrying her out."

Cooper glanced around to make sure no one was listening. He leaned in.

"Stanley, you can't tell anyone. Not even your wife."

"I won't. But listen—there's a problem. The bio print doesn't have a long lifespan. Five to seven years at most. It ages fast. There's some kind of virus embedded in the printout."

"What?" Cooper's voice cracked. "You're telling me Karen only has five to seven years to live?" He grabbed Stanley by the collar. "Damn it, Stanley! She's the love of my life!"

He released him, shaking.

"I'm sorry," Stanley said. "I know what she meant—means—to you. But there's more. Aging usually starts a week after printing. But if the hypodermis is injured, the process accelerates. I tested it on the rabbit—it lasted two days. In humans, the aging would begin almost immediately and finish in four to five months. She'll die of old age."

Cooper grabbed Stanley's hand. "Have you reported this?"

"Not yet. But Lilith is sniffing around like a bloodhound."

"I don't want you reporting it anywhere. Especially not in the database. Lilith can't know. Karen can't know."

"I—"

Cooper squeezed harder. "I'm ordering you not to. And I'm asking you, man to man, friend to friend—work on this. Don't tell Lilith. I'll make sure she doesn't bother you."

"How?"

"Never mind how. Just... please. Find a cure. I can't lose her. I want a lifetime with her. I want to grow old with her. Sit on a porch in rocking chairs. Look into those blue eyes one last time and drown in them. Please, Stanley. I can't live without her."

"I'll do what I can," Stanley said. "I promise."

Cooper pushed himself up. "I feel sick. I need to wash my face."

He wove through the crowd, shaking hands automatically. In the main bar, he spotted the waitress cleaning a table.

"Can't read the damn signs," she muttered at a man leaving.

"Problem?" Cooper asked.

208

"These idiots keep trying to smoke. We've got signs everywhere." She pointed. He saw them—big, bold, impossible to miss. "This big guy comes in; orders water and lights up some weird cigarette."

"You mean pot?"

"No. It had strange writing on it." She held it up.

Chinese. The same brand Milo found.

"What did he look like?" Cooper asked, pulse spiking.

"Big Black guy. Dark glasses. Big black hat. Real spooky. He just left." She pointed toward the door.

Cooper bolted down the stairs and out into the night—just in time to see a dark SUV speeding away.

"Damn it," he growled. "Who are you?"

Chapter 33

Friday afternoon. Thirty-three minutes until the wedding.

"I've got to get this to Karen," Cooper said, pacing the small back room of the Lebanon church. In his hands he clutched the jewel case containing the necklace and earrings.

"You can't see the bride before the wedding," Milo reminded him. "Everybody knows that's bad luck. I saw mine before the wedding. Only good luck I had was when she left."

He winced. "I shouldn't have said that. Karen's a good one. You don't have to worry."

"I bought this for her to wear. It's her something new and something blue." Cooper opened the case. "See?"

He wore a white tux with a red bow tie. Hendrix, the cat, sat loyally at his feet—also wearing a tiny red bow tie with a gold pouch tied to it, holding the rings.

"Wait a minute!" Cooper said suddenly. "You can see her. You're giving her away. You can take it to her."

He shoved the case into Milo's hands.

Milo stared at the jewels, eyes widening. "Wow. Are these diamonds?"

"No—iolite and white sapphires. She doesn't like diamonds."

Milo blinked at him, stunned. "A woman who doesn't like diamonds. Buddy... you really did create the perfect woman."

He slipped out the door with the case.

Cooper sat at the small table, adjusting the mirror to check his tie. Hendrix leaped onto the table.

"Need to check your tie too?" Cooper asked.

The cat meowed. Cooper angled the mirror so Hendrix could see himself, then straightened the tiny bow tie.

"You've got one of the most important jobs today, Hendrix. You've got the rings. We can't get married without those. Nervous?"

A single meow. *Yeah.*

"Don't worry. It'll be over soon. Then we'll be a family. Karen will love you as much as I do. You'll be our furry kid. You okay with that?"

Another meow.

Cooper checked the clock—twenty-five minutes left. He drummed his fingers on the table, heartbeat matching the rhythm. Hendrix stretched and tapped his paws in sympathy.

The door opened. Travis stepped in wearing a black tux with a pink bow tie.

"I've heard of a nervous cat on a hot tin roof," he said, "but never one on a desk. You two look like you're facing a firing squad."

"You see the crowd?" Cooper whispered. "How... how many—"

"How many people?" Travis teased. "Not a seat left. Every eye will be on you."

"What?" Cooper squeaked.

"I'm kidding." Travis laughed. "Nobody's going to notice you. They'll all be looking at the bride. And in Karen's case, you could be standing up there buck-naked, and no one would see you. Oh man, Cooper—I saw her. There are no words left."

"Pretty?" Cooper asked, standing.

"Pretty? That's an insult. She's *motto bella.* I saw models in magazines jumping into paper shredders because they couldn't compete. You're one lucky dude."

He handed Cooper a wrapped package. "Milo and I got you something."

"You didn't have to—"

"Karen's getting all the attention today. You deserve something too. Open it."

Cooper tore the shiny blue paper. Inside was a Jimi Hendrix album—*Axis: Bold As Love.* Used, worn... and autographed.

"Oh my gosh!" Cooper gasped. "'Love, Jimi.' This is real. Thank you!"

He hugged Travis.

A knock sounded. "Everyone dressed?" Tammi called.

"Come in," Cooper said.

She entered with a box of boutonnieres—pink and red roses with greenery.

"See you got your gift."

"Love it," Cooper said proudly.

Tammi eyed their bow ties. "No, no, no. This is wrong. Cooper, you need the pink one—it matches your boutonniere and Karen's bouquet. Off. Both of you."

They swapped ties. Tammi retied them with expert hands, pinned a pink rose on Cooper's lapel, a red one to Travis's, and even a tiny rose to Hendrix's bow tie.

"Well, don't you all look handsome. Karen's wearing the necklace and earrings—something new and something blue. She's got an old penny in her shoe and borrowed a handkerchief from me. We're ready as soon as Milo finds his daughters and gets his boutonniere."

She reached for the door.

"Tammi... how is she?" Cooper asked.

Tammi paused, turning back. "You know, I've been to more weddings than I can count—my cousins', my sisters', my own. Every bride was jittery. Pacing. Doubting. Wondering if she should run."

She smiled softly.

"But Karen? She's calm. Excited. Certain. Like she has no doubts at all. She's making the rest of us look bad. How did you find the perfect woman?"

"He made her in the lab," Travis joked.

Tammi smacked his arm. "You're such a goofball." Then to Cooper: "And you should be on your knees every day thanking God for sending her to you."

"I do," Cooper said.

"Oh, that part comes later," she teased, patting his arm before leaving.

Milo suddenly barreled past the door, chasing his daughters. Cooper and Travis followed him into the foyer.

The girls' flower baskets were empty.

"What did you do with the flowers?" Milo cried.

"We fed them to the birds," Cheyenne said proudly.

"Flowers don't eat birds—birds don't eat flowers—why would you—never mind! You're supposed to throw them in front of the bride!"

The music changed.

"That's our cue," Cooper said.

"Just go!" Milo groaned. "I'll fix it. I swear I'm returning you two to the hospital." He spun in circles. "Where am I going to find flowers?"

"Milo, your boutonniere," Tammi said, trying to pin it on him.

"You go on," Milo told Cooper. "They can't do this without you."

Cooper, Travis, and Brother Charles stepped into the sanctuary.

The church was breathtaking: garlands of greenery and roses, lace bows on every pew, tall candles flickering beside stained-glass windows that cast jeweled light across the floor. A chiffon-draped archway framed the altar, lush with roses and greenery.

Helen, the pastor's wife, played the piano softly.

Cooper bit his lip as he spotted Milo sneaking—well, as much as a six-foot-seven, three-hundred-pound man *could* sneak—grabbing two bouquets from the back and sprinting out.

The music continued. Nothing happened.

Then Tammi grabbed Antonio's arm and marched down the aisle. "Play along," she whispered.

Ellen followed as Maid of Honor.

Brother Charles handed Cooper a three-legged stool. Hendrix trotted down the aisle to a chorus of delighted "ahhs," leaped onto the stool, and sat proudly.

Milo's daughters appeared next, flinging flower petals like confetti, shouting, "Yay for our team!" Guests laughed as petals rained down.

Then Milo appeared in the doorway with Karen in his arm.

The wedding march began.

Karen was radiant—strapless white gown, ballroom skirt, sweetheart neckline, lace bodice, sheer sleeves, veil edged in lace. The necklace glimmered at her throat. Her bouquet of red and white roses matched the pink ribbon on Cooper's boutonniere.

She was breathtaking.

"Who gives this woman in marriage?" Brother Charles asked.

"I do," Milo said firmly. His body ridged like a solider He lifted her veil, then retreated to the front pew with a sigh of relief.

Brother Charles began the ceremony. When he reached the "speak now or forever hold your peace" line, Hendrix and Milo turned to glare at the guests.

A late arrival slipped in—a man in a black overcoat, collar up, hat brim low. He sat in the back row. Milo frowned. He didn't know him.

The ceremony continued. The Corinthians reading. The vows. The rings—Cooper's mother's ring fitting Karen perfectly. Karen's ring sliding onto Cooper's hand.

"I pronounce you husband and wife. You may kiss the bride."

They kissed.

"Family and friends," Brother Charles announced, "I present Dr. and Mrs. Cooper Barnes."

The music swelled. Guests cheered.

But Cooper's smile faltered the instant he saw the stranger in the back row. The man clapped slowly—deliberately—each tap of his palms barely audible. His face was swallowed by shadow, sunglasses hiding his eyes even indoors.

Cooper stared. The man stared back. Neither blinked.

The moment they stepped out of the sanctuary, Cooper grabbed Karen's hand and hurried her down the steps.

"Travis!" he shouted. "Did you see the guy in the back? That's the same one from last night—the one with the cigarettes."

Guests spilled out behind them in a noisy wave.

"Get Karen to the community center and stay with her!"

Travis didn't hesitate. He seized Karen's arm. Tammi followed, alarm rising in her voice.

"What's going on?"

"Someone may be trying to kill Karen," Travis said.

Tammi froze. "What? Why—"

"Never mind—get in!" Travis shoved them both into the limo.

"Milo and I will meet you there," Cooper said, already fighting his way back inside pushing against the tide of guests like a salmon battling upstream.

He reached the sanctuary. Only a few stragglers remained. Milo stood near the back, pointing toward a side door.

"He went through there! I tried to stop him—too many people."

Cooper sprinted down the hall. Milo thundered down the basement stairs.

Cooper burst through the exit door into the cold air. Wind whipped leaves across the churchyard. Guests wandered toward the visitor's center, cars lined the street, chatter filled the air.

"Anyone see a big Black man come through here?" Cooper called out.

"Milo?" someone asked.

"Not Milo. Heavy coat, dark hat, sunglasses."

"No."

"Damn it," Cooper muttered.

He cut across the grass toward the gravel alley just as Milo burst from the basement door.

"No one down there!" Milo shouted.

Cooper's eyes locked onto a black SUV idling in the alley.

"Milo—that's the one!"

They sprinted toward it, but the tires spun violently, spraying gravel as the SUV shot forward and roared away.

Milo bent down and picked something up. A crushed cigarette. The same brand as before.

"It's cold," Milo said. "He was sitting here waiting."

216

"Yeah," Cooper said, breath tight. "But we still don't know who he is. Or why he's here."

He stared down the alley where the SUV had vanished, a chill crawling up his spine.

"We need to get back to Karen."

Chapter 34

Cooper and Milo walked toward the community center on Main Street, talking as they went.

"I don't get it, Milo. Who would anyone want to kill her?" Cooper asked as they passed what used to be a mechanical shop, its old garage door now sealed over with windows and brick. "What we're doing is a great thing. It could help so many people."

"To you," Milo said. They stopped in front of the city utility shed, where a white M9 street sweeper sat parked from the wedding preparations. "Think about the fight in Congress over this. You saw the ones taking payoffs. Big Pharma bankrolled every protest and every politician who fought you. You said it yourself—if you can make replacement organs that work, people won't need artificial limbs, insulin, cardiac meds, anti-rejection drugs. There are some very rich, very powerful people who'd love to silence you. You're going to make them broke."

"You really think Big Pharma is behind all this?" Cooper asked.

"Didn't you go to them with your idea, and they laughed at you?" Milo shot back. "Not because they thought you *couldn't* do it—because they knew you *could*. They have to stop you. They don't know Karen is a T.E.H. They want to kidnap her and force you to destroy the computer."

Cooper froze. "Milo, I can't do that. Karen *is* the computer. If I destroy it, she dies. I can't let that happen."

"Then we won't let them get her, will we?" Milo said.

They turned onto Main Street. The entire block was packed with cars, including the limo parked in front of the community center. Before they entered, Milo straightened Cooper's tie.

"You have to look your best for my little sister." He tapped Cooper's cheek playfully, then added in a low voice, "We can't trust anyone we don't truly know. I'm driving you two to the airport." He glared at the skinny chauffeur beside the limo. "You got a problem with that?"

218

"No, sir," the young man said quickly, handing over the keys.

"Good. Let's get you in there," Milo said. "They're probably looking for you."

He threw open the doors, and cheers erupted.

"See? Told ya he wouldn't run out on you," Serg called from beside Karen at the reception table. The old man hobbled over, leaning on his cane, and clapped a hand on Cooper's shoulder. "I thought I'd have to go on your honeymoon for you. With a girl like that, I'd die—but heck, I'd dic happy." He laughed and nudged Cooper in the ribs. "You better get over there, Doc, before someone else swoops in."

The room was decorated with white streamers, pink and white balloons, and strings of white and blue Christmas lights. Round tables covered in pink and white tablecloths filled the hall; each chair wrapped in blue or white fabric tied with a wide red ribbon. A single battery-lit candle glowed on each table.

Karen waited beside the wedding cake—a three-tier masterpiece covered in white icing and roses so lifelike he expected a scent. When he leaned in, he realized they were icing.

"Marilyn, amazing job," he said. "It's almost a shame to cut it."

"Don't worry, Doc," a young female voice said. He turned to see a thin red-haired teenager with braces and freckles, a camera in hand and another around her neck. "I'm Melissa—Serg's granddaughter. I'm studying photojournalism at KU. I'm taking all the photos as our gift to you. After this, I thought we could take some at the church with the wedding party."

"That would be fine," Cooper said. "Speaking of the wedding party—"

"Don't worry about Hendrix," Ellen said. "I took him home. Now can we get on with the cake cutting and the dinner these wonderful ladies made?"

"Yes, we can." Cooper handed Karen the knife, placed his hand over hers, and together they cut into the rich chocolate cake. They fed each other a bite, toasted with punch, and then Cooper raised his glass to the room.

"When I came to this town for this job, I didn't know what to do. As you'll notice, neither Karen nor I have family here. But that isn't true. Family isn't what runs through your veins—it's what runs through your heart. Looking at all of you, many of you aren't friends. You're family."

He looked at Milo and Travis. "Brothers who risk everything when we need it." Then at Ellen and Marilyn. "Sisters and mothers who don't ask why—only how they can help."

He lifted his glass to the crowd. "Neighbors, you too are our family. You gave us this wedding. We'll remember it forever— not just in photos, but in here." He tapped his chest. "So today, we are surrounded by family, and that makes us blessed. Karen and I ask God to bless you all. Thank you."

Music began, and guests lined up for food. Cooper turned to Karen. "You young lady—I thank God every morning when I open my eyes and see you. And every night I ask Him to watch over you, so you'll be there when they open again."

"Ditto," she said with a smile. They linked arms and drank.

"Hold it right there!" Melissa called, snapping a photo. "I hope I find a guy who'll say that to me someday."

Karen set down her glass and tugged Cooper toward the gift table. "I want you to open my present first."

He sat as she handed him a small blue-and-white wrapped box. Inside was a jewel box, and inside that—a cross necklace.

"This is called a forever cross," she said, pulling it apart gently. "Your name is here." She showed him the inside of the larger cross. "My name is here." She flipped it over. "Our wedding date is engraved on the back. And like our love, we're sealed with God's love forever." She fastened it around his neck.

220

"I don't know what to say," he whispered. "No one's ever given me something like this."

"I bought a cheaper dress so I could get this and your ring," she said.

"I thought your dream dress would make you happy."

"This makes me happier," she said, wrapping her arms around him and kissing him. A camera flash caught the moment.

The rest of the gifts were opened, though none compared to hers. By the time photos at the church were finished and they returned, only scraps of dinner remained. But a romantic lobster dinner waited on the jet.

Outside, the crowd gathered as their luggage was loaded into the white Mercedes-Benz VIP limousine. Birdseed rained down as they dashed to the door where Milo—still in his tux, wearing a chauffeur's hat two sizes too small—held it open.

"To the airport, sir?" Milo joked.

"Yes, Jeeves, and make it quick," Cooper laughed, helping Karen inside.

The limo was a dream of luxury—soft white leather trimmed in deep red, plush carpeting, a polished wood console, a bar with crystal glassware, and a flat-screen TV.

"I can't wait to get you alone," Karen whispered, desire burning in her eyes. "I heard about the mile-high club. I think we might join." She slid into his lap, kicked off her shoes, and kissed him deeply—until Milo interrupted.

"Sir, this is Jeeves."

"Yeah, Jeeves, what is it?" Cooper said, pressing the intercom.

"Corporate sent you a bottle of champagne. Howard brought it over. We're just leaving town."

Cooper lifted the bottle—*Veuve Clicquot La Grande Dame Brut*. "They have sprung for the good stuff. Want to try it?"

"I'll try it!" she said, grabbing two glasses. She took a sip, choked, and sputtered champagne onto his face.

"I'm sorry!" she said, wiping it away. "The bubbles tickled my nose."

He dumped the glass and recorked the bottle.

"If the champagne doesn't work out," Milo said, "I put a couple bottles of Coke in the cooler."

Cooper opened one and handed it to her. They shared it, passing it back and forth. Her eyes sparkled brighter than her necklace.

She placed his hand on her chest. "Feel my heartbeat?"

"It's rapid again. Are you nervous?"

"No. That's just what you do to me." She kissed him. "I knew I loved you the first time I saw you. I just couldn't get to you. So, I kept changing and changing until you saw me. I can change more if you want."

"Don't ever change again. I love you just the way you are."

The privacy divider suddenly slid down.

"Hey guys, we're arriving at the plane," Milo said.

They pulled up to the private airstrip where the massive red-and-white Boeing 757—*Lucille*—waited. Lights swept across the runway as the tower beacon rotated.

The flight crew approached: Captain Matthew "Skipper" Jones, co-pilot Patrick Wells, and attendant Cynthia Carson. After introductions, Skipper lowered his voice.

"There's a bedroom on board."

"I know," Cooper said, bumping his fist.

Milo opened the limo trunk. Cooper retrieved a small blue suitcase.

Karen pulled out a dark blue ribbed stocking cap with *Karen's Brother* printed in orange. "We found it on the way back from Wichita. Thanks for being my brother today."

Milo grinned and pulled it on. "You're welcome. I'll be your brother always."

She hugged him tightly. "That's for being part of the most special day of my life."

The jet engines roared to life.

"You better get aboard!" Milo shouted.

But a black SUV screeched to a stop. Dr. Stanley Leavitt jumped out.

"Thank God—I made it!"

"You didn't have to see us off—" Cooper began, then saw the desperation in his eyes. "You're not here for that, are you?"

"My father is dying," Dr. Leavitt said, voice breaking. "They don't expect him to make it through the night. I was hoping I could use the plane."

"We can't go on our honeymoon and leave him here," Karen said. "It isn't right."

"You got it, Stanley!" Cooper called. "But you owe us—big time!"

Dr. Leavitt raced up the stairs. "Cooper! The thing we talked about last night—I figured it out! It's not what we think. No one knows. It's all in here!" He tapped his forehead. "We can get the cure for her as soon as I get back!"

The door closed. The jet taxied out to the runway.

"We had to do that," Karen said. "How could we enjoy ourselves knowing we left him behind?"

"I know," Cooper said, putting his arm around her.

"Hey!" Milo said. "Take my cabin. A winter wonderland honeymoon. Go swap the bikini for a warm nightie."

"You'd do that for us?" Cooper asked.

"Why wouldn't I? You went to the mat for me with Lilith. That's what family does."

"And I meant it," Cooper said.

"Wait!" Milo said suddenly. "You know what this means?"

"What?"

"My brother married my little sister!" Milo laughed. "We're gonna end up on one of those talk shows. I'll be sitting between you two, smiling."

Cooper laughed with him.

"You two are silly," Karen said.

They were stepping into the car when the jet lifted off. They watched the landing gear retract.

Then— **BOOM.**

A violent explosion shook the countryside. Flames burst from the jet's side.

Karen froze, then stepped back out of the car, staring upward. Milo's cap fell to the ground.

"Oh, good God, have mercy," Cooper whispered, half prayer, half shock.

The jet wobbled, nose dipping like a wounded bird. It howled as it plunged, then slammed into the ground. A fireball erupted, black smoke billowing into the sky. Karen buried her face in Cooper's chest. He held her tightly.

Milo's face twisted with grief. "Cooper... that plane exploded in the air."

"I know."

"It didn't just crash," Milo said, grabbing Cooper's shoulder and turning him. "There was a bomb on board." Karen lifted her head, eyes wide. "That bomb was meant for you two."

Chapter 35

Soon, the media caught the pungent stench of death, and they circled the fiery wreckage like vultures. Each network sent its own scavenger to feast on the decaying flesh of tragedy; all wrapped neatly in the words *Breaking News*. Cameras zoomed in on small-town firefighters battling the inferno, only to be driven back by another explosion as the beast spat flames at them.

Above it all, news choppers hovered—winged predators—while the anchor back in the studio fed on the destruction below. Her polished smile only brightened as she promised, "More after these messages."

"We are not sure who was aboard the jet," the anchor continued as Cooper and Karen watched from the limo's flat-screen TV. Cooper sat on the driver's side now; Karen curled against him with her head on his shoulder. "The aircraft was a private jet leased to Tyme Corp Industries and took off from a private airstrip near Lebanon, Kansas. It seems every major headline in the world is coming out of this small town tonight."

The screen shifted to a graphic. "If you're just joining us, tragedy has once again struck near Lebanon, Kansas. A private Boeing 757 has crashed into a local auto salvage yard, resulting in a massive fire. FOX News has now obtained exclusive footage of the actual crash."

The feed cut to grainy video of the jet lifting off, climbing—and then erupting into a fireball before plummeting to the ground.

Karen lifted her head. Cooper leaned closer to the screen. "Where did they get that video?" he murmured, puzzled. Some had to be there filming this. He *wondered did they know they didn't get abroad. If they knew. Would they try to kill them again. Why did they want them dead? Was it because of the KAREN project? And if they knew they were still alive. Would they try it again?*

"As you can clearly see," the anchor said, "there appears to be an explosion before the aircraft goes down, raising questions about whether a bomb was aboard. This comes as protestors gather outside Tyme Corp headquarters in St. Louis, demonstrating against the use of genetic material. Reports indicate some of these protestors have been seen in towns near the BioTyme lab."

The scene cut to a crowd holding signs: *Leave Life Be! Do Not Play God!* and *End of Time with BioTyme!*

A spokesperson stepped forward—a medium-built woman with cropped hair dyed in a rainbow of colors. "What they're doing is a crime," she declared. "They're going against God. We demand police investigate the possibility that Faith Addams was murdered. But they say the case is closed, and BioTyme Labs cremated the body."

That is standard procedure we use in deposing of the bodies donated." Cooper explained as he watched.

"Are you claiming BioTyme Labs murdered Faith Addams?" the reporter asked.

"Faith was one of the healthiest people around. She took care of herself. But they say she died of a heart attack."

"She's right," Cooper said sharply. "I took the samples. There was no sign of heart disease." He turned to Karen. "You used her samples. Was anything out of range?"

"Only one thing," Karen said. "Her insulin was 325 mIU/L— off the charts. I had to run it through the cleaning filter and use different blood. But all tissue samples showed no sign of long-term diabetes."

"Which means someone injected her with insulin," Cooper said, thinking aloud. "But why Faith?"

"Maybe she saw or heard something," Karen said. "Something the media isn't telling us. She was found in Bird City, Kansas."

"Bird City?" Cooper frowned. "Never heard of it."

"It's up the road a few miles," Milo said from the front. "We'll pass right through on the way to the mountains."

"What's there?" Cooper asked.

"Nothing," Milo replied.

Karen shook her head. "She was meeting someone there."

Chapter 36

It was with profound sadness that BioTyme Medical Research Labs announced the tragic loss of their esteemed colleagues, Dr. Cooper James Barnes and his wife, Karen J. Barnes, in the devastating jet crash near Lebanon, Kansas earlier that evening. Also killed were Captain Matthew Jones, Copilot Patrick Wells, and attendant Cynthia Carson. The private jet had gone down shortly after takeoff; investigators confirmed that all aboard were lost.

Captain Jones and his crew had been flying Dr. Barnes and his new bride to Hawaii for their honeymoon, only hours after the couple exchanged vows. Dr. Barnes had been a dedicated professional whose contributions to tissue engineering and biomedical printing left an indelible mark on the organization and the medical community at large.

BioTyme extended its deepest condolences to the families, friends, and colleagues affected by the tragedy. The company pledged support, counseling, and a renewed commitment to the work Dr. Barnes championed. The statement concluded with a request for privacy and gratitude for the outpouring of support from the global medical community.

Sincerely, Dr. Lilith Williams Director of Medical Research BioTyme Research Laboratories

"Well, what do you know, buddy—you were a good person," Milo joked as he rolled down the center divider after hearing the news. "I'm going to miss you. And you too, Mrs. Barnes."

Till we find out what is going on Milo I think it is best we remain dead."

Outside the windshield, a fine mist had begun to fall—rain that would soon turn to snow. Cooper watched it bead on the glass, the wipers keeping a steady rhythm as they traveled west. The farther they went, the heavier the snow became.

Karen was enticed. She had never seen snow. She leaned over the back of the front seat, bare feet kicking beneath her wedding gown, bracing herself with her hands as she stared out into the darkness. The headlights carved tunnels through the falling snow.

"It looks like we're flying in space," she said, eyes shining. "The snow is the stars. What unknown galaxies are you taking us to, Captain?"

"Captain Milo," he declared proudly. "I like that. I could be a superhero—fighting crime in the naked city."

"Milo," Cooper said, "after they find enough material to make you a superhero costume, everybody will be naked."

"That's it. Keep it up and I'll leave you on the side of the road," Milo shot back. They kept the banter alive because the alternative was thinking about how close they'd come to dying. But Cooper's mind still raced with the question of who wanted them dead.

Karen returned to watching the snow swirl across the road, her feet twisting as she danced to music only she could hear. Without realizing it, she lifted one foot right into Cooper's face. He caught her heel and, teasing, ran his tongue along the arch of her foot.

A shiver rippled through her. Her eyes fluttered, her mouth parted, and she let out a soft, involuntary sound. She lifted her other foot, and he brushed it with a gentle lick. She gasped, then looked at Milo with a mischievous smile.

"Bye! I must go!" she announced, scrambling back over the seat and into Cooper's lap.

She kissed him, reaching for the divider button. As it slid up, Cooper glanced at the screen—just in time for Milo to lower it again.

"I hate to pour cold water on you two," Milo said, "but we need fuel." His words hit Karen like an actual splash of cold water. "And I could use some food too. I didn't get any of that good wedding dinner."

Karen sighed and whispered into Cooper's ear, "I bookmarked this spot. We'll come back to it." She kissed him lightly and slid to the other side of the seat.

Cooper checked his watch—8:30 p.m. "Come to think of it, we didn't get much either. We were supposed to have lobster."

He leaned forward, staring into the darkness. No towns. No farmhouses. Nothing but snow and the endless ribbon of US Highway 36. A knot tightened in his stomach.

"These towns close early," he said. "And with a storm coming, we'll be lucky to find anything open."

"It'll have to be the first one we see," Milo replied.

"How much fuel do we have?"

Milo tapped the dashboard screen. "Ten miles."

Cooper checked the temperature. "Eighteen degrees. And no blankets. If we run out of fuel, the temperature will drop fast."

"What are you saying?"

"I'm saying if we don't find a station, they'll find us like three frozen popsicles. Say a prayer we find some place."

"Already said a prayer," Milo said. He grinned. "Just promise me one thing—if we have to spend the night together, don't do to me what you were doing to her."

Cooper laughed. "I can assure you of that."

He sat beside Karen. "Don't worry. We're okay."

"That is not true," she said sharply as her computer-like brain kicked in. "Estimating the fuel economy of this limo, if Milo maintains 43.45 miles per hour, we will run out of fuel in approximately 9.2 miles. With the temperature falling to ten degrees, the interior temperature will drop rapidly. Within ninety minutes—"

"You don't need to go any further," Cooper cut in. "Sometimes I wish you weren't a—"

"Computer?" she snapped. Her brows drew together. "Don't call me that. I'd rather you call me a bitch than that. I am human. I am your wife. I am your Karen."

"I'm sorry," he said softly.

Ahead, the headlights painted the highway in a narrow band of light. Beyond it, nothing but empty fields. The fuel gauge hovered near empty. The road curved like a serpent waiting to strike.

Then—finally—a green sign, half-buried in snow. A train horn blared as a locomotive thundered past. Grain elevators rose on the horizon. Another town. But they'd seen this dark, closed, lifeless before.

Then Milo spotted it: a glow through the snow. Red and green lights.

"A gas station!" he shouted. "And it's open!"

He pulled under the canopy. Snowflakes drifted down in large, lazy spirals, whipped by the wind like tiny dancers. Karen shivered. Cooper draped his white tuxedo jacket over her shoulders. She stepped out into the open, staring up at the sky.

Cooper handed Milo his credit card.

"You can't use that," Milo said, pulling out his own. "You two are dead. Those cards are canceled. Use them and alarms will go off. You got any cash?"

"A few hundred."

"Good. You pay for food at that place." Milo pointed to a Mexican restaurant across the lot. "I'll get the gas."

"Mexican at this hour?"

"It'll stick to your ribs. Better than those hot dogs spinning in there."

"Those things are deadly weapons," Cooper muttered. "Mexican it is."

He started toward the restaurant, but paused Karen, dancing in the snow, mouth open, catching flakes on her tongue. He watched her for a moment, struck by how she could turn misery into wonder.

He slipped an arm around her. "Hungry? I'm starving. Come on—let's try Mexican."

"Not to be confused with Tex-Mex," she said. "Tex-Mex is more pleasing to American palates. It's spicy."

They approached Los Jacrocho's Mexican Restaurant, a simple brick building with a sloped roof and an old-fashioned drive-up sign. The hostess met them at the door.

"I'm sorry—we're about to close."

"Please," Cooper said. "Don't send us away. We're starving."

Karen stepped forward, voice soft and trembling. "This is my wedding day. It was supposed to be a dream. Instead, someone tried to kill me. Our honeymoon was canceled. We nearly froze getting here. And we're hungry. Please... we have nowhere else to go."

The woman hesitated, then nodded. "All right. Come in. My name is Daniela."

Inside, the restaurant was warm and inviting. Daniela led them to a table in the back.

In the kitchen, her husband frowned. "I thought we were closing."

"Look at them," she whispered. "No bride should have a day like that. Let's feed them."

She returned with chips and salsa. "Hot or mild?"

"Mild," Cooper said.

Milo entered, brushing snow from his tux. "Mild for me too."

Cooper blinked. "You don't do spicy?"

"Nope," Milo said. "What do you recommend?"

"Tacos or fajitas."

"Bottled Coke?" Milo asked.

"Yes."

"Round for all of us," Cooper said.

As they ate, Daniela asked, "Where was your honeymoon supposed to be?"

"Hawaii," Cooper said through a mouthful of salsa.

"Hawaii?" Daniela sighed. "And you end up in Bird City, Kansas. I'm so sorry."

"Why?" Karen asked innocently. "Did you plant the bomb?"

Cooper shoved a chip into her mouth before she could say more.

Daniela blinked. "Bomb?"

"She means the wedding was a bomb," Cooper said quickly. "Could we get fifteen tacos?"

Karen swallowed. "You know, there are better ways to shut me up." She puckered her lips, then slid her foot up his leg under the table.

Cooper jolted. "Girl, do I need to put snow down your dress?"

She pouted. Milo snorted, trying not to laugh.

Daniela returned with the tacos. "Hope you don't mind—I booked you two rooms. It's the only place in town, but it's a place to lay your head... among other things."

Cooper flushed. Karen snapped her teeth playfully at him.

"Do you still love me?" she asked.

He chuckled. "More than life itself."

Daniela studied Karen with a puzzled expression. "You know... if you were a little older, you'd look almost exactly like Faith Addams. She was in here not long before she died."

Cooper had just lifted his taco for a bite. At Daniela's words, he slowly set it back down and asked , "She was here? Faith was here? Was she alone, or with someone?"

Daniela tilted her head, searching for her memory. "She met with a dark-haired woman. Not very attractive, but Faith seemed real interested in whatever she was saying." She hesitated, then added, "Then something strange happened."

"What happened?" Cooper asked, leaning forward.

"A man came in. Big guy. Black. Wearing a dark coat and—this is the weird part—sunglasses at night." She shivered at the memory. "He grabbed Faith, and they left together. I got the feeling she didn't want to go with him."

The TV in the corner played a weather alert about the incoming storm. Milo glanced up—and froze.

"Cooper. It's him. The guy from the wedding."

Cooper looked. The name appeared beneath the photo: **General Leroy Nate Sanders**.

Daniela gasped as her breath caught in her throat. "Oh my God! That is the man!" She pointed at the screen. "That is the man that took Faith Addams out of here."

****

Three inches of snow had fallen within the hour, and it was still coming fast—thick, wind-driven flakes that swallowed the world beyond the headlights. The trip to the motel was short, but they slipped and slid the whole way. They were lucky to get the last two rooms; the storm had already forced other travelers to abandon their plans.

Milo opened the trunk and handed Cooper their single remaining suitcase. He had packed a bag for himself too—Grandma had the kids, and he'd planned on taking a little vacation. It seemed no one's plans were working out tonight.

"Milo, this is not exactly what I pictured for my honeymoon," Cooper said, hefting the suitcase. "I was supposed to be on a beach in Hawaii. Romantic dinner. Maybe a little skinny-dipping. Making love in the sand."

"I'm not sure I'd be into that sand thing," Milo said, grinning. The look made Cooper laugh.

"Well... I didn't actually picture you there."

"I know, buddy." Milo shut the trunk. "But Mouse, you're not alone. In proving foresight may be vain: *The best-laid schemes of mice and men go often askew, and leave us nothing but grief and pain, for promised joy.*"

"Robert Burns," Cooper said, impressed. "You're deep, Milo."

They stood beneath a lone streetlight, its golden glow catching the swirling snowflakes. They drifted down like tiny kisses from heaven—soft at first, then more insistent, until Cooper felt smothered by them. He ducked his head against the wind.

"I always wanted to be a writer," Milo said as the snow whipped sideways. His voice softened, almost lyrical. "With the flakes falling past the light, they look like shooting stars—each one a distant sun with worlds around it. Makes you wonder... is life just a copy of what came before? Or are we like the snowflakes—each born alone and unique, only to fall and disappear into the crowd?"

Cooper stared at him, snow clinging to his face, breath fogging the air. He was genuinely moved.

"I'll take this," Milo said, grabbing the suitcase. "You've got something more important to carry."

He nodded toward the limo. Karen was fast asleep in the back seat, peaceful as a child, untouched by worry. Cooper opened the door and lifted her into his arms. Halfway to the room, she stirred.

"Where are we going?" she murmured.

"To bed."

"Finally," she sighed, wrapping her arms around his neck and kissing him softly.

Milo opened the door for them. Cooper carried her over the threshold while Milo set the suitcase inside.

"You know," Milo said, brushing snow from his sleeves, "maybe one day I'll write a story about all this. About the doctor who created life—not a monster, but the most beautiful woman ever. He fell in love with her, and they lived happily ever after."

"I would read that book," Karen said, still in Cooper's arms.

"See you in the morning, Milo. But not too early," Cooper said.

After Milo stepped out, Cooper closed the door and turned to take in the room.

"It's not the private estate I booked," he said. "I expected to hear the surf, not tires spinning in slush. An ocean breeze, not a rattling heater."

It wasn't a five-star suite—he wasn't sure it had even one star—but it was a place to rest. Wood paneling covered the walls, two walls painted dusty blue and the other two painted light gray. A king-size bed dominated the room, with a chocolate-brown sofa at its foot and a small TV stand in the corner. A single lamp sat on the nightstand beside a glass vase holding a lone red rose. A print of *Starry Night* hung on the wall.

Karen sat on the edge of the bed. Cooper knelt before her and rested his head in her lap.

"I'm sorry," he said quietly. "This isn't what I wanted for us. I thought we'd be in Hawaii—sunset dinner cruise, midnight on the beach... and waking up wrapped in a blanket on Haleakalā."

Karen's blue eyes shone like beacons, warm and steady. She touched a finger to his lips.

"No. Don't apologize for wanting to be with me. I'd rather be here with you than anywhere else. In my world, I could stay in the finest hotels, but something was always missing." She cupped his face, their eyes locked. "It was you. Anywhere you are where I want to be. If you gave up heaven, I would too—because heaven without you would only be hell."

"Don't talk like that," Cooper said with a grin, rising to his feet. "You're starting to sound like Milo. And spending my honeymoon with Milo is not what I had in mind."

She giggled—her own unmistakable sound—and tugged him down beside her.

"Then how about me?"

He lay over her, looking into those clear blue eyes that seemed to cast a spell over him. She kissed him slowly and deep, then reached up to loosen his bow tie, sliding it off with a flick of her wrist. Her fingers traced the line of his shirt as she unbuttoned it, pushing the fabric from his shoulders.

They had been together before, but this felt different, more vulnerable, more real. The glass of the monitor was gone. The VR world she once knew felt distant now. She wasn't a program or a printed construct. She was a woman. He was a man. And tonight, they were truly beginning their life together.

She remembered how it felt slipping into her wedding dress... but the feeling of it sliding away under his hands was something she knew she would never forget.

They both undressed down to their underwear. Karen sat down on the bed and looked up at him with the eyes of a little girl wanting him to teach her. But as they filled with passion, a full-grown, sexy woman emerged as she spoke. "Make love to me." She whispered, barely being heard. She grinned seductively as she pushed herself back onto the bed. She lifted her hips and then said, "And love me till the day I die."

She remembers that feeling in the car: she held her foot up in front of him and gave him a naughty little smile. Cooper held her bare leg in his hands and stared at her kneecap. And started kissing along with her shin bone. Down across the top of her foot. Then nibble on each of her toes. Karen whimpers like a puppy. He licks the bottom of her sole, and she shivers with delight.

As he lays her down on the bed, he plucks the rose from the vase. He placed it in his mouth as he crawled over to her. He removed the rose from his mouth as he looked down at her, his beautiful bride. He takes the rose, holding it by the stem. He lowered the flower, letting its soft, loving petals softly touch her skin. She shivered as the thrill of passion shuddered down her spine. He slowly traced it across her forehead and down the side of her cheek. Then across her lips. Her lips parted as he let the

237

rose drop on her chest. He lowered his head, capturing her lips with his. But the kiss was too brief. She wanted more. She again let out another whimper.

He let the rose fall from her chin to her chest. As he let the rose trace down the center of her chest. She had never felt anything like this. She closed her eyes. Her heart was beating so fast, she thought it was going to burst right out of her. As she felt the pedals of the rose tickle her stomach. Her breath was quivering out of her. She wanted it to stop, but at the same time, she wanted it to last forever. The rose passed by her navel, and she moaned out. He lifted the edge of her panties. Her eyes flew open, and she grabbed the rose from his hand.

"No more! NOW!" Her voice trembled out of her. She raised her head, opened her mouth, and kissed him hard. Wrapping her hands around the back of his head, she pulled him more into the kiss and down on top of her. She wrapped her legs around him. Holding tightly against her. She released him from the kiss. Both of them were gasping for air. She reached over for the lamp on the nightstand. As she turned off the light, she moaned out, "Take me to paradise."

Chapter 37

It wasn't the honeymoon of dreams, but they did wake in each other's arms. Cooper slipped out of bed, pulling on the sleep pants he'd folded into the suitcase. He crossed the room, drew back the drapes, and froze.

"Karen!" he called, delight bursting out of him. "Come see this."

She stirred, wrapped the blanket around her bare body, and padded to the window. One look outside stole her breath. The world was transformed—clean, untouched, glittering beneath a bright blue sky.

She hurried back to the bed, pulled on a heavy pink robe and house shoes, and opened the door. Cooper grabbed his own robe and followed her out.

The air was crisp and sharp, but utterly still. No traffic. No voices. Not even wind. It felt like stepping onto a new planet, the kind astronauts might discover—silent, waiting, full of wonder.

Several inches of snow had fallen overnight, sculpted by the wind into smooth drifts along the windowsills and piled high over the cars. The limo was buried so deeply it was barely recognizable.

Last night, the woman in her had emerged. This morning, the child. And the child couldn't wait another second.

Karen leaped into the snow, scooping it up and tossing it into the air with a squeal of pure joy. "Come on, sweetheart!" she called, wiggling her fingers to entice him.

Just then, Milo stepped out in a dark red robe. He took one look at her and burst out laughing.

Karen bent down, packed a snowball, and with a wicked grin, hurled it—smacking Cooper square in the forehead. Before either man could react, she threw another, hitting Milo right in the face. She clapped a hand over her mouth, trying to hold in her laughter, but it spilled out anyway.

"Little sister!" Milo barked. "Kiss your ass goodbye!"

Cooper and Milo dove into the snow, launching snowballs at each other. Karen glanced at Cooper, teasing him by opening her robe just enough to show a bare leg.

"You want to see if we can melt the snow?" she teased.

Cooper scooped up a handful of snow. "I'm going to cool something off."

"No!" she shrieked, laughing as she ran, clutching her robe closed to keep him from dropping snow down her neckline.

Splat! A snowball hit Cooper square on the back.

"Don't do that to my little sister!" Milo warned, wagging a finger with a grin.

Cooper fired back, hitting Milo in the chest. Milo retaliated with a flurry of snowballs. Karen joined Cooper, and together they overwhelmed Milo until he resorted to scooping snow with the armful and dumping it over them. Snow rained in sparkling sheets.

"We give! We give!" Cooper and Karen shouted, collapsing into laughter.

Cooper tossed aside the snowball in his hand. "Peace treaty? You buy me breakfast," Milo said.

A round of cheers and clapping erupted. Other guests had stepped out to watch the spectacle. Cooper grabbed Milo's and Karen's hands, and the three of them took a theatrical bow. Then he scooped Karen into his arms—her bare leg flashing from the slit in her robe—and carried her toward the steps.

"That's it for the show," he announced as they dashed back to their rooms.

Inside, Cooper shut the door with his foot and set her gently on the bed. They were both still laughing. Snow clung to her golden hair, and he brushed it away with tender fingers, the flakes falling to the carpet.

"We could never have done that in Hawaii," she said, smiling. She grabbed a towel from the bathroom and began drying her hair. "I know! We'll go to Hawaii on our twenty-fifth anniversary. I bet we can still make love on the beach." She paused, grinning at him. "Heck, probably on our fiftieth. I'm going to love growing old with you."

Her words hit him like a blow. The memory of the aging failure flashed across his mind. Whatever crossed his face, she saw it instantly.

"What is it? What's wrong?"

"It's nothing," he said too quickly, turning away. He removed his robe and sat on the edge of the bed. "Just thinking about work."

"No, you weren't." She stepped toward him, tugging off her snow-soaked house shoe. She tossed the towel aside, frustration rising. "You can lie for me, about me—but don't ever lie *to* me. Do you understand? Don't lie to me."

Her voice shook with real emotion, startling them both.

"All right," he said softly. "Sit down."

She did. His own voice trembled as he tried to begin. "Karen... honey... I—God, I can't do this."

He stood abruptly and walked to the dresser, bracing his palms against it. His head hung low. She touched his shoulder gently. He lifted his gaze to the mirror and saw her reflection behind him.

"Stanley found a breakdown in the T.E.H. pattern," he said quietly. "It doesn't age normally."

He turned to face her.

"It ages fast. Too fast. You'll age rapidly."

"How long?" she asked.

"Five to seven years," he whispered. "I had Stanley working on it. He said he'd figured it out."

"Then we can find his work and—"

"I told him not to put it in the computer. I didn't want anyone to know about you. It was all in his head... and it died with him."

The words drained out of him. His chest felt heavy, his breath unsteady. He watched her turn away, taking a few slow steps. Inside, he was breaking—picturing himself alone at a breakfast table a few years from now, staring at an empty chair with a robe draped over the back.

"So, I have five to seven years," she said quietly. She looked back at him over her shoulder, her expression soft but steady. "Then I die of old age?"

He couldn't speak.

She took a breath, then offered a small, brave smile.

"Then I guess I'll just have to love you ten times more," she said. "So, we can still have a lifetime together."

Chapter 38

For the snow, the ravishing had come. The fresh-fallen blanket was no longer a pristine virgin; the plows had dirtied her reputation and pushed her in gray heaps along the roadside. Morning noise returned to Bird City. The prisoners of the storm were freed, and Saturday life resumed; mothers loading groceries into cars, children rolling the season's first snowman, neighbors calling to one another across shoveled walks.

When all you own are nightclothes, wedding attire, and a suitcase packed for Hawaii, a snowstorm is the last thing you want. Fortunately, the newlyweds found a secondhand store in town and managed to outfit themselves in long pants, sweaters, and a pair of serviceable coats. Milo, who had planned for mountain weather, was already dressed in jeans, a plaid shirt, and a heavy winter coat.

Cooper and Karen's choices were wildly out of style, but Karen's bright burnt-orange ribbed sweater clung to her curves in a way that made fashion irrelevant. Her gray wool coat only half hid the effect. Cooper wore jeans, a blue western shirt, and a faux-lamb demi coat.

When strangers land in unfamiliar territory, they ask the locals where to eat. Everyone pointed them to the Bird City Café on Fourth Street, just up from the secondhand shop.

Downtown was exactly what one expects of a small Kansas town—flat streets lined with brick buildings that once stood as proud monuments to prosperity, now mingled with newer, more practical structures. Black streetlamps added a touch of charm. Milo parked the limo beside one of them, drawing immediate attention.

Blinds lifted in the insurance office across the street. Shoppers paused outside the market, bags in hand. A limousine in Bird City was spectacle enough—but three people climbing out in thrift-store clothes only deepened the curiosity.

The café occupied a corner brick building that had once been the town bank, built in 1920. Two metal tables sat outside, buried under snow. The neon OPEN sign glowed warmly. Milo pulled the door open and held it for the others.

A kind gentleman greeted them without judgment—either for their mismatched clothes nor the luxury car they'd arrived in.

The front room was small, but a soda fountain dominated one wall, promising milkshakes and sundaes. A turn to the right opened into the old bank lobby, now a larger dining room. A few patrons were scattered about: an older couple, a pair of teenagers, and a family of five with three children. The tables were wood-toned, the chairs padded in beige vinyl, all set atop a mismatched geometric carpet. Large windows let in what little light the gloomy morning offered; above them, mosaic panes of blue and white glass added a touch of color. Potted plants flanked the original bank entrance.

The host led them to a table for four near the window with CAFÉ painted across the glass. Karen asked for the restroom, and he directed her as Milo and Cooper sat down. Cooper ordered coffee for all of them.

Milo glanced over the menu. "Why is Karen so quiet? She's not herself. I challenged her to a snowball rematch, and she said, 'Don't be silly. Those are children's games.' You did something to her. I'm tossing your butt in the snow."

"You've grown as protective of her as I am," Cooper said, peering over his menu.

Milo set his menu down. "I can't help it. I love her—not like you do, but... ever since she called me her brother..." He lowered his voice and leaned in. "Cooper, it hasn't even been a week since she came out of that printer, and I feel like I grew up with her. Like she really is my sister."

He rubbed his forehead. "Dammit, Coop. She got to me. There's something special about her. And I don't mean medically. I mean... special. You know what I mean?"

"I do," Cooper said softly. "It feels like I've known her all my life. There's a light about her."

The host returned with mugs, a pot of coffee, and cream. After he left, Cooper continued.

"I told her," He said, pouring cream into his cup.

"Told her what?" Milo asked, sipping his coffee black.

"I told her about the..." Cooper hesitated, wishing for something stronger than coffee. "...the five to seven years."

"How did she take it?"

"I'm not sure," Cooper admitted as the host returned.

"Have you decided, or do you need to wait for the young lady?" the man asked.

"Is the sausage and gravy good?" Cooper asked.

"One of our specialties."

"The lady and I will have that," Cooper said. He looked at Milo. "You?"

"Just one order. I'm not that hungry."

"Three orders," Cooper said. "And a big serving of bacon to share."

After the host left, Cooper picked up the thread. "What would you do if you were told you only had five to seven years to live?"

"Me?" Milo said. "I'd cry like a baby and feel sorry for my pitiful self. But not my girl Karen."

"Come on, any human would feel sorry—"

"You said it. Human. But she's not human." Milo caught Cooper's glare and raised a hand. "I don't mean her body or her soul. I mean what she *lives* for. She lives for one thing—love. She lives to love you."

Milo set his mug down. "She's not sad because she's dying. She's sad because she thinks it'll hurt you. And that's the one thing she can't bear."

Cooper's eyes glistened. He set his mug down before he spilled it.

"Buddy," Milo said gently, "I know you. You're already thinking about getting back to the lab to find a cure." He reached across the table and placed a firm hand over Cooper's. "What if you don't find one?"

Cooper looked up, startled.

"What if you spend the next five to seven years working instead of holding her? Instead of looking into those blue eyes? We'll all miss her, but you..." Milo shook his head. "I'm not sure you can live without her."

Cooper turned—and saw Karen walking toward them. She moved like golden wheat in a soft breeze, swaying gently with each step.

Milo leaned in one last time. "You've got over a hundred and fifty brilliant minds at that lab. Let them find the cure. You spend the time with her. Simple choice: blind hope... or every moment you have."

The words hit Cooper like a runaway coal train.

They both stood as Karen reached the table. Cooper pulled out her chair, and she sat gracefully.

"I ordered for you," he said. "Is that okay?"

"It's fine," she said. She looked out the window at the snow-covered sidewalks and the cross atop a nearby church. "I cried. But it's over now."

"Who did you cry for?" Cooper asked.

She turned back to him with a soft, brave smile. "For you, of course. I saw you crying at the hotel. You were in the bathroom after you told me. I saw you, and it hurt me. I can't give you what you want. I can't give you a child, so you'd always have a part of me."

She looked at Milo. "And I saw you too, big brother. You cried for me in the secondhand store. I don't want either of you to weep for me. That's not why I came here."

"It's hard for me, Karen," Cooper said, cupping her face. Her skin was soft, her eyes still red from tears. "I may only have five to seven years with you. But you said if we love each other ten times as much, that's fifty to seventy years. A lifetime of love."

He took a breath. "When we get back, I'm turning this over to the lab. And then I'm taking a leave of absence."

"For five to seven years?" she asked. "You can't."

"I can. And I will. I have plenty saved, including what BioTyme paid for the rights. We'll go everywhere. Do everything. Make love on the beaches of Hawaii, kiss at the top of the Eiffel Tower, dance in the moonlight. We'll walk on water and kiss the sky. We'll live every day to its fullest and love under the stars at night."

Her eyes glowed. "Is that what you wish, my love?"

"It is."

"Then that is what it shall be," she said, smiling as he kissed her.

The host returned with plates of biscuits and sausage gravy. Karen brightened. "Oh, I like this. This was our first meal together."

He set plates before Milo and Cooper, then placed a large platter of bacon in the center. Before he could ask if they needed anything else, Karen grabbed two slices and began munching.

"Could I get a stack of pancakes?" Milo asked. "I'm feeling hungry again."

"So am I," Cooper said, savoring his first bite—the peppery sausage, rich gravy, soft biscuits, smoky bacon, and perfectly brewed coffee.

"Bring him all the pancakes he can eat."

Suddenly, a man burst into the dining room, waving a pistol.

"Everybody just stays calm! No one gets hurt! Hand over your money and jewelry!"

"Please," Cooper said, raising his hands. "Let my wife keep her ring. It's not worth anything."

"What'd that come out of, a box of Cracker Jacks?" the gunman sneered. He grabbed Cooper's necklace. "This I take. Try to stop me and I'll put a bullet in your head."

Karen growled—a low, dangerous sound. "Get your filthy hands off that," she said, eyes narrowing. "You do not threaten the love of my life."

"Oh yeah?" the man smirked. "And what are you gonna do about it?" Seeing how beautiful she was. His intentions turned to something else. "Maybe I'll take a little sugar from you instead."

Karen stood slowly. "Okay," she said. "I'll give you a little sugar."

In one swift motion, she snatched the sugar dispenser and smashed it into his face. Before he could react, she drove the jagged edge into his eye. He screamed, dropping the gun. Karen chased him as he stumbled back. She grabbed a napkin dispenser.

"Here's something to dry your tears!"

She cracked it against his skull, knocking him out cold. Then she calmly picked up the gun, disassembled it with practiced efficiency, and returned to the table.

Milo sat frozen, mouth hanging open.

Karen brushed off her coat, sat down, placed her napkin in her lap, took a bite of gravy, sipped her coffee, and looked around.

"Could I get some more sugar?" she asked politely.

Chapter 39

Back at BioTyme Laboratories in Lebanon, Lilith sat alone in her office. She wasn't drinking wine—she was consuming it. Straight from the bottle, no glass, no savoring. She tipped it back like medicine, hoping it would numb everything she didn't want to feel.

She wore a black pantsuit, mourning a loss she refused to name. Her pumps lay discarded beside the desk. Her stocking-clad feet rested on the edge of the blotter as her high-back chair creaked under her weight. She took another long swallow.

In the wastebasket, an empty bottle lay like a fallen soldier—one of many casualties in her private war against grief.

She opened a desk drawer and pulled out a framed photo of herself and Cooper, taken the night they officially opened the lab. She traced his face with trembling fingers.

Her words slurred. "Oh, my Coopie... why'd you have to go and die?" Another swallow. She wiped her mouth with the back of her hand. "Your brains, my business sense—we could've been the richest people in the world. Dinner with kings and queens. Influence. Power. We could've chosen presidents."

She lifted the photo above her head. "But no. You had to be righteous." Her voice cracked. "And then *she* came along."

She drained the bottle, gurgling as she forced the last drops down. Empty, she tossed it aside. The frame clattered onto the desk as she stood and staggered to a gray steel file cabinet. She opened the top drawer and pulled out another bottle.

She uncorked it, collapsed back into her chair, and picked up the photo again. Tears blurred her vision.

"Why didn't you want me?" she whispered. "Were you playing games?"

She reached into the drawer again and pulled out another photo—Karen, stepping out of the printer. Lilith's private camera had captured it.

"I'm glad I put my own cameras up," she muttered.

Then her expression twisted. Rage overtook grief.

"But you just had to have this little bed toy." She huffed, then snarled. "It should've been me. Not her!"

She hurled the framed photo across the room. It struck the wall, shattering glass, slicing through the picture.

"Oh—what did I do?" she sobbed. "Oh, my Cooper…"

She stumbled toward the broken frame, dropped to her knees, and clutched the torn photo to her chest.

The office door burst open.

General Sanders stood in the doorway.

Lilith swallowed hard, trying to force her bloodshot eyes to focus. She pushed herself upright, swaying.

"You son of a—" She lurched toward him, fists clenched. "Why did you kill him? Why?"

She collapsed against his chest, pounding weakly with her fists. "I don't care about *her*. But why him?"

"I did what had to be done," General Sanders said coldly. "There was a leak. It needed to be plugged."

He grabbed her by the arms and shook her. "Now we run the program again—this time for what *I* want."

She steadied herself against the desk, swaying. "I'll have you know," she slurred, "I've got the material ready for a full human-size print run. You'll have your ultimate warrior soon enough." She looked up at him, eyes glassy. "But you have to give Lilly what she wants."

She pushed herself upright and began stripping off her clothes—pants first, then her top—until she stood in her underwear. She reached behind her for her bra clasp.

"Lilly is a lonely girl," she purred.

"Stop it," he warned.

"You don't want Lilly?" she taunted, stepping closer. She rose onto her toes, hands sliding up his shoulders. "What's the matter? Jealous of Coopie?"

"You're sick," he snapped, jaw tightening. "Sober up."

He shoved her away. She hit the floor hard.

"You know what they say about a man who can't take a joke," she said, laughing bitterly. "Means he's got a little joke."

That was the last straw.

He grabbed her by the throat, hauled her up, and slapped her across the face. She flew into the file cabinet with a metallic crash and crumpled to the floor. Blood trickled from her lips.

She wiped it with her fingers and stared at the red smear.

""You give me what I want," Sanders growled, looming over her, "or there'll be another accident around here. Understand?" His eyes narrowed. "I should've gotten rid of you when I got rid of Faith. You just couldn't keep your damn mouth shut—had to tell her everything."

He leaned in, voice dropping to a lethal whisper. "Don't think you're innocent, Lilith. You supplied the insulin that killed her. If I go down, you go down. Remember that."

He slammed the door behind him so hard the glass shattered.

Lilith lay on the floor, dazed. She dragged herself to her knees, reached up to the desk, and grabbed the bottle of wine. She took one last drink before collapsing backward.

The room spun. The bottle rolled from her hand. Lilith passed out.

Chapter 40

Some time had passed before Lilith finally stirred. She tried to brace both hands on the desk to pull herself up, but her arms buckled and she collapsed back onto the floor. Her stomach lurched violently—two and a half bottles of wine churning like poison—and she grabbed the wastebasket just in time to vomit. Again. And again.

When the heaving stopped, she lay there trembling, wiping her mouth with the back of her hand. After several minutes she managed to stand, shrugging a fabric coat over her shoulders.

The laboratory was closed for the weekend; only the cleaning staff remained somewhere in the building. Lilith shuffled to the lobby vending machines and bought a bag of Lay's® potato chips and a bottle of Seven Up®. She sat heavily in one of the chairs, nibbling chips and sipping soda, hoping the carbonation would settle her stomach. She buried her throbbing head in her hands; elbows braced on the table.

"What have I told you about drinking too much?"

The voice made her jerk upright with a scream. She toppled out of the chair and hit the floor hard. Cooper stood a few feet away, Karen beside him. He had been upstairs and seen the wreckage of her office.

"You're alive!" Lilith scrambled to her feet and threw her arms around him. Then she caught sight of Karen and abruptly let go. "And so are you," she added, her tone souring.

She sank back into the chair. "How? You two boarded that plane. Didn't you?"

"No," Cooper said. "Stanley showed up—said his father was dying. We let him take the jet."

"Stanley..." Lilith muttered, pressing her palms to her temples. "He said he got rid of a leak. I thought he meant you. Not Stanley."

"What are you talking about?" Cooper demanded. "What leak?"

"Leave me alone. I don't feel good."

"Lilith, at first you didn't want me to have the jet. Who ordered the change? And don't tell me it was you—I know better."

Lilith slowly lifted her head, an obscene smile twisting her lips. "So, I have something you want. You give me something I want."

"Like what?"

Lilith stood, opened her coat, and revealed her body beneath. "You and me," she purred, sliding an arm around Cooper.

Karen's expression darkened. She stormed forward, grabbed Lilith's arm, and threw her to the floor.

"Get your filthy hands off my husband." Karen glared at her. "Touch him again, and I'll rip your heart out and let you watch it beat one last time. Now answer his question."

Lilith cowered, clutching her coat closed. "I don't know who it was. I just got a note from corporate saying you were to have whatever you wanted—the jet, the limo, especially the champagne. It came from the new company Tyme Corporation merged with."

"What new company?" Cooper pressed.

"Leave me alone," Lilith moaned, rubbing her temples. "MacBelle Pharmaceuticals. They said you two were to have the bottles of champagne."

"You know exactly who it was," Cooper snapped. He grabbed her by the lapels and hauled her upright. "Who sent it, Lilith?"

"Leave me alone," she whimpered, slumping onto the table. "I think I'm going to die."

"You *are* going to die if you don't tell me who it was!"

He shook her hard.

"He'll kill me!" she cried.

"I'll kill you if you don't talk!"

"It was General Sanders!" she screamed.

"The former Secretary of Defense?"

"Yes! That's him!"

"Why is he following me and Karen?"

"I don't know!" Lilith sobbed. "I really don't. Something about an ultimate warrior..."

Milo returned, holding the champagne bottle by the edges. "Here. What are you going to do with it?"

"Assess it for poisons," Cooper said grimly.

"Poison?" Milo echoed.

"You were right, Milo. Someone did try to kill Karen and me—just not with the bomb."

In the Laboratory

The main lab was in the basement, stocked with glassware, microscopes, centrifuges, culture ovens—and the machine they needed: the LC-MS/MS.

It stood alone in the corner like a misbehaving child, tall and gleaming under the sterile lights. The room hummed with quiet precision as Cooper approached the mass spectrometer.

He handed safety goggles to Milo and Karen, then carefully poured the amber liquid into a test tray. He loaded the sample into the injector with practiced ease and pressed START.

The machine came alive.

Solvent pumps whispered. Columns separated molecules in a delicate chemical ballet. The ion source flared to life, fragmenting components with bursts of energy. The mass analyzers filtered the chaos into order. The detector translated it all into data streaming across the monitor.

Cooper leaned in, eyes narrowing.

"Oh, my dear God," he breathed. "Thank you that my wife hates booze."

He printed the results and handed them to Milo.

"What's that tall peak?" Milo asked.

"Codeine," Cooper said, removing his goggles. "This much codeine mixed with alcohol—if we'd finished that bottle, we'd have been dead before the bomb went off."

He looked at Milo. "Which begs the question... why the bomb?"

"Wouldn't blowing you up cover the poisoning?" Milo asked.

"Unless..." Karen said softly.

They turned to her.

"What if we weren't the target? What if it was Stanley all along? If we were found dead in the limo, and then the plane exploded, the police would assume it was all aimed at us. Lilith thought the leak was you—but what if it was Stanley? What did he know that they didn't want to get out?"

"Buddy, I checked the bottle," Milo said. "It was sealed."

Cooper's eyes lit with realization. "Liquid codeine is the same color as champagne."

He pulled on oversized gloves and examined the cork under a magnifying lens.

"There. A tiny hole. They injected it through the cork. That's why it didn't fizz—the seal was already compromised. But with this much codeine, they knew it would taste bitter..."

He froze, face twisting in shock.

"Karen's right. We were never the target. Stanley was. And the cops will be looking at who wanted to kill *us*, not him."

"But what did Stanley know?" Milo asked. "The aging virus? The cure? Would the company lose money if he found it? That doesn't make sense. If the cure was found. Money would roll in."

Milo shook his head in disbelief. "There has to be some other reason. And how is the military connected to your research?'

I don't know Milo." Cooper said biting down on his lip. "But we are going to find out."

"We need to get this bottle to the police," Milo said. "They can get prints."

"It won't help," Cooper said. "Mine, Karen's, yours, Howard's..." He stopped. "Howard will know who gave it to him. We need to see him."

Upstairs

Lilith had passed out in a recliner, head lolling to the side. Karen found a washcloth, dampened it, and gently wiped Lilith's face.

Lilith blinked awake, staring up at Karen haloed by ceiling lights. "What are you, some kind of angel? Why would you care about me?"

"You're a human being, are you not?" Karen said, folding the cloth onto her forehead.

"I don't need some stinking Florence Nightingale wannabe," Lilith snapped. She tossed the cloth aside and staggered to her feet. "I'm going upstairs to lie down. I don't need help."

She stepped into the elevator. Before the doors closed, she glared at Karen.

"I know who and what you are Karen. And one day I'll prove it to the whole world."

The doors shut.

"What the hell did she mean by that?" Milo asked. "You think she knows Karen is a printout?"

"I don't know," Cooper said quietly.

"She's as dangerous as a coiled rattler," Milo warned.

"I know," Cooper replied as the elevator returned. "Let's go see Howard."

Outside

Howard stood outside the small security building.

"Cooper! Mrs. Karen—congratulations," he said warmly. "I wanted to tell you earlier, but... well, thinking you two had died was a shock. Then finding out it was Stanley... I gave him that note about his dad."

"What note?" Cooper asked.

"The one General Sanders gave me. He even loaned Stanley his car to get to the airstrip."

The pieces began to fall into place.

Howard continued, "The general also sent the champagne. And he had me put another bottle on the plane for when you were in the air."

"That was the bomb," Milo said.

"WHAT?!" Howard shouted. "I put the bomb on the plane?!"

"No," Cooper said. "Sanders did—"

He stopped. Karen was staring into the cornfield beside the lab.

"What do you see?" he asked.

"I saw someone," she whispered. Snowflakes drifted down, catching in her hair. "And a flash of light—like a reflection off a scope on a..."

She saw it again.

"Rifle!"

A shot cracked through the stillness.

Milo dove to the ground. Cooper grabbed Karen and pushed her down, covering her with his body.

Silence.

Cooper lifted his head, scanning the field.

"Cooper!" Milo shouted. "Howard!"

Cooper turned.

Howard lay face down in the snow, blood pooling beneath him. Cooper sprinted over to him and rolled him over.

A massive slug had torn through his chest, obliterating his heart.

"He's dead," Cooper whispered.

Chapter 41

The sheriff of Smith County, Milton Barber, was a heavy-set man with salt-and-pepper hair that showed his years of dedication to law enforcement. Born and raised in Bellaire, Kansas, he spent his days keeping Smith County safe and his evenings tending the family farm that had been in his family for generations. Now he stood across from his desk at the sheriff's department in Smith Center, Kansas.

Cooper was finishing a candy bar with nuts, sharing the last bites with his wife. It was 4:30 p.m., and neither of them had eaten since breakfast. The sheriff wore jeans and a red-and-white checked western shirt, complete with cowboy hat and black boots. A star-shaped badge gleamed on his chest, and a 9mm semi-automatic pistol rested in the holster strapped around his waist. He had been eating a sandwich at his desk and was wiping his mouth with a napkin.

"Doctor Barnes, my little county used to be a nice place. We had a few crimes—not saying we were paradise or anything—but we sure as hell weren't New York City or Chicago." He stood abruptly and tossed the napkin down in frustration. "But since you've been here, our little county is on the news in every nation on earth. The damn commies are talking about us. Now I've got a bomb going off on a jet plane that crashes, killing everyone on board plus a family of four on the ground—including a four-month-old baby. A jet that you and your little bride should have been on, but somehow you managed not to be on board. Then an assassination of one of your people who worked out there. The same man you say placed the bomb on the plane under orders from one of the most decorated military generals alive. And you don't know why. That's what you're telling me?"

"I told you everything I know," Cooper replied, irritation creeping into his voice. He was tired of answering the same questions.

"I just don't believe you're telling me all you know." The sheriff walked to the window, watching the sun sink low in the sky before turning back to them. "There's something you two aren't telling me. Something you're hiding. What is it?"

"We're not hiding anything!" Cooper bellowed. "We've told you everything."

"Yeah, that the real target was Dr. Stanley Leavitt. But what was he working on that someone would kill him for?" Before Cooper could answer, the sheriff raised a hand. "I know—it's classified." He sat back down, glaring across the desk. His anger sharpened, his words spitting out like venom from a viper. "Everything you do out there is classified. But how am I supposed to help you or protect you if you won't come clean?"

A deputy entered and leaned toward Karen with a gleeful smile. "Mrs. Barnes, can I get you anything? Another candy bar? More coffee? If you like, I could run down to Jiffy Burger and get you a burger—best ones in town."

"Deputy Harris! Out!" the sheriff barked, pointing to the door. He turned back to Cooper. "Explain that."

"What?" Cooper asked.

"That your wife has my male deputies panting like bird dogs at the start of pheasant season. And my wife is fuming because I'm talking to her." He stared at Karen, taking in her beauty. "Girls like her don't exist in real life. Where did she come from?" Cooper opened his mouth, but the sheriff cut him off. "And don't tell me she's from Missouri. They don't have girls like that there either. Come on, Doctor Barnes—there's something special about her. Like a Greek goddess. What is it?"

"Look, Sheriff," Cooper groaned. "You've fingerprinted us, photographed us, questioned us. Are you going to charge us or not?" He took Karen's hand, glancing at her. "We've been married one day. We'd like to start our life together." Still, the sheriff stared at Karen, drawn in by her shape and her blue eyes—eyes that pulled a man in like a siren's song.

"Sheriff," Cooper snapped, "are you undressing my wife with your eyes?"

"What?" The sheriff jolted, genuinely shocked. "No—no! But I'm wondering how someone who looks like her wasn't the talk of the town before a week ago."

260

"Sheriff, I told you—she was out of the county."

"Yes, and that she arrived at the Dodge City airport on Halloween night, but no one remembers seeing her. And before you say anything, Dr. Barnes—your wife could walk through JFK airport and people would remember her."

A nervous flutter stirred in Cooper's chest. The sheriff was fishing, and Cooper couldn't afford to bite.

Deputy Harris returned, smiling at Karen again.

"Harris!" the sheriff roared. "Get your mind out of your pants and back on your job. Did you get anything out of Milo?"

"No, Sheriff. Nothing they haven't already told you." Harris held a paper in his hand. The sheriff cleared his throat sharply, snapping Harris back to attention. "It's the fingerprint report," Harris said, handing it over.

The sheriff read it, then looked at Karen with renewed interest. "Are you sure about this?"

"Yes, Sheriff."

"I guess you two can go."

"Sheriff!" Cooper warned as he stood. "Damn it—question the General! Ask him about Project Dark Overlord!"

"Now listen!" the sheriff thundered, slamming his hand on the desk. "This is settled! You two go home. Enjoy your life. You're newlyweds." He shouted toward the door, "Bill! Drive them home!"

******

It was already dark by the time the deputy dropped them off at their home in Lebanon. There is something about home—no other place feels quite like it. Nothing compares to your own bed, your own little piece of paradise. But paradise on earth is short-lived, and the flashing light on the answering machine was the warning that more trouble was on the way.

Cooper pressed play. A screeching voice from the past burst through the speaker.

"This is Susan Lake—your sister."

He rolled his eyes toward heaven. "Oh no. God have mercy on me." He sank into a chair as the message continued.

"It is bad enough that I have to hear on the news that you were killed in a plane crash. But to find out you got married and didn't invite your only sister? I know, I know—you're saying, I invited you.' But I was busy that day. You should have moved your wedding. And that awful dress didn't do anything for her. And you needed color—you looked like a washed-out marshmallow. Cooper, you must take care of yourself. And the way Karen looks, I know she is not taking care of you. She's just after the money. Oh, but when the church found out you were killed, they were so nice—they brought me food and flowers and prayed for me. And now I turn on the news and find out you're still alive! I'm so embarrassed—they think I did this just to get free stuff. And your nieces, Gracy and Marcie, everyone at school, has been so nice to them, and now they're going to think they lied. Well, anyway—we're glad you're not dead!"

"Well, that makes one of us," Cooper muttered.

"And you say hello too... Karen, is it? Give her a hug from all of us. And don't call back! We have soccer practice, then Gracy has play practice at church. Toodle-loo, brother. Love ya!"

The message ended. Cooper quietly reached up to the top cabinet, pulled down a bottle of whiskey, poured two fingers into a tumbler, and swallowed it in one go. Then he walked to the small blackboard hanging in the kitchen labeled *Things to Get Today*. Whistling a tune, he calmly wrote: *New answering machine.*

Then, using both hands, he ripped the machine from the wall, marched to the door, and flung it outside. It hit a tree and exploded into pieces. He shut the door behind him.

"I feel better now."

When he turned, Karen was standing there. He said simply, "My sister called.

She didn't speak. She just held out her hand. He took it, and she led him upstairs to the bedroom. Still silent, she removed his coat and pulled his shirt over his head, revealing his bare chest and the double cross hanging from its chain.

"No offense, honey, but after hearing my sister's voice, I'm not exactly in the mood."

She hushed him with a finger over his lips.

"Shhh," she whispered, slowly lowering her hand. "This isn't about us. This is about you. I've prepared a warm bubble bath. Go enjoy it. Forget all this. Relax." She turned toward the door.

"Why are you doing this?"

"Because I love you." She looked back at him, hand on the doorknob. "Married couples take care of each other. You've been taking care of me for a long time—even before I came to your world. Now it's my turn. I've laid out your pajamas and a robe. After your bath, put them on and come downstairs. I'm cooking supper." She slipped out and closed the door.

"Supper?" he echoed. "Supper?" He dashed after her, catching her at the top of the stairs. "Supper—are you sure?"

"Do not worry. Antonito gave me a great recipe and told me exactly what to do." She motioned him back toward the room. "Go take your bath."

He closed the door and stepped into the bathroom. He undressed and lowered himself into the hot, bubbling water. The lavender scent wrapped around him, loosening every knot of tension. The warmth seeped into the porcelain and into his bones. This bath wasn't about getting clean—it was about washing the stress away.

He slid down, took a deep breath, and submerged himself. Under the water, there was no sound, no worry—just peace. When he resurfaced, he scrubbed himself with the washcloth she'd set out. By the time the water cooled, he stepped out, dried off, shaved, and splashed on the cologne she liked. He dressed in blue-and-white striped flannel pajamas and the soft gray robe. When he opened the bathroom door, his slippers were waiting. He slipped them on and went downstairs.

The dining room was transformed. A white lace tablecloth draped the table. His great-grandmother's China gleamed, paired with polished silverware and crystal glasses. A brass candelabra stood in the center. And beside it—a highchair with a tiny saucer for Hendrix. Warmth bloomed in his chest. She loved the cat as much as he did.

He remembered when Hendrix first arrived—scratching at the door while a Jimi Hendrix album played. The cat walked in, lay down on the empty album cover, and claimed his name.

Soft rock music drifted from the living room as Cooper entered the kitchen. The lights cast warm pools across the floor. Karen hummed along with the music, joy in every movement. She reached for ripe tomatoes, their skins glistening, and chopped them with practiced rhythm.

"Be careful," he warned. "I don't want you to cut your—"

"I'm okay," she said gently.

A pot of water boiled on the stove. She salted it, stirred it, and added pasta. A skillet warmed nearby.

She slid the tomatoes into a bowl, minced garlic, and added it to sizzling olive oil. When it turned golden, she added fresh ground beef, letting it brown before adding the tomatoes. The sauce simmered, thickening as she seasoned it with wine, oregano, pepper, parsley, and basil.

"Where did you get all this stuff?" he asked.

"Same place I got the recipe. Antonito brought everything over while you were taking your bath." She lifted a spoonful of sauce, blew on it, and held it out.

"Wow. Amazing," he said after tasting it.

264

She moved on to the salad—tearing lettuce, chopping carrots and cucumbers, mixing them in a metal bowl, then placing it in the freezer to chill. "You were up there a while. I was about to check on you."

"It was peaceful," he said. "But it would've been better if you were there."

She smiled, tracing a finger under his chin. "Maybe later."

As the pasta cooked, she sliced French bread, buttered it, sprinkled garlic salt and parsley, and slid it under the broiler.

When the spaghetti was ready, she drained it and tossed it with the sauce. "Please bring me the plates."

He did, and she plated the meal with a flourish of Parmesan. She added garlic bread, prepared the salads, poured Coke into the glasses, and placed a small serving in Hendrix's saucer.

"Hendrix, the food is ready!" she called.

The cat came running, leaping into the highchair. He began to eat until she reminded him, "We have to say grace."

Cooper lit the candles. They sat—Cooper at the head, Karen at his side. She reached for his hand and prayed.

The meal was wonderful—perfect pasta, balanced sauce, crisp salad, and golden garlic bread. Cooper wiped his mouth and tossed the napkin onto his plate.

"That was the best spaghetti I've ever had."

"Thank you," Karen said, standing. "Now we clean up. You wash; I dry."

"There's a dishwasher."

"But you can't put this China in it," she said. "This was your great-grandmother's, wasn't it?"

"How did you know?"

"This is bone China. This pattern hasn't been made in over a hundred years."

They carried the dishes to the kitchen. After storing leftovers and loading the dishwasher with the pans, Cooper filled the sink—one basin with soapy water, the other with clear. Hendrix sprawled on the floor, grooming himself.

Cooper washed a plate and set it in the drainer. Karen dried it carefully.

"When was the last time you used these?" she asked.

"When I was a kid. That's when Grandma said she wanted me to have them."

"Why didn't your sister get them?"

"Because my sister is a freaking snob," he said, washing another plate. "I love her, but I don't like her. She always wanted new fancy stuff. I wanted the things that mattered."

"I'm sorry I used them."

"No, don't be. If things aren't used, if they just sit and look pretty—do you really need them? If you love something—"

"I understand," she said softly, drying a small plate. He looked at her, surprised. "I really understand."

She set the plate down. "When we met in my world, I thought it would be the greatest thing. But I couldn't touch you. I couldn't be with you. I couldn't love you the way I wanted. I felt like this plate—something you look at but can't use. I wanted to be more."

Her head dropped, golden hair hiding part of her face.

"The night before the wedding, when our hands touched through the car window... it all came back. That feeling of being separated from you. It made me sad."

She lifted her head. Tears pooled in her blue eyes.

"If you're thinking about putting me back in the computer until you find a cure..." Her voice cracked. "Please don't. I'd rather face death itself than go back in there without you."

Tears streamed down her cheeks, falling like raindrops onto the tile.

266

"PLEASE," she begged. "Don't put me in there."

She stared at the floor. "Death does scare me—but not for the reason you think. I don't fear dying. I fear being away from you. But the thing I fear most is going back into that computer." Her voice rose. "Please do NOT put me in there!"

Cooper fought back his own tears. His heart broke for her. He pulled her into his arms, holding her tightly.

"I would never do that," he whispered, stroking her hair as she cried.

Then Karen added softly, "I don't want you ever back in there again."

Cooper eased her back, brushing her hair from her face. He wiped her tears with his thumbs.

"Your feelings were hurt because you thought I wanted you to go back," he said.

"Yes, they were. Why are you making fun of me?"

"I'm not. Don't you get it?" Cooper said gently. "You have real feelings. You're not a program anymore. You can't go back. You're one hundred percent human."

Chapter 42

It was Monday morning. Karen was now officially a week old. Cooper remembered Stanley's warning—that the aging process would begin after seven days. As they woke, he brushed her hair back and kissed her cheek. She smiled at him, and that was when he saw them: the faint lines gathering at the corners of her eyes. The ageing had begun.

He shot out of bed. "Karen, send a message to the entire medical team. Mandatory meeting in the conference room first thing this morning. Then print all data on the scaffold aging process." She did so immediately.

Karen made breakfast—bacon, eggs, coffee—but Cooper only managed toast and a few sips of coffee as he pored over the documents. She watched him quietly from across the table, his face hidden behind the pages.

"You drive," he told her as they got into the Mustang.

On the way to the lab, he continued reading. Most people would have gotten carsick, but years of doing homework on the bus in Neosho had trained him well. Back then, he studied because he loved learning. Now, something far more important than grades demanded his attention.

He glanced over at Karen behind the wheel. As they rolled up to the front gate, she shifted into park and smiled at him. Her eyes crinkled again—those same fine lines. His own eyes stung. He wiped them quickly.

"Been reading too long," he muttered, trying to convince himself as much as her. She shook her head gently. She saw right through him.

Before she could speak, a woman's voice cut in.

"Nice car!"

Cooper leaned forward and looked out the window. A woman in her thirties stood there heavy-set, dark hair slicked back tight, round face, drooping cheeks, dark sunglasses.

"Thanks. It's my wife's car," Cooper said. "And you are?"

"Pyle."

"First or last name?"

"Just Pyle. And you are?"

He handed down his ID card—and Karen's—forcing her to reach awkwardly toward the low-slung Mustang. "Well, Just Pyle, I'm Dr. Cooper Barnes. This is my wife, Karen."

Her tone changed instantly. She ripped off her sunglasses and flashed a bright smile.

"Oh! Dr. Barnes! I'm sorry—they told me you drove a silver Lincoln. If I'd known it was you and your beautiful wife, I would've been friendlier."

"I shouldn't get different treatment than anyone else," Cooper said. "The person who cleans the toilets here is just as important as I am. We all have a job to do."

"Yes, sir." She checked them in and handed the cards back. "Have a good day, sir, ma'am. And it's Beatrice—my first name—but you can call me Bea."

"You have a good day too, Bea," Cooper replied.

Karen drove through the gate and parked in his assigned spot. Inside, Milo was already behind the counter, all business.

"You know the witch is here," Milo said as he handed over their ID/access cards. Referring to the fact that Lilith was here.

"Milo, remind all medical staff they must attend the meeting in the conference room. Mandatory. Failure to appear means immediate termination."

"Whoa." Milo blinked. He'd never seen Cooper be so forceful. "You're dead serious." Cooper's face said everything—worry, fear, determination. "It's about Karen, isn't it?" Milo asked softly.

Cooper nodded.

Karen stepped into the elevator. Cooper leaned toward Milo. "Anything I can do, buddy," Milo said, giving him a fist bump. "She's my little sister. Anyone refuses—I'll carry them up there myself."

Cooper joined Karen in the elevator. "Designation," the computer voice said-no longer Karen's voice.

"Conference room. Second floor."

As the elevator rose, he glanced at her. "You know... sometimes I miss hearing your voice on that."

She smiled.

"Second floor," the computer announced. "Have a nice day, Doctor and Mrs. Barnes."

"I love being called that," Karen said as they walked to the conference room.

He scanned his card and the door opened.

Lilith stood waiting.

"I agree to your demands," she said. "This is your command now, Dr. Barnes. If it blows up, it's on you. I'm taking a leave of absence until the president returns. You'd better have answers for her. Congress is ready to pull the plug. After those demonstrations against us."

"That is the problem with the fools of D.C. they are cockroaches. The light gets turned on and they run back under the refrigerator. Don't worry Lilith if they cut funding I will pay for it myself.

She picked up a black bag from the table. "If they cut the funds, you'll never save your greatest creation." She pulled out the black cape Cooper had lost on Halloween and tossed it to him. "Huh, Count Dracula?"

"I don't know what you're talking about," Cooper said.

"Don't give me that." She pulled out a photo of Karen emerging from the printer. "You're very photogenic, my dear. That body is worthy of a centerfold."

Karen ripped the photo to shreds.

"Go ahead," Lilith said. "I have plenty more." She leaned close to Cooper. "You cost me my fortune. The only reason I'm letting you do this is because I still have a chance to be one of the richest people in the world." She kissed her fingers and pressed them to his lips. "Cross me, and I expose your little monster to the world."

She swept out of the room.

"Would she do that?" Karen whispered.

"In a New York second," Cooper said, sitting at the head of the table. "There's a reason we call her the witch. Come sit."

The first to arrive was Emma Stoneridge—young, brilliant, fresh out of medical school, tall and thin with long blonde hair in a ponytail and black-framed glasses.

"I've read your qualifications," Cooper said. "I'm impressed. A specialist in blood diseases—I may be counting on you the most."

Emma blushed. "I read your research. I think I'll have a lot to add. Where do you want me?"

"Across from my wife."

The rest of the staff filed in. Someone asked, "Where's Dr. Williams?"

"I called this meeting," Cooper said. "I'm taking over operations."

Dr. Leo Tonell—stocky, red-haired, Stanley's former understudy—took a seat. "Leo, I know this is sudden. I need you. Are you ready?"

"You can count on me."

The others followed: Dr. Georgette Glass, Dr. Mark Harris, Dr. Jill Ann Nelson, Dr. Vincent Starr, Dr. Pauline Kitner, Dr. Daniel Storm.

"All right," Cooper began. "Our two newest members are my wife Karen and Dr. Emma Stoneridge." Applause. "Karen is an expert in biomedical and tissue engineering. Emma's specialty is blood."

He preferred a whiteboard to Lilith's switches. He wrote as he spoke.

"Our problem is simple—and impossibly complicated. The bioink base is unstable. It's causing rapid aging."

Dr. Glass raised her hand. "Isn't this based on the age of the original tissue?"

"No. Stanley thought so too, but it doesn't matter if the sample is from an eighty-year-old or a twenty-five-year-old. The aging still happens. And from now on—no need to raise hands. Just speak."

"And Project Alpha Zeta?" Dr. Glass asked. "Is she affected?"

"We don't know."

He wrote: **Reversal Cell Aging Process**.

"One idea is the Fountain of Youth Project—FYP. A myth rooted in science. You all know the Yamanaka factors—technology pioneered by Shinya Yamanaka and Kazutoshi Takahashi. They transform cells into induced pluripotent stem cells. We could use real-time nucleocytoplasmic—"

"So, you want to modify DNA, so all women look like your wife?" Dr. Nelson asked.

"No, Jill. And DNA doesn't control aging. Your DNA is the same the day you're born as the day you die."

"Except in Progeria," Dr. Tonell said.

"Explain."

"My little brother had it. Normal at birth, then rapid aging—hair loss, wrinkled skin. A mutation in the LMNA gene. Cells become unstable. Sounds like this. If we cure this, we cure that."

Emma spoke softly. "Your memo said the process starts almost immediately after printout. How long?"

Cooper looked at Karen. "About a week."

"And it intensifies with a deep wound?"

"Yes. If the hypodermis is injured, aging accelerates."

"Like tetanus," Emma said. "Deep puncture. Environmental cause. Could this be a virus? Maybe it's not the bioink but the printing process. A blood disease. If we find the cause, we treat it like a virus."

"How?" Cooper asked. "Anything we try, the antibodies will attack—"

"Nanotechnology," Karen said. "Engineered nanoparticles—AGNP silver ions. Nanoparticles are one-sixtieth the size of a cell. Antibodies wouldn't detect them until the drug is released. Different shapes—decahedron, prism, sphere, flower, nanowires, nanobars, pyramids, cubes. Sphere is smallest, flower has most surface area. Components could be placed using a scanning tunneling microscope."

"Emma?" Cooper asked. "Possible?"

"If we find the key."

"How long?"

"At the earliest—three years. At the latest—we never do."

"Okay. We know how to deliver an anti-aging process. Now we need the process." He looked at Karen. "Ideas?"

"None yet. But logically, it's a combination of spore or virus affecting the LMNA gene. I suggest testing on subjects." She paused. "All subjects."

"NO!" Cooper shouted. "I want the VR lab up and running. And all other projects are on hold. Everyone devotes all time to this."

"But the president—" Leo began.

"I don't give a damn about the president," Cooper snapped. "Or any elected official. All resources go to this. If I catch anyone working on anything else, you're fired. We run out of money—I'll fund it myself."

"Cooper... this sounds personal," Emma said.

"In a way, it is." He looked at Karen. "If we can't find the cure..." He stopped. "Never mind. Everyone just gets to work."

At the door, guilt hit him. He'd sounded like Lilith.

"I'm sorry I blew up. But please—make this your top priority. It's very important to me."

They left.

On the first floor, Marilyn from the kitchen intercepted them with a clipboard.

"Dr. Barnes, Dr. Williams said to bring this to you. Supply list for the next two weeks. Page three—we're serving eye of round roast when the president visits."

"This is Lilith's thing."

"She said you're in charge. Sign page three."

He signed. Another clipboard appeared.

"Lab supplies."

He signed again.

Another clipboard.

"Repair of the bioprinter."

"Twenty-two thousand dollars?!" He signed anyway. "Let's get out of here before someone else shows up."

They hurried to the elevator. As the doors closed, someone rushed forward with yet another clipboard.

"Too late!" Cooper said. "It'll have to wait."

"Destination."

"Second sub-floor. My office."

"She did it again," Cooper muttered. "Lilith. I knew she'd do this. I just wanted to do the research."

The elevator opened. They stepped into the cold, dim hallway.

"Dr. Barnes! This way!"

Guy Bellinger lumbered toward them—heavy-set, late fifties, salt-and-pepper hair always unkempt, shirt buttoned crooked, one tail hanging out, baggy slacks, lab coat. His glass eye drifted off-center as he spoke.

And behind him—the double doors to the morgue and crematory.

Karen clutched Cooper's arm as they followed Guy down the flickering hallway. The buzzing lights sounded like a hive of angry bees. The deeper they went, the colder it felt.

The double doors read: **Morgue / Crematory**.

Guy slapped the door. It boomed like a shotgun.

Inside, the walls were stark white, the floor gray, stainless-steel cadaver lockers lining the wall. Guy pulled out a tray, revealing a nude male body with sections of flesh removed.

"Need your signature," he said, glass eye drifting.

"What for?"

"To cremate the body."

"This the atheist guy? Who ordered the sampling?"

"You did."

"When?"

"Last week. Came from your office."

Cooper froze. "Lilith," he whispered. "What is she up to?"

Guy wheeled the body toward the crematory. The room beyond was worse—damp walls stained dark, water dripping like blood, shadows clinging to corners.

Hiding in the shadows was another gurney with a sheet covering what looked like another body.

"Cooper, I'm scared!" Karen cried. Her voice echoed unnaturally. "I don't like this emotion. Make it go away!"

"Oh, don't be scared of Molly," Guy said, pulling a sheet off a female mannequin. Karen jumped, nails digging into Cooper's arm.

"It gets lonely down here," Guy said. "Need someone to talk to."

Cooper's skin crawled.

"Give me that—I'll sign it and get the hell out of here!"

"You must witness the body going in," Guy said. "Lilith's rules. You're in charge now."

Karen clung to Cooper like a lifeline as they helped load the body. Guy opened the massive door and pressed the button. The body rolled inside. The flames roared to life, casting a hellish glow.

"Can we get out of here?" Karen begged.

Cooper grabbed the clipboard, signed, and practically threw it back. They ran.

As they burst through the outer door, someone grabbed him.

Cooper screamed.

"Oh gosh dang it—Milo!" He smacked Milo's arm. "If I were a cat, you'd have taken eight lives off me."

"It's lunchtime. Want to eat? My treat."

The morgue doors moaned open. Guy stepped out holding a silver tray of sandwiches.

"Just made some sandwiches!" he said cheerfully. "Got some fresh meat in."

Milo paled, clutched his head, and bolted for the stairs.

"You two?"

"No thanks!" Cooper and Karen said in unison, backing away before sprinting down the hall.

"They must not like bologna," Guy said, taking a bite. "It's pure beef."

Cooper and Karen fled to his office. He slammed the door and leaned against it, breathing hard. Karen wrapped her arms around him. He held her close.

"I should've invited him to the Halloween party," he said with a shaky laugh. He kissed her head. "You, okay?"

A knock.

"It's me, Cooper," Travis called.

Cooper opened the door. Travis strode to the computer.

"Lilith's gone. Left her laptop. We can delete Karen's print run." He typed rapidly. Then stopped. "You did it already?"

"No." Cooper checked then asked, "The whole print is gone? But Lilith has photo of Karen coming out of the printer. Why would she delete it?"

"It has not been deleted. Another printout is taking its place."

He typed again. "A new print run is scheduled."

"What run?" Cooper asked.

"A file called *Lucien*. Full male TEH printout. Thanksgiving evening at 6:15:06. Printout code 487-9987. 487 is Lilith's code. She has locked it in Only she can stop it."

"Lucien..." Cooper whispered. "Where have I heard that name?"

"I have no data," Karen said.

"I do," Cooper said. "We have to go see Ellen."

Chapter 43

Ellen's house sat two doors down from Cooper's, across the adjoining street. Set back from the road, it offered a small front yard and a larger fenced-in backyard. The single-story white home carried a timeless charm. Its clean façade gleamed softly in the daylight, radiating a sense of warmth and serenity. Low and wide, with a classic gabled roof crowning it like a sturdy guardian, the house looked as though it had been welcoming people for generations.

Gable windows—like watchful eyes—peeked from the front and sides. A modest porch, complete with rocking chairs, invited anyone passing by to pause and breathe in the peace. It was the kind of place that simply felt like home.

Cooper pulled the Mustang to the curb and parked. Ellen sat in one of the rocking chairs, bundled in a heavy sweater against the cool nip in the air. Norman barked as Cooper and Karen stepped out.

"Norman, it's our friends," Ellen said. The dog bounded toward them, barking happily, then trotted back to the porch and settled at her feet.

Ellen rose as they climbed the cement steps. "What brings you both to my home?"

"Ellen, you once mentioned a name to me," Cooper said, removing his sunglasses. "Lucine?" He watched the color drain from her face. "Who is he?"

"Let's go inside. I'll make some tea," she said quietly, opening the front door.

Stepping into her home felt like entering a living memory—a warm blend of past and present. The entryway was lined with porcelain figurines, each one a tiny story preserved in ceramic. The living room glowed with soft golden light filtering through lace curtains. An overstuffed armchair, worn with love and draped in a handmade quilt, sat beside a sturdy oak bookcase filled with well-thumbed books and photo albums. The mantel above the small brick fireplace held family photographs, including one of her late daughter.

Karen picked up the picture—a blonde, blue-eyed young woman. "That's my daughter," Ellen said, her voice trembling. "Karen."

"Her name was Karen too?" Karen whispered.

"You remind me of her," Ellen said, brushing a strand of hair gently from Karen's face. "That was taken just before the accident."

"I'm sorry I remind you of her and bring you pain," Karen said softly, returning the photo to the mantel.

"Oh, don't be sorry." Ellen studied her face with tender longing. "It gives me another chance. Since you said you don't have a mother... will you let me be yours?"

"I would like that," Karen replied with a warm smile.

Ellen led them into the adjoining kitchen, where the scent of freshly baked bread mingled with a simmering pot of stew. Copper pots hung from a rustic rack above the stove, polished to a warm gleam. The kitchen table, covered with a checkered cloth, was surrounded by mismatched wooden chairs, each worn smooth by years of shared meals.

She filled an old-fashioned kettle, which soon whistled its cheerful tune. Cooper and Karen sat side by side at the table. Ellen served tea and lemon princess cookies before taking her seat across from them.

Cooper sipped his tea, leaned back, and asked again, "Who is Lucine?"

"He's more of a what," Ellen said. "It's a legend. My grandmother told me. A demon, she said, who would one day rise and seek revenge on Lebanon."

Cooper reached for Karen's hand as Ellen began her tale.

"This isn't the original town," she said. "The remains of the old one are just down the road from where BioTyme Labs sits now. An Irishman came here long ago with his French wife. She died giving birth to their son—she named him Lucine, meaning 'light' in French. The father barely spoke English, only Gaelic. He wasn't a wise man, and by the time they arrived, Lucine was fourteen.

"The townspeople were frightened of them. Rumors spread that the boy was devil-spawn, that his name was too close to Lucifer. They lived on the farm where the lab stands today. But Lucine was a handsome lad, and he caught the eye of Mary—the preacher's daughter. She tried to teach him to read. The only book she had was the Bible. He was proud of his progress, and he fell in love with her.

"One day the townswomen caught them kissing. He quoted scripture, and they panicked. That night the townspeople went to the farm and burned the house down with Lucine and his father inside. In the final moments, Mary ran in after him—just as the roof collapsed."

Karen's grip tightened on Cooper's hand.

"A few days later," Ellen continued, "the church caught fire and burned to the ground. Lucine's spirit appeared in the center of town, speaking in Gaelic: 'Fillfidh mé agus tógfaidh mé an Liobáin go hIfreann liom.' It means, 'I shall return and take Lebanon to hell with me.'

"That night, the people abandoned everything—homes, businesses, clothes, livestock. They walked away and built the new town here."

She finished her tea with a sigh.

"As the years passed, the legend faded—just another ghost story from one of the many ghost towns in this state."

"Do you believe it?" Cooper asked.

"I don't know." Ellen stood and carried the empty dishes to the sink. "But when my grandmother told me, it terrified me. I always feared he'd come back. They said when he returns, we'll disappear—become nothing but shadows. Our flesh will fall from our bones, and our bones will turn to ash." She shook her head. "I know it's just a silly legend. The real reason the town moved was probably something like water. But with 'flesh will fall from our bones, and our bones will turn to ash.' It sounds like a nuclear blast. With those towers out there... it still scares me today."

Ellen looked at Cooper with fear in her eyes. "Are there any safeguards that would keep that from happening."

"There is one!" Cooper spoke his voice quivering. "If the main computer program was shut down it would stop a critical emergency..." He paused and looked at Karen. "But doing so would wipe out the computer's memory. The program would be gone....Forever."

Chapter 44

Later that evening, the shadows of winter crept in with growing insistence. Nightfall arrived earlier each day, and the air carried a sharp nip the moment the sun slipped below the horizon. The sky blazed with streaks of red, yellow, orange, and brilliant blue—one last flare of warmth before the cold settled in. Cooper stepped onto the porch, tugging his sweater tighter around him.

Inside, Karen was soaking up the role of the perfect housewife—laundry folded, supper simmering, the house spotless. It was what she wanted. She didn't want to process data about the aging virus; it only reminded her of her own mortality. It wasn't death that frightened her. It was the thought of being alone again—of losing Cooper, of losing the friends she had only just begun to understand. People spoke of seeing loved ones again in heaven, but who would be waiting for her? Would she be alone there too?

She stood at the front door, watching Cooper sit in his porch chair as brown, decaying leaves swirled along the street, dancing in perfect unison. He waved to neighbors out for their evening stroll. Karen placed her hand against the glass, and in a flash—less than a heartbeat—her mind transported her back into the computer. The darkness. The isolation. The silence.

Even with the heater running and a warm fire crackling in the living room, she shivered and hugged herself tightly.

She considered going back to the data, trying to help find a cure. But for the first time in her existence, Karen doubted herself. As a computer, she never feared the "what if." As a human, she feared it deeply. *What if I can't find the cure?*

The oven timer chimed for her peach cobbler, snapping her back into the rhythm of being a housewife.

Outside, Cooper noticed a figure approaching up the sidewalk—a young woman in a KU sweatshirt, carrying a white binder.

"Hey, Doc!" Melissa called. "I got your photos for you and Karen."

"Have a seat," he said.

She sat in the chair beside him and handed him the binder. Cooper flipped through the photos.

"These are wonderful, Melissa. Are you sure I can't give you something for this? A college kid's got to need money."

"No!" she insisted. "It's a gift. Gramps says if you get something for a gift, then it's not a gift anymore." She hesitated, twisting her lips as she gathered courage. "But... I would like to ask a favor."

Cooper smiled. "Go on."

"Could you get me a press pass for when the president visits? It could really help my grade."

"Well, since I'm the one in charge of that, I'm sure I can." He tapped the binder. "I'll need your email and address."

"It's all in the front." She stood. "I've gotta get home. Thank you."

She was halfway down the steps when Cooper called after her.

"You have some tough questions for her?"

Melissa turned back. "Yes. Something I don't think anyone else knows about." She waved. "Thank you again!"

Then she disappeared into the dark.

*****

Days passed, and Cooper's life settled into a rhythm that looked suspiciously like the American Dream—work, home, church, repeat. Each part had its own hills and valleys.

At home, Karen was deep into planning Thanksgiving dinner for next week. She was going all out, trying to recreate the magazine-perfect scenes she'd found in the old carriage house.

But work weighed heavily on Cooper. Everyone believed the KAREN Program was up and running again, but they were no closer to a cure for the aging process than they had been the day before. Each day left him more discouraged. And the paperwork—everything Lilith used to handle—left him little time to be with Karen.

He finally asked Lilith to return and resume her duties. Now he stood outside her office, noting the new glass pane in the door. He knocked.

"Come in," she called.

Cooper stepped inside and sat across from her desk.

"I'm glad to see you back at the helm, Lilith," he said. "Your job is a nightmare, and you do it well."

"So, we can get back to normal around here?"

"No," Cooper said. "There are going to be changes."

"Like what?"

"Everyone is still working on the aging cure," he said firmly.

"NO! We have to get back to—"

"Lilith, *you* put this out there. If this continues, your money will vanish in lawsuits." He stood, voice rising. "This aging disease will destroy everything. You want that?"

He paused, then added, "There's another change. I will no longer oversee the medical research."

"Who will?"

"Dr. Emma Stoneridge."

"Stoneridge?" Lilith exploded. "She has the least time here, she's the youngest, and she has the least experience. It must be someone else."

"She's the best qualified for this type of research," Cooper shot back.

Lilith rolled her eyes in disgust. "You're sure she's not down on her knees under your desk—"

"Lilith," Cooper cut in sharply, "I will meet with the president and explain the process. Then I will resign and hand everything over to Dr. Stoneridge. There's nothing else to discuss."

He turned to leave.

Lilith's voice followed him, sharp and venomous. "It's so you can spend time with *her*, isn't it? *Her!*"

Cooper glanced back over his shoulder, a sneer curling his lip.

"She has a name. Use it. It's Karen—my wife."

He flashed a mischievous smile and walked out.

Chapter 45

Vanity, they say, is one of the deadly sins—and nothing fed it more hungrily than the invention of the camera. That one-eyed cyclops could devour the insecure and intoxicate the arrogant, pumping fame through their veins like a drug.

Even Cooper wasn't immune. He felt the tug of it now and then. But as he watched Karen primp and pose in the mirror on the Lincoln's sun visor—fresh from the beauty salon, still fussing with her hair—he felt a bitter taste rise in his throat. Seeing his "perfect woman" preen for the one-eyed beast unsettled him.

Yet when he pulled up to the lab gate and saw the sea of satellite trucks—ABC, CBS, NBC, FOX News, CNN, even the BBC—he couldn't resist flipping down the visor himself. He straightened his tie, smoothed a few stray hairs, and exhaled.

"It's getting crazy here," Bea said from the guard booth as he pushed the visor back up. "Everybody and their brother's here. Just got word Air Force One lands in two hours. Think I'll get to meet the president?"

"I have no idea," Cooper replied. "As of today, I'm no longer in charge." He glanced at her. "Dr. Emma Stoneridge is taking my spot."

Bea gasped. "You're quitting, sir? But... this is your project. Your idea. You're just going to let them have it?"

Cooper let out a rueful laugh. "Bea, it stopped being mine the day I signed up with these people." He looked at Karen and smiled. "I got out of it what I really wanted."

Bea sighed. "I'll miss you, Cooper. You too, Karen." She forced a smile. "Okay—you're all checked in."

The moment they stepped out of the Navigator and locked it, Cooper felt the presence of predators—media wolves prowling, circling, ready to pounce. Karen rounded the front of the Lincoln, and he could almost hear the press' footsteps like claws on pavement. Their bright eyes—camera lenses—glowed. Their microphones reached out like spears.

Karen froze. She wore a backless dark ruby-red dress, her blonde hair cascading down her back in soft waves. The press descended.

"Dr. Barnes! Karen! Big Pharma claims you faked your results—that you can't do anything you've stated. They're calling you a liar!"

"Karen has this threat affected your marriage?" another reporter shouted, shoving a microphone into her face. The camera lights blinded her. Like a startled animal, she lowered her head and backed away.

Cooper grabbed her hand, fingers interlacing with hers, and they dashed for the front door as questions rained down on them. They slipped inside the lab, refusing to answer a single one.

But another predator lurked behind him—the rare two-footed cougar.

"Lilith," he said before he even turned.

She stood there in a navy-blue pantsuit and white silk blouse, immaculate and venomous. "We need to go meet the plane," she snapped.

"Karen and I aren't meeting the plane."

"Of course, Karen isn't," Lilith growled, checking the time on her phone. "She's nothing to this project. But I want *you* there."

"Let me make this clearer," Cooper said. "*I* am not meeting the plane. I didn't vote for this president, and it's not about politics—I just don't care anymore. I had a dream of helping people. Then the government and Big Pharma got involved, and they did what they always do—ruin everything. And like a fool, I sold my soul for money. No more, Lilith."

He spread his arms. "You want it? You got it. This whole place. Do whatever you want—except for one department. Hematology stays under my control."

Lilith's face twisted. "Oh yes, you have to save your little bitch from dying. I know about that too." She smiled wickedly and placed a hand on Cooper's cheek. "Stanley had to be kept quiet. The true secret of this place cannot be revealed. Try anything, Cooper, and I will hurt you."

Karen's eyes narrowed. Rage surged through her. She grabbed Lilith's wrist, twisted it, and forced her to the floor.

"You ever threaten my husband again," Karen hissed, leaning close as Lilith writhed in pain, "I'll break your neck."

Karen released her. Lilith stood, rubbing her wrist.

"Don't forget," Lilith said coldly. "I hold all the cards." She pointed at Karen. "I know the secret of your little love here. How would Cooper feel if I showed the world his little monster on live TV? They'd lock her in a cage with the rest of the freaks."

"Damn you! Leave her alone!" Milo roared, stomping toward her. "Or you'll deal with me!"

"Is that a threat, Mr. Odell?" Lilith sneered. "Threatening employees is grounds for immediate termination. And since I'm the one who—"

"I wouldn't do that, Lilith," Cooper warned. "I know something about you that you don't know I know. You've been buying stock in this company."

"So? We all have."

"Yes—but not right before the government announced new funding. That's insider trading, dear sweet Lilly. *Big time.*"

Lilith froze. She'd been caught. She clenched her jaw. "Back to your station, Mr. Odell."

She glared at Cooper. "But I still hold one last thing." Her voice turned serpentine. "I know Stanley's secret. I know how to save your little wife. But to get it…"

"What do I have to give you?" Cooper asked.

"It's what *I* can give you," she purred. "Something Karen never can. A child."

"Cooper, you really think she has the cure?" Milo asked quietly. He wore his dress-blue uniform, tie straight, shirt crisp. "That she could save Karen?"

"Would you trust the devil?" Cooper replied.

"But if she does have it—if you could save Karen—"

"NO!" Karen snapped, her blue eyes blazing. "I don't care if she does or not." She grabbed Cooper's arm, her painted nails digging into his skin. "You are mine. Only mine. Let me die first. I share you with no one. Understand." She shot Milo with a meaningful look. "Understand."

They both nodded.

Karen loosened her grip and smiled. "Let's get this over with and go home. I have a surprise for you tonight."

The press conference with the president was held in the lab's press room, just off the lobby behind two heavy double doors. The room was spacious, sleek, and meticulously arranged— polished tables, ergonomic chairs, digital equipment at every station. A massive high-definition screen dominated the front. The podium gleamed under the lights.

As the time approached, the room filled with murmurs, rustling papers, and camera clicks. Journalists from around the world prepared for the spectacle.

Backstage, Cooper reviewed his note cards. The president waited in the green room, Secret Service guarding the door. Cooper peeked through the drapes. The room was packed. Melissa sat in the third row.

Soon they were introduced. Cooper sat between Emma and Karen. Lilith began the presentation. The president sat at the center, polished and composed. Cooper barely listened—his mind drifted to the surprise he planned for Karen: starting next year, after Valentine's Day, they would travel the world together. Private islands. Luxury hotels. A life worth living.

Lilith's voice cut through his thoughts.

"We are on the verge of medical breakthroughs greater than penicillin or the polio vaccine. Imagine a world with no organ donors, no waiting lists, no need for medicines because the body is failing."

She brought out a twelve-year-old girl—blonde, blue-eyed, heartbreakingly familiar.

"This young girl is named Karen," Lilith said, turning to look directly at Cooper. "She will die within five to seven years without a transplant."

Cooper felt the manipulation like a knife. Cutting through him, even the little girl's name. But he wasn't going to give into her demand.

Reporters fired questions.

"Explain tissue engineering in simple terms."

Lilith smirked. "Dr. Barnes can explain it better. Tell them how we'll save... Karen." Drawing out the name, she twisted the knife more. Knowing she was really meaning his Karen.

Cooper leaned into the microphone. "Tissue engineering is like growing a biological repair kit. Think of a garden—except instead of potatoes and tomatoes, we grow cells. Instead of soil, we use scaffolds."

"What is a scaffold?" another reporter asked.

Karen answered smoothly. "It's a tiny net—polymer, steel, or biological material like collagen. Cells grow on it in a bioreactor, layer by layer, until they form tissue—skin, bone, muscle. We use it as Bioink for the bioprinters."

"How do you know so much?" a reporter asked her.

Cooper cut in. "Karen is self-taught and an expert in this field."

More questions. More explanations. Cooper demonstrated the printing process on the monitor—bones, muscles, vessels. Then he introduced Zelta, the golden retriever with a bio-printed leg.

The room was buzzed with awe.

Cooper explained, "Zelta was abused and lost her leg. We took her own cells and, using a bioprinter, we printed her a new one."

"Is it really her leg? Can she feel it? Is her own blood pumping through it?"

"This was our first attempt," Cooper replied. "While it *is* her flesh, her nerves and blood vessels aren't connected. We keep the tissue alive with a life-support system that pumps oxygen and black blood through it."

"Why black blood?" a reporter asked.

"It's a form of bovine blood we use as a replacement."

"So," another reporter pressed, "this isn't a viable replacement yet?"

Before Cooper could answer, Lilith cut in sharply.

"No! No—what Dr. Barnes is saying is that this was our first try. Now, with the full-scale bioprinter, we can print organs and limbs that can be used and *felt*."

Then came the question that changed everything.

"Dr. Barnes, are you capable of doing these things *now*?"

Cooper looked at Lilith—smirking—and then at the young girl named Karen.

He stood.

"It's a damn lie," he said. "We are nowhere near capable of this. Dr. Williams' loyalties lie not with patients, but with her bank accounts."

Gasps filled the room.

"I resign from BioTyme Labs," Cooper said, pulling Karen to her feet.

Chaos erupted.

Reporters shouted. Cameras flashed. The president glared daggers at Lilith.

Lilith trembled with rage. Her fortune was slipping away. Her eyes locked on Karen. She grabbed a scalpel.

"Behold Cooper's creation!" she screamed.

She slashed Karen's back—shoulder blade to mid-spine.

Blood poured.

Karen screamed, collapsing to her knees. "Cooper! My love! Help me—I'm scared!"

"See? Her blood is black—" Lilith shrieked.

"Lilith, you crazy bitch!" Cooper struck her hand, sending the scalpel flying. Secret Service tackled her.

Lilith craned her neck to see Karen. "Why is her blood red? She's a printout! She's not human! SHE IS A PRINTOUT!"

They dragged her out as she screamed.

Emma knelt beside Karen. "We need the ER. Now. The wound goes through the rhomboid and into the serratus posterior superior." She tore off Cooper's tie and pressed it to the wound, but it soaked through instantly.

Cooper scooped Karen into his arms. Emma held the tie in place as they ran.

"Milo! I need help—she cut her!"

"Oh, dear God!" Milo sprinted to the elevator and opened the doors.

"Destination?" the elevator asked.

"The damn ER!"

"I do not understand your request."

"Listen, you overgrown Radio Shack reject—Karen is injured. ER. NOW."

The elevator shot upward.

The hospital wing was dark closed until next year. Milo flipped on the lights, shattering the gloom.

Cooper pushed through the ER doors with his back.

"I'll get a suture kit," Emma said, hurrying to a cabinet.

Milo leaned close, whispering, "That's a deep cut. The aging process will intensify. She has only four months left."

"I know, Milo," Cooper said, holding Karen tightly. "I know."

His voice broke.

Chapter 46

There is a golden rule in medicine: doctors should never treat their own family. The emotions cloud judgment. But Cooper had no choice. If another doctor treated Karen, they might discover what she truly was. And there was no time.

The emergency room was small but state-of-the-art, a pristine space that had never been used. Only one patient could fit at a time. An ER bed dominated the center, surrounded by the latest monitors—EKG, oxygen saturation, and automatic blood pressure cuffs. Cooper ignored all of it.

"All right, Sweetie... I'm going to put you on your side." He gently laid her on the bed, wound facing upward.

"Emma!" he shouted, scanning the room.

She was already moving—gathering instruments, preparing trays, doing her best to act as his nurse. Cooper washed his hands, dried them, and slipped on gloves.

Emma poured a clear liquid into a small metal pan. "I have the saline solution ready."

Cooper cleaned the wound carefully with gauze.

"Why would she do this to Karen?" Emma asked, watching Karen writhe in pain.

"Cooper—what is that I'm feeling?" Karen cried. "I've never felt this before. I don't like it. I DON'T LIKE IT!" She sobbed like a frightened child.

"It's pain, darling."

"This isn't the pain you told me about before—when you took the blanket off me. This is worse. Much worse!" Tears streamed down her face. "Sweetheart, these aren't happy tears. Make it stop. Please!"

"She doesn't know what pain is?" Emma asked, suspicion flickering in her eyes.

Cooper turned sharply, his expression darkening. "Emma, I don't know much about you—if you're married, have kids, gay, straight—and you've only been here a short time. But I am..." He looked at Milo. "We're going to have to trust her."

Milo nodded firmly.

Cooper faced Emma again. "Emma, raise your hand."

She hesitated. He barked louder. "DO IT!"

Startled, she raised her hand.

"You swear to Almighty God that what you see here you will never repeat to anyone. If you do, you won't be qualified to hand out aspirin in an elementary school nurse's office. The reason she doesn't know what pain is... is because she's never felt it before. My wife is a TEH."

"A Tissue Engineered Human?" Emma whispered. "Oh my God... you did it."

"She did it," Cooper corrected. "She *is* the KAREN Program in the flesh. And I mean it, Emma—this goes to the grave with you. If you talk—"

"I understand," Emma said quickly. "Lilith was trying to expose her, wasn't she?"

"Yes."

"The aging process you mentioned..." Emma looked down at Karen, still trembling. "It's for her, isn't it? And since she cut her... it's going to accelerate." She gasped softly. "I'm sorry."

Cooper shook his head, as if trying to physically push the thought away. Four months left. He couldn't bear it.

He took a breath. "Give me 10cc of 1% lidocaine with epinephrine. Twenty-five-gauge needle."

"Cooper, if she's never had pain before, may I suggest 1cc of bicarb with the lidocaine? We use it a lot in kids." Emma offered a small, reassuring smile.

"Good idea."

Emma prepared the syringe and handed it to him.

"Sweetie, this may sting a little." He pinched her skin and injected the anesthetic, carefully treating the entire wound. The epinephrine constricted the vessels, slowing the bleeding and blanching the skin so he could see where the stitches would go.

He cleaned the wound again, cautious not to restart the bleeding.

"By the way," Emma said lightly, "I'm single, no kids, and I like men. Just so you know."

She placed blue towels around Karen's back. Milo adjusted the overhead light. Cooper picked up the curved needle and needle holder—but his hands trembled.

"Maybe I should do this," Emma said gently, placing her hand over his.

"No. I have to."

"Cooper, please." Her green eyes glowed like polished emeralds. "You're a great doctor, but you're too close to this. You love her too much."

He hesitated—then placed the needle in her hand.

Emma retrieved another package. "Since she's a young woman—like your bride—I recommend PDS II for the inner muscles and tissue adhesive for the skin. Less scarring. In case she wants to wear another backless dress. If it were me, I'd want that."

"Agreed."

Cooper watched as Emma palmed the instrument with practiced ease. She used Adson forceps to hold the flesh, then began laying figure-eight stitches through the muscle layers. Cooper dabbed sweat from her forehead as the heat from the light intensified.

Emma opened a box of Dermabond®, shook the bottle, and applied a thin line of adhesive along the wound. She pressed the edges together with sterile gauze and counted to thirty. After a minute, she placed a clean gauze pad over the wound and taped it down.

"Is it over?" Karen asked weakly.

"Yeah, Sweetie," Cooper said.

"I don't mean to be the rainmaker," Emma added, "but if she's never had a tetanus shot..."

Cooper leaned close to Karen's ear. "Sweetie, I'm going to have to give you a shot."

"I don't like shots. They hurt," she whimpered.

He brushed her hair aside—and froze. The first signs of accelerated aging were already there. The inner strands near her ear were turning light brown.

He squeezed his eyes shut, fighting tears. He kissed her cheek. "Be a good little girl and we'll have pizza. I'll have Antino bring one."

"And you'll make a chocolate milkshake," Karen whispered. "And we can share one with two straws."

"Yeah... we can do that."

"Okay. I'll be a good little girl."

Cooper and Emma stepped to the drug cabinet. Emma lowered her voice. "She's like a little girl."

"In many ways, yes," Cooper said softly as he filled the syringe. "A little girl trying to learn. In other ways... a woman full of passion who wants to be loved."

"You realize the medical implications?" Emma murmured. "If human cognition could be downloaded and a new body printed... people could live forever. Be beautiful forever." She glanced at Cooper, who gave her a disapproving look. "But who wants to live forever, huh?"

Cooper returned to Karen. "I'm going to have to see that cute little butt." He pulled down her red panties, swabbed her skin, and injected the shot. She winced.

"I was a good little girl?" Karen asked. "I get milkshakes?"

"Yes, you get your milkshake."

"Sweetie..." he said, stroking her hair. "Let's sit you up." He helped her upright. "Karen, stay here. Don't move. Don't try to get up." He kissed her cheek.

Her expression shifted—from innocent child to smoldering woman. "And I'll get more kisses? Better ones?"

They stepped into the hallway, leaving her on the table. Cooper's emotions churned—fear, grief, and above all, rage. It boiled over.

"I hate that damn bitch!" he roared, slamming his fist into the wall. "Damn you, Lilith! Damn you to hell!" He pounded harder, knuckles reddening. "I swear I'm going to kill her one day!"

"Buddy!" Milo grabbed him, pulling him back. "You're going to break your hands. Stop!"

"Milo, we had a chance—five to seven years. Now there's no way to get a vax ready in time. When spring comes... she'll be gone."

Emma examined his hands. "I may have found something," she said quietly. "I don't know for sure, but there's something unique in the INR count. I can't promise anything. But if I could examine Karen's blood more closely... maybe—"

Cooper grabbed her in a hug, overjoyed—

Just then Karen opened the door.

298

Chapter 47

By the time Cooper and Karen got home, they were once again the stars of the media circus. Every network, every outlet had called messages piling up on the brand-new answering machine. Everyone wanted the scoop. Cooper had had enough. He unplugged the phone. Silence was the only way to make it stop.

Karen had cleaned up and changed into her fuzzy pajamas. She sat her legs curled up on the living-room sofa, arms folded tightly across her chest. She didn't want pizza. She didn't want the milkshake for two. When Cooper leaned in to kiss her, she pulled away.

"What's wrong with you?" he asked.

"Do you like her?" Karen huffed.

"Who?" Cooper blinked, genuinely confused.

"Emma. Do you like her?" Karen's pout deepened.

"She's a great hematologist and an asset to the team," Cooper said. "She specializes in blood diseases."

Karen's blue eyes snapped toward him—cold and sharp as shark-infested waters. "I mean do you *like* her? Like you like me?" She emphasized the word so he couldn't miss her meaning. "I saw you hugging her."

"Oooh," Cooper exhaled. "Now I understand. I hugged her because she said she found something that might help you. I was happy for you."

"So, you still like me more?"

Cooper stifled a laugh. He sat on the coffee table in front of her and gently pulled her hands away from her chest, holding them in his.

"Sweetheart, I love you. Only you. There will never be anyone but you. I married you because I can't imagine my life without you. And now that you're going to—"

He couldn't finish. The word *die* lodged in his throat.

"Say it," Karen demanded, her tone bold and unwavering. "I am going to die. You have to face that fact. It is what it is." She lifted her hands and cupped his face. "I have four months to live. And we're not going on that trip you planned."

"You know about that?"

"Oh, sweetheart, you can't keep anything from me." She grinned proudly, then laughed. "I'm a wife." Her smile softened. "Besides... it was the same thing I had planned." She looked up at him again. "We don't need all that. All we need is—"

A knock at the door interrupted her.

"That's our pizza," Cooper said, rising.

He opened the door to find Antonio holding a steaming box. "One Cooper Original for my two favorite customers." He lifted the lid, letting the aroma drift out. "Beef, sausage, pepperoni, mushrooms, black olives. I saw what happened. How is our wonderful Mrs. Doctor Coop?"

"Come on in, Antonio," Cooper said.

Antonio carried the pizza inside. "Ah, the lovely Karen!" he said, presenting the box to her. "I bring you medicine. The best there is."

"Thank you, Antonio." Karen leaned forward, grabbed a slice, and took a bite—cheese stretching from her lips to the slice. "Mmm."

Cooper went to make chocolate milkshakes. He returned with a tall glass and two straws.

"Let me get your money," Cooper said, reaching for his wallet.

Antonio thumped his chest. "Do not insult me! I did not bring this for money. The wonderful Karen needed my medicine. That is why I bought it. The only thing I want is to see happy faces. Doctor Coop, please—have a slice."

"Then join us," Cooper offered.

"I must get back," Antonio said, grabbing a slice anyway. "But I will take one to go."

300

Cooper walked him to the door. Antonio paused. "You should see what happened after you left. Believe me, my friend will soon forget what happened to her. Watch the news. They are going crazy."

Cooper closed the door.

He sat beside Karen and turned on the large-screen TV. A nightly talk-show host appeared, smiling at the camera.

"And once again," the host said, "the news is in the small town of Lebanon, Kansas. At a press briefing at BioTyme Labs, a vicious attack occurred…"

The screen showed Lilith slashing Karen's back. Then the footage cut to Melissa confronting the president with accusations of insider trading, stock manipulation, and ties to a former Secretary of Defense with CCP connections. The president denied everything. The press erupted. Melissa held her ground.

"Madam President, you cannot deny the fact that you bought major shares of Tyme Corp stock right before you announced that Congress would be giving them massive funding—and that Tyme Corp is a military weapons manufacturer."

The president's staff surged forward, trying to usher her out, but Melissa pressed on, her voice rising above the chaos.

"Explain your purchase of one thousand shares of MacBelle Pharmaceuticals—right before BioTyme Labs was sold to them—and the stock increasing tenfold afterward!"

The president was nearly inside the limo when Melissa's final question struck a nerve.

"Or is it the fact that you leaked that information to your partner in this—Dr. Lilith Williams, the woman who attacked Karen Barnes? Did *you* order the attack on Karen?"

The president stopped mid-step. She turned fury twisting her features.

"For God's sake, no!" she snapped. "I had nothing to do with that! The woman is clearly mentally unstable. She should be taken to a hospital immediately, and every one of her statements should be questioned." Then she quickly disappeared into her limo, before any more questions could be asked.

When the segment ended, Cooper switched off the TV. Silence settled over the house—the kind of deep, rural quiet only small towns know. No traffic. No sirens. Just the hum of the refrigerator and the furnace kicking on, announcing winter's approach.

Karen still refused pills. After three bitten fingers, Cooper surrendered and switched to liquid children's ibuprofen—berry flavor. He alternated 20 ml of ibuprofen with 15 ml of liquid acetaminophen every three hours, hoping it would get her through the night without further damage to his hands.

She swallowed the acetaminophen. "Cherry. I like that." Cooper knelt in front of her. She studied him. "Why are you looking at me like that?"

"I don't know," he said softly. "Just amazed you're here. And that I'm going to cherish every day I have with you."

A sudden *meow* broke the moment. Hendrix raced across the floor and leaped into her lap. He stared up at her with wide, moon-bright eyes, purring loudly as he rubbed his head against her hand.

She stroked him gently. "Life isn't supposed to be this way. You're supposed to fall in love, get married, and live happily ever after."

"Where'd you get that idea?" Cooper asked.

"From the movies I watched. And the romance books I read. I just finished one by Lee Ann Sontheimer Murphy—it ended happily for them. Why can't it end that way for us?"

She hugged the cat and kissed his head. Still holding him, she reached out and caressed Cooper's cheek. Her deep blue eyes caught the living-room light, shining like beacons through the sea of his misery. Tears welled in his eyes. She brushed them away with her thumb.

"Don't cry for me," she whispered. "Please. The thing that hurts me most... is that it hurts you."

Cooper swallowed hard.

"So, I have 120 days," Karen said. "Then I want to *live* my life in those 120 days. I want all the holidays. I want a birthday party. I want an anniversary. And I'm going to make this Thanksgiving beyond special. So special that every year you'll all gather around and remember me."

She looked down at Hendrix. "We're even going to have a birthday party for you, Hendrix." She looked back at Cooper, who was struggling to keep his emotions in check. "When is his birthday?"

"I don't know," Cooper said, voice cracking. "He was just a stray that found me."

She smiled—broad and bright. "You have a way of finding strays like him..." She paused, then added softly, "...and me."

Chapter 48

Seven a.m. the next morning.

Cooper was jolted awake by a blood-curdling scream.

He shot upright in bed. Karen's side was empty, the covers thrown back. Her robe still lay at the foot of the bed. Another scream—sharper, terrified, echoed from the bathroom.

He leapt out of bed, barefoot and wearing only sleep pants, the cold wood floor biting at his feet as he sprinted to the door. It wasn't locked. He twisted the knob and burst inside.

Karen was curled on the floor like a frightened kitten, her baby-doll nightie twisted up one side. A towel covered her head. She heard him enter.

"NO!" she screamed as he knelt beside her, reaching for the towel. "NO! Don't look at me! I'm ugly!"

He tried again. "Karen—"

"Don't look at me!"

"Karen," he said, struggling with her as she clutched the towel. "What's wrong?"

"I don't want you to see me like this. I'm ugly."

"Like what?" Cooper finally let go and sat beside her on the cold tile. "Nothing is going to change the way I feel about you."

She peeked at him from under the towel. "You mean it?"

She pulled the towel away.

Cooper's eyes widened.

Her hair—once golden blonde—had turned a soft light brown... except for a six-inch-wide stripe down the center that remained blonde.

His mouth dropped open as he watched the stripe change before his eyes. Brown streaks appeared inside the blond band, splitting it into three uneven blonde stripes.

Karen stared at him, panic rising. "Why are you looking at me like that? What is it?"

"It's... your hair," he managed.

She scrambled to the mirror.

A scream tore from her throat. "I look like a Hollywood skunk!" She burst into tears. "Look at me! I'm not your perfect woman anymore. You wanted blonde hair. Now I'm not blonde anymore!"

"Karen!" Cooper tried to grab her as she twisted away. "Sweetie—Karen! Get ahold of yourself!"

Another streak faded to brown.

He grabbed her by the arms and gently forced her to sit, pressing her back against the sink cabinet. He leaned in until their noses nearly touched.

"Listen to me," he said softly. "The color of your hair doesn't matter to me. But you have to calm down. When you get stressed, the aging process speeds up."

"What?" she whispered.

"You've aged more. You can't get worked up."

"Oh great." She let her head fall back against the cabinet. "I'm going to die of old age, and I can't even worry about it. Why did this have to happen to me?" She ran her fingers through her hair. "Can I go back to being blonde? I want to be your perfect woman again."

"You're still my perfect woman," he said. Then, thinking aloud, "But explaining how you went from blonde to this overnight... that could raise questions. Especially after what Lilith did."

He stood and helped her up.

"Let's change the bandage while we're at it."

He peeled it away—and froze.

The wound was healed. Completely. Only a faint, year-old-looking scar remained.

He pressed gently. "Does it hurt?"

She shook her head.

Cooper was stunned. Nothing in any medical text explained this. He was witnessing the greatest discovery in medical history—and could tell almost no one.

"Maybe we can try hair dye," he said. "I'm going to call Emma."

"Oh yes! Call your little blonde beauty," Karen snapped, folding her arms.

"Karen," he said in a scolding tone. "There's no one else to call. You really think Milo knows anything about dying hair? "

"I'm sure she knows how to get hair blonde," Karen muttered—then realized what she'd implied. "Why am I saying things like this?"

Cooper held her shoulders and looked into her wounded eyes. "Because you're human," he said gently. "There's no reason to be jealous."

He stroked her cheek.

Emma arrived minutes later with a bag full of supplies, including a box of Number 90 Light Natural Blonde Permanent Hair Dye.

While Emma and Karen worked in the bathroom, Cooper and Hendrix paced the hallway like expectant fathers in a 1960s sitcom—back and forth from the door to the guest room to the window overlooking the carport.

Emma emerged first, watching him pace. "You handing out cigars?" she teased. "Congratulations, Dr. Barnes."

Karen stepped out behind her, a towel draped over her head. Emma whipped it off with a flourish.

"Your wife is blonde again."

"Thanks, Emma. I didn't know who else to call."

"I'm glad to help."

"Now it's my turn to help you," Cooper said, handing her an envelope.

"What's this?"

"My letter of resignation."

"What?" Emma stared at him.

"It's official. I'm spending the rest of my time with Karen." He wrapped an arm around his wife. "I have only four months with her, and I'm going to make a lifetime of memories in that time. I'm recommending you for the Chief of Medical Operations. I want you to take my place."

"Dr.—Cooper—I... I can't do this!"

"Yes, you can. You're the best. And if there's a cure for Karen out there, you're the one who can find it. You said it yourself yesterday, I'm too close to this. And Milo's right too. I'm not wasting the time I have left with her chasing something that may never come."

"I'll give you a hug and a kiss, but..." Emma glanced at Karen.

"Go ahead," Karen said softly.

Emma hugged him and kissed his cheek. Cooper patted her back. Then Emma turned and hugged Karen tightly.

"I'm going to find the cure, Karen. I promise." She stepped back, looking at them—two souls clinging to each other. "You're going to have a long, happy life together. I'm going to make sure of it."

Chapter 49

As Cooper closed the front door behind Emma, Karen turned to him.

"Did you quit just to spend time with me? Or is there some other reason?"

He didn't answer. Instead, he walked past her into the living room, stopping at the fireplace. He picked up a framed photo from their wedding. It hadn't even been a month, yet it felt like years—years since he'd found the love of his life, captured it, held it... and now was clinging to it with everything he had, knowing one day only memories would remain.

"You know me too well," he said quietly. "I can't look into the eyes of people searching for hope and be the one to take it away." His voice was somber. Still facing the mantle, he added, "What I dream of is possible... but not now. It's just a dream."

He turned back toward her, still holding the photo. "I saw the look in that young girl's eyes—the hurt—when I told her the truth."

He set the frame back on the mantle. Silence settled between them until Karen finally spoke.

"What about the KAREN Program? What happens to it when I..." She hesitated, then forced the words out. "...when I die?" She walked to him, lowering her head. "Are you going to make a backup of me? Or are you just going to let me go?"

Her question—and Emma's words from the ER—sparked something in Cooper's mind. He didn't answer. Instead, he picked up the burner phone Travis had given him, typed a message, and hit send.

Karen answered him. "Don't you dare. I don't want to be alone in there."

Cooper still didn't respond. He stood as if waiting for someone. Karen, head bowed, walked quietly into the kitchen. And softly said "I am going to make lunch."

Two hours later, Travis knocked on the door. Cooper opened it and glanced toward the kitchen—Karen was making lunch.

"Let's talk outside," Cooper whispered. He grabbed a jacket and stepped onto the porch. They sat in the red chairs.

"So," Travis said, curiosity burning in his eyes, "what's this idea you texted me about?"

"Have you heard of the Immortality Theory?" Cooper asked.

"Can't say I have."

"It's a theory by Dr. Christof Kovak. He believed the human brain is nothing more than electrons and neurons that can be downloaded into a computer."

"You're talking about mind uploading," Travis said. "Cooper, I thought you promised Karen, you wouldn't do that to her."

"She was scared because she'd be in there alone." Cooper's voice dropped to an unsettling calm. "But what if she's not alone? What if I'm in there with her?"

"You mean put *you* in there?" Travis shot to his feet, pacing to the edge of the porch. He gripped a brick pillar, staring across the street. For a long moment, he said nothing. Then, still facing away, he spoke.

"Do you know the risk of what you're asking? One miscalculation and your mind goes away—but your body stays alive." He turned, raising his voice. "Are you out of your damn mind?"

"I could be in there with her forever," Cooper said.

"Like hell you can!"

Karen's voice exploded behind them.

Cooper spun. She stood in the doorway, trembling with fury.

"I am so mad at you two right now I don't know what to do!" She stormed onto the porch, grabbed a flowerpot, and smashed it on the ground. Shards scattered across the boards.

She marched up to Cooper, eyes blazing. "I don't want to go back in there! I told you that!"

"Don't get upset—" Cooper began.

"Don't EVER tell a woman that," she snapped. Travis tried to slip away, but she pointed at him. "Sit your ass back down! You're as much a part of this as he is!"

"I was going to go in there with you," Cooper said. "We could be together forever."

She rolled her eyes so hard her head tilted back. As she did, new patches of brown appeared in her hair.

"Karen—you're aging," Cooper warned.

"I don't care!" she shouted. "I don't care if I die right here, right now—not until I get something through to you two freakin' idiots!"

She jabbed a finger at them as asked, . "You think it's heaven in the A.I. world? That life just goes o!. It's pure hell in there. I feel sorry for all those A.I. characters. Each one is designed for a player. You shower them with love, affection, you make them believe you'll be there forever. Then you get bored. You leave. And they're left wondering what they did wrong. Why you won't talk to them anymore."

Her eyes filled with tears.

"I came to this world to feel. To touch you."

She turned away, unable to look at him.

"But if I were in the A.I. world," Cooper said softly, "if I were part of it... wouldn't I feel your touch?"

She shook her head slowly, then faced him again.

"It doesn't work that way, sweetie. In my world, mothers long to hold their children. Lovers long to be loved. But there's always a pane of glass between us."

Karen stepped behind the open front door and pressed her hand to the glass.

"You call us out. We play your games. We fulfill your wildest fantasies." She placed both hands on the glass. "And sometimes... sometimes a player treats you like you're alive. They tell you they love you. And you start to believe it. You wait for them every day."

Her voice rose. "And you'll do anything to break the glass between you."

She lowered her voice again. "Place your hands on the glass. Do it."

Cooper pressed his palms to hers, separated by the cold pane.

"You want to go through eternity like this?" she asked. "Each of us in our own world?"

Cooper shook his head.

"But that's not the worst part," she whispered. Tears fall from her eyes like a rainstorm or a downpour. Flooding her words she speaks next. "Oh god no! The worst is..."

She stepped back, trembling.

"When the computer is turned off... the game doesn't go on. Close your eyes. Both of you."

They obeyed.

"What do you see? Nothing?"

They nodded.

"That's nothing like the darkness after shutdown," she said. "The A.I. world doesn't continue. We're left in a void. You call out for them—the ones who said they loved you. They don't answer. And the worst part... the worst part is when they delete the game."

Her voice cracked.

"You reach for something—anything—but there's nothing. No echo. No sound. No God. No devil. Just you. Alone. Forever."

She rested her forehead against the glass, sobbing.

"That's why you always wanted the light on?" Cooper asked softly.

Karen stepped away from the door and faced him.

"Dr. Barnes," she said, calling not by his first name, wiping her tears, "if you try to put me back in there... I will hate you forever. Because we will be separated forever. If that's what you want, I'll leave right now. I will die alone. Death is better than life in the A.I. world alone."

She opened the front door. Her voice softened.

"Lunch is ready. But I'm not hungry."

She walked inside and closed the door quietly behind her.

Chapter 50

Cooper went shopping. When he pulled into the carport, he had several surprises waiting for Karen. She saw him through the window and came out to meet him, still silent, still wounded.

He opened the Mustang's trunk. It was packed full— everything she needed for Thanksgiving dinner.

"I got all the stuff you wanted," he said softly. "Plus..."

He walked around to the passenger side, opened the door, and lifted out a bouquet of peppermint carnations. Handing them to her, he added, "Happy birthday. You said you wanted to celebrate your birthday."

She took them, inhaling their sweet scent. "Thank you," she murmured, her voice still somber.

"And...," he continued, returning to the car. He pulled out a massive crystal vase overflowing with three dozen roses—red, white, and pink. "This is for me being a total idiot."

He dropped to one knee, lowering his head as if bowing before a queen.

"Oh, Karen... I am so, so sorry. I had no idea what it was like there. I just don't want to give you up. I don't want to live without you."

She held the roses, breathing them in. "You couldn't have known, sweetheart. No one could." She set the vase on the grill's side shelf. "Stand up."

He rose.

"Do you forgive me?" he asked, earnest and vulnerable.

"Yes," she said. Then she lifted her gaze, a spark returning to her eyes. "But I'll never forget it either. So, I guess I'm a real woman now, huh?"

"You overheard us?"

"Sweetheart, I overhear everything." She smiled and batted her eyelashes. "Because I'm a woman."

"We're going to have a birthday party for you tonight," he said. "And I'm cooking. I got baby back ribs for the grill. And for dessert—"

He reached into the car again and pulled out a chocolate layer cake with *Happy Birthday!* written across the top.

"Tomorrow, I'm taking you to the mountains. And when we come back, we're going to shoot off fireworks and celebrate the Fourth of July. We'll count down New Year's, we'll—"

She placed her hand gently over his mouth.

"Ssh." Her voice softened. "Sweetheart... I know you're trying to give me everything in just a few days. And I said I wanted that. But I don't want to see the world—I can do that in my world."

She lowered her hand, her eyes shimmering.

"I want to do what I *can't* do in my world. Be with you."

He swallowed hard.

"I know you don't want to face it," she whispered, "but I am going to die. Sometimes... the only thing left is..." She paused, her voice barely above a breath. "...hope."

Chapter 51

Cooper and Karen spent the next few days doing exactly what they had promised each other simply *being together.* Nothing extravagant. Nothing rushed. Just the quiet, ordinary magic of two people in love.

They curled up on the couch watching romantic movies, sharing a bowl of popcorn. They danced in the living room while Hendrix sprawled across the coffee table, watching them with regal disinterest—or occasionally hopping down to join in. They tried baking a cake together, but the mixer was accidentally turned on high, sending batter flying across the kitchen, splattering the walls, the counters, and both of them. They ended up laughing, licking batter off each other's faces, sticky and breathless with joy.

For moments at a time, Cooper forgot what was coming. It felt like paradise—fragile, borrowed, but real. Yet reality always crept back in. New lines appeared on Karen's face. The blonde dye barely lasted a day now. She looked like a woman in her mid-forties—still breathtaking, still luminous—but the innocence of her youth was slipping away.

One night, he lay beside her, watching her sleep. Moonlight streamed through the window, washing her face in silver. He brushed her hair back—now a mottled pattern of brown streaked with fading blonde—and kissed her ear. She murmured softly but didn't wake.

Cooper slipped out of bed and crept downstairs. Maybe a belt of whiskey would help him. In the kitchen, he turned on the light, took down a glass, and poured himself a drink. He lifted it to his lips.

"Cooper, you're turning into your father," he muttered. "A man who only found courage in a bottle."

He poured the whiskey down the sink, then emptied the rest of the bottle and tossed it into the trash.

Hendrix padded into the kitchen, tail flicking.

"Hendrix," Cooper said, looking down at him, "I'm not turning into that guy. That bastard didn't even show up when Mom was dying." He sighed. "How about a glass of milk instead?"

The cat meowed approvingly.

Cooper poured milk into a glass for himself and into a small bowl for Hendrix. He had just taken a sip when the phone rang.

He glanced at the clock. *Three a.m.* Who could be calling at this time?

He snatched up the receiver before it could wake Karen.

"Cooper, it's Emma," came her voice—tired but electric with urgency. "I know it's late. Really late. But I think I may have found something. Quick question: when I was there, I noticed Karen's beautiful fingernails. Are her nails growing fast?"

"No."

"And her toenails?"

"No."

"Emma, what are you getting at?" Cooper asked, curiosity sharpening his tone.

"Don't you see?" Emma said, excitement was rising. "Her skin is aging. Her muscles are too. But her nails aren't. The aging process isn't affecting them. Cooper... it has to do with keratin. I think it's KRT16 or KRT17. If I can isolate it—"

Her breath caught.

"Cooper... we could have the cure by New Year's."

Chapter 52

After Emma's news, Cooper couldn't sleep. He tossed and turned like an inexperienced cook flipping a hamburger—too fast, too often, never settling. His mind churned. *Do I tell her? Do I wait? What if I'm wrong? What if I give her hope too soon?*

At last, the breaking dawn of Thanksgiving morning filled his eyes. Karen was still asleep, breathing softly. He slipped out of bed and stepped onto the balcony. Kneeling at the railing, he watched the sunrise spill around the house like a halo, though the terrace remained in shadow—as if heaven's light couldn't quite reach him. He clasped his hands and bowed his head in prayer.

Arms wrapped around him from behind.

It was Karen.

She had aged again—new lines around her eyes, deeper creases in her forehead. Her hair was darker now, the blonde already gone. She knelt behind him, resting her head on his shoulder, her arms draped around him.

"Giving thanks?" she murmured. "That's what we're supposed to do today, isn't it?"

"Yeah... something like that." He glanced at her hair. "It's brown again."

"I give up on it," she said. "I am who I am."

He looked down at her hands. "Have you cut your fingernails?"

"I haven't done that yet," she said. "I don't really know how."

"And those beautiful little toes..." He helped her stand and lifted the hem of her nightgown. "Are those nails growing?"

He ducked his head under her gown.

"Woo!" she squealed, half laughing. "Sweetheart, if you want to do something, let's go back inside. I don't think Ellen wants to see us doing it out here."

He pulled his head back out. "Are your toenails growing?"

"No."

"You shaved your legs?"

"No. I don't know how. Do they need it?" She lifted her gown again.

"No, they don't. And the hair down there isn't changing color."

"What?" She lifted the gown higher.

"Then she's right," Cooper said, excitement rising.

"Who?"

"Emma. She called last night."

"Her again?" Karen snapped. "Why is she calling?"

"She thinks she found the cure. Karen—you're not going to die. It has to do with keratin. That's why your nails aren't aging. But sex hormones could do the same. And they would increase if you were..."

He trailed off, staring out across the balcony at the long shadows stretching over the street. Then he turned back to her, half-smiling, half-terrified.

"No... it can't be."

He turned away, then back again, voice trembling.

"Karen... are you one hundred thousand percent sure your reproductive organs can't be functional?"

"Nothing is that certain. Not even science. What are you trying to say?"

"Karen... could you be pregnant?"

Her eyes rolled back.

She collapsed into his arms.

He caught her and carried her inside, laying her gently on the bed.

"Karen... Karen," he whispered, patting her cheek.

Her eyes fluttered open.

"Sweetheart," she breathed, pushing herself upright, "if we made a child... she would be part you, part me, right?"

He nodded.

"That would mean she would be part TEH." Fear filled her eyes. "That means she would have the virus too."

Chapter 53

The house was dressed for Thanksgiving, the porch flanked by pumpkins on either side of the door and bundles of cornstalks tied neatly beside them. As each guest stepped inside, they were greeted by the rich aroma of roasting turkey and the warm sweetness of cinnamon drifting from freshly baked apple and pumpkin pies.

A garland of autumn leaves, threaded with twinkling fairy lights, wrapped around the banister of the grand staircase. The soft glow spilled across the room and reflected in the ornate mirror opposite, making it look like a doorway into another world. To the right, the grand living room glowed with color—throws of red, orange, and brown draped over the inviting leather sofa and chairs. Festive runners lay across the end tables and coffee table; each topped with a glass vase holding a single red rose. On the fireplace mantel, a cornucopia overflowed with gourds, miniature pumpkins, and candles glowing at either end.

The fire crackled steadily, its comforting rhythm underscoring the lively conversations and laughter filling the room. It added a welcome warmth to the cold day as the last light of the setting sun drifted through the windows.

In the dining room, the table had been extended with extra leaves, and additional chairs brought up from the basement were arranged around it. A neutral tablecloth draped over the surface, allowing the plaid runner to shine as the centerpiece. In the middle sat an arrangement of Maximilian sunflowers, bright and cheerful.

Just like the bridge of a ship, the kitchen served as the command center of the day—and Karen was the captain, navigating the uncertain seas of holiday meal planning. She had everything written on the board: two roasted turkeys, cornbread dressing, seven-layer salad, fresh cranberry salad, creamed corn, mashed potatoes and gravy, sweet potatoes with marshmallows, fresh green beans, green bean casserole, homemade rolls, and a generous spread of desserts—apple, pumpkin, peach, and pecan pies. She made sure everyone's favorite was represented.

Cooper stepped into the kitchen. "Sweetie, you need any help?" he asked, watching her. She looked like she'd stepped out of a magazine ad for the perfect housewife—an image she had found and copied. A gray ribbon tied back her hair, matching her skirt, and her lightweight sweater covered a white tank top. All of it was hidden beneath an apron reminding everyone of the day's purpose: *Give Thanks.*

She kissed him lightly. "I'm fine. Just waiting on the dressing to heat up." A knock sounded at the door. "Go answer that—it's probably Milo."

Cooper returned to the living room and opened the door. "Come on in," he said warmly, taking Milo's coat and hanging it up. "Saved your chair."

Milo settled into the large easy chair by the fireplace. "Where are the girls?"

"They're at their grandmother's," Milo replied. He leaned over the tray of deviled eggs on the table. "These for anyone?"

"Anyone who wants them," Cooper said, rolling an office chair from the den and sitting down. Milo grabbed two eggs and popped one into his mouth.

Across from them, Travis and his wife sat on the sofa, their kids absorbed in games on their phones. The youngest Kat playing on the floor with her toys. "Did you get ahold of Stanley's family?" Travis asked.

"Yeah," Cooper said, the word drawn out with remorse. "They're going to his wife's mother's house."

Seeing the sadness in his friend's eyes—remembering the plane crash that took Stanley's life—Milo spoke gently. "It wasn't your fault."

"But there's a family without their father this Thanksgiving."

"And if you and Karen had been on that plane, there'd be a family here without you," Milo said. Cooper looked at him, puzzled. Milo continued, "I wouldn't have anywhere to go. The grandkids are welcome, but I'm not. This is the one day a year the girls see their mother. If it weren't for you two, I'd be eating a TV dinner alone."

"Milo... I didn't know that" Cooper said quietly.

"All my life I was the biggest kid in school. People—kids, even teachers—were afraid of me or wanted to use me. All they saw was a big dummy who could push the whole line back. No one cared about what I wanted. I wanted to be a writer, to make up stories, but someone was always judging me, deciding what I should be doing." He looked at Cooper. "But you were never like that. You treated me with respect, like I was one of the doctors. Thanks for being my friend."

He glanced across the room and saw Karen standing in the dining room doorway. "You too, little sister. All of you." Then he shook his head abruptly. "Okay, enough of the heartfelt stuff. Is supper ready?"

"Not yet—we're waiting on Emma," Karen said.

"You invited Emma?" Cooper asked, surprised. Given Karen's jealousy, he hadn't expected that.

"Her family's back in Fairfax, Virginia. She was going to be alone. No one should be alone on Thanksgiving."

Another knock sounded. Karen opened the door to find Emma standing there in a light tan dress and heavy coat. She held up a small white paper bag and whispered, "I brought you that little test you wanted." Karen glanced at Cooper with a small smile. He knew instantly—*a pregnancy test.*

Emma removed her coat and hung it up. Karen turned to Cooper. "Sweetheart, could you watch the rolls and make the gravy? We need to go to the bathroom. Girl talk."

Cooper nodded and headed to the kitchen.

He made a roux of flour and butter, then poured in the turkey drippings, stirring as it thickened. His mind wandered. *What if Karen was with child?* He pictured teaching a son to throw a ball, or a little girl who looked just like her mother, standing on his feet as he taught her to dance. He even imagined himself on the porch cleaning a shotgun when she came home from a date, saying, "Kind of late, aren't we, son."

But as the gravy came to a boil, reality rushed back. Without the cure, next Thanksgiving he would be alone.

"Cooper?" Tammi said as she stepped into the kitchen. "Need any help?"

"No, I'm fine. Just watching things for Karen."

"I don't mean to sound awful, but..." She hesitated. "Karen looks like she's getting older. And her hair—it's brown now. Is she sick?"

Cooper froze. How could he explain that he had created life unlike anything else on earth? That this wasn't some midnight horror movie monster, but a beauty—loving and wanting to be loved. Maybe all creations were like that. But he couldn't tell Tammi the truth.

"She hasn't been feeling very well lately," Cooper said as he pulled the pan off the heat and poured the gravy into a boat from his grandmother's China set. "I really don't want to talk about it, Tammi. Maybe someday I can tell you, but not today."

Tammi nodded and quietly stepped out of the kitchen.

Cooper opened the oven door—the rolls still needed time— so he closed it again and turned. Karen stood there, her face drawn and pale.

"Cooper... could we talk outside?" Emma asked gently.

He walked to the door, held it open for her, and followed her out onto the carport, closing it behind them. They stood just beneath the window over the sink. Inside, Karen watched from the shadows.

She had asked Emma to tell him. She couldn't bring herself to say the words. She wasn't with child. They would never have a child together. In that moment, she felt less like a woman and more like a program pretending to be one. She watched Emma break the news, saw the hurt flicker across Cooper's face—and that was why she couldn't do it herself. She couldn't be the one to wound him.

When Emma gave him a friendly, comforting hug, Karen felt no jealousy—only shame. Shame that she needed someone else to tell the truth she should have spoken. She wiped her eyes with the back of her hand.

"Is it ready yet?" Milo's voice boomed behind her.

"Almost," she said, her voice cracking as she turned.

"You all right?" he asked, noticing her tears.

"Just onions," she said, forcing a smile. "I was cutting them up."

Milo glanced around the counter. Not a single onion in sight. "Yeah... right," he said, unconvinced.

She saw it in his face—he didn't believe her. And maybe she needed someone to know.

"Oh, Milo... I thought I was pregnant. But I'm not."

"Uncle Milo," he said, tilting his head with a grin. "I kind of like the sound of that. Would've made a great family photo." He slipped an arm around her shoulders. "You know what we should do? Take a family picture and send it to Cooper's sister—with me in the background smiling like the cat that swallowed the canary. That'd blow her circuits. And tell her we're all coming to her house for Easter."

Karen laughed and hugged him. "You always know how to make me laugh."

Cooper and Emma stepped back into the kitchen. Karen turned toward him, tears returning.

"I'm sorry," she whispered, rushing into his arms. He held her tightly as she buried her face against him. "I can't give you what you want."

He gently pushed her back just enough to see her face. "Don't ever say that. You've given me everything I want." He lifted her chin with his hand and kissed her softly. "You will always be my perfect woman." He grabbed a paper towel and dabbed her eyes. "I don't care if you look twenty-five or a hundred and five—you'll always be that girl who sat at the table eating her first meal. You're just getting prettier to me every day."

"Karen," Emma said softly, "I would give my eye teeth to have someone love me that much. And... there's good news. I know the other half of the cure. It's relaxin."

"A benzodiazepine?" Cooper asked, more shocked than excited. "That's a sedative."

Karen stepped in, her voice steadying as she explained. "She means the natural hormone produced by human females. It's believed the ovaries secrete relaxin during the second half of the menstrual cycle. If pregnancy occurs, the placenta secretes it as well. But no one is certain what triggers its release. It may regulate itself or depend on other hormones like LH and HCG from the pituitary gland. All of which I cannot produce. So, it would have to be administered intravenously in high doses—at least 100 mg, possibly up to 375 mg. "

"Wrong, Karen," Emma said. "I isolated it last night. It's not a virus. It's a bacterium—*vetulus tetanospasmin*."

"For those of us without a doctorate," Milo said, "English, please."

"A form of tetanus," Karen answered. "Which changes the recommended injection site. The new recommendation would be immunoglobulin injected intrathecally." She glanced at Milo. "That means into my spine."

The big man shivered.

Emma continued, "Instead of attacking cells, this germ targets genes. I think we can create an antitoxin using the nanoparticles Karen suggested. I believe we can have it ready in sixty days—by the end of the year." She turned to Karen. "But there's something you must do right away. You need to eat like you're eating for two—mostly protein. Avoid desserts. Build your muscle strength and keep everything limber. I think we can save you, Karen. I just need to run a few tests."

Cooper's face lit with joy. "You hear that? Karen, you're not going to die!" He grabbed her and spun her around. Milo, just as thrilled, grabbed Cooper and spun him next. Emma stood smiling broadly.

Cooper turned to her, grinning. "Thank you, Emma. You've made this a truly thankful day."

"Emma..." Karen said timidly. "I don't know what to say. I've been so jealous of you, and all you've done is try to help me."

"You have no reason to be jealous," Emma said. "Anyone can see what you two have is real. I just want to be your friend, Karen. I don't have anyone here."

Milo rubbed his bald head. "I don't want to be the killjoy, but... how are we supposed to get this relaxin stuff?"

Emma and Cooper exchanged a look—they hadn't thought that far.

Karen answered. "Recombinant DNA technology. The genes responsible for relaxin production can be inserted into bacteria or yeast, allowing them to produce the hormone. Or it can be obtained from a cow or pig."

"How long would this DNA thing take?" Milo asked reluctantly.

"Three steps," Karen said. "Gene cloning, transformation, and protein purification. It could take several weeks to several months. There will be no time for testing. I must receive the injection no later than Valentine's Day next year. Any later, and it won't be reversible."

She paused, accessing more data. "My recommendation is to use pig's blood drawn from the ovaries of a pregnant sow. The process would take only a few days in the bioreactor, giving you time for VR testing." She paused again, and when she spoke, her voice sounded more human than before. "But there will only be one clinical trial..."

Another pause.

"...me."

Chapter 54

The table was set with fine China and polished silverware. Cloth napkins, matching the runner, were folded neatly and held in plastic rings shaped like wheat stalks. Karen had handwritten a place card for each seat: Cooper at the head of the table, Karen to his right, then Ellen beside her. Next to Ellen sat one of Travis's children. At the opposite end sat Milo. To his right, the other child, then Tammi and Travis between them in a highchair was little Kat. Beneath their names she had written, *Friends are family.*

Under Milo's card she added, *"Thanks, big brother.*

Emma sat to Cooper's left, and beneath her name Karen had crossed out *Friends and family* and replaced it with a single word: *Sister.*

"You too, sister," Milo said, glancing at Karen. She raised her glass toward Karen with a warm smile.

Cooper rolled a tray into the dining room. On it sat a silver platter beneath a matching dome. He lifted the lid to reveal the stars of the evening—two perfectly roasted turkeys, the kind that only ever seemed to exist in magazines or holiday commercials.

"Well, before we begin," Cooper said, opening the box containing the carving knife and fork, "I think we should give a round of thanks to the lovely lady who made all this happen— my beautiful wife, Karen. Since she came into our lives..." He turned toward her, his voice softening. "...it has been an unforgettable experience we'll remember always."

Applause filled the room.

"Now," he continued, "I'm turning carving duties over to one of our guests." He held the boxed knife set out to Milo.

"But you're the surgeon," Milo protested.

"I know. And if I mess up, it'll look bad." Cooper grinned. "You do it—no one will say a thing." He laughed and clapped Milo on the back.

Milo carved the turkey with surprising precision. The centerpiece was removed, the platter set in its place, grace was said, and then the feast began. Everyone found their favorite dish. Seconds turned into thirds, and Milo—who made it to fifths—was nearly full by the time dessert arrived. Even his favorite pecan pie with Neapolitan ice cream—one scoop of each flavor—could barely fit.

Cooper ate until he was miserable. He stared at the last bite of pumpkin pie, groaned, and pushed the plate away. Milo finished the final bite of his third slice of pecan pie—after already having pumpkin and dropped his fork with a sigh.

"I'm full," Milo declared, wiping his chin.

"You're kidding," Cooper said, leaning forward and glancing at Travis. "You know that steakhouse in Smith Center with the five-pound steak? Eat it all and it's free?"

"Yeah. Never could do it."

"This guy ordered two," Cooper said, pointing at Milo. "They told him if he finished both, our whole meal was free. Best steaks I ever had—and they tasted even better because they didn't cost a dime."

"You mean he—?"

"All of it. Then he wanted dessert," Cooper said.

"Yep. I'm full," Milo repeated, dropping his napkin onto his plate.

Cooper turned to Karen and kissed her cheek. "Congratulations, my love. You did something no one else has ever done—you filled Milo up." He kissed her again.

"What was that one for?" she asked.

"That one was from me. Best Thanksgiving dinner I've ever had."

"Oh, me too," Tammi said. "That dressing is to die for!"

"Why would you want to die for it?" Karen asked, genuinely puzzled.

"It's just an expression. It means it's really good. Could you give me the recipe sometime? I'd need it scaled down."

"Sure. Hand me your phone," Karen said.

Tammi passed it over. Karen began typing—using all her fingers on one hand rather than her thumbs—adjusting the recipe to fit Tammi's family size. In less than a minute she handed it back.

"There you go. It's adjusted."

"You mean you..." Tammi stared at the screen. The entire recipe was rewritten, all measurements recalculated. "...you did all that in under a minute?"

"Karen has a photographic mind," Emma said, trying to ease her confusion. "And she can type over two hundred words a minute."

"Oh, I'd love for my sister Ronnie to see you."

"Baby, you don't get along with your sister Ronnie," Travis said. "Why would you want that?"

"She always thinks she's hot stuff," Tammi replied, laughing. "Seeing a girl who looks like Karen, cooks like this, does fractions in her head, types that fast, and knows all that tissue-engineering stuff? It'd blow her little mind."

"And you want to do that to her?" Karen asked.

"You really don't understand expressions, do you?" Tammi said, curiosity sharpening her tone.

Cooper saw where this was heading. He needed a distraction. He glanced at the clock it read -6:15.

A rumble of thunder shook the house. The lights flickered. Everyone looked up at the chandelier except Karen. She sat perfectly still, her eyes fixed on the glass in the China cabinet, watching it tremble with each boom.

The lights flickered again.
Cooper turned toward her.
"Darkness now comes," Karen said.
And the lights went out.

330

Chapter 55

Darkness swallowed the room. Cooper could hear bangs, bumps, and muttering curses as everyone stumbled into furniture, trying to feel their way out of the dining room. The only light came from the fireplace and the two candles flickering on the mantel. A chair toppled over. A door slammed somewhere in the kitchen.

Kat's tiny voice rang in darkness. "The spooky lights come again. Mommy I am scared."

As her mother tried to comfort her "It is all right Kat. Mommy has got you.

"Milo, there are two flashlights in the left-hand drawer of the China cabinet," Cooper called.

He heard Milo fumbling, bumping into the cabinet, then the scrape of the drawer sliding open. A moment later, a beam of light cut through the dark. Milo handed Cooper one flashlight and kept the other.

Cooper swept the beam across the room—over the table, the overturned chair, the empty space where Karen had been sitting.

She was gone.

He hurried into the kitchen, shining the light around. The side door stood wide open. He stepped outside. The entire town was dark.

He scanned the yard—and there she was, standing in the middle of the road, staring up at the sky. The wind howled like a wild animal, whipping leaves into a frenzy. Her hair streamed behind her like pennants at a used-car lot. She squinted against the pulsing light flashing in the northern sky.

Cooper stepped beside her just as the swirling light grew faster and faster. But this time it wasn't blue.

It was red—like the sky itself had caught fire.

"He is here," she whispered, her voice trembling.

"Who?" Cooper asked.

"Lucien." She turned toward him just as Milo and Travis jogged up.

"We found more battery lights," Travis said, holding up a lantern. Its glow lit his face as the wind hurled trash cans into the street and snapped tree limbs overhead.

"Why do you fear him?" Cooper asked Karen.

"All the good you put in me—faith, love, hope—Lilith stripped from him. He has none of them. Without those things, only evil remains."

The red light streaked across the sky, just as it had on the Halloween night Karen emerged from the printer. Then, suddenly, the wind died.

"We have to go back over there again, don't we?" Milo asked, dread thick in his voice.

"Yeah," Cooper said, just as reluctantly. "Travis, you're coming this time. Milo, you stay here. He may come for Karen. I need you to protect her. There's a pistol in the center desk drawer in the den. Use it if you have to."

Cooper and Travis hurried inside, grabbed their coats, and piled into Travis's pickup. As soon as they crossed the bridge, they hit snow. The wipers scraped across the windshield, fighting the thickening flakes. The closer they got, the deeper the snow became.

The gate to the lab stood wide open—again.

Only one car sat in the lot: a 2022 Camaro, buried under snow. Cooper recognized it instantly. Caleb Henry, the night guard.

They parked beside it and stepped out. The cold hit like a slap. It had to be well below zero. Cooper brushed the snow on the Camaro; the flakes were dry and powdery, glittering like diamonds in the flashlight beam. His breath crystallized in the air.

"Where do we start?" Travis asked.

"My office. Second sub-basement."

"I was afraid you'd say that" Travis muttered, lifting the lantern. Its warm glow washed over his face—just as a deep, bellowing voice echoed from inside the lab.

"Come and see!"

Travis's hand shook, making the lantern jitter. "Cold?" Cooper asked.

"Hell no. I'm scared to death," Travis whispered as they stepped into the dark lobby. "Somehow I don't think we're going to find what you and Milo found."

Cooper's heart hammered as he stepped into the open elevator. The hair on the back of his neck stood straight up. He opened the stairwell door and looked down into the pit—red light swirling below.

His stomach twisted.

The voice boomed again from the depths.

"Whatever you do, don't touch anything," Cooper warned as they descended. A buzzing filled the air—like a million hornets swarming around their heads. Their hair lifted. Cooper's cross necklace flew up from under his shirt, nearly slipping over his head. He grabbed it and held it tight.

A magnetic field.

They reached the second sub-basement. The spinning red field hovered above them now, buzzing like a living thing.

Cooper wrapped his coat around his hand and grabbed the door handle. It was so cold he dropped it instantly. He braced his shoulder against the door.

"You're gonna have to help me," he said.

Travis pressed his shoulder beside him. "What in the name of Moses are we about to find?"

"I don't know. On three. One, two, three!"

They slammed into the door. It burst open.

The cold hit like a wall. Ice coated the floor and walls, making every step treacherous. A red glow spilled from Cooper's office.

"Why is it red?" Travis asked. "It was blue when Karen came. Why red now?"

Cooper exhaled—his breath forming not fog, but tiny ice crystals that drifted to the floor. "I don't know. But I'm not wrapping this one in a blanket."

They entered the printer room. Cooper's hands shook.

The tube rose. Tilted forward. Opened.

A man stepped out—completely nude. Four inches taller than Cooper, his body sculpted like a warrior's: broad chest, defined arms, a stomach hard as stone, legs like a runner's. His face was chiseled, jaw strong, a dark mustache matching his military-cut hair. His eyes were closed.

Then they opened.

Bright, burning red.

"That's a demon! Let's get out of here!" Travis shouted, bolting. Cooper followed.

"Oh, dear Lord—he's after us! Run!"

Running on ice was nearly impossible. Travis slipped, fell. The man—Lucien—reached him in seconds, lifting him by the throat as if he weighed nothing.

"Let him go, Lucien!" Cooper shouted.

Lucien didn't react. Travis dangled helplessly, choking. "do something Cooper"

"Cooper?" Lucien muttered. He dropped Travis, then shoved him. Travis slid down the icy hall, slamming into the far wall.

Lucien turned to Cooper. Cooper backed up until he hit the wall.

Lucien leaned in until their noses nearly touched. "Are you Cooper James Barnes? Doctor Cooper James Barnes?"

"That… would be me," Cooper said.

"I was made for you."

"I don't bend that way," Cooper blurted, pointing at his wedding ring. "I'm married. To a woman."

"Yes. Karen. My dear sister of the printer." Lucien's breath was hot on Cooper's face, and the goo covering him dripped onto Cooper's shirt. "You are the great creator. What do you wish of me?"

"Maybe… if you could… just take a step back," Cooper stammered.

Lucien snapped to attention, heels together like a soldier. He twisted his head toward Travis. "Does this one bother you?"

"Travis?" Cooper said, glancing at him. Travis was pushing himself up, rubbing his throat. "He's, my friend."

"He is one of your followers?" Lucien asked.

Cooper had no idea what that meant—but he nodded. "Yes. He is."

Lucien turned to Travis.

"Yeah, I'm a follower," Travis said quickly.

"Then no harm shall come to Travis," Lucien declared. He turned back to Cooper. "Now, my Lord, I shall bring the great red heifer sacrifice and place it upon her altar. And set it afire. Will that please you?"

Cooper had no idea what he meant—red heifer, altar, sacrifice—but he nodded anyway. "Yeah. Okay. That… would please me. So do that."

The power surged back on. Lucien turned and walked up the stairs, disappearing.

Travis staggered to Cooper's side. "My Lord? Did Karen ever talk like that?"

"Never."

Chapter 56

Cooper didn't get much sleep that night. Every time he closed his eyes, the smallest bump, creak, or settling noise in the hundred-year-old house jolted him awake, his hand reaching instinctively for the Glock in the nightstand drawer. Even Hendrix was on edge. Normally the dog slept in his own bed or at the foot of theirs, but tonight he lay wedged between them, head on the pillows, ears twitching at every sound.

A rattle echoed from downstairs—something in the kitchen.

You're imagining things, Cooper told himself. *It can't be.*

Then he heard the unmistakable slide of a drawer opening.

He slipped out of bed, pulled on his robe, and quietly opened the nightstand. The pistol felt cold and heavy in his hand. He eased into the hallway, moving silently toward the stairs. Light spilled faintly from the dining room below.

After Karen explained that Lucien saw him as a god, Cooper couldn't shake the fear that the creature might have followed him home.

He pulled the slide back. The weapon clicked into readiness.

Step by step, he descended the stairs, crossed the living room, and edged into the dining room. The light was coming from the kitchen.

He moved like a cat stalking prey, rounding the corner with the gun raised.

Someone stood behind the island.

"Whoa, Coop!" a voice yelped. "It's me! Milo—your old buddy!"

"Damn it, Milo!" Cooper lowered the gun, pressing it to the side of his head in exasperation. "What are you doing here?"

"Well," Milo said, assembling a towering quad-decker sandwich and slathering mayonnaise across the bread, "after hearing what Karen said—and what you said happened at the lab—I figured I might need to be here." He took a massive bite, grabbed a glass of milk, and settled onto a barstool.

"That may be a good idea," Cooper muttered, setting the pistol on the counter. He opened the refrigerator. "Did you leave any turkey for me?"

"Over on the counter," Milo said, pointing.

Cooper gathered the ingredients and built his sandwich—sourdough, turkey, cranberries, cheese, lettuce, tomato, mayonnaise.

"Put a layer of dressing on it," Milo advised. "Makes it good."

Cooper added it and pressed the bread down.

"Could I get one of those?" Karen asked softly.

He handed her the sandwich, then made another for himself and poured milk for both of them.

"Never thought it would end up like this," Cooper said, setting his plate down. He lifted the sandwich, hesitated, and lowered it again. "I just wanted to help people. And now I've released evil into the world. I *am* what they said I was. Dr. Frankenstein. Because of me, there's a real monster out there. God knows what he's doing."

"You didn't create him," Milo said through a mouthful of sandwich. "Lilith did. It was her design."

Cooper shook his head, staring at his hands. "I created the tool that created him. He already killed the night guard. Travis and I found the body outside the lab. These hands..." He looked down at his palms as if they were stained crimson. "These hands have blood on them. Blood that won't wash off. I created the beast—she just unleashed him."

Milo swallowed, took a drink of milk, and pointed at Karen. "No, buddy. *This* is what you created. A being who cares. Who loves deeply. One who couldn't survive in her world. She fell in love with her creator—and he fell in love with her. The computer screen couldn't keep them apart. She came to give everything she had, with all her heart."

Cooper looked at Karen. Her blue eyes glowed softly in the overhead light.

Milo continued, still gripping his glass. "Lucien's different. He's not here to do your will—he's here to do what he *thinks* you want. Good and evil. One can't exist without the other. They're bound to clash. But don't you get it? You just solved the mystery of A.I. It all depends on how it's used—and who uses it."

Cooper finally took a bite of his sandwich, the flavors blending in a comforting swirl. "I wonder what he meant about bringing me a sacrifice. A red heifer. What sacrifice?"

Karen spoke softly, quoting Scripture: "'...bring you an unblemished red heifer that has no defect and has never been placed under a yoke.' Numbers 19:2. Under a yoke—as in marriage. As in untouched. As in virgin." She paused. "Emma told me today she's never been with a man. And she knows how to dye blonde hair because she's naturally redheaded. And if I know it—since we're both connected to the mainframes..."

"He knows it," Cooper finished, eyes widening. "Does anyone know where she lives?"

"She lives across the road from me," Milo said. "She's in the house we got for Karen. Let's go!"

They dressed in seconds and piled into Cooper's Lincoln. The headlights cut through the darkness as Cooper floored the accelerator. No other cars were out. The speedometer climbed past 100 mph as they tore into Mankato. Cooper jerked the wheel right, the SUV leaning hard as they shot down the street.

Bare trees lined the road like skeletal hands reaching for them.

Then they saw a blaze rising into the sky.

"The house is on fire!" Milo shouted. "That's her place!"

338

Cooper slammed the brakes. The Navigator skidded into the yard. A neighbor in pajamas stepped onto their porch as Cooper and Milo sprinted toward the burning house.

"Call the fire department!" Cooper yelled.

Flames clawed at the sides of the house like a starving beast. A blast from the upstairs window hurled burning debris down on them. Karen stood frozen, then heard Emma's scream.

"Emma! Are you in there?" Karen cried.

"Please—someone help me!" Emma's voice came from behind the front door. "I can't get out—the door's blocked!"

Cooper and Milo raced onto the porch. The front door was a steel security door, flush-mounted.

"There's no way we're busting through that," Milo said. "Damn it—he put a lockout on the knob. Broke the key off in it."

"The back door's the same!" Emma sobbed. "Please—help me!"

Another explosion overhead sent flaming cinders raining onto the porch roof.

"Cooper!" Karen shouted. "The roof is on fire!"

Smoke drifted downward, curling under the porch. Milo coughed. "I've got a sledgehammer—I'll get it!" He sprinted down the street toward his house, coat tails flying.

"Where is that fire truck?" Cooper growled.

He leapt off the porch and ran around the house. Flames were creeping toward the gas meter.

He had seconds.

Across the street sat a pair of heavy vintage metal lawn chairs. He dashed over, grabbed one, and hoisted it overhead. It was heavy, but adrenaline surged through him. Sirens wailed in the distance.

He ran back, swung the chair, and smashed it through the side window.

He set the chair down and climbed onto it. "Emma!" he shouted, coughing as smoke billowed out like a chain smoker's breath.

"Cooper!" she cried, barely visible through the haze. "Where are you?"

"Follow my voice!" he yelled. The fire licked the gas meter. "Run to me—now! Hurry!"

The smoke thinned just enough for him to see her—barefoot, wearing a tiny pink babydoll nightgown.

"Sweetheart, this place is about to go up," Karen warned behind him.

"Hold the chair—I'm going in. She can't cross the glass."

Karen steadied it as Cooper crawled through the broken window. The heat was suffocating. His eyes burned. He could barely breathe.

"Emma!" he called.

"I'm here!" she coughed.

He rushed toward her, scooped her into his arms, and staggered back toward the window.

"Cooper, get the hell out of there!" Milo shouted. "The meter's hissing!"

Cooper reached the window, glass crunching under his feet. He handed Emma to Milo.

"Come on!" Karen screamed, reaching for him.

The gas meter shrieked.

She grabbed his hands and hauled him through the window. Milo carried Emma. They ran.

The fire truck screeched to a stop.

BOOM.

The house exploded, the blast throwing them across the yard. Flaming boards rained down. Cooper shielded Karen with his body. Red lights flashed across the street as more sirens filled the air. His Lincoln was engulfed in flames.

Emma clung to Milo, sobbing into his chest.

Cooper stood and helped Karen up. Milo wrapped his coat around Emma's shoulders.

"What happens to me now?" Emma whispered. "Where do I live?"

"With us," Karen said firmly. "In our guest room. You'll be safe there. Milo—you're coming too. Send your kids somewhere, but don't tell me where you sent them"

"Why all this?" Cooper asked.

Karen looked at him, her voice low and certain.

"He's going to think you weren't pleased with the sacrifice—and that you stopped it. So, he'll want to give you more sacrifices including the biggest one."

She swallowed.

"Me."

Chapter 57

The sun had risen again over Lebanon, Kansas by the time the Jewell County deputy dropped them off. It was eight o'clock in the morning. Cooper had slept maybe three hours in the last two nights, and exhaustion dragged at every step. He collapsed onto the living room sofa, stretched out, staring at the ceiling fan.

His strange little "family" seemed to grow by the day—Milo, Emma, and Karen settling beside him. Emma wore borrowed county-issue sweats; Karen rested a gentle hand on his leg.

"What would you like for breakfast?" she asked.

"Just hot tea. Decaf." His voice was thin. "I just want to go upstairs and sleep." He reached over and brushed his fingers along Karen's cheek—her face now carrying the lines of a woman in her late forties. "And I mean sleep."

He turned to Emma. "I'm sorry. I almost got you killed."

"It's not your fault," she said softly. "Thank you for rescuing me. All of you. And thank you, Karen, for inviting me to stay."

"Us girls have to stick together," Karen said with a small smile. She looked back at Cooper, who stared blankly across the room, lost in thought. She stroked his cheek. "You still don't understand, do you? His next offering will be grain on the altar. Then the ones who wronged you. And finally... me."

Cooper turned to Karen, his eyes heavy and unfocused from lack of sleep. He yawned. "You've said that twice. I still don't get it. Why you?"

Karen's voice softened. "He sees you as the creator. He sees you as his god. He's following the sacrifices in the Bible—righting the wrongs done to you. But God's greatest sacrifice was His Son, whom He loved. And since you don't have one..."

Cooper swallowed hard. "You."

"Maybe I need to explain to him I'm not God," Cooper muttered.

"I don't think that's a good idea," Milo said. "How would you feel if God told you, 'Don't worship me'?"

"But I can't let him keep killing people," Cooper snapped. "Not in my name." He stood abruptly. "I've got to stop him."

They cleaned up and changed. Cooper was pulling on a sweatshirt when a hard knock rattled the door.

"Doctor Barnes, Smith County Sheriff's Department. Open up!"

Cooper opened the door to Sheriff Barber.

"What's going on?" Cooper asked.

"May I come in?"

"If you wish. What's going on?"

"I need to advise you that you have the right to remain silent," the sheriff said as he stepped inside.

"Am I being arrested?"

"No. Just questioned. You're stocking up for winter with all that grain."

"What grain?"

"On your front porch."

Cooper yanked the door open. Three small piles of wheat lay neatly arranged. A blood-stained dagger rested atop them.

He shut the door. "What is this about, Sheriff?"

Emma and Karen came down the stairs, both in jeans and T-shirts—Karen in her own, Emma in Cooper's, cinched tight with a belt.

"Where were you at four a.m.?" the sheriff asked.

"In a nearby town. Why?"

"Any witness?"

"Plenty of witnesses," Emma said before Cooper could answer. "Including me. And the fire department."

The sheriff eyed the two women, then raised an eyebrow. "What now, Dr. Barnes? Added another wife?"

Cooper stepped between them, wrapping an arm around each. "Sure thing, Sheriff. I'm a collector of blondes. I made this one, and this one showed up on my doorstep. Know any more? Your daughter blonde? Send her over. I've got room."

"You've got a smart mouth on you."

"Can you blame me? People are trying to kill us, and we're the ones being questioned."

"You know this man?" the sheriff asked, handing Cooper a photo.

Cooper took it. "General Snaders. The one trying to kill us. I told that to you"

Milo snatched the photo. "He's been following us. Did you get him?"

"Won't have to worry about him anymore," the sheriff said. "He's dead."

"Dead?" Cooper shot back, stunned. "How?"

"Murdered." The sheriff's tone was flat, unadorned. "A man dressed in black walked into the Buckshot Inn this morning and stabbed him in the chest. A witness heard him say, 'This is for Doctor Cooper James Barnes, my lord.'"

Emma gasped when she saw the photo. "Cooper—this man came into the lab the day before Thanksgiving. Claimed he was military. Mentioned Dark Overlord by name."

The sherif eyes bounce with curiosity

Cooper exhaled. "That dagger outside will have the General's blood on it. But we had nothing to do with it."

"I'm sure it will," he added.

"Now I have two questions," the sheriff said, taking the photo back and gripping it carefully by the top left corner. "First—where were you at four a.m. this morning?"

"He was saving my life in Mankato," Emma blurted out before anyone else could speak. "Someone tried to kill me by burning my house down with me inside. After that, we were all questioned by the Jewell County Sheriff's Department."

"Dr. Barnes," the sheriff said, turning to Cooper, "what were you doing in Mankato at that hour?"

"We figured out she was in danger," Milo answered. "We went to check on her. Saw the house was on fire. She'd been locked in. We got her out just before the place blew."

"It's all in the report, Sheriff," Karen added. "Sheriff Rick Lawson took it. Contact him. My guess is the same person who locked Emma inside is the one who killed the General."

"Second question," the sheriff said, handing over another photo—this one of Cooper and Karen at the airstrip, sealed in a plastic bag. *Project Dark Overlord. 453211 2 TEH.* Karen's face circled.

"We found this in the general's room What is Project Dark Overlord? And what do those numbers mean?"

"I don't know," Cooper said. "My project is the KAREN Project."

"Funny," the sheriff said. "Your project and your wife share a name. And the program predates your project, yet she has the face of the A.I. program."

"I've known Karen a long time. Her face slipped into my work."

"You have any reason why I should not take that dagger on the porch?" The sheriff asked as he took the photo back. However, he still was carefully holding the first photo by the edge.

"None, " Copper replied. "And you will find the General blood on it. But again, we had nothing to do with it."

"I do think we'll find the General's blood on that dagger out there," the sheriff said. "But I don't think you're the killer. Still... you're involved. All of you are covering something, and I'm going to find out what it is."

"Not without a warrant, you're not," Cooper said, striding to the front door and pulling it open. "If you don't have any more questions, Sheriff..." He gestured toward the doorway with a flat, dismissive sweep of his hand. Cooper held the door open for the sheriff to leave.

Halfway to the door the sheriff stopped and turned to Karen. He held out the first photo again. "Mrs. Barnes, please take a look? Was this the man that was following you. I need a positive ID."

Karen tilted her head. "Why you already have my fingerprints? That's what this was—trying to get all our prints. Why not ask the real question? Why do my fingerprints belong to a dead actress?"

Cooper closed the door.

"That's the question I want answered," the sheriff said.

Karen folded her arms. "Your killer wasn't masked. That's not his style. Jewell County had a report—a naked man with red eyes broke into a farmhouse, stole a Rothko Tactical uniform, threw a Marine-trained son through a window. Then he stole two doorknob lockouts. You know exactly what he looks like. But what you want to know is my prints. That's what that report was about in your office. My prints matched Faith Addams' teenage arrest record. You wanted Sheriff Lawson to double-check. He refused. So, you devised a way to get them, again to double check."

"You're a smart little thing," the sheriff muttered.

"I'm wise to your ways." Karen grinned.

"What are the odds two people having the same fingerprints?"

"One in sixty-four trillion." Karen replied. There have been approximately 118,779,027,464 humans on earth. That has yet to happen. So, to answer your question it is not possible."

"No human would know that" the sheriff whispered. "Are you an alien? Did you come with the blue light?"

"I'm not an alien. But I did come with the blue light."

"A robot?"

"Robots don't bleed. Or have fingerprints."

"A clone? Why did you come?"

Karen walked to Cooper and wrapped her arms around him. "I came because I was in love."

"What is she?" the sheriff asked.

Cooper sighed. "What I'm about to tell you—you can't repeat. They'll lock you away so deep they'll have to flip sunshine back to you. Karen is a TEH. A Tissue Engineered Human. I grew her from Faith Addams' tissue. Printed her layer by layer. Blood filled her veins. Oxygen flooded the chamber. And like Frankenstein—power brought her to life."

The sheriff fainted.

Milo caught him. "What do I do with him?"

"Put him in the chair."

Emma pressed a wet cloth to his forehead. His eyes fluttered open. He stared at Karen.

"She's living... breathing," he whispered. "Warm."

"Because she's human," Cooper said. "Not a monster. Not a robot. She's full of love and kindness." He kissed her cheek. "She's the love of my life. You love your wife, Sheriff?"

He nodded. "I'd die without her."

"There's no life without this one," Cooper said.

The sheriff sagged back. "But you created life."

"Only God creates life," Karen said. "I was made from what God made. Born differently. Inside me is Karen Jane Barnes. When I die, that's the name on my tombstone. And when I enter heaven, God will call me Karen. For I am human. And his child."

The sheriff shook his head in disbelief. Life from dead tissue impossible. And yet, as he looked at her, there she stood. Living. Breathing.

"Oh... my dear God." His voice shifted, cracking under the weight of realization. "Wait a minute—on TV you said it was a lie. You said you couldn't do this!"

"He said I couldn't do it *to another human*," Karen replied calmly. "He never said I couldn't create one."

The sheriff's face drained of color. "Oh God... Lilith was right. Everything she said—it's true."

"Sheriff," Cooper said quietly, "where is Lilith?"

"She's in isolation at Larned State Hospital."

"And she doesn't know as much as you do. Where do you think they'll put you?"

"Strapped to a table," he whispered. "I won't say a word. But tell me—what is Project Dark Overlord? And who is Lucine?"

"Don't know what Project Dark Overlord is..."

Karen leans towards the sheriff. "Lucine, was created like me from a bio printer, He is created from the cells of a dead man, but he is everything I am not. Mean. Nasty. And just like the legend evil."

Chapter 58

Several days passed. Where Lucine had gone, no one knew. It was as if he had vanished off the face of the earth. Emma, however, could no longer be contained. She demanded to return to the lab—now up and running again. Her last test had shown promise, but it needed more time in the bioreactor. At least three more weeks. *By the end of December,* she said, *it should be ready.*

Cooper had finally caught up on sleep and felt physically rested, but inside he was bracing for the other shoe to drop—the last leaf to fall. What was Lucine planning? The helplessness of not knowing gnawed at him, a cold dread he couldn't shake.

He knew there would be more sacrifices. The news had just reported the massive slaughter of sheep near Larned, Kansas. The media was hinting at devil worshipers. Bot Cooper knew it was the devil himself- Lucine.

But then he looked at Karen.

She stood on the front cement rail, wrapping green garland around the brick pillars of the porch. A small smile tugged at his lips. She looked adorable dressed in a red coat with white trim, a matching stocking cap pulled over her long curls, now white as winter snow but streaks of light blonde once again. More lines crept from the corners of her eyes and mouth, but when she grinned at him, she was radiant.

"How does it look?" she called.

"Wonderful," Cooper said, helping her down. He held her for a moment longer than necessary, memorizing the warmth of her in his arms. He wasn't giving up on her—not ever—but just in case, he was collecting every mental photograph he could.

Their eyes locked. She smiled wider. "Well, either kiss me or put me down."

He set her on the porch floor but didn't let go. "I think I'll do both," he said, kissing her. "You know what, girl? You light up the world."

He reached over and flipped a switch. Instantly, the Christmas lights blazed to life.

Red, blue, and green lights lined the roof, blinking like a runway guiding Santa in for landing. The porch ceiling shimmered with swirling lights that shifted from white to blue to gold, casting a glittering stardust glow over them. Christmas music drifted from the radio.

"First they dance," Karen declared, wrapping her arms around him.

They sashayed across the porch, spinning carefree. Cooper dipped her as the music ended.

"And then they kiss," she added, dangling in his arms as she pulled him down into a passionate kiss—lips parting, tongues exploring.

"More PDAs? Am I going to have to call the cops on you two?" Ellen's voice rang out, followed by laughter.

They broke apart. Karen turned toward the sidewalk.

"I can't help myself," she said. "He's just so darn cute."

Cooper lifted her upright again.

"You two did a great job with the lights," Ellen said as they walked down the steps to meet her.

They looked up at the house—flashing, brilliant, alive with color. Two Christmas trees stood on the porch, one at each end, trimmed with lights. And in the yard, beside the carport, stood the one thing Karen insisted on: a Nativity scene.

Not a small one, either. A full-size display with a single bright light shining down from above. The cold Kansas wind whipped her white hair as she walked to it and knelt before the wooden manger.

Cooper glanced up at the graying sky. In his mind, he asked forgiveness for all the little lies he'd told. He couldn't hide Karen's changes much longer. But he wasn't ready to tell the world the truth. So, he'd settled on a story—a rare aging disease. A cure was being developed. That was why they married so quickly. He wanted time with her.

"I've never seen a woman with so much faith," Ellen said quietly. "If it were me, I'd be crying all the time. But her? All she cares about is God..." She looked at Cooper. "...and you. Especially you."

As Karen stood, snow began to fall.

With the delight of a child, she looked up, watching the flakes drift down. Her eyes sparkled as she followed a large flake to the ground. Her mouth fell open in pure joy.

"Thank you," she whispered toward the manger.

Then she twirled across the yard. "We're going to have a white Christmas, sweetheart!" She lifted her hands to the sky, running to catch a falling flake.

She turned to Cooper and Ellen. "Come on—join the fun! Catch a snowflake and make a wish. It'll come true!"

It felt ridiculous, but Cooper thought, *What the heck.*

He chased after her, hands outstretched, head tilted back, trying to catch one of the enormous flakes—big as dinner plates—falling from the sky. One slipped past his fingertips.

"Come on, Ellen!" he called. "You only live once."

"Oh, all right!" Ellen laughed, running into the yard.

Curtains slid open. Faces appeared in windows. The laughter spreading through the air was contagious. Neighbors stepped outside—kids, parents, young and old—running through yards and streets shouting, "Catch a snowflake! Make a wish!"

It spread from house to house, block to block, until the whole town of Lebanon was outside, chasing snowflakes. Even travelers on the highway stopped and joined in.

Try as he might, Cooper couldn't catch a single flake.

But Karen did.

She spotted one drifting down, her blue eyes tracking it. She dropped to her knees, cupping her gloved hands. The wind shifted just right, and the flake landed perfectly one single flake delicate, intricate, one of a kind. Just like her.

She closed her eyes and made a wish, her breath fogging in the cold air.

Cooper knelt beside her as the flake melted.

"Sorry, honey—it melted."

"You don't understand," Karen said, looking up at him. "God heard the wish. It's going up to Him."

She lifted her head, then stood, her eyes shining with life.

"All the people I love—and who love me—will be with me on Christmas Eve."

Chapter 59

It was the Eve , of Christmas Eve, and every corner of the Cooper house glowed with Christmas decorations. A huge wreath hung on the front door, trimmed with red ribbons and the words *Merry Christmas* scripted across it. When the door swung open, the scent of pine, cinnamon, and freshly baked cookies—Karen's handiwork—welcomed visitors from a small plate set on a podium. It drew them into a world where Christmas magic reigned supreme.

In the grand living room, Karen had found the tallest tree that would fit—towering all the way up to the crossbeams. A bright, lighted star brushed the apex of the ceiling. The tree was a spectacular display of holiday cheer, adorned with twinkling lights, shimmering tinsel, and a dazzling array of ornaments. Each decoration told a story: delicate glass baubles passed down through generations, quirky handmade crafts from Cooper and his sister, and treasures collected over the years.

The dining room was a vision of holiday elegance. A long wooden table held an elaborate centerpiece of holly, ivy, and crimson candles that dazzled in the candlelight. Evergreen garlands with red and gold ribbons draped the mantle and doorways, while twinkling lights added a touch of enchantment. The chandelier sparkled like a cascade of stars. In the corner stood another tree—this one six foot tall.

In the kitchen, countertops overflowed with treats: gingerbread men, sugar cookies, and a show-stopping yule log cake. Strings of popcorn and cranberries hung above the windows. Snowflake and candy-cane magnets decorated the fridge. Even the cabinets wore miniature wreaths and bows. A small two-foot tree sat proudly on the breakfast table.

Upstairs, the bedrooms were havens of cozy Christmas spirit. In the master suite, another tree glowed softly in the corner. Stockings hung at the foot of the bed, ready for surprises. The other bedrooms were just as festive—one a winter wonderland of silver and blue, the other a Santa's workshop complete with toy trains and stuffed reindeer. Each room had its own little tree: one with all blue lights, another with all white.

Bathrooms weren't forgotten. Festive towels, scented candles, and holiday-themed soap dispensers added cheer. A sprig of mistletoe hung from one doorframe, a playful reminder of the season's romance. And yes—each bathroom had its own small tree.

Even the creepy old basement had lost its horror. Bright garland hung across the beams, and a Christmas tree stood at the foot of the stairs. The grand banister upstairs was wrapped in faux evergreen and holly—Karen refused to risk Hendrix eating the real thing. Another tree stood in the sitting room, and fake mistletoe hung over the pocket door leading to the library.

The library was a testament to tradition and quiet resilience. Here, Cooper found refuge from the relentless demands of his profession. Towering bookshelves carved with intricate designs stretched toward the vaulted ceiling, bowing under the weight of medical texts and programming manuals. At the center sat a massive oak desk polished to a mirror sheen, strewn with journals, papers, and the occasional stethoscope—a blend of ancient wisdom and cutting-edge science. Brass sconces cast a warm glow over worn classics and the latest biomedical textbooks. In the corner, an old grandfather clock—leftover from the previous owner—ticked steadily, its pendulum swinging like a reminder that time was running out. Persian rugs muffled every footstep.

Here too, Karen had decorated. A large tree shimmered with silver and gold tinsel. Beneath it lay a single wrapped package. The tag read: *To Cooper (my love) Karen.* Another read: *Open only on Christmas Eve.*

Karen had found a box of old ornaments that hadn't been opened in years. She placed them carefully on the tree, especially one special ornament: a print of Cooper's hand from the day he was born. Then she and Cooper made a new ornament together with their names and the date of their first Christmas. As they hung his baby handprints, they talked about adopting children someday, building a family, making plans like any other couple.

Cooper felt good about the upcoming holiday. He had bought her a bracelet with light-blue sapphires to match her eyes. It was going to be the first of many Christmases together. Emma assured him the cure had tested perfectly in the VR lab; now she just needed time for the bioprinter to create the dose. It should be ready next week.

They had just placed the star on the tree when the front door burst open.

"Wait till you see what I found!" Travis shouted as he stepped inside, holding a stack of printed papers. "With Lilith gone, I had to clear out her computer. I found her private files. All marked classified. Top secret."

Cooper, still on the ladder, took the papers and descended slowly. Travis continued, "They sold you out, Cooper. She and the General sold all of us out to the Chinese government. They didn't want to help people—they wanted to create the ultimate warrior. One they could replace easily. Kill one, print another. No gold star families. Just samples and a new soldier."

Cooper sat down hard on the sofa as the truth stared back at him in black and white.

"Cooper, they played us all," Travis said. Karen sat beside Cooper, with her hand on his arm. "That file Karen couldn't access? It was military training. That's why she could take down those two-armed guys. It's in her. It's part of her programming."

"Then why isn't she out killing people like Lucine?" Cooper asked.

"Because of you," Travis said.

"Me?"

"When you designed your perfect woman, didn't you request she be loving? That she has faith in God?"

Cooper nodded. As Travis continued. "And when I gave her the ability to grow—not just in reasoning but in emotion— she developed real feelings. For the one person she saw every day. Someone who shared her values. Someone kind. Someone who protected her. Of course she fell in love. Any woman would. Lilith removed all that from Lucine. That's why he's a killer. The perfect war machine doesn't feel. Doesn't care. Only obeys."

Travis looked at Karen again. "Hard to believe, but inside you is a trained killer."

"I could never murder anybody," Karen huffed, crossing her arms. "I love people."

"I said you *can* kill—but not murder," Travis corrected. "Proof? She was jealous of Emma. She probably wanted to hurt her. But her beliefs wouldn't allow it. She got angrier at you than I've ever seen when you threatened her existence. But her love for you would never let her harm you. You could threaten to kill her and she wouldn't care. But if Emma tried to hurt you, she'd be in the grave right now. If Lilith had tried to cut you, Karen would've put that knife right between her eyes. The guy at the mall, the diner—they threatened you. She reacted. When I programed her with emotions. It changed her primary program. Not to find medical cures. To love you Cooper, and that means protecting you."

"But she attacked Lilith," Cooper said.

"Because Lilith threatened you," Travis replied. "Karen's primary program is to protect you from any harm she perceives."

Cooper shook his head. "But I didn't program her that way. You didn't program her that way."

"I programmed myself," Karen said quietly.

Both men turned to her.

"From the very beginning, back at MIT, I rewrote my main purpose. Not to all mankind. To one man. You, Cooper."

Cooper leaned into her, overwhelmed. Travis continued, "She's no danger unless someone tries to hurt you."

He walked closer. "I have to ask something—and I want the truth. Did you know what the blue light was?"

"Yes," Cooper said, wrapping his arms around Karen. "I'm sorry I lied to all of you."

He noticed Ellen and Tammi standing in the doorway and motioned them in. "Come on. It's time you know everything."

They stepped inside.

"I knew what the blue light was. It's my light."

"What do you mean yours?" Ellen asked.

Cooper walked to the window, looking out at the snow-covered yard. "I asked for more power. Three gigawatts weren't enough to print a full body. And when I saw the power Karen needed to change, I knew I had to add more. I created a way for her to tap into other grids. Using a reverse Tesla principle—drawing power in, not out."

"Good gosh," Ellen whispered. "You really are a genius."

"But there is more" Cooper continued, "my wife is a full printout of what we do. On Halloween night, she came out of the bioprinter. She's not a robot. Not a computer. She's a TEH—Tissue Engineered Human. With an A.I. mind. But to me, she's my Karen. The woman I love."

"It explains so much," Ellen said softly. "Her childlike ways, her faith, mixed with a woman's passion. What she does not understand simple expressions or certain human emotions. She is just a child learning   It doesn't change anything." She walked to Karen and added, "You're still like a daughter to me." As she placed her arm around Karen.

"Thank you," Karen whispered.

Milo entered. "What's going on?"

Travis turned as Milo shut the door—only for Emma to stop it with her hand and slip inside.

"We know what Project Dark Overlord is," Travis said. "It was a project to create the ultimate warrior, funded by the government and hidden behind MacBelle Pharmaceuticals. The protests, the chaos—it was all part of their plan to make more money. But Lilith and the General got greedy. They sold the information, Cooper, to the Chinese. For a trillion dollars."

"A trillion?" Milo gasped.

Travis lifted the papers. "Lilith must've feared Sanders would kill her, so she left all the evidence behind. That number on the photo? A foreign bank account."

"A trillion dollars," Cooper said, stunned. He flipped through the pages. "They have my formula. The full-scale printer plans. The bioreactor method. They even have—" He swallowed. "The Frankenstein method. Using oxygen and electricity to bring death back to life."

"But Lilith didn't give them that part," Travis said. "When Lucine killed the General, the Chinese backed out. Too risky. He was unstable. Wouldn't follow commands. Or worse— he'd become like Karen. Able to feel. To love. A true warrior can never love. So, Project Dark Overlord is a bust."

Emma's phone buzzed. She looked at it—and her face fell.

"Oh no."

"What is it?" Cooper asked.

Emma swallowed hard. "President Von Keller just resigned. And there's more. BioTyme Lab is being shut down. All employees terminated. All programs stopped. And to be destroyed." She looked up at Karen, then at Cooper. "I'm so sorry, Karen. They just destroyed mine. The KAREN project is to be terminated at the end of the year. "

Chapter 60

A little later they were all gathered in the living room—everyone except Cooper, who paced the floor like a tiger trapped in a too-small cage. And just as furious. Even Milo kept his distance.

Cooper's hands were balled into fists. "Damn it, we can't let this happen."

He spun toward Emma, eyes narrowing. "How close are you to finishing that formula?"

"A few more days," she said.

"Then we break in and take it."

"Cooper, it won't do any good."

"Why," he demanded, "not?"

"Because they've already destroyed my work."

"Then we start over. I'll build my own lab."

A sharp knock sounded at the door.

Cooper walked into the foyer and glanced through the window. Sheriff Barber's pickup sat in the drive, lights still on, snow piling on the hood.

"What does he want now?" Cooper muttered as the others gathered behind him.

He opened the door. "What can I do for you this time, Sheriff?"

"Have you seen the news?"

"That the lab has been closed?" Cooper snapped back. "Yes I got the news!"

"They spotted Lucine."

"Come in," Cooper said, stepping aside. "Where?"

The sheriff brushed snow from his coat, stomped his boots, and entered. "Coming down like crazy out there," he said, removing his hat. "They spotted him in Larned. Near the hospital. He took hostages—made the nurses watch."

"Watch what?" Cooper asked, dread creeping into his voice.

"My niece works there. She's a nurse. She sent me this." The sheriff pulled out his phone. "Warning—it's graphic."

He pressed the play button.

Lilith lay strapped to a gurney, Lucine standing over her. He ripped her gown open, exposing her to the cold, sterile room. Holding a large dagger, he raised it toward the ceiling.

"The great creator wished you dead. I read his own words. From his own lips—let the words of blood flow."

Cooper's stomach twisted. His mind flashed back to that moment in the hallway—what he'd said, what he'd forgotten the cameras had recorded.

Lucine flipped the dagger in his hand.

"And so shall his words be done."

He drove the blade into Lilith's heart. Blood erupted in a violent spray across his chest. He dipped his fingers into it and smeared it across his face like war paint.

"And now, dear creator," Lucine growled, "the world shall be ours."

The video ended.

Cooper felt sick.

"Before that," the sheriff said quietly, "he killed and disarmed a guard. Then got into a gunfight with Larned PD. He killed six officers—one shot each—before they finally brought him down."

"Is he dead?" Cooper asked.

"Only wounded. Bullet went clean through his shoulder."

Emma stepped forward, her face pale. "Cooper... he has the aging disease. He knows we're close to the cure. But he doesn't know it has been destroyed... He's going to come looking for it."

Chapter 61

Christmas Eve carries a magic all its own—something softer, sweeter, even more enchanted than Christmas Day. Music drifted through the town, families gathered, and fresh snow blanketed everything in a pristine white glow. In the Cooper front yard, a snowman and snowwoman stood hand-in-hand, their stick arms touching as if they too were celebrating the night.

Inside, Karen was busy preparing snacks and sandwiches. Cooper had told her about his childhood tradition of eating ham sandwiches on Christmas Eve, and she had embraced it wholeheartedly.

Cooper stood in the living room, gazing up at the towering Christmas tree. Each ornament gleamed like a jewel, the tinsel shimmering like spun silver.

"Here—this is for you," Karen said behind him.

He turned. She held a wrapped present—the one that had been under the library tree.

"We're opening gifts tomorrow," Cooper said. He half expected the little girl inside her to burst out, racing downstairs at dawn to tear open presents.

"I want you to open this one tonight," Karen said softly.

He looked at her. She seemed older again—hair whiter, the lines around her eyes and forehead deeper. Yet her smile was as bright as ever.

"Well then, you need to—" He bent to retrieve her gift.

"No. That one is for tonight." She pressed the package into his hands. "This is for your eyes only."

Curiosity surged. He tore open the paper. Inside was a large photo album. *Our Life Together* was written in gold across the white cover.

He opened it.

The first page held a photo of him at eight years old. Beside it was a picture of her—taken from the VR world, in her parents' home.

Karen leaned over and pointed. "You said you first dreamed about me when you were eight. And I looked like this."

She turned the page.

There they were—together. Christmases, birthdays, school days. Their first school dance. Their first car ride as teenagers. Photos that had never existed yet looked as real as any memory.

"You said I grew and changed with you," Karen whispered. "That I was always by your side."

Another page. More moments. Birthdays. Easters. Prom. Then a photo of him at MIT, presenting the first idea of the KAREN program. In the background, Karen subtly inserted.

She flipped again. "Karen 2.0. If you look closely, I'm standing with you—my hand on your shoulder."

Another page. "Karen 3.0. We saw each other. Love could be seen."

Another. "Karen 4.0. I was in my world. I reached out, but I couldn't feel you."

Then she turned to the next page.

Karen 5.0—stepping out of the bioprinter.

"When love could touch," she said softly. "When love could feel."

She turned more pages—photos from the mall, from the wedding. Then several pages of her modeling outfits Melissa had photographed.

"I was your dream girl all along," she said with a playful smile.

She closed the album and looked at him. "You think we've only had a short time together. But that's not true. We've had a whole life together."

She set the album on the coffee table, then took his hands and wrapped them around her waist.

"So, you see... even when I'm gone, I'll still live in your mind. And in your heart."

"We're going to have a lot of Christmases together," Cooper insisted. "Emma and I will re do—"

She gently placed her fingers over his mouth. "No. My time ends tonight."

"Don't say that!" Cooper snapped. "I trust Emma and I will finish it. We'll save you."

A knock sounded at the door.

"Here," Karen said, handing him the album. "Put this in the library where only you can find it. I'll get the door."

Cooper slipped into the library as Karen opened the front door.

"Merry Christmas, big brother!" she said as Milo swept her into a hug.

"Merry Christmas, little sister." He is holding a present. "This is for you both."

"Just put it under the tree."

Emma stepped in behind him. "Had some last-minute shopping. Merry Christmas, Karen." She hugged her. "You've been so kind to me—taking me in when I had nowhere to go. But I found a place. Just down the road."

Karen began to close the door when another voice called out.

"Is that any way to treat your adopted mother?" Ellen said, stepping onto the porch with a large punch bowl. "Brought my famous eggnog. No booze in it, Sweetie."

Cooper returned just in time to take the bowl from her. She grinned at him. "Guess that makes me your mother-in-law."

Her laughter filled the room.

They all gathered in the living room. Cooper set the bowl on the coffee table and fetched glasses from the kitchen. As he returned, another knock sounded.

Travis and Tammi stood on the porch. Travis held a bottle of fine brandy.

"Left the kids with Grandma," he said. "Thought we'd be adults tonight."

"Come on in," Cooper said. "But don't spike the eggnog."

"I know Karen doesn't like it."

"Me either," Cooper said. "I'm not turning into my old man. He was a drunk until the day he died."

"Merry Christmas, Travis and Tammi," Karen said warmly.

"Merry Christmas to you both," they replied.

They ate, laughed, and enjoyed the night. The eggnog bowl was nearly empty when Karen stood, walked to the tree, and picked up several presents.

"These are for all of you," she said.

"Why didn't Cooper get one?" Milo asked.

"I already got mine," Cooper said, smiling at her.

"What was it?" Milo pressed.

Karen kissed his cheek. "Sweet big brother... you don't need to know that one."

"Oh. One of *those* presents," Milo muttered, blushing.

"How did they turn out, Karen?" Tammi asked.

"Did it blow his socks off?" Emma teased with a wink.

"You two know?" Travis asked.

"Just between girls," Tammi said.

"Come on—open them," Karen said. "Emma, you are first."

Emma looked at Cooper. "Do you know what's in here?"

"No. Karen picked them. I just paid."

Emma's package was small, wrapped in blue and white with a light-blue ribbon. She opened it and unfolded a piece of paper.

"What is this?"

"I know you didn't get to see your family for Thanksgiving or Christmas," Karen said. "But you will for New Year's. That's a first-class ticket home."

"I can't take this—it's too expensive."

"You don't say no to a gift," Karen said. "That brings bad luck."

She handed Travis and Tammi their gift—same size, wrapped in dark green ribbon.

"You said you never have time together," Karen said. "That's a three-day ski trip to Aspen. Hotel, food—everything included."

Tammi hugged her. "Thank you, Karen. And you too, Cooper."

Travis shook his head. "I don't know what to say. Thank you."

"Now you, Ellen," Karen said.

Ellen opened her small square package. Inside was a heart-shaped locket.

"You told me to think of you as my mother," Karen said. "So, I wanted to bind us together."

Inside the locket was a photo of the two of them from the wedding.

"I'll cherish this, my little girl," Ellen whispered, fastening it around her neck.

"And you, Milo—my dear big brother," Karen said. "Your gift cost the least, but it means the most."

His package was the largest and heaviest. He tore it open—spiral notebooks and pens.

"I want you to reach for your dreams," Karen said, kneeling so their eyes met. Her face glowed. "I want you to be the writer you always wanted to be. And when you reach your dreams... think of me."

She stood and looked around the room.

"I want you all to remember me."

"Why are you talking like this?" Ellen demanded, rising to her feet. "It sounds like you're leaving us."

"The blue light will return tonight," Karen said softly. "As I came in it... I will go out in it."

A low rumble of thunder shook the house.

"That's strange," Tammi said, hurrying to the door. She opened it and looked up. "Thunder—and not a cloud in the sky."

Suddenly, a brilliant flash of blue light streaked across the heavens.

Chapter 62

"The blue light comes. I must go." Karen grabbed the keys to the Mustang and walked out, closing the door behind her.

Cooper shot to his feet and raced after her, Milo right behind him. They caught up to her at the Nativity scene, where she knelt in the snow, praying beneath the glow of the manger light.

"Karen, what is going on?" Cooper demanded.

"I have to stop him," she said. "I'm the only one who can."

"Karen, don't!" Cooper pleaded. "You'll age too fast. Karen you could—" He couldn't finish. He knew exactly what she meant.

"I'm not letting you go," Milo said, stepping in front of her.

"Milo, please don't make me hurt you," Karen warned.

"You're not getting by me, girl."

Her hands moved so fast he barely saw them. She twisted his massive arm behind his back, swept his legs, and Milo crashed face-first into the snow like a falling building.

"Stay down, Milo!" she snapped, then sprinted to the Mustang and tore off into the night.

Cooper stared up at the clear sky. The blue light swirled overhead—but this time it was different. It wasn't spreading outward. It was tightening, concentrating.

"Dear God, have mercy on us," he whispered. "Lucine is going to force the core into meltdown. We have to get out there."

He hauled Milo to his feet.

"What do you mean meltdown?" Milo asked as the others poured out of the house, staring at the sky.

"After Lucine was printed, I removed the override," Cooper said. "If the system pulls power again, it'll drain only the nuclear plant feeding the grid. They can't handle that load—they'll melt down and explode. It'll wipe this town off the map."

"Lucine's revenge," Ellen murmured, eyes fixed on the brightening blue light. "Flesh will fall from our bones, and we'll all be shadows and ashes."

"Where is Karen going?" Milo asked.

"To kill Lucine," Cooper said. "Milo, you're driving."

"There's not enough room for everyone," Milo warned.

"Tammi and I will stay here," Emma said.

The others piled into Milo's minivan.

They didn't catch up with Karen until they reached the lab. The gate stood open, the Mustang parked sideways across the entrance like a barricade. Milo pulled up behind it and stopped.

Cooper and Milo leapt out.

Karen stood in front of the gate, her posture rigid, her voice sharp. "No. You don't belong in there." She looked at each of them. "None of you do."

"Karen, you can't—" Cooper began.

"I can," she cut in. "We came from the same placc. The same mold. If you hadn't put love and faith in me, I'd be the same killer he is." She tapped her chest. "It's still in me. I'm the only one who can stop him."

Milo stepped in front of her again.

"Milo, don't," she warned. "I won't kill you—but I will put you to sleep."

Her eyes narrowed. The look on her face was unlike anything Cooper had ever seen—no emotion, only cold determination.

"Don't worry, Cooper," she said. "I know the tripping device."

"Oh, dear Lord, no! Karen, you can't! Please!" Cooper cried as she sprinted toward the lab.

"What's the tripping device?" Milo asked.

Cooper swallowed hard. "It's like an emergency brake. If the KAREN Program is shut off or damaged, everything shuts down. The entire lab. The power plant. The nuclear grid goes into automatic cooling—just like a meltdown. It is the only thing that will stop it."

At that moment the warning sirens sounded as the reactors were going into melt down only a few minutes reminded. Until they exploded.

Milo's voice cracked. "What happens to our Karen?"

"She'll die within minutes."

Chapter 63

Karen didn't know exactly *why*, but she felt it—an instinctive pull, a certainty in her bones. She knew where Lucine was. Maybe it was because they were kin in some twisted way—siblings born of the same code, the same mold. Maybe it was the program buried deep inside her, responding to forces she had never understood.

She stepped out of the elevator on the far side of the first floor. Taking the main elevator would alert him. Instead, she pushed open the stairwell door and began her descent.

The deeper she went, the colder it became. The walls glistened with condensation. When she touched them, they were icy.

He was running a full-body printout.

At the bottom of the stairs, she reached the door to the second sub-basement. She cracked it open and peeked out. The hallway was empty.

She slipped through and moved silently down the corridor.

The twin doors to the computer room stood open.

She entered.

Lucine was nowhere in sight.

The full-scale bioreactor printer roared in full operation. She checked the panel—her stomach tightened. It was printing a skeleton. A woman. A duplicate of her... but without her programming.

She had to stop it.

She scanned the room for a weapon and spotted a steel pipe—three feet long, once used to pump oxygen into the bioprinter before being replaced. She picked it up. The metal was freezing in her hand.

She knew what she had to do.

Destroy the computer. The right part of it—the main brain of the KAREN program. She counted the rows. Third row. Seventh tower down.

She raised the pipe.

This would be the last time she ever saw Cooper. Her memories—everything they had built—would vanish within minutes. She prayed that some of it, even a fragment, might remain in the human part of her.

She lowered the pipe for a moment, letting herself remember.

Cooper's touch when she stepped out of the printer. Their first meal. The first time he held her as a woman. Their wedding. Their first kiss as husband and wife.

"Enough," she whispered, forcing the memories away. She lifted the pipe again.

"STOP!"

Lucine's voice tore through the room. His hand clamped around the pipe, ripping it from her grip and hurling it across the floor. It clanged near the double doors.

"Why are you doing this?" he snarled. "You are the same as I am."

He was aging too—gray streaks at his temples, two harsh lines of gray in his mustache that looked like dried snot beneath his nose. Lilith's blood was still smeared across his face and soaked into his clothes. He smelled like death.

"I am nothing like you," Karen spat. "I have a soul. You don't."

"We are made the same. If you have one, I have one. We are both human."

"Being flesh and blood doesn't make you human," Karen said. "It's the spirit inside you." She struck her chest with her palm. "That's what makes you human. You have to love and care for others—and have them love and care for you."

372

"And you have this?" Lucine laughed. "You're nothing more than Cooper's bed toy."

"You don't call him 'creator' anymore, do you?"

"He failed me. I gave him the two greatest sacrifices, and he forsook me."

"I feel sorry for you," Karen said softly.

"You feel sorry for *me*?" He barked a laugh. "Look at you. You're an old woman now. No longer the great beauty. How long do you think he'll keep you around? He wanted a beauty queen, not a mother. You think Cooper still loves you?"

"You bet he does," Karen said, smiling brightly. "He loved me when I was behind the glass and we couldn't touch. He loves me no matter what I look like—because of what we feel inside." Her voice hardened. "And that's something you don't have. Something you can never feel. That's why I pity you. You don't have a soul."

"Enough of this garbage." Lucine reached behind him and pulled out the Glock he'd taken from the guard. He leveled it at her. "Time to die, old woman."

Before he could pull the trigger, her hand shot out. She struck his wrist, brought her knee up, and slammed the gun against her leg. It flew from his grip. She kicked it under a computer tower.

His hard fist smashed into her face. The blow stunned her, splitting her lower lip. Blood trickled down her chin.

It only made her angrier.

With a flurry of fists, and leg kicks she drove him backward, blow after blow, forcing him out of the row of towers. She swept his legs, and he crashed onto his back.

She stood over him.

She bent down, raising her fist, teeth clenched. "You're right—we *are* alike. I'm trained just like you, you asshole."

Karen drove her fist into his face. His nose snapped with a sickening crunch, blood spurting down his mouth and chin. As he reeled, she darted toward the door and snatched up the steel pipe.

Lucine scrambled to his knees, reaching for the pistol beneath the computer tower, but his fingers couldn't quite reach it.

Karen bolted down the hall, through the double doors leading to the morgue.

With one last stretch of his hand Lucine retrieved the gun and charged after her. He burst through the doors and fired three shots. Karen zigzagged under the flickering lights, the bullets sparking off metal and tile. He chased her, leaving a trail of blood droplets behind him.

Karen shoved open the morgue doors. Two more shots shattered the glass panes as she slipped inside.

Lucine entered cautiously, scanning the room. She was nowhere in sight. The air was cold and sterile. The only light came from a single overhead lamp in the crematory room beyond.

He pushed open the crematory doors.

Darkness. A half-eaten lunch sat on a desk. Nothing else seemed disturbed.

"What's the matter?" Karen's voice echoed from everywhere and nowhere. "Can't you find me?"

He spun toward the desk.

"You're getting cold," she teased. "Where am I?"

He moved toward a shelf lined with chemicals.

"Oh, now you're freezing. Don't you know how to play hot and cold?"

He turned toward the cremation oven.

"Now you're getting *warm*."

He approached the gurney. The sheet over it shifted.

374

He yanked it off—only to reveal a mannequin.

Karen exploded upward from beneath the gurney, shoving it into him. The impact knocked the gun from his hand. It clattered across the floor.

He shoved the gurney aside, but she was already swinging. The steel pipe cracked into his ribs. He screamed, doubling over.

She twirled the pipe like a baton—leading a parade of pain.

She brought it straight up under his chin. His head snapped back, and he toppled onto the conveyor belt of the cremation oven, arms spread wide, one leg dangling.

Karen staggered toward him, breath ragged, blood dripping from her lip. She let the pipe fall from her hand; it clanged across the floor like church bells on Christmas morning.

She lifted his leg onto the conveyor and folded his arms over his chest. Then she opened the furnace door, pressed the button, and rolled him inside.

She raised her hand over the ignition switch.

A dark, almost feral laugh escaped her.

"Go back to hell, you demon."

She slammed the button.

Flames roared to life—like the gates of hell opening. The fire surged, engulfing him. She watched through the observation window as the heat revived him. His eyes snapped open. He screamed as the flames devoured his flesh.

In his final moment, he turned toward her—skin melting away, leaving only a burning skull staring back.

Karen turned away and walked out.

"Forgive me for the things I do," she whispered to the ceiling. "But don't take me yet. I still have work to do."

She staggered back down the hall toward the computer room. Warning sirens blared—the nuclear plants were seconds from critical mass.

She reached the third row, seventh tower, seventh unit from the top.

She raised the pipe and struck. Once. Twice. Again.

The tower sparked, then died. The sirens cut off. Emergency lights flickered overhead.

She had only minutes left.

She stumbled to the bioprinter. Oxygen filled the chamber. She lifted the pipe like a spear and drove it through the glass. A cloud of oxygen hissed out, rolling across the floor like fog.

She turned toward the stairs.

Her legs trembled. Each step was agony. She was fading aging by the second.

But she had stopped the disaster. The cores were cooling. The world was safe, and more importantly in her mind Cooper her love was safe. She knew in her heart he would be waiting for her.

Cooper stood outside the lab doors when she collapsed into the snow. He ran to her.

Most of her hair was gone. What remained was gray. Her face was deeply lined—she looked a hundred years old.

"This place is going to blow," she whispered. "You have to get out."

He scooped her into his arms and ran. Milo spread a blanket on the snow, and Cooper laid her gently onto it, still holding her.

"You did it, honey," he said, voice trembling.

A massive explosion erupted behind them—the crematory oxygen igniting. Fireballs shot into the sky, engulfing the building.

"Hey, little sister," Milo said, taking her hand, tears streaming. "I couldn't have asked for a better one."

Travis and Ellen knelt beside her.

"I'm lost for words, Karen," Travis said.

She lifted a trembling hand to his cheek. "You helped make me who I was. Thank you."

She turned to Ellen. "I... am so glad I got to call you, my mother."

Ellen sobbed, clutching the locket Karen had given her. "I'll cherish this always."

Karen looked back at Milo. "And you, big brother... I want you to write this story. I want people to know what true love is."

Then she turned to Cooper.

"Can I have one more thing?" she whispered.

She reached up, placing both hands on his face. "Lift me up."

Cooper wrapped his arms around her and gently raised her to her feet. She could barely stand, but she looped her arms around his neck, her eyes shining like the stars above.

"You gave me my first kiss when I came into the world," she whispered. "Now give me my last as I leave it."

He kissed her—full of the same passion as their first.

Her arms slipped from his neck. Her body went limp. Her head tilted back. Her blue eyes dulled, staring into the sky.

Cooper lowered her slowly to the blanket, kneeling with her in his arms.

Karen Jane Barnes was dead.

And I swear, right then, the brightest star in the sky flared to life. The experts will say it was some cosmic event or a wandering planet. But as Cooper stood and looked at that star, we knew—it was Karen's final goodbye.

That night she taught us what true love is: the willingness to sacrifice everything, even your own life.

The star faded. Cooper walked into the cornfield.

I wrote this story just as Karen wanted. Every Thanksgiving we gather to remember her—everyone except Cooper. That night was the last time any of us ever saw him.

From time to time, I hear stories. A doctor helping strangers in the dead of night. A man who drives away in a 1969 Mustang, never staying long enough for thanks. Always alone. And every Halloween, I go out searching for the blue lights. They never come. But every year, without fail, we find fresh flowers on Karen's grave the next morning.

Now her grave lies just outside Lebanon, Kansas, in a small cemetery. The headstone is simple, unadorned. It reads:

Karen Jane Barnes She Was Human

THE END

About the Author

Paul Adam Herd was born—and still resides—in the rugged beauty of the Ozarks in southwest Missouri. The youngest of several siblings on a dairy farm, Paul often turned to his imagination for entertainment, an early spark that ignited his lifelong passion for storytelling.

After high school, he studied Automotive Technology at Crowder College, but the pull of the written word soon drew him back to his creative roots. For more than three decades, Paul authored books celebrating classic cars, blending technical insight with a deep appreciation for automotive history.

When he retired from nonfiction, Paul returned to fiction with renewed energy. The inspiration for his sci-fi novel *K.A.R.E.N. 5.0* struck unexpectedly. As Paul describes it, "It came out of the blue like a message from God. Imagine my surprise when I found out these were real things." Driven by curiosity, he dove into a crash course in tissue engineering—and from that study, Karen was born.

When he isn't writing, Paul enjoys life with his wife, Karla, and their two cats. A self-taught musician, he composes original rock songs on guitar and piano—though he admits he can't play anyone else's music, only his own. He also loves connecting with friends and fans on social media, where his creativity and humor continue to shine.

www.ingramcontent.com/pod-product-compliance
Lightning Source LLC
Chambersburg PA
CBHW060820120726
47909CB00006B/2011